DARKFEVER
'A wonderful dark fantasy . . . give yourself a treat and read
outside the box'
Charlaine Harris

'Moning launches a remarkable new series that's exotic and treacherous'
Romantic Times

BLOODFEVER
'Addictively dark, erotic, and even shocking'
Publishers Weekly

'Moning brilliantly works the dark sides of man
and Fae for all they are worth'
Booklist

FAEFEVER
'The newest installment of this supernatural saga will have you
panting for the next. Breathtaking!'
Romantic Times

'A seductive mix of Celtic mythology and dark, sexy danger'
Chicago Tribune

DREAMFEVER
'This book is absolutely riveting. By far, the most fascinating book
I have read this year'
Penelope's Romance Reviews

'Freaking fabulous! So utterly wonderful that you must be
reading this series, if you're not already'
Literary Escapism

D1494405

Also by Karen Marie Moning from Gollancz:

Darkfever

Bloodfever

Faefever

Dreamfever

Shadowfever

KAREN MARIE
MONING

FAEFEVER

A MACKAYLA LANE NOVEL

BOOK 3

First published in Great Britain in 2011 by
Gollancz
An imprint of the Orion Publishing Group
Orion House, 5 Upper St Martin's Lane, London WC2H 9EA
An Hachette UK Company

1 3 5 7 9 10 8 6 4 2

A CIP catalogue record for this book is available
from the British Library

ISBN 978 0 575 10853 0

Printed in Great Britain by Clays Ltd, St Ives plc

The Orion Publishing Group's policy is to use papers that are natural,
renewable and recyclable products and made from wood grown in
sustainable forests. The logging and manufacturing processes are
expected to conform to the environmental regulations of the country
of origin.

www.karenmoning.com
www.orionbooks.co.uk

This one's for the Moning Maniacs –
the best fans any writer ever had.

"And I will show you something different from either
Your shadow at morning striding behind you
Or your shadow at evening rising to meet you;
I will show you fear in a handful of dust."
T. S. Eliot, *The Waste Land*

"Do not go gentle into that good night...
Rage, rage against the dying of the light."
Dylan Thomas

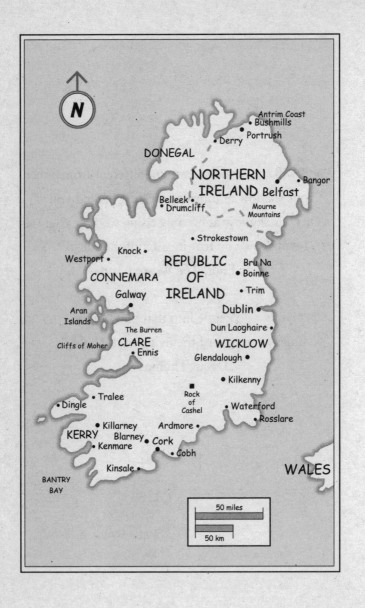

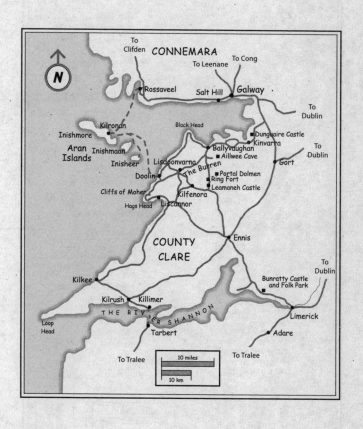

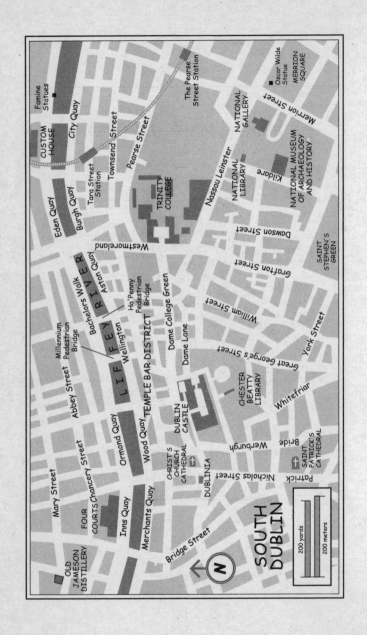

PART ONE

Before Dawn

"I keep expecting to wake up and find it was all a bad dream.

Alina will be alive,

I won't be afraid of the dark,

Monsters won't be walking the streets of Dublin,

And I won't have this terrible fear that

tomorrow dawn just won't come."

—*Mac's journal*

Prologue

'd die for him.

No, wait a minute...that's not where this is supposed to begin.

I know that. But left to my own devices, I'd prefer to skim over the events of the next few weeks, and whisk you through those days with glossed-over details that cast me in a more flattering light.

Nobody looks good in their darkest hour. But it's those hours that make us what we are. We stand strong, or we cower. We emerge victorious, tempered by our trials, or fractured by a permanent, damning fault line.

I never used to think about things like darkest hours and trials and fault lines.

I used to fill my days with sunning and shopping, bartending at The Brickyard (always more of a party than a job, and that was how I liked my life), and devising ways to con Mom and Dad into helping me buy a new car. At twenty-two, I was still living at home, safe in my sheltered world, lulled by the sleepy, slow-paddling fans of the Deep South into believing myself the center of it.

Then my sister, Alina, was brutally murdered while studying abroad in Dublin, and my world changed overnight. It was bad enough that I had to identify her mutilated body, and watch my once happy family shatter, but my world didn't stop falling apart there. It didn't stop until I'd learned that pretty much everything I'd been raised to believe about myself wasn't true.

I discovered that my folks weren't my real parents; my sister and I were adopted; and despite my lazy, occasionally overblown drawl, we weren't southern at all, but descended from an ancient Celtic bloodline of *sidhe*-seers, people who can see the Fae—a terrifying race of otherworldly beings that have lived secretly among us for thousands of years, cloaked in illusions and lies.

Those were the easy lessons.

The hard lessons were yet to come, waiting for me in the *craic*-filled streets of the Temple Bar District of Dublin, where I would watch people die, and learn to kill; where I would meet Jericho Barrons, V'lane, and the Lord Master; where I would step up to the plate as a major player in a deadly game with fate-of-the-world stakes.

For those of you just joining me, my name is MacKayla Lane, Mac for short. My real last name might be O'Connor, but I don't know that for sure. I'm a *sidhe*-seer, one of the most powerful that's ever lived. Not only can I see the Fae, I can hurt them and, armed with one of their most sacred Hallows—

the Spear of Luin, or Destiny—I can even kill the immortal beings.

Don't settle into your chair and relax. It's not just my world that's in trouble; it's your world, too. It's happening, right now, while you're sitting there, munching a snack, getting ready to immerse yourself in a fictional escape. Guess what? It's not fiction, and there's no escape. The walls between the human world and Faery are coming down—and I hate to break it to you, but these fairies are *so* not Tinkerbells.

If the walls crash completely...well, you'd just better hope they don't. If I were you, I'd turn on all my lights right now. Get out a few flashlights. Check your supply of batteries.

I came to Dublin for two things: to find out who killed my sister, and to get revenge. See how easily I can say that now? I want revenge. Revenge with a capital *R*. Revenge with crushed bones and a lot of blood. I want her murderer dead, preferably by my own hand. A few months here and I've shed *years* of polished southern civilities.

Shortly after I stepped off the plane from Ashford, Georgia, and planted my well-pedicured foot on Ireland's shore, I probably would have died if I hadn't stumbled into a bookstore owned by Jericho Barrons. Who or what he is, I have no idea. But he has knowledge that I need, and I have something he wants, and that makes us reluctant allies.

When I had no place to turn, Barrons took me in, taught me who and what I am, opened my eyes, and helped me survive. He didn't do it nicely, but I no longer care how I survive, as long as I do.

Because it was safer than my cheap room at the inn, I moved in to his bookstore. It's protected against most of my enemies with wards and assorted spells, and stands bastion at the edge of what I call a Dark Zone: a neighborhood that has been taken over by Shades, amorphous Unseelie that thrive in darkness and suck the life from humans.

We've battled monsters together. He's saved my life twice. We've shared a taste of dangerous lust. He's after the *Sinsar Dubh*—a million-year-old book of the blackest magic imaginable, scribed by the Unseelie King himself, that holds the key to power over both the worlds of Fae and Man. I want it because it was Alina's dying request that I find it, and I suspect it holds the key to saving our world.

He says he wants it because he collects books. Right.

V'lane is another story. He's a Seelie prince, and a death-by-sex Fae, which you'll be learning more about soon enough. The Fae consist of two adversarial courts with their own Royal Houses and unique castes: the Light or Seelie Court, and the Dark or Unseelie Court. Don't let the light and dark stuff fool you. Both are deadly. However, the Seelie considered the Unseelie *so* deadly that they imprisoned them roughly seven hundred thousand years ago. When one Fae fears another, be afraid.

Each court has their Hallows, or sacred objects of immense power. The Seelie Hallows are the spear (which I have), the sword, the stone, and the cauldron. The Unseelie Hallows are the amulet (which I had and the Lord Master took), the box, the Sifting Silvers, and the highly sought-after Book. They all have different purposes. Some I know; others I'm not so clear on.

Like Barrons, V'lane is after the *Sinsar Dubh*. He's hunting it for the Seelie Queen Aoibheal, who needs it to reinforce the walls between the realms of Fae and Man, and keep them from coming down. Like Barrons, he has saved my life. (He's also given me some of the most intense orgasms of it.)

The Lord Master is my sister's murderer; the one who seduced, used, and destroyed her. Not quite Fae, not quite human, he's been opening portals between realms, bringing Unseelie—the worst of the Fae—through to our world, turning them loose, and teaching them to infiltrate our society. He *wants* the walls down so he can free all the Unseelie from their icy prison. He's also after the *Sinsar Dubh,* although I'm not certain why. I think he may be seeking it to destroy it, so no one can ever rebuild the walls again.

That's where I come in.

These three powerful, dangerous men *need* me.

Not only can I see the Fae, I can sense Fae relics and Hallows. I can feel the *Sinsar Dubh* out there, a dark, pulsing heart of pure evil.

I can hunt it.

I can find it.

My dad would say that makes me this season's MVP.

Everybody wants me. So I stay alive in a world where death darkens my doorstep daily.

I've seen things that would make your skin crawl. I've done things that make my skin crawl.

But that's not important now. What's important is

starting at the right place—let's see...where was that?

I peel the pages of my memory backward, one at a time, squinting so I don't have to see them too clearly. I turn back, past that whiteout where all memories vanish for a time, past that hellish Halloween, and the things Barrons did. Past the woman I killed. Past a part of V'lane piercing the meat of my tongue. Past what I did to Jayne.

There.

I zoom down into a dark, damp, shiny street.

It's me. Pretty in pink and gold.

I'm in Dublin. It's nighttime. I'm walking the cobbled pavement of Temple Bar. I'm alive, vibrantly so. There's nothing like a recent brush with death to make you feel larger than life.

There's a sparkle in my eyes and a spring in my step. I'm wearing a killer pink dress with my favorite heels, and I'm accessorized to the hilt, in gold and rose amethyst. I've taken extra care with my hair and makeup. I'm on my way to meet Christian MacKeltar, a sexy, mysterious young Scotsman who knew my sister. I feel *good* for a change.

Well, at least for a short time I do.

Fast-forward a few moments.

Now I'm clutching my head and stumbling from the sidewalk, into the gutter. Falling to all fours. I've just gotten closer to the *Sinsar Dubh* than I've ever been before, and it's having its usual effect on me. Pain. Debilitating.

I no longer look so pretty. In fact, I look positively wretched.

On my hands and knees in a puddle that smells of

beer and urine, I'm iced to the bone. My hair is in a tangle, my amethyst hair clip bobs against my nose, and I'm crying. I push the hair from my face with a filthy hand and watch the tableau playing out in front of me with wide, horrified eyes.

I remember that moment. Who I was. What I wasn't. I capture it in freeze-frame. There are so many things I would say to her.

Head up, Mac. Brace yourself. A storm is coming. Don't you hear the thunderclap of sharp hooves on the wind? Can't you feel the soul-numbing frost? Don't you smell spice and blood on the breeze?

Run, I would tell her. Hide.

But I wouldn't listen to me.

On my knees, watching that … *thing* … do what it's doing, I'm in the stranglehold of a killing undertow.

Reluctantly, I merge with the memory, slip into her skin …

ONE

The pain, God, the *pain*! It's going to splinter my skull!

I clutch my head with wet, stinking hands, determined to hold it together until the inevitable occurs—I pass out.

Nothing compares to the agony the *Sinsar Dubh* causes me. Each time I get close to it, the same thing happens. I'm immobilized by pain that escalates until I lose consciousness.

Barrons says it's because the Dark Book and I are point and counterpoint. That it's so evil, and I'm so good, that it repels me violently. His theory is to "dilute" me somehow, make me a little evil so I can get close to it. I don't see how making me evil so I can get close enough to pick up an evil book is a good thing. I think I'd probably do evil things with it.

"No," I whimper, sloshing on my knees in the puddle. "Please...no!" Not here, not now! In the past, each time I'd gotten close to the Book, Barrons had been with me, and I'd had the comfort of knowing he wouldn't let anything too awful happen to my unconscious body. He might tote me around like a divining rod, but I could live with that. Tonight, however, I was alone. The thought of being vulnerable to anyone and anything in Dublin's streets for even a few moments terrified me. What if I passed out for an hour? What if I fell facedown into the vile puddle I was in, and drowned in mere inches of... ugh.

I *had* to get out of the puddle. I would not die so pathetically.

A wintry wind howled down the street, whipping between buildings, chilling me to the bone. Old newspapers cartwheeled like dirty, sodden tumbleweeds over broken bottles and discarded wrappers and glasses. I flailed in the sewage, scraped at the pavement with my fingernails, left the tips of them broken in gaps between the cobbled stones.

Inch by inch, I clawed my way to drier ground.

It was there—straight ahead of me: the Dark Book. I could feel it, fifty yards from where I scrabbled for purchase. Maybe less. And it wasn't just a book. Oh, no. It was nothing that simple. It pulsated darkly, charring the edges of my mind.

Why wasn't I passing out?

Why wouldn't this pain *end*?

I felt like I was dying. Saliva flooded my mouth, frothing into foam at my lips. I wanted desperately to throw up but I couldn't. Even my stomach was locked down by pain.

Moaning, I tried to raise my head. I had to see it. I'd been close to it before, but I'd never *seen* it. I'd always passed out first. If I wasn't going to lose consciousness, I had questions I wanted answered. I didn't even know what it looked like. Who had it? What were they doing with it? Why did I keep having near brushes with it?

Shuddering, I pushed back onto my knees, shoved a hank of sour-smelling hair from my face, and looked.

The street that only moments ago had bustled with tourists, making their merry way from one open pub door to the next, was now scourged clean by the dark, arctic wind. Doors had been slammed, music silenced.

Leaving only me.

And *them*.

The vision before me was not at all what I'd expected.

A gunman had a huddle of people backed against the wall of a building, a family of tourists, cameras swinging around their necks. The barrel of a semi-automatic weapon gleamed in the moonlight. The father was yelling, the mother was screaming, trying to gather three small children into her arms.

"No!" I shouted. At least I think I did. I'm not sure I actually made a sound. My lungs were compressed with pain.

The gunman let loose a spray of bullets, silencing their cries. He killed the youngest last—a delicate blond girl of four or five, with wide, pleading eyes that would haunt me till the day I died. A girl I couldn't save because I couldn't fecking *move*.

Paralyzed by pain-deadened limbs, I could only kneel there, screaming inside my head.

Why was this happening? Where was the *Sinsar Dubh*? Why couldn't I see it?

The man turned, and I inhaled sharply.

A book was tucked beneath his arm.

A perfectly innocuous hardcover, about three hundred and fifty pages thick, no dust jacket, pale gray with red binding. The kind of well-read hardcover you might find in any used bookstore, in any city.

I gaped. Was I supposed to believe *that* was the million-year-old book of the blackest magic imaginable, scribed by the Unseelie King? Was this supposed to be funny? How anticlimactic. How absurd.

The gunman glanced at his weapon with a bemused expression. Then his head swiveled back toward the fallen bodies, the blood and bits of flesh and bone spattered across the brick wall.

The book dropped from beneath his arm. It seemed to fall in slow motion, changing, transforming, as it tumbled, end over end, to the damp, shiny brick. By the time it hit the cobbled pavement with a heavy *whump*, it was no longer a simple hardcover but a massive black tome, nearly a foot thick, engraved with runes, bound by bands of steel and intricate locks. Exactly the kind of book I'd expected: ancient and evil-looking.

I sucked in another breath.

Now the thick dark volume was changing again, becoming something new. It swirled and spun, drawing substance from wind and darkness.

In its place rose a...*thing*...of such...terrible essence and pitch. A darkly animate...again, I can only say *thing* ...that existed beyond shape or name: A malformed creature sprung from some no-man's-land of shattered sanity and broken gibberings.

And it *lived*.

I have no words to describe it, because nothing exists in our world to compare it to. I'm glad nothing exists in our world to compare it to, because if something did exist in our world to compare it to, I'm not sure our world would exist.

I can only call it the Beast, and leave it there.

My soul shivered, as if perceiving on some visceral level that my body was not nearly enough protection for it. Not from this.

The gunman looked at it, and it looked at the gunman, and he turned his weapon on himself. I jerked at the sound of more shots. The shooter crumpled to the pavement and his weapon clattered away.

Another icy wind gusted down the street, and there was movement in my periphery.

A woman appeared from around the corner as if answering a summons, gazed blankly at the scene for several moments, then walked as if drugged straight to the fallen book *(crouching beast with impossible limbs and bloodied muzzle!)* that abruptly sported neither ancient locks nor bestial form but was once again masquerading as an innocent hardcover.

"Don't touch it!" I cried, goose bumps needling my flesh at the thought.

She stooped, picked it up, tucked it beneath her arm, and turned away.

I'd like to say she walked off without a backward glance, but she didn't. She glanced over her shoulder, *straight at me,* and her expression choked off what little breath inflated my lungs.

Pure evil stared out of her eyes, a cunning, bottomless malevolence that *knew* me, that understood things about me I didn't, and never wanted to know. Evil that celebrated its existence every chance it got through chaos, demolition, and psychotic rage.

She smiled, an awful smile, baring hundreds of small, pointy teeth.

And I had one of those sudden epiphanies.

I remembered the last time I'd gotten close to the *Sinsar Dubh* and passed out, and reading the next day about the man who'd killed his entire family, then driven himself into an embankment, *mere blocks* from where I'd lost consciousness. Everyone interviewed had said the same thing—the man couldn't have done it, it wasn't him, he'd been behaving like someone possessed for the past few days. I recalled the rash of gruesome news articles lately that echoed the same sentiment, whatever the brutal crime—*it wasn't him/her; he/she would never do it.* I stared at the woman who was no longer who or what she'd been when she'd turned the corner and entered this street. A woman possessed. And I understood.

It *wasn't* those people committing the terrible crimes.

The Beast was inside her now, in control. And it

would retain control of her until it was done using her, when it would dispose of her and move on to its next victim.

We'd been so wrong, Barrons and I!

We'd believed the *Sinsar Dubh* was in the possession of someone with a cogent plan who was transporting it from place to place with a purpose, someone who was either using it to accomplish certain goals or guarding it, trying to keep it from falling into the wrong hands.

But it wasn't in the possession of anyone with a plan, cogent or otherwise, and it wasn't being moved.

It was *moving*.

Passing from one set of hands to the next, transforming each of its victims into a weapon of violence and destruction. Barrons had told me that Fae relics had a tendency to take on a life and purpose of their own in time. The Dark Book was a million years old. That was a lot of time. It had certainly taken on some kind of life.

The woman disappeared around the corner, and I dropped to the pavement like a stone. Eyes closed, I gasped for shallow breaths. As she/it moved farther away, vanishing into the night where God only knew what she/it would do next, my pain began to ease.

It was the most dangerous Hallow ever created—and it was loose in our world.

Creepy thing was, until tonight, it hadn't been aware of me.

It was now.

It had looked at me, seen me. I couldn't explain it, but I felt it had somehow *marked* me, tagged me like a pigeon. I'd gazed into the abyss and the abyss had gazed back, just like Daddy always said it would: *You want to know about life, Mac? It's simple. Keep watching rainbows, baby. Keep looking at the sky. You find what you look for. If you go hunting good in the world, you'll find it. If you go hunting evil ... well, don't.*

What idiot, I brooded, as I dragged myself up onto the sidewalk, had decided to give *me* special powers? What fool thought I could do something about problems of such enormity? How could I *not* hunt evil when I was one of the few people who could see it?

Tourists were flooding back into the street. Pub doors opened. Darkness peeled back. Music began playing, and the world started up again. Laughter bounced off brick. I wondered what world *they* were living in. It sure wasn't mine.

Oblivious to them all, I threw up until I dry-heaved. Then I dry-heaved until not even bile remained.

I pushed to my feet, dragged the back of my hand across my mouth, and stared at my reflection in a pub window. I was stained, I was soaked, and I smelled. My hair was a soppy mess of beer and ... *oh!* I couldn't bear to think about what else. You never know what you'll find in a gutter in Dublin's party district. I plucked the clip from my hair, scraped it back, and secured it at my nape where it couldn't touch much of my face.

My dress was torn, I was missing two buttons

down the front of it, I'd broken the heel off my right shoe, and my knees were scraped and bleeding.

"There's a lass that gives a whole new meaning to falling-down drunk, eh?" A man sniggered as he passed by. His buddies laughed. There were a dozen of them, wearing red cummerbunds and bow ties over jeans and sweaters. A bachelor party, off to celebrate the joy of testosterone. They gave me wide berth.

They were so clueless.

Was it really only twenty minutes ago I'd been smiling at passersby? Walking through Temple Bar, feeling alive and attractive, and ready for whatever the world might decide to throw at me next? Twenty minutes ago, they'd have circled around me, flirted me up.

I took a few lopsided steps, trying to walk as if I weren't missing three and a half inches of spike beneath my right heel. It wasn't easy. I ached everywhere. Although the pain of the Book's proximity continued to recede, I felt bruised from head to toe, from being held in the crushing vise of it. If tonight turned out anything like the last time I'd encountered it, my head would pound for hours and ache dully for days. My visit to Christian MacKeltar, the young Scot who'd known my sister, was going to have to wait. I looked around for my missing heel. It was nowhere to be seen. I'd *loved* those shoes, darn it! I'd saved for months to buy them.

I sighed inwardly and told myself to get over it. At the moment, I had bigger problems on my mind.

I hadn't passed out.

I'd been within fifty yards of the *Sinsar Dubh*, and I'd stayed conscious the entire time.

Barrons was going to be so pleased. Delighted, even, although delight is a difficult expression to read on that dark, arresting face. Chiseled from savagery by a sculptor-savant, Barrons is a throwback to a lawless time, and looks as stoically primitive as he behaves.

It appeared recent events had "diluted" me, and I was now more like the Book.

Evil.

On my way back to the bookstore, it began to rain. I limped miserably through it. I hate the rain. For many reasons.

One, it's wet, cold, and nasty, and I was already wet and cold enough. Two, the sun doesn't shine when it's raining and I'm an unapologetic sun-worshipper. Three, it makes Dublin at night even darker than usual, and that means the monsters get bolder. Four, it makes me need an umbrella and when people carry umbrellas they have a tendency to pull them down really low and hunch behind them, especially if the rain is being blown into their faces. I'm no different. And that means you can't see what's coming toward you, which in a busy street usually results in people careening off one another with muttered apologies, or bit-off curses, and in Dublin means I could run smack into a Fae (their glamour doesn't physically repel me like it does normal people) and betray myself, all of which adds up to: When it rains here, I don't dare carry an umbrella.

Which wouldn't be so bad except it rains here *all the freaking time*.

Which means I get completely soaked and that leads me to the fifth thing I hate about rain: My makeup runs and my hair becomes a mop of cowlicks.

But every cloud really does have some kind of silver lining and, after a good, hard drenching, at least I no longer smelled quite so bad.

I turned down my street. It's not really my street. *My* street is four thousand miles away in the rural Deep South. It's a sunny, lushly overgrown street, framed by waxy-leaved magnolias, brilliant azaleas, and towering oaks. My street doesn't rain all the time.

But I can't go home now, for fear of leading monsters back to Ashford with me, and since I need someplace to call my own, this rainy, gloomy, dreary street will have to do.

As I approached the bookstore, I scanned the façade of the old-world, four-story building carefully. Exterior spotlights mounted on the front, rear, and sides bathed the tall brick building in light. The brightly painted shingle proclaiming **BARRONS BOOKS AND BAUBLES** that hung perpendicular to the building, suspended over the sidewalk on an elaborate brass pole, creaked as it swung in the increasingly chilly night breeze. The sign in the old-fashioned green-tinted windows glowed soft neon: **CLOSED**. Amber torches in brass sconces illuminated the deep limestone archway of the bookstore's grand, alcoved entrance. Ornate, diamond-paned cherry doors nestled between limestone columns gleamed in the light.

All was well with my "home." The lights were on, the building protected from my deadly neighbors. I stopped and stared for a moment down the street, into the abandoned neighborhood, making sure no Shades had made inroads into my territory.

The Dark Zone at the edge of Barrons Books and Baubles is the largest one I've seen so far (and the largest I hope to ever see!), encompassing more than twenty city blocks, crammed to overflowing with lethal dark shadows. Two things characterize a Dark Zone: darkness and death. Creatures of night, the Shades devour everything that lives, from people, to grass, to leaves, even down to the worms in the soil, leaving behind a wasteland.

Even now, they were moving restlessly, writhing like flies stuck on tape, desperate to exchange their lifeless shadows for the fertile, well-lit neighborhoods beyond.

For the moment I was safe. The Shades can't tolerate light, and near the bookstore, I was bathed in it. However, if I were to wander twenty feet down the street, into the gloom where the streetlamps were all out, I'd be dead.

I'm obsessed with my neighbors. They're vampires in the truest sense of the word. I've seen what they do to people. They consume them, leaving only piles of clothing, jewelry, and other inanimate objects, topped by a small, dry papery husk of whatever human matter they find unpalatable. Like leaving the tail of a shrimp, I guess; part of us is too

crunchy for their taste. Not even I can kill them.
They have no real substance, which makes weapons
useless. The only thing that works against them is
light, and it doesn't kill them, it just holds them at
bay. Penned in on all sides by the lights of surround-
ing neighborhoods, this Dark Zone had remained
roughly the same size for several months. I know; I
scout its perimeter regularly.

If you're not a *sidhe*-seer, you can't even see them.
The people who die in a Dark Zone never know the
face of their executioner. Not that the Shades have
faces. Featureless is their middle name. If you are a
sidhe-seer, they're still difficult to separate from the
night, even when you know what you're looking
for. Darker than the darkness, like inky black fog,
they slither and slide, creeping over buildings, oozing down drainpipes, twining around broken streetlamps. Although I've never gotten close enough to
test my hunch and hope I never do, I think they're
cold.

They come in all shapes and sizes, ranging from
as small as a cat to as large as—

I blinked.

Surely *that* wasn't the one that had cornered me
in the back parlor the night Fiona, the woman who
used to run the bookstore, had tried to kill me, by
letting a horde of them inside while I slept! The last
time I'd seen it, roughly five weeks ago, counting
the month I'd lost in Faery, it had been about twenty
feet long and nine feet high. It was now *twice* as
large, a dense cloud of oily darkness stretching
nearly the entire length of the deserted building adjacent to Barrons.

Did they grow from eating us? Could one get as big as a small town? Maybe hunker down on top of it and swallow it whole?

I stared. For a thing that had no face, it certainly seemed to be staring back at me. I'd flipped this thing off a time or two. Last time I'd seen it, it had shaped itself into an almost human form and shot the insult right back at me.

I wasn't about to teach it any new tricks.

I gave myself a brisk shake, and immediately regretted it. My head hurt so badly my brain felt bruised, and I'd just jostled it from side to side against the inner walls of my skull. Though the rain had finally stopped—or rather taken one of those all too brief Dublin hiatuses—I was wet and freezing, and had better things to do than stand out here brooding over one of my many enemies. Things like eating a half a bottle of aspirin, and standing under a scalding shower. Things like clearing my head so I could ponder the ramifications of what I'd seen tonight, and finding Barrons to tell him all about it. I had no doubt he would be as astonished as I was by the Book's method of locomotion. What dark agenda was it pursuing? Were random chaos and violence purpose enough?

As I stepped into the alcove and began digging in my purse for my keys, I heard footsteps behind me. I glanced over my shoulder and scowled.

Inspector Jayne joined me in the arched entry, dashing rain from his coat with a gloved hand. I'd passed him earlier in the street, on my way to see Christian, before my encounter with the *Sinsar Dubh*. He'd given me a look that had promised harassment, but I'd figured I'd had a day or two before he got around to making good on that promise.

No such luck.

Tall and burly, with brown hair neatly combed to a side part, his craggy face was set in harsh lines. Brother-in-law to the late Inspector Patty O'Duffy— the inspector who'd originally handled my sister's murder case, and who'd had his throat cut while clutching a scrap of paper with my name on it— Jayne had recently hauled me down to the Garda station and held me all day on suspicion of murder. He'd interrogated and starved me, accused me of having had an affair with O'Duffy, then turned me out into the dark heart of Dublin, minus my Shade-repelling flashlights, to walk home by myself. I wasn't about to forgive his callous treatment.

I'm going to be tape to your ass, he'd told me.

He'd been proving true to his word, following me, staking me out, watching my every move.

Now, he looked me up and down and gave a snort of disgust. "I'm not even going to ask."

"Are you here to arrest me?" I said coolly. I quit trying to pretend I had a heel and leaned lopsidedly against the door. My calves and feet hurt.

"Maybe."

"That was a yes or no question, Jayne. Try again." He didn't say anything and we both knew what that meant. "Then go away. The store is closed. That makes it private property right now. You're trespassing."

"Either we talk tonight, or I come back in the morning when you have customers. You want a homicide detective hanging around, interrogating your clientele?"

"You don't have any right to interrogate my clientele."

"I'm the Garda, lady. That gives me all the rights I need. I can and *will* make your life miserable. Try me."

"What do you want?" I growled.

"It's cold and wet out here." He cupped his hands, blew on them. "How about a cup of tea?"

"How about you go screw yourself?" I flashed him a saccharine smile.

"What, my overweight, middle-aged brother-in-law was good enough for you, but I'm not?"

"I did *not* have sex with your brother-in-law," I snapped.

"Then what the fuck *was* he doing with you?" he snapped back.

"We've already been through this. I told you. If you want to interrogate me again, you're going to have to arrest me, and this time I'm not saying a word without an attorney." I glanced over his shoulder. The Shades were moving restlessly, vigorously, as if stirred up by our discord. Our arguing seemed to be...exciting them. I wondered if anger or passion made us taste even better to them. I forced the macabre thought from my mind.

"Your answers were no answers at all, and you know it."

"You don't *want* the real answers." *I* didn't want the real answers. Unfortunately, I was stuck with them.

"Maybe, I do. However...difficult to believe... they might seem."

I gave him a sharp look. Though he wore his usual determined dog-with-a-bone expression, there was a subtle new component to it that I'd missed before. It was the same component I'd glimpsed in O'Duffy's eyes the morning he'd come to see me, the morning he'd died, a wary, maybe-my-world-isn't-quite-what-I-thought-it-was look. A sure sign that, like O'Duffy, Jayne was about to start poking into matters that were probably going to get him killed. Although O'Duffy's method of death seemed to imply a human murderer, I had no doubt he'd been killed for what he'd been learning about the new kids in town—the Fae.

I sighed. I wanted out of my nasty, wet clothes. I wanted to wash my disgusting hair. "Let it go, will you? Just let it go. I didn't have anything to do with O'Duffy's murder, and I don't have anything else to tell you."

"Yes, you do. You know what's going on in this city, Ms. Lane. I don't know how or where you fit into things, but I know you do. That's why Patty came to see you. He didn't stop by that morning to *tell* you anything about your sister's case. He came to *ask* you something. What was it? What had been burning such a hole in his brain all night that he couldn't wait until Monday to talk to you, that he sent his family on to church and missed Mass? What did Patty ask you the morning he died?"

He was good. I'd give him that. But nothing more.

"Will I die, too, Ms. Lane, now that I've come to

see you?" he said roughly. "Is that how it works? Should I have woken my children and kissed them good-bye before I left this morning? Told my wife how much I loved her?"

Stung, I said, "It's not my fault he died!"

"Maybe you didn't kill him, but maybe you didn't save him, either. Did you answer his questions? Is that why he died? Or if you had, would he still be alive?"

I glared at him. "Go away."

He reached inside his coat and withdrew a handful of folded maps from an inner pocket.

I glanced away sharply, hating everything about the moment. This was a déjà vu I never wanted to revisit.

Patty O'Duffy had brought me maps, too. That Sunday morning he'd come to see me at the bookstore, he'd illustrated in cartographic detail a graphic impossibility, a discovery I'd beat him to by nearly two weeks: Parts of Dublin were no longer being printed on the maps. They were disappearing, falling off the plats and out of human memory, as if they'd never existed. He'd discovered the Dark Zones. He'd been scouting them out, going into them, a mere dusk away from dying.

Jayne leaned closer until his nose was inches from mine. "Looked at any of these lately?"

I said nothing.

"I found a dozen of them on Patty's desk. He'd circled certain areas. It took me a while to figure out why. The Garda have a warehouse on Lisle Street seven blocks from here. You can't find it on a single map published in the last two years."

"So? What's your point? That in addition to murder, I'm part of some vast mapmaking conspiracy? What will you charge me with next, colluding to get tourists lost?"

"Funny, Ms. Lane. I took a long lunch yesterday and went to Lisle Street. I tried to take a cab, but the driver insisted there was no such address and refused to go there. I ended up having to walk. Care to hear what I saw?"

"No. But I'm pretty sure you're going to tell me anyway," I muttered, massaging my temples.

"The warehouse is still there, but the city around it seems to have been . . . forgotten. I mean, *completely* forgotten. The streets aren't being cleaned. The trash isn't being collected. The lamps are out. Sewage has backed up into the gutters. My cell phone couldn't get a signal there. Right in the middle of the city, I couldn't get a bloody signal!"

"Not getting what this has to do with me," I said in my most bored voice.

He didn't hear me, and I knew he was walking the desolate, debris-filled streets in his mind again. A Dark Zone doesn't just look abandoned; it oozes death and decay, makes you feel slimy with it. It leaves an indelible mark on you. It will wake you up in the middle of the night, heart in your throat, terrified of the dark. I sleep with all the lights on. I carry flashlights, 24/7.

"I found cars abandoned in the middle of the streets with the doors wide open. Expensive cars. The kind that get stripped for parts before the owner can even return with petrol. Explain that," he barked.

"Maybe Dublin's crime rate is decreasing," I offered, knowing it for the lie it was.

"It's skyrocketing. Has been for months. Media's been crucifying us over it."

They certainly had. And after what I'd seen tonight, the local escalation in violent crime was a fact I was especially interested in. I had an idea germinating.

"There were piles of clothing outside the cars with wallets in the pockets. Some of them were stuffed with cash, just waiting to be stolen. For Christ's sake, I found two Rolexes on the sidewalk!"

"Did you pick them up?" I asked with interest. I'd always wanted a Rolex.

"But you know what the strangest thing was, Ms. Lane? There were no people. Not a single one. As if everyone had agreed at exactly the same moment to vacate twenty-some city blocks, right in the middle of whatever they were doing, without taking a single thing, not their cars, not even their clothes. Did they all walk out naked?"

"How would I know?"

"It's happening right here, Ms. Lane. There's an area missing on these maps right next to your bookstore. Don't tell me you never look down that way when you leave."

I shrugged. "I don't leave much."

"I follow you. You leave all the time."

"I'm pretty self-engrossed, Inspector. I rarely look around." I glanced behind him, for the dozenth time. The Shades were still behaving shadily, trapped in their darkness, licking thin, dark, nasty Shade lips.

"Bullshit. I interrogated you. You're smart and sharp, and you're lying."

"Okay, you explain it. What do you think happened?"

"I don't know."

"Can you think of anything that might explain what you found?"

A muscle worked in his jaw. "No."

"Then what do you expect me to tell you? That evil creatures of the night have taken over Dublin? That they're right down there"—I flung my arm out to the right—"and they're eating people and leaving the parts they don't like behind? That they've claimed certain territories as their own, and if you're stupid enough to walk or drive into one after dark, you'll die?" There, that was as close to warning him as I could get.

"Don't be a fool, Ms. Lane."

"Ditto, Inspector," I said sharply. "You want my advice? Stay out of places you can't find on maps. Now go *away*." I turned my back on him.

"This isn't over," he said tightly.

It seemed, lately, everyone was saying that to me. No, it certainly wasn't, but I had a sinking feeling I knew how it was going to end: with one more death on my conscience to occupy my already sleepless nights. "Leave me alone, or go get a warrant." I slid the key into the door and unlocked it. As I opened it, I glanced over my shoulder.

Jayne was standing on the sidewalk, in almost exactly the same spot I'd occupied five minutes earlier, staring down into the abandoned neighborhood, brows drawn, forehead furrowed. He didn't know it, but the Shades were staring back, in that faceless, eyeless way they have. What would I do if he began walking down there?

I knew the answer and I hated it: I'd whip out my flashlights and follow him in. I'd make a complete and utter spectacle of myself rescuing him from something he couldn't and wouldn't ever be able to see. Probably get locked up in the mental ward at the local hospital as thanks for my trouble.

My headache was turning brutal. If I didn't get aspirin soon, it was going to spike right back up to vomiting pain.

He looked at me. Although Jayne had perfected what I call cop-face—a certain imperturbable scrutiny coupled with a patient certainty that the person they're dealing with will eventually sprout several extra assholes and turn into a complete one—I've gotten better at reading people.

He was scared.

"Go home, Inspector," I said softly. "Kiss your wife, and tuck your children in. Count your blessings. Don't go hunting for curses."

He looked at me a long moment, as if debating the criteria of cowardice, then turned and stormed off toward Temple Bar.

I heaved a huge sigh of relief and limped into the bookstore.

Even if it hadn't been a much-needed sanctuary, I would have loved BB&B. I've found my calling, and it isn't being a *sidhe*-seer. It's running a bookstore, especially one that carries the best fashion magazines, pretty pens, stationery, and journals, and has such an upscale, elegant atmosphere. It embodies all the things I always wanted to be myself: smart, classy, polished, tasteful.

The first thing that strikes you when you step inside Barrons Books and Baubles, besides the abundance of gleaming rich mahogany and beveled glass windows, is a mildly disorienting sensation of spatial anomaly, as if you've slid open a matchbox and found a football field tucked neatly inside.

The main room is about seventy feet long and fifty feet wide. The front half vaults straight up to the roof, four grand stories. Ornate mahogany bookcases line each level, from floor to molding. Behind elegant banisters, platform walkways permit catwalk access on the second, third, and fourth levels. Ladders slide on oiled rollers from one section to the next.

The first floor has freestanding shelves arranged in wide aisles on the left, two seating cozies, fore and aft, with an elegant, enameled gas fireplace (in front of which I spend a great deal of time trying to thaw out from Dublin's chilly weather) and a cashier station on the right, behind which is a fridge, a small TV, and my sound dock. Beyond the rear balconies on the upper levels are more books, including the very rare ones, and some of those baubles the sign mentions, secured in locked display cabinets.

Costly rugs drape the hardwood floors. The furniture is old-world, sumptuous, and expensive, like the authentic tufted Chesterfield sofa I like to curl up on and read. The lights are antique sconces and recessed bulbs of a particular amber hue that cast everything in a warm buttery glow.

When I cross the threshold from the cold, wet, crazy streets outside and step into the bookstore I feel like I can breathe. When I open for business and begin ringing up purchases on the old-fashioned cash register that tinkles a tiny silver bell each time the drawer pops open, my life feels simple and good, and I can forget all my problems for a while.

I glanced at my watch, and kicked off my ruined shoes. It was nearly midnight. Just a few hours ago, I'd been sitting in the rear conversation area with the enigmatic owner of the bookstore, demanding to know what he was.

As usual, he hadn't answered me.

I really don't know why I bother. Barrons knows virtually everything about me. I wouldn't be surprised if somewhere he has a little file that encompasses my entire life to date, with neatly mounted, acerbically captioned photos—*see Mac sunbathe, see Mac paint her nails, see Mac almost die.*

But whenever I ask him a personal question, all I get is a cryptic "Take me or leave me," coupled with a broody reminder that he keeps saving my life. As if that should be enough to shut me up and keep me in line.

Sad fact is, it usually does.

There's an intolerable imbalance of power between us. He's the one holding all the trump cards while I'm barely managing to hang on to the few lousy twos and threes life deals me.

We might hunt OOPs, or Objects of Power— sacred Fae relics, like the Hallows—together, fight and kill our enemies side by side, and, recently, even try to tear each other's clothing in a case of lust as sudden and searing as the unexpected sirocco I'd somehow glimpsed in his mind while kissing him—but we sure didn't share personal details of our lives or schedules with each other. I had no idea where he lived, where he went when he wasn't around, or when he might come around next. It irked me. A lot. Especially now that I knew he could find *me* anytime he wanted, using the brand he'd tattooed on the back of my skull—his fecking middle initial Z. Yes, it had saved my life. No, that didn't mean I had to like it.

I peeled off my dripping jacket and hung it up. Two flashlights crashed to the floor and went rolling. I needed to find a better way to carry them. They were cumbersome in my pockets and constantly falling out. I was afraid that pretty soon I'd be known as "that crazy flashlight-carrying chick" around the parts of Dublin I frequented.

I hurried to the bathroom at the back of the store, gingerly toweled my hair, and wiped gently at my smudged makeup. There was a bottle of aspirin upstairs shouting my name. A month ago, I would have immediately fixed my face. Now, I was just happy I had good skin and glad to be out of the rain.

I stepped from the bathroom and through the set of double doors that connected the bookstore to the private residence part of the building, calling for Barrons, wondering if he was still around. I pushed open the doors and checked in all the rooms on the first floor, but he wasn't there. There was no point in searching the second and third floors. He kept all the doors locked. The only open rooms were on the fourth floor, where I slept, and he never went up there, except once, recently, to trash my bedroom when I'd disappeared for a month.

I considered calling him on my cell phone, but my head hurt so bad that I vetoed the idea. Tomorrow was soon enough to tell him what I'd learned about the *Sinsar Dubh*. Knowing him, if I called him tonight and told him, he'd try to make me go back out and hunt it, and there was no way I was going anywhere but straight into a hot shower and a warm bed.

I was headed up the back stairs, when something moved in my peripheral vision. I turned, trying to pinpoint the source. It couldn't have been a Shade; all the lights were on. I backed down a step and scanned the rooms I could see. Nothing moved. I shrugged and started back up.

It happened again.

This time I got a weird feeling, not quite a tingle of my *sidhe*-seer senses, more like a prelude to it. I glanced in the direction that was bothering me: Barrons' study. After poking my head in, I'd left the door ajar. Beyond it, I could see the ornate fifteenth-century desk, and part of the tall mirror that filled the wall behind it, between bookcases.

It happened again and I gaped. The silver reflection of the mirror had just *shivered*.

I backed down the stairs, never taking my eyes off it. From a safe vantage in the hallway outside the room, I watched it for a few minutes, but the event didn't reoccur.

I pushed the door open all the way and stepped

into the room. It smelled like Barrons. I inhaled deeply. A trace of dark, spicy aftershave lingered in the air, and for a moment I was in the caves beneath the Burren again, where I'd almost died last week, when the vampire Mallucé had abducted me and taken me deep into the labyrinthine tunnels, to torture me to death as vengeance for a gruesome injury I'd inflicted on him not long after I'd arrived in Dublin. I was lying on the ground, beneath Barrons' wild, electric body, ripping his shirt open, and splaying my hands over the hard, muscled abdomen tattooed black and crimson in intricate, alien designs. Smelling him all around me. Feeling like he was inside me, or I was inside him. Wondering how much more inside him I'd get if I let him inside *me*.

Neither of us had mentioned that night. I doubted he ever would. *I* sure wasn't going to bring it up. It disturbed me on levels I didn't pretend to understand.

I focused on the room. I'd searched his study once before. Peered into every drawer, looked in the closet, even snooped behind the books on the shelves hunting for I don't know what, any secret I could dig up on the man. I'd found nothing. He maintains an antiseptic existence. I doubt he permits so much as a hair to lie around that might be used for DNA analysis.

I walked over to the mirror and traced my fingertips across the glass. Elegantly framed, it filled the wall from floor to ceiling, and was hard and smooth, made of nothing that could shiver.

It shivered beneath my fingertips. This time my *sidhe*-seer senses trumpeted alarm. Yanking my hand

away, I stumbled back against the desk with a muf-
fled cry.

The surface was now shivering in earnest.

Did Barrons know about this? I thought wildly.
Of course, he did. Barrons knew everything. It was
in his bookstore. But what if he didn't? What if
Barrons wasn't as omniscient as I believed? What if
he was dupable, and someone—like, oh, say, the
Lord Master—had planted some kind of spelled
mirror in his path, knowing his penchant for certain
antiquities...and Barrons had bought it, and the
crimson-robed leader of the Unseelie was spying on
him through it, or something? How had I failed to
sense it? Was it Fae or not?

Smoky runes appeared on the surface, and the
perimeter of the glass darkened abruptly to cobalt,
framing the mirror with a three-inch-wide border of
pure black.

It was definitely Fae! The black edges were a dead
giveaway. If they'd been visible earlier, I'd have
known instantly what the mirror was, but the true
nature of the glass had been camouflaged behind
some kind of illusion that even my *sidhe*-seer senses
hadn't been able to penetrate. I'd been in this room
half a dozen times, and never gotten the faintest tingle. Who could craft such flawless illusion?

This was no mere mirror. It was one of the glasses
fashioned by the Unseelie King himself as a means
of moving between the realms of Man and Fae. It
was part of the Unseelie Hallow known as the
Sifting Silvers, and it was in my bookstore! What
was it doing here? What else might be concealed in
the store from me, hiding in plain sight?

I'd seen part of this Hallow before. Nearly a dozen of the eerie silver apertures with black edges had adorned the walls of the Lord Master's house at 1247 LaRuhe, in the Dark Zone. There'd been terrible things in them. Things I still had nightmares about. Things like...well, like that hideously deformed thing currently morphing into shape before my very eyes.

When I'd told Barrons about the mirrors I'd seen at the Lord Master's house, he'd asked if they'd been "open." If this was what he'd meant, they had been. When they were open, could the monsters inside them come out? If so, how did one "close" a Sifting Silver? Could it be as simple as breaking it? Could it *be* broken? Before I could glance around for something to try it with, the thing of stunted limbs and enormous teeth was gone.

I exhaled shakily. I now understood why BB&B had that strange sense of spatial distortion. I'd felt a similar thing in the Lord Master's house, the day I'd gone into the Dark Zone and discovered my sister's ex-boyfriend was Dublin's Big-Bad, but I hadn't put two and two together. These mirrors, these dimension-connecting portals, somehow affected the space around them.

Now something else was coming, moving deep in the glass, whirling silver gusts back with its inexorable stride. I retreated to a safer distance.

Dark shapes drifted over the surface of the shivering mirror. Shadows that lacked definition yet tugged at primal fears. It was one of those times when running probably would have been a really good idea, but the problem was, I didn't have anyplace to run to. This *was* my sanctuary, my safe haven. If I couldn't stay here, I couldn't be anywhere.

It was closer now, the thing that was coming.

I stared into the mirror, down the narrow, silvery lane fading into blackness at the edges, lined with skeletal trees, cloaked in wisps of jaundiced fog, littered with monstrous creatures forming and re-forming in the mist. It reeked of wasteland worse than a Dark Zone, and I somehow knew the air inside the mirror was a chilling, killing cold, physically and psychically. Only a hellish, inhuman half-life could endure in such a place.

As the dark shape glided down the nightmarish path, the shadow-demons reared back with soundless screams.

More smoky runes materialized on the shivering glass. I couldn't tell if what was coming walked upright, or stalked on all fours. Perhaps it scuttled on dozens of claws. I strained my eyes trying to identify the shape of it, but the sickly fog concealed its attributes.

I knew only that it was huge, dark, dangerous... and almost here.

I exited the room on tiptoe, and pulled the door shut, leaving the smallest of slivers through which to peer, braced to yank it shut and run like hell.

The mirror belched an icy gust of air.

It was *here*!

Long black coat fluttering, Jericho Barrons stepped out of the glass.

He was covered with blood that had iced to crimson frost on his hands, face, and clothing. His skin was pale from extreme cold, and his midnight eyes blazed with an inhuman, feral light.

In his arms he carried the brutally savaged, bloody body of a young woman.

I didn't need to feel her pulse to know that she was dead.

TWO

]'d like to speak with Inspector Jayne, please," I said into the phone, early the next morning. As I waited for him to pick up, I gulped down three aspirins with my coffee.

I'd hoped to be done with the insufferable inspector for a while, but after last night I'd realized I needed him. I'd devised a plan that was simple yet brilliant, and I lacked only one thing to implement it: my unsuspecting victim.

After a few moments and a series of clicks, I heard, "Jayne here. How can I help you?"

"Actually, I'm the one that can help you."

"Ms. Lane," he said flatly.

"The one and only. You want to know what's going on in this city, Inspector? Join me for tea this afternoon. Four o'clock. At the bookstore." I caught myself on the verge of adding, in a deep announcer's voice, *and come alone.* I'm the product of a generation that watches too much TV.

"Four it is, but Ms. Lane, if you're wasting my time..."

I hung up, in no mood for threats. I'd accomplished what I needed. He'd be here.

I'm not much of a cook. Mom is such a great one, and well, let's just call a spade a spade and get it over with, until a few months ago I was so spoiled and lazy that if the thought of fending for myself *had* occurred to me, I would have promptly thrust it away in favor of beautifying myself and coaxed Mom into making me one of my favorite snacks. I'm not sure who's guiltier, me for doing it, or her for putting up with me.

Since I've been on my own, I've been eating a lot of popcorn, cereal, instant noodles, and snack bars. I have a hot plate in my bedroom, a microwave, and a small fridge. That's the kind of kitchen I know how to get around in.

But today I'd donned my chef's hat, limp and unused though it was. I might have purchased the tray of rich, buttery shortbreads at a pastry shop down the street, but I'd made the sandwiches myself, cutting loaves of fresh bakery bread into pretty little shapes with fancy edges, preparing the filling, and spreading my special recipe between the slices. My mouth watered just looking at the bite-size snacks.

I glanced at my watch, poured water over Earl Grey to steep the tea, and carried cups to the table near the rear conversation area, where a fire crackled brightly, chasing the chill from the gloomy

October day. Though I was loath to lose business or break routine, I'd closed the shop early because I had to conduct this meeting at a time when I knew my employer was unlikely to show up.

I'd gotten a major wake-up call last night when I'd watched Jericho Barrons step out of the mirror.

I'd fled up the stairs faster than a Fae sifting space, locked my door, and barricaded it, heart pounding so hard I'd thought the top of my skull might blow off.

It was bad enough that he was keeping an Unseelie Hallow in the store, hidden from me, and using it, probably regularly, considering it was in his study, but... the woman... God, the woman!

Why had Barrons been carrying a blood-covered body in his blood-covered arms? Logic screamed: Duh, because he'd killed her.

But why? Who was the woman? Where had she come from? Why was he bringing her out of the Silver? What was inside that mirror? I'd examined it this morning, but it had been flat, impenetrable glass again, and whatever the way inside, only Barrons knew it.

And the *look* on his face! It had been the look of a man who'd done something that he'd found in, if not pleasure, *some* kind of comfort. In his face there'd been a certain... grim satisfaction.

Jericho Barrons was a man it wouldn't be hard to romanticize (overlooking the toting around of savaged bodies, of course). Fiona, the woman who'd run the bookstore before I'd come along, had been so blindly in love with him that she'd tried to kill me to get me out of her way. Barrons was powerful, broodingly good-looking, insanely wealthy, frighteningly intelligent, and had exquisite taste, not to mention a hard body that emitted some kind of constant low-level charge. Bottom line: He was the stuff of heroes.

And psychotic killers.

If there's one thing I've learned in Dublin, it's that there's a very fine line between the two.

I wasn't about to romanticize him. I knew he was ruthless. I've known that since the day I met him, and saw him staring at me across the length of the bookstore with cold, old eyes. Barrons does exactly and only whatever serves Barrons best. Period. Keeping me alive serves him best. Period. But one day it might not. Exclamation mark!

Why did he have an Unseelie Silver in his study? Where did he go in it? What did he do? Besides carry dead women around.

The shadow-demons in the mirror had behaved just like the Shades in the Dark Zone had when he'd walked through it: yielding to his passage, giving him wide berth. The Lord Master himself had taken one look at him recently, and walked away.

Who *was* Jericho Barrons? *What* was Jericho Barrons? Possibilities crowded my mind, each worse than the last.

I had no way of knowing what he was, but I knew what he wasn't. He *wasn't* someone I was going to be telling anything about what I'd learned about the *Sinsar Dubh* last night. He kept his secrets? Fine. I was keeping mine.

I had no desire to be the one responsible for putting Jericho Barrons and the Dark Book in the same place together. He walked in one Unseelie Hallow and was hunting another. Gee, might that make him Unseelie of some kind? Maybe one of those dainty, transparent ones that could slip inside human skins and take them over, that I called Grippers? Was it possible one had possession of him?

I'd considered the idea once before but swiftly discarded it. Now I had to admit that I'd had no basis for dismissing it, other than that...well...I'd been romanticizing him, telling myself Jericho Barrons was too tough to be possessed by anyone or anything. Who was I to say that was true? I'd watched a Gripper walk straight into a young woman in the Temple Bar District not so long ago. The moment it had entered her, I'd no longer been able to sense Unseelie within her. She'd passed for human to my *sidhe*-seer senses.

What if he was secretly working for the forces of darkness, conning me as cunningly as the Lord Master had seduced my sister into hunting the Book? It would explain virtually everything about him: his inhuman strength, his knowledge of the Fae, his familiarity with and ownership of one of the Dark Glasses, the Shades avoiding him, the Lord Master not confronting him—after all, they'd be on the same side.

I blew out a frustrated breath.

The only time I'd ever felt like I could take care of myself, since I'd come to Dublin, was the night

Mallucé had nearly killed me, and I'd eaten Unseelie to survive. Revolting as it was, Fae flesh bestowed a degree of Fae power upon the person eating it; made them superstrong, healed mortal wounds, even supposedly granted power in the black arts.

I'd felt like I finally had an edge that night and hadn't needed anyone else to protect me. I'd been able to kick ass like all the other big bad men around me. I'd been Mallucé's equal. I'd been nearly as deadly as Barrons himself, perhaps *as* deadly, just not as well trained. I'd finally felt like a force to be reckoned with, someone capable of demanding answers, of throwing my weight around, without the constant fear of getting hurt or killed.

It had been exhilarating. It had been freeing. But I couldn't eat Unseelie every day. It had too many downsides. Not only did it temporarily cancel out all my *sidhe*-seer powers, and make me vulnerable to my own spear (the Hallow killed anything Fae, even if you'd only eaten it; I'd learned that from watching Mallucé rot), but I'd realized over the past week that eating Unseelie was addictive, and a single meal was enough to birth that addiction. Mallucé hadn't been weak. The lure of Fae power was strong. I'd been dreaming about it at night. Carving off chunks of live Rhino-boy...chewing... swallowing...feeling their incredible dark half-life entering my body...electrifying my blood...changing me...making me invincible again...

I snapped out of my reverie to find a dainty sandwich perched at my mouth. A bit of flour from the bakery bread was on my lip.

I thrust the sandwich back on the tray, carried the snacks to the table, and arranged the spread invitingly, near flowered paper plates and napkins I'd picked up on my way back from the pastry shop.

Genteel southern Mac was shamed by my lack of china and silver.

Spear-toting Mac cared only that there might be leftovers and food should never be wasted. People were starving in third-world countries.

I glanced at my watch. If Jayne was a punctual man, he'd be here in three minutes, and I would put my plan into action. It was risky but necessary.

Last night—between nightmares in which I was chasing the Book and each time I got close to it, it morphed into, not the Beast, but Barrons—I'd lay awake, sorting through and discarding ideas until I'd struck upon one that had impressed even me with its cleverness.

The key to finding the *Sinsar Dubh* was tracking the most heinous crimes. Where chaos and brutality reigned, It would be found. At first, I'd decided to try to get my hands on a police radio, but the logistics of stealing one, and monitoring it 24/7, had defeated me.

What I needed, I'd realized, I already had.

Inspector Jayne.

Mom always told me not to put all my eggs in one basket, and that was exactly what I'd been doing with Barrons. Who had I cultivated as my backup plan? No one. I needed to diversify.

If I could persuade one of the Garda to call whenever they received a report of the type of crime that fit my parameters, I'd get an instant lead, without being tied to a radio. I could rush to the crime scene, hoping the Book was still close enough that I could sense it, and use my *sidhe*-seer senses to track it. Most of the tips would probably prove fruitless, but eventually, I was bound to get lucky, at least once.

Jayne was going to be my informant. One might wonder how I planned to achieve such a monumental twist on the usual police/civilian relationship. That was the brilliant part of my simple plan.

Of course, I had no idea what to do if I managed to actually locate the *Sinsar Dubh*. I couldn't even get close to it, and if I managed to somehow, I'd seen what happened to people who touched it. Still, I had to hunt it. It was one of those things programmed into my genes along with my innate fear of Hunters, knee-jerk reaction to Hallows, and constant urge to run around warning people about the Fae, even though I knew I'd never be believed.

Today, I needed to be believed. Jayne wanted to know what was going on.

Today, I would show him.

The voice of my conscience protested thinly. I quashed it. Conscience wasn't going to keep me alive.

I eyed the tray. My mouth watered. Those were no simple egg, tuna, or chicken salad sandwiches, those scrumptious little confections I'd worked so hard to make, and was now dying to eat. Dreaming of eating. Hungering for in a way I'd never hungered for human food.

Those wriggling little delicacies were *Unseelie* salad sandwiches.

And Jayne was about to get one great big, eye-opening look at his city.

It went about as well as train wrecks do.

The inspector ate only two of my tiny sandwiches: the first because he hadn't expected it to taste so awful; the second, I think, because he'd thought surely the first must have been a mistake.

By the time he'd swallowed the second one, he could see that the sandwiches were moving on his plate, and there'd been no chance of getting a third one into him. I wasn't sure how long the effects of such a small amount of Unseelie would last, but I figured he had a day or two of it. I hadn't told him about the superstrength, regenerative powers or skill in the black arts that resulted from eating Unseelie. Only I knew he was currently strong enough to crush me with a single blow.

My hands had trembled when I'd forced myself to flush the rest of the uneaten delicacies down the toilet before we'd left. I'd set two aside, in case of emergency. Halfway out the door I'd called my own bluff and gone back to flush those, too. I'd caught a glimpse of myself in the mirror, white-faced with the strain of denying myself what I so badly wanted, the bliss of strength, safety from my countless enemies roaming the streets of Dublin, not to mention being able to hold my own with Barrons. I'd clung to the edge of the toilet, watching the chunks of meat swirl around in the porcelain-cradled whirlpool, until they'd disappeared.

We stood on the outskirts of the Temple Bar District, and I was exhausted.

I'd been with Jayne for seven long hours, and I didn't like him any better now than before I'd fed him Unseelie, and forced him to see what was going on in his world.

He didn't like me any better, either. In fact, I was pretty sure he was going to hate me for the rest of his life for what I'd made him confront tonight.

I'd drugged him, he'd insisted, shortly after I'd commenced our little monster-tour. Given him hallucinogens. He was going to have me arrested for trafficking in narcotics. He was going to have me kicked out of Ireland and sent home to prison.

We both knew he wouldn't.

It had taken hours of steering him around Dublin, showing him what was in the bars, driving the cabs, and running the vendor stands, to get through to him, but I'd finally managed. I'd had to coach him the entire time on how to act, how to sneak looks and not to betray us, unless he wanted to end up as dead as O'Duffy.

Regardless of what I might think of his methods of handling me, Inspector Jayne was a fine cop, with sound instincts—whether he liked what they were telling him or not. Though he'd insisted none of it was real, he'd nonetheless employed the stealth of twenty-two years of investigative procedure. He'd regarded the mouthless, sad, wet-eyed monsters and the leather-winged gargoyles and the hulking masses of deformed limbs and oozing flesh with the perfect impassivity of a nonbeliever.

He'd slipped up only once, a few minutes ago.

I'd quickly nulled and stabbed three Rhino-boys in the dark alley we'd been using as a shortcut.

Jayne stood there, staring down at their gray-limbed bodies, absorbing the lumpy faces with jutting jaws and tusklike teeth, the beady eyes and elephant skin, the open wounds, revealing pinkish gray flesh marbled with pus-filled cysts. "You *fed* me this?" he said finally.

I shrugged. "It was the only way I knew to show you what you needed to see."

"Pieces of these...*things*...were in those little *sandwiches*?" His voice rose; his ruddy face was pale.

"Uh-huh."

He looked at me, his Adam's apple convulsing, and for a moment I thought he was going to vomit, but he got it under control. "Lady, you are one sick fuck."

"Come on. There's one more thing I want you to see," I told him.

"I've seen enough."

"No, you haven't. Not yet." I'd saved the worst for last.

I concluded our sightseeing tour at the edge of a new Dark Zone on the north side of the river Liffey that I'd been planning to scout, so I could ink its parameters on the map I'd nailed up on my bedroom wall. "Remember those places you couldn't find on the maps?" I said. "The area next to the bookstore? The ones O'Duffy was checking into? This is what they are." I waved a hand down the street.

Jayne took a step toward the darkness and I barked, "Don't leave the light!"

He stopped beneath a streetlamp and leaned against it. I watched his face as he watched the Shades slithering hungrily at the edge of the darkness.

"And you expect me to believe these shadows eat people?" he finally said, tightly.

"If you don't believe me, go home, get one of your kids, and send them in. See what happens." I didn't feel as cold as I sounded when I said it, but I had to get through to him, and to do that, I needed to hit him where he lived, bring the threat as close to home as I could.

"Don't you ever mention my children to me again!" he shouted, turning on me. "Do you hear me? Never!"

"When this wears off," I pointed out, "you'll no longer know where the Dark Zones are. Your children might walk to school through one, and never come home again. Will you go looking for their piles? Will you even know where to look? Will you die trying?"

"Are you threatening me?" Big hands fisting, he bristled toward me.

I stood my ground. "No. I'm offering to help you. I'm offering you a deal. In a day, give or take a little, you won't be able to see any of this anymore. You won't have any idea where the danger to your family lies, and it's all around you. I can keep you informed. I can tell you where the Dark Zones are, where the majority of the Unseelie are gathering, and how best to keep your wife and children safe. If it gets really bad, I can tell you when to get out of town, and where to go. All I want in exchange is a little information. It's not like I'm asking you to help me commit crimes. I'm asking you to help me try to prevent them. We're on the same side, Inspector. Until tonight, you just didn't know what was on the other side. Now you do. Help me stop what's happening in this city."

"This is insane."

"Insane or not, it's real." I'd had a hard time accepting that, too. The bridge connecting the sane world to this dark, Fae-infested Dublin had taken me many faltering steps to cross. "It killed O'Duffy. Will you let it kill you?"

He looked away and said nothing. At that moment, I knew I'd won. I knew he would call me the next time a crime was radioed in. He would hate every minute of it, he would tell himself he was crazy, but he would make the call, and that was all I needed.

I left Jayne at the Garda station on Pearse Street, assuring him the vision would wear off soon. As we parted, I saw the same hollow expression in his eyes I sometimes glimpsed in my own.

I felt sorry for him.

But I needed someone on the inside at the Garda, and now I had him.

Besides, if I hadn't opened his eyes tonight and forced him to see what was going on, he'd have ended up dead in a matter of days. He'd been nosing around too much. He'd have spotted an abandoned car down some back alley and walked into a Dark Zone at night, or whoever'd slit O'Duffy's throat to silence him would have slit Jayne's next.

He'd been a walking dead man. Now, at least, he had a chance.

THREE

I'd die for him.

There's nothing else to say.

I'd give the last breath in my body and the last hope in my heart to keep him alive. When I thought I was crazy, he came to me and made sense of it all. He helped me understand what I was, showed me how to hunt and hide. He taught me that there are necessary lies. I've been learning a lot about those lately. Every time Mac calls I get more practice. I'd die for her, too.

He's made me see myself differently. He lets me be the woman I always wanted to be. Not the perfect daughter and honor student who feels like she has to do all the right things to make Mom and Dad proud, or the perfect big sister who always tries to set a shining example for Mac, and keep the nosy neighbors from ever turning their sharp, gossipy tongues our way. I hate small town busybodies! I always wanted to be more like Mac.

She doesn't do anything she doesn't feel like doing. When people call her lazy and selfish, she doesn't care, she's happy. I wonder if she knows how proud of her I am for that?

But things are different now.

Here, in Dublin with him, I can be anyone I want to be. I'm no longer trapped in a small town in the Deep South, forced to be the good girl. I'm free!

He calls me his Queen of the Night. He shows me the wonders in this incredible city. He encourages me to find my own way, and to choose what I think is right or wrong.

And the sex, God, the sex! I never knew what sex was until him! It's not soft music and candle-light, a choice, a deliberate action.

It's as involuntary as breathing, and as impossible not to do. It's slammed up against a wall in a dark alley, or flat on my back on cold concrete because I can't stand one more second without him. It's on my hands and knees, dry-mouthed, heart-in-my-throat, waiting for the moment he touches me, and I'm alive again. It's punishing and purifying, velvet and violent, and it makes everything else melt away, until nothing matters but getting him inside me and I wouldn't just die for him—I'd kill for him, too.

Like I did tonight.

And when I see her tomorrow.

I hated him.

Oh, I'd hated my sister's murderer before, but now I hated him even more.

Here, in my white-knuckled hand, was proof that the Lord Master had used his dark powers on Alina, turned her into someone she wasn't, before killing her: A page torn from her journal, penned in the beautiful, gently sloping hand she'd begun perfecting before I'd even learned to read.

A page so unlike Alina that it couldn't have been more obvious he'd brainwashed her, done that Voice thing to her he'd done to me the other night in the caves beneath the Burren, when he'd demanded I give him the amulet and come with him, and I'd been unable to resist or deny him. With the power of a few mere words, he'd turned me into a mindless automaton. If not for Barrons, I would have trundled off behind him, enslaved. But Barrons, too, was skilled in the Druid power of Voice, and had freed me from the Lord Master's spell.

I knew my sister. She'd been happy in Ashford. She'd loved being the person she was: bright, successful, and fun, idolized by me and most everyone else in town, the one whose smiling face was always in the newspaper for some honor or another, the one who did everything right.

He calls me his Queen of the Night.

"Queen of the Night, my petunia." My sister had never wanted to be queen of anything, but if she had, it certainly wouldn't have been the night. It would have been something festive, like Ashford's annual Peach & Pumpkin Parade. She would have worn a shiny orange ribbon and a silver tiara, and been on the front page of the Ashford *Journal-Constitution* the next day.

I always wanted to be more like Mac. She'd never

once said she wished she was more like me! *When people call her lazy and selfish, she doesn't care.* Had people really said that about me? Had I been deaf back then, or just too dumb to care?

And what she'd written about sex was definitely not my sister. Alina didn't like it doggie-style. She'd considered it demeaning. *On your hands and knees, babe. Yeah, right,* she'd say, and laugh. *Up yours.*

"See, not Alina," I told the page.

Who had my sister killed the night she'd written this entry? A monster? Or had the Lord Master brainwashed her into killing one of the good guys for him? Who had she been going to see the next day? Had she been planning to kill her, too? Were they humans she'd been killing, or Fae? If they were Fae, *how* had she been killing them? I had the spear. Dani, a courier for Post Haste, Inc., the false front for the organization of *sidhe*-seers run by the Grand Mistress, Rowena, had the sword. Those were the only two weapons I knew of that could kill a Fae. Had Alina discovered some other weapon I didn't know about? Of all the pages in her journal, why had someone sent me *this* page?

Most important and troubling of all: *Who* had sent it to me? Who had my sister's journal? V'lane, Barrons, and Rowena all denied ever having met her. Might the Lord Master himself have sent it, thinking perhaps, in his twisted arrogance, that it would make me find him as attractive as my sister had? As usual, I was adrift in a sea of questions and if answers were lifeboats, I was in imminent danger of drowning.

I picked up the envelope and studied it. Plain,

off-white vellum, thick and tasteful enough to have been custom-ordered; still, it told me nothing.

The address, neatly typed in generic font, could have come from any inkjet or laser printer, anywhere in the world.

MacKayla Lane c/o Barrons Books and Baubles, it said.

There was no return address. The only clue it offered was a Dublin postmark, dated yesterday, and that was no clue at all.

I sipped my coffee, thinking. I'd gotten up early this morning, dressed, and hurried down from my bedroom on the top floor of the shop so I could stock the new dailies and monthlies, but I'd gotten distracted by the stack of mail piled on the counter. Three bills into it, I'd found the envelope containing the page from Alina's journal. The pile of mail teetered; the monthlies were still boxed.

I closed my eyes and rubbed them. I'd been hunting for my sister's journal, desperate to find it before someone else did, but it was too late. Someone else had gotten to it before me. Someone else was privy to her innermost thoughts, and had at their disposal all the knowledge she'd gained since she'd arrived on Ireland's Fae-infested shores.

What other secrets did her diary contain, besides unflattering personal insight into me? Had she written about the location of any of the Hallows or relics we needed? Did someone else know about the *Sinsar Dubh,* and how it was moving around? Were I and my anonymous foe both hoping to track it the same way?

The phone began to ring, a local number. I ignored

it. Everyone that mattered to me had my cell phone number. Seeing Alina's handwriting, hearing her words spoken aloud in my mind, as I'd read them, had left me feeling raw. I was in no mood to talk books to a customer.

The phone finally stopped ringing, but after a three-second pause, began again.

The third time it started ringing, I picked it up, just to shut it up.

It was Christian MacKeltar, wondering what had happened to me the other night, and why I hadn't returned any of his calls. I could hardly tell him it was because I'd been a little busy being driven to my knees by a sentient Book; watching my murderous employer tote a dead body around; serving addictive, cannibalistic tea to a homicide detective in order to turn him into my informant, then steering him around the city, forcing him to see monsters; and just now, reading up on how my sister had loved having sex with the very monster responsible for bringing the rest of the monsters through to our world.

No, I was quite certain all of that would only alienate a man I was hoping might prove a valuable source of information.

So I offered him a colorful bouquet of lies, and made a new date with him for tonight.

By the time I left to go see Christian, Barrons still hadn't put in an appearance, and I was glad. I wasn't ready to face him yet.

As I locked up the bookstore, I scanned the Dark

Zone. Three Shades toed the edge of the light. The rest slithered and slid in the shadows. Nothing had changed. Their prison of darkness still held.

I turned briskly to my left and headed for Trinity College, where Christian worked in the Ancient Languages Department. I'd met him several weeks ago, when Barrons had sent me to pick up an envelope from the woman who ran the department. She hadn't been there, but Christian had.

Then we'd run into each other a second time, a week ago, in a pub, where he'd stunned me by telling me he'd known my sister, and even knew what she and I were. Our conversation had been rudely interrupted by Barrons, who'd called to warn me Hunters were in the city, and told me to return to the bookstore. I'd been planning to call Christian the next day and find out what else he knew, but on my way home, I'd been cornered by Hunters and abducted by Mallucé and, needless to say, I'd had my hands a little full battling for my life. Then, the other night, the debilitating appearance of the *Sinsar Dubh* had prevented us from meeting again. I was anxious to find out what he knew.

I pushed my curls back from my forehead and fluffed them with my fingers. I'd dressed up again tonight, wound a brilliant silk scarf through my hair and tied it, letting the brightly colored ends trail over my shoulder, and drape softly in my cleavage. I was nothing if not determined; at least twice a week I would wear bright, pretty clothes. I was afraid if I didn't, I'd forget who I was. I'd turn into what I felt like: a grungy, weapon-bearing, pissy, resentful, vengeance-hungry bitch. The girl with long blond hair, perfect makeup, and nails might be gone, but I was still pretty. My shoulder-length Arabian-night hair curled flatteringly around my face, complementing my green eyes and clear skin. Coupling red lipstick with my darker 'do made me look older, sexier than I used to.

I'd chosen clothes tonight that hugged my curves and showed them to their best advantage. I was wearing a cream skirt, with a snug yellow sweater in honor of Alina (beneath a short, stylish, cream raincoat that concealed eight flashlights, two knives, and a spear), high heels, and pearls. Dad said the day they'd picked us up from the adoption agency, Alina had been dressed like a sunbeam, and I'd been a rainbow.

Alina.

Her absence in my life was so painful that it was a presence. Grief still kicked me awake in the morning, kept me company all day, and crawled into bed with me at night.

Dublin was a constant reminder of her. She was here in every street, in the face of every young coed who had no idea what was walking right alongside her, masquerading as human. She was laughing in the pubs, and dying later in the dark.

She was all the people I couldn't save.

I skirted the busy *craic*-filled streets of Temple Bar and headed straight for the college. Last night I'd walked through the heavily trafficked tourist zone that boasted over six hundred pubs, but tonight I was in no mood to be reminded that there were only two known weapons that could kill Fae and hundreds, if not thousands, of Unseelie in the city. My encounter with the *Sinsar Dubh* had sobered me. The sheer evilness of the thing had served as a grim reminder that, although I might have recently triumphed in an against-all-odds type of situation and walked out of it stronger, there was worse in store for me yet.

When I arrived at the office that housed the staff of the Ancient Languages Department, Christian met me at the door, looking young, hip, and hot in faded jeans, rugged boots, and a sweater, his long, dark hair pulled back at his nape in a leather thong. He gave me a charged, appreciative look, making me glad I'd taken care with my appearance. A woman likes to know her efforts are paying off.

He took my arm and suggested we go somewhere else. "They're discussing the budget," he advised in a deep, husky brogue, adjusting his stuffed backpack over a well-muscled shoulder.

"Don't you need to stay?"

"Nah. Only full-timers have to suffer the meetings. I'm part-time." He flashed a killer smile that made me stand up straight. Christian was the kind of good-looking that hit you over the head, made you keep stealing second and third glances at him: the five-o'clock shadow on the strong jaw, the broad shoulders, the flawless dark skin, and the striking tiger-eyes. There was an easy grace to his long-limbed body that hinted at maturity beyond his years. "Besides, it's not a place I'm comfortable talking, and we've a great deal to talk about, lass."

I hoped that meant someone was finally going to tell me something useful about my sister. He led me to a windowless study room off a vending area in the nearly deserted basement of the building. We settled into folding metal chairs, beneath the hum of fluorescent lights, where I imagined Alina might have sat and studied a time or two. I wasted no time asking Christian how he'd met her. I wondered if he'd been one of the boys she'd dated when she'd first come over, before she'd been brainwashed by the Lord Master. I sure would have. In another life. A normal one.

"She came to the ALD, looking for someone to translate a page of text."

"What kind of text?" I thought instantly of the *Sinsar Dubh*.

"Nothing I could translate. My uncles couldn't, either."

I assumed his uncles were linguists and said so.

He smiled faintly, as if amused by the question. "They're historians, after a fashion, knowledgeable about antiquities and such. I've never stumbled across a text they couldn't translate."

"Did you ever find out what it was?"

"My turn, Mac. I've a few questions of my own. What happened to you the other night? Why'd you cry off?"

"I told you. My dad called, and we got to talking about Mom and how she's getting worse and I lost track of time. Then, by the time I got off the phone, something I ate for dinner wasn't agreeing with me and I felt so sick I just went to bed."

"Nice try," he said dryly. "Now tell me the truth."

"I just did."

"No, you didn't. You're lying. I hear it in your voice."

"You can't hear whether I'm lying in my voice," I scoffed. "Body language might tell you a thing or two, but—"

"Yes, I can." He cut me off with a faintly bitter flash of that killer smile. "Literally. You lie, I hear it. And I wish I didn't. You have no idea how often people lie. All the bloody time, about everything, even stupid things that make no sense to bother lying about. Truth between us, Mac, or nothing at all. Your choice. But don't bother trying to fool me. You can't."

I began to ease off my coat, remembered my arsenal, and thought better of it, settled back in my chair, and crossed my legs, one high heel swinging. I searched his face. My God, he was serious. "You really know when people are lying?"

He nodded.

"Prove it."

"Got a boyfriend?"

"No."

"Is there a man you're interested in?"

"No."

"You're lying."

I stiffened. "I am not."

"Yes, you are. He may not be a boyfriend but there's someone you're interested in enough that you're thinking about having sex with him."

I glared. "I am not. And you can't possibly know that."

He shrugged. "Sorry, Mac, I hear the truth even when the person isn't admitting it to themselves." One dark brow lifted. "I don't suppose it might be me?"

I blushed. He'd just made me think it. Us. Naked. Wow. I was a perfectly healthy woman, and he *was* a gorgeous man. "No," I said, embarrassed.

He laughed, gold eyes glittering. "Lie. A whopper. Gotta love that. Have I told you I'm a big believer in fulfilling a woman's fantasies?"

I rolled my eyes. "I *wasn't* thinking it before you said it. You put the thought in my head and then, there it was, and I was thinking it." And that worried me, because I could think of only two other people—and I was using that term loosely about both—that I might have been thinking of having sex with *before* he'd made me think about having sex with him, and both were terrible choices. "This doesn't prove anything."

"Guess you'll have to take me on faith then, until you get to know me. I take you on faith. I don't ask you to prove that you see the Fae."

"People think about having sex all the time," I said irritably. "Are you aware of every time you're thinking about it, and who with?"

"Bless the saints, no. I wouldn't get anything done. Most of the time it's just background music, you know, sex-sex-sex-find-it-have-it-drown-in-it-before-more-perfectly-good-sperm-die, playing in my head, to an easy, sensuous beat, then somebody like you walks in and it ratchets up to that Nine Inch Nails song my uncle plays all the time for his wife." He grimaced. "We leave the castle and go somewhere else when he does that."

"Your uncle listens to Trent Reznor?" I blinked. "You live in a castle?" I didn't know which thought was weirder.

"Big. Drafty. Not as impressive as it sounds. And not all my uncles are as cool as Dageus. Men want to be him. Women adore him. It's irritating, actually. I never introduce my girlfriends to him."

If he was anything like Christian, I could see why.

"Point is, Mac, don't lie to me. I *will* know. And I won't put up with it."

I pondered his claim. I knew what it was like to be capable of doing something others would consider impossible. I decided to take him at face value, and see what came of it. Time would tell. "So, is it a gift of birth, like me being a *sidhe*-seer?"

"You don't think being a *sidhe*-seer is a gift. Nor is my . . . little problem, and yes, much to my parents' inconvenience, I was born this way. There are necessary lies. Or, at least, kind ones. I never got to hear any of them. I don't get to hear them now."

Alina had said the same thing: necessary lies. "Well, look on the bright side of it, you don't get to hear any lies, but nobody around you gets to tell any, either. Do you think it's easy to be around someone that you have to tell the truth to all the— oh!" I drew up short. "You don't have many friends, do you?" Not if he spoke his mind freely, and he looked like the kind of guy that did.

He shot me a cool look. "Why'd you cry off last night?"

"I had a close call with a Dark Hallow, and they make me too sick to function if I get too close."

He leaned forward, elbows on his knees, and stared at me with fascination. "Now *that* was a celestial choir of truth, lass! You saw a Dark Hallow? Which one?"

"How do you know about the Dark Hallows? Who *are* you and what's your involvement in this?" I didn't need any more mystifying men in my life.

"How much truth will you give me?"

I hesitated only briefly. Of all the men I'd met in Dublin, he seemed the most like me; essentially normal, but afflicted with an unwanted, life-altering talent. "As much as I can, if you do the same."

He nodded, satisfied, then settled back in his chair. "I come from a clan that, in ancient times, served the Fae."

The Keltar, Christian told me, had once been High Druids to the Tuatha Dé Danaan, many thousands of years ago, during that brief time in which the Fae had attempted to play nice and coexist with man. Something had happened that shattered the fragile peace—he skimmed over this part—but whatever it was had caused Fae and Man to go their separate ways, and not amicably.

A Compact was negotiated to permit both races to exist on the same planet but keep the realms separate, and the Keltar were given the duty of performing certain rituals to maintain the walls between them. Over the millennia, they performed them faithfully with few exceptions, and if they failed in some small way, they always managed to make up for it in the nick of time.

But in recent years, the rituals stopped going as expected. On those preappointed nights of the year when the Keltar were to perform their magic, some other dark magic had risen up and prevented the pledge from being reinforced, and the tithe from being fully paid. Although this other magic hadn't been able to collapse the walls between our worlds, it had seriously weakened them. Christian's uncles believed the walls would not hold through another incomplete ritual. The queen of the Seelie, Aoibheal, who in the past had always appeared in times of crisis, had yet to be seen, although they'd invoked her by every spell they had at their disposal.

I was riveted by the story. The thought that, for thousands of years, a clan in the Highlands of Scotland had been protecting Mankind from the Fae fascinated me. Especially if they were all like Christian: gorgeous, sexy, self-possessed. It was comforting to know there were other bloodlines out there in the world with special, unusual powers. I wasn't alone in my awareness of what was happening to our world. I'd found someone besides Barrons who had more information than me, and he was willing to share it!

"My uncles believe something has happened to the queen," he said, "and as her power diminishes, another's grows. The walls continue to weaken, and if we don't figure out something by the time the next ritual must be performed, they'll come down."

"What'll happen then?" I asked in a hushed voice. "Will the Compact be broken?"

"My uncles believe the Compact already *is* broken, that the walls are holding only because of the increasing tithes they keep paying. Fae magic is strange stuff." He paused then said tightly, "At the last rites, we had to use blood, Keltar blood, in a pagan ritual. It's unheard-of. We've never used blood before. Uncle Cian knew how to do it. It was dirty magic. I could feel it. What we did was wrong but it was the only thing we could do."

I understood that feeling. What I'd done to Jayne would never sit entirely well with me, but I'd been unable to think of an alternative. It hadn't been dirty magic, just dirty tea. Manipulative. Ruthless. But I've begun to understand that you can only afford to play nice when there's not much at stake. "And if the walls come down completely?" I reiterated my earlier question. I wanted to know just how bad things might get.

"When the Fae walked among us before, only the Seelie did. The Unseelie have been imprisoned for so long that mere whispers of myths remain. If the walls come down completely, *all* the Unseelie will be freed, not just the lower castes that are currently managing to get through somehow. The most powerful of the Unseelie Royal Houses will escape." He paused and when he spoke again, his voice was low, urgent. "Myth equates the heads of those four houses, the dark princes, with the Four Horsemen of the Apocalypse."

I knew who they were: Death, Pestilence, War, and Famine. The Unseelie I'd seen so far were bad enough. I had no desire to ever encounter a royal dark Fae.

"It'll get bad, Mac. They'll turn our world into a living nightmare. My uncles believe the Seelie may not be able to reimprison the Unseelie if they escape."

Was this why everyone was after the *Sinsar Dubh*? Did it contain the spells necessary to imprison the

Unseelie, maybe even keep the walls from coming down in the first place? It would certainly explain why V'lane and the Queen wanted it, why Alina had wanted me to find it before the Lord Master did. No doubt if he got his hands on it, he'd hurry up and destroy it to make sure no one could ever imprison his army again. I wondered where Barrons fit in. Would he really sell it to the highest bidder?

I couldn't dwell on the possibility of Unseelie overrunning our world. Keeping my thoughts tightly focused on my goals was the key to keeping my fears in check. "Tell me more about Alina." At my swift change of subject, he looked relieved, and I realized I wasn't the only one who felt like I was charged with an impossible task. It was no wonder Christian seemed mature beyond his years. He was. He had his own fate-of-the-world issues to deal with.

"I'm sorry, Mac, but I don't have much more to say. I tried to make friends with her. Although my uncles couldn't translate the text, they knew where it had come from, and we needed to know how she'd gotten it. It was a photocopy of a page from an ancient book—"

"—called the *Sinsar Dubh*." *The Beast,* I thought, and my soul shivered.

"I wondered if you knew about it. What do you know? Do you know where it is?"

I didn't know *exactly* where it was at the moment, and brandished that thought like a shield when I answered, "No," in case he really was a walking, breathing lie detector. Because he was searching my gaze far too intently for my comfort, I added quickly,

"What happened when you tried to make friends with my sister?"

"She rebuffed my efforts. She was deeply involved with someone and I got the impression he was very possessive. Didn't like her talking to anyone."

"Did you ever meet him?"

"No. I caught a glimpse of him once. Fleeting. Don't remember much, which makes me believe he was Fae. They mess with your head if they don't want you to see them."

"Did you tell my sister the stuff you just told me?"

"I didn't get the chance."

"If you never became friends, how did you find out she was a *sidhe*-seer? How did you find out about me?"

"I followed her a few times," he said. "She was always watching things that weren't there, studying empty spaces. I was raised on stories of *sidhe*-seers. My family is...into old myths and lore. I put two and two together."

"And me?"

He shrugged. "You were poking around Trinity asking about her. Besides, family's a matter of public record, if you know where to look."

With all my enemies, those were records I'd like destroyed. I was grateful my parents were four thousand miles away.

"Which Dark Hallow did you have a close call with last night?" he asked casually.

"The amulet."

"Lie."

I tested him. "The scepter."

"Lie again. And there is no such thing."

"You're right. It was the box," I said heavily.

"I'm waiting for the truth, Mac."

I shrugged. "The *Sinsar Dubh*?" I offered, like I didn't really mean it.

He exploded out of his chair. "What the—are you *kidding* me? No, no need to answer that, I know you're not. You said you didn't know where it was!"

"I don't know. I saw it in passing."

"Here? In Dublin?"

I nodded. "It's gone. I have no idea where it was . . . taken."

"Who—" Christian began.

"Hi, guys. What's up?"

Christian's gaze slid past me, to the door. He stiffened. "Hey, man, I didn't hear you come in."

I hadn't, either.

"How long've you been standing there?"

"I just opened the door. I thought I heard you in here."

I turned in my chair. The second time he'd spoken, I'd recognized the voice. The dreamy-eyed guy I'd seen in the museum and then run into later on the street the day I'd been interrogated by Inspector Jayne was filling the doorway with his dark, dreamy good looks. He'd told me he worked at the ALD, but I'd put him out of my mind. Like Christian, in another life, I'd have dated him in a heartbeat. Why, then, had it been Barrons I'd ended up kissing?

"Hey, beautiful girl. Fancy seeing you here. Small world, isn't it?"

"Hey." I blushed a little. I do that when a good-looking guy calls me beautiful. Especially now that every time I look in a mirror, I hardly recognize myself. Ironically, when your world comes completely unglued, it's the paste of the everyday, meaningless little things that suddenly seem like real gems.

"You two know each other?" Christian looked baffled.

"We've run into each other a time or two," I replied.

"They're looking for you back at the office, Chris," said the dreamy-eyed guy. "Elle wants to talk to you."

"Can't it wait?" said Christian impatiently.

He shrugged. "She didn't seem to think so. Something about misappropriated funds or something. I told her I'm sure it's just a bookkeeping error, but she's on one."

Christian rolled his eyes. "That woman is impossible. Will you tell her I'll be there in five?"

"Sure, man." His gaze cut to me. "Is this the boyfriend you meant?"

I shook my head.

"But you have one?"

"Dozens, remember?"

He laughed. "See you around, beautiful girl. Five minutes, Chris. You know how Elle gets about you." Dragging a finger across his throat, he grinned and left.

Christian hurried to the door and shut it. "Okay, we've got to talk fast because I need this job for the time being and lately Elle seems to be looking for any reason to fire me. There's something you need to see." He opened his backpack and pulled out a leather notebook, tied with knotted cord. "My uncles sent me to Dublin for a reason, Mac. Well, several, but only one immediately concerns you. I've been watching your employer."

"Barrons? Why?" What had he learned? Something that might help me sort through my own worries about who and what he was?

"My uncles are collectors. Everything they've been trying to collect for the past few years your employer has been going after, too. Some of it he's gotten, some of it my uncles have gotten, and still other items have gone to a third party." He withdrew a file from his notebook and handed me a magazine folded open to a page. "Is that Jericho Barrons?"

A brief glance was enough. "Yes." He was nearly lost in the shadows, standing behind a group of men, but the flash had caught his face at just the right angle to bathe it starkly in light. Though the photo was grainy, there was no mistaking him. Barrons is unusual. He says his ancestry is Basque and Pict. Criminals and barbarians, I'd mocked when he'd told me. He certainly looks the part.

"How old would you say he is?"

"In this picture?"

"No, now."

"He's thirty. I saw it on his driver's license." His birthday was coming up; on Halloween he'd be thirty-one.

"Look at the date on the magazine."

I flipped to the cover. The photo had been taken seventeen years ago, which meant he'd been thirteen at the time of the photograph, if the date on his driver's license was to be believed. Obviously, it wasn't. No thirteen-year-old boy in the world looked that mature.

Christian handed me another magazine, this one featuring a gathering of wealthy socialites at a gala at a British museum. Again, Barrons was unmistakable in it, even half turned as he was from the camera. Same hair and faultlessly tailored clothing, same expression on the haughty old-world face: a mixture of boredom and predatory amusement.

I flipped to the cover. This photo had been taken *forty-one* years ago. I flipped back to the photo and studied it carefully, looking for anomalies. There were none. It was either Barrons, or he had a grandfather who'd been his identical twin, and if this was Barrons in the photo, he was currently seventy-one years old.

Next, Christian passed me a photocopy of a newspaper article with a faded black-and-white photo of a group of uniformed men. Barrons was the only one not wearing a uniform. As was the case in the last two photos, he was angled slightly away, as if trying to slip off before the shot could be snapped. And, as was the case in the last two photos, he didn't look a day older or younger than he did today.

"Do you know who that is?" Christian pointed to the big, rawboned, thirtyish man in the center of the photograph.

I shook my head.

"Michael Collins. He was a famous Irish revolutionary leader."

"So?"

"He was killed in 1922. This picture was taken two months before he died."

I did some rapid math. That would mean Barrons wasn't seventy-one, he was an extremely well preserved one hundred and fifteen. "Maybe he had a relative," I offered, "with a strong genetic resemblance."

"You don't believe that," he said flatly. "Why do people do that? Say things out loud they don't even remotely believe?"

He was right. I didn't believe it. The pictures were too identical. I'd spent enough time with Jericho Barrons that I knew the way his limbs moved, the way he stood, the expressions he wore. It was him, in all those pictures. Inside, a part of me went very still.

Barrons was old. Impossibly old. Being kept alive by Gripper possession? Was that possible? "Are there more of these?" I wondered how far back Christian's uncles had traced him. I wanted to take these photographs with me, slap them against Barrons' chest and demand answers, even though I knew I'd never get any.

He glanced at his watch. "Yes, but I have to go."

"Let me hold on to these a few days."

"No way. My uncles would kill me if Barrons got his hands on them."

I relinquished them reluctantly. I could begin research of my own, now that I knew what to look for. I wasn't sure I needed to. What difference if Barrons were a hundred, a thousand, or *several* thousand? The point was: He was inhuman. The question was: How bad was whatever he really was?

"I'm leaving for Inverness tomorrow and won't be back for a week. There are...things at home I need to take care of. Come and see me next Thursday. I believe you and I can help each other." He paused, then said, "I believe we may *need* to help each other, Mac. I think our purposes may be tied together."

I nodded as we walked out, although I had my doubts. I'd been turning into a real bottom-liner lately and, regardless of how much Christian might know, or his involvement in maintaining the walls between realms, or how much I might enjoy his company, the bottom line was he was a man who couldn't see the Fae, and that meant, in a fight, he'd be a liability, one more person I'd have to worry about keeping alive, and lately, I was having a hard enough time keeping *myself* alive.

I shouldered past tourists, wound my way between Rhino-boys and assorted Unseelie, and was a few blocks from the bookstore, passing one of the countless pubs that characterize Temple Bar, when I glanced in the window, and there she was.

Alina.

Sitting with a group of friends in a low-backed corner snug, tipping back a bottle of beer. Lowering it and laughing at something the guy next to her had just said.

I closed my eyes. I knew what this was, and he needed to get some new tricks. I opened them and glanced down at myself. At least I wasn't naked.

"V'lane," I said. Did I ever have a bone to pick with him!

"MacKayla."

Ignoring the reflection of the tall, erotic golden creature behind my shoulder, I focused that ancient, alien, *sidhe*-seer place inside my brain on the illusion: *Show me what is true,* I demanded. The vision of Alina ruptured with the suddenness of a bubble bursting, revealing a group of boisterous rugby players toasting their latest victory.

I turned and was slammed upside the head with death-by-sex Fae.

My knees got soft, my nipples got hard, and I wanted sex on the sidewalk, sex bent over that nearby car, sex up against the wall of the pub, and who cared if my naked petunia got smashed up against the window for all to see in the process?

V'lane is a prince from one of the four Seelie Royal Houses, and it's difficult to look at him directly when he's in high glamour. He's gold and bronze, velvet and steel, and his eyes blaze with the stellar grandeur of a wintry night sky. He is so unearthly beautiful that it makes a part of my soul weep. When I look at him, I hunger for things I don't understand. I ache to be touched by him. I'm terrified of his touch. I think sex with him might undo my essential cellular cohesion, and shatter me into fragments of a woman that could never be pieced back together again.

If V'lane were a signpost, it would read Abandon All Personal Will, Ye Who Tread Here, and while I never thought much about will back home in

Ashford, here I've begun to think it's all I really have to call my own.

I tried regarding him with slightly peripheral vision. It didn't help. My clothing was painfully constricting, and I battled the overwhelming urge to remove it.

Fae princes drip such raw eroticism that it provokes a woman's senses beyond anything she was meant to experience, turning her into an aroused animal, willing to do anything for sex. While that might sound like it promises the kinkiest escapades and most incredible orgasms of your life, Fae don't grasp basic human concepts like death. Time has no meaning to them, they don't need to eat or sleep, and their sexual appetite for human women is enormous, all of which leads to one inevitable outcome: A woman caught in a Fae prince's spell usually gets fucked to death. If she survives it, she's *Pri-ya:* an addict, a void of insatiable sexual need that exists for one purpose, to serve her Master—and that's determined by whoever is currently giving her sex.

The first few times I encountered V'lane I'd begun stripping where I stood. I was getting better at resisting, because I was catching my hand every time it moved to the hem of my sweater, *before* I began pulling it off over my head. Still, I wasn't sure how long I could keep it up.

"Mute it," I demanded.

A slow smile curved his lips. "I *am* muted. Whatever you feel is not coming from me."

"You're lying." I briefly visited Christian's charge that I was thinking of having sex with someone. V'lane was not a someone. He was a some*thing.*

"I am not. You have made it clear you will not abide my...sexing you up. Perhaps you are...how do you humans say it...in heat?"

"We say that about animals, not people."

"Animals, people, what difference?"

"Seelie, Unseelie, what difference?"

Silvery flakes crystallized in the air between us, icing the night with royal displeasure. "The difference is too vast for your puny mind to comprehend."

"Ditto."

"You are not naked, on your hands and knees, offering me your pretty little ass, MacKayla, which is what you do when I use the *Sidhba-jai* on you. Would you like a reminder?"

"Try it and I'll kill you."

"With what?"

I yanked my hand from the button at the back of my skirt and went for the spear holstered beneath my arm, but it was gone. He'd taken it the last time we'd met, too. I wanted to know how he was doing it. I had to find a way to stop him.

He paced a circle around me. By the time he'd completed it, his gaze was as chill as the night air. "What have you been up to, *sidhe*-seer? You smell different."

"I've been using a new moisturizer." Could he smell my recent cannibalization of his race? Though I no longer suffered the dramatic effects of it, did a residue stain my skin, as it had tarnished another, less tangible part of me? I'd eaten Unseelie, not Seelie; would that make a difference to him? I doubted it. The bottom line was I'd eaten Fae to steal the power of the Fae. And I'd just fed it to another human. And I would never admit either of those facts to *any* Fae. "Like it?" I said brightly.

"You are powerless to defy me, yet stand before me dripping defiance. Why?"

"Maybe I'm not as powerless as you think." What would a bite of Seelie royalty do to me? I'd find out if I had to. Surely I could Null him long enough to sink my teeth in somewhere. The thought was a little too tempting. All that power... mine in one tiny bite. Or ten. I wasn't certain exactly how much I had to eat to get superstrength, when I wasn't mortally wounded to begin with.

He considered me a moment, then laughed, and the sound made me feel suddenly ebullient, drunk with euphoria.

"Stop it," I hissed. "Quit amping up my feelings!"

"I am what I am. Even when I 'mute myself,' as you say, my presence overwhelms mere humans—"

"Bull," I cut him off. "When you were kneeling on the beach in Faery, and touched me, you felt like a man and only a man." That wasn't entirely true, but it had been better than this. He could tone himself *way* down if he chose. "I know you can do it. If you want my help finding the *Sin*—er, the Book, turn it off, and turn it *all* off. Now. And keep it off in the future." I'd picked up a superstition from Dani, the young *sidhe*-seer I'd met recently who'd warned me about casting certain words on the wind I didn't want traced back to me, so now, whenever I spoke of the *Sinsar Dubh* aloud, out in the streets, especially at night, I tried to remember to call it simply "the Book."

V'lane shimmered, flashed brilliant white, then faded and resolidified. I tried not to gawk. Gone were the iridescent robes, the eyes that burned with a thousand stars, the body that radiated the fire of Eros. A man stood before me in faded jeans, a biker jacket, and boots; the sexiest man I'd ever seen. A golden, horny angel stripped of wings. *This* V'lane I could deal with. This Fae prince I could keep my clothes on around.

"Walk with me." He offered his hand.

Sidhe-seer walk with Fae? My every instinct screamed no. "I'll Null you if I touch you."

He considered me a moment, as if debating whether to speak. Then he shrugged, but not well. The human gesture only made him look more alien. "Only if you wish, MacKayla. The desire to Null or the instinct to defend yourself must be present. If you do not desire it, you may touch me." He paused. "I know of no other Fae who would permit such intimacy and risk. You speak to me of trust. I am giving it to you. Once you touch me, you could alter your intent and I would be at your mercy."

I liked that: him at my mercy. I took his hand. It was a man's hand, warm, strong, nothing more. He laced his fingers with mine. I hadn't held hands with anyone in a long time. It felt good.

"You spent time in my world," he said, "now I will spend time in yours. Show me what it is you care for so deeply that you would die for it. Teach me of human ways, MacKayla. Show me why I should care, too."

Teach this ancient creature who, in his most recent incarnation, was over one hundred and forty-two thousand years old? Show him why he should care about us? Right. And I was born yesterday. "You never stop, do you?"

"Never stop what?" he said innocently.

"Trying to seduce. You just switch tactics. I'm not stupid, V'lane. I couldn't teach you to care about us in a million years. But you know what really pisses me off? I shouldn't have to justify our existence to you, or any Fae. *We* were here first. We have the right to this planet. You don't."

"If might makes right, we have all the right to this world we need. We could have exterminated your kind long ago."

"Why didn't you?"

"It is complicated."

"I'm listening."

"It is a long story."

"Got all night."

"Fae decisions are not for humans to know and understand."

"There you go, getting all superior again. You can't fake nice for more than a few seconds."

"I am not faking, MacKayla. I am trying to know you, to earn your trust."

"You could have earned some of my trust by being around when I needed you. Why didn't you save me?" I demanded. I'd been scarred by my hellish time beneath the Burren in ways I didn't fully understand and, although my body had healed, and I felt stronger than ever, I wasn't certain I was necessarily the better for it. "I almost died. I begged you to come."

He stopped abruptly and spun me to face him.

Though his body was as warm and solid as mine, his eyes blazed inhuman fire. "You begged me? Did you cry my name? Pray to me?"

I rolled my eyes. "Figures that's what you'd hear." I stabbed him in the chest with a finger. It sent erotic recoils up my arm. Even "turned off" he was turning me on. "The important part in there is that I almost *died*."

"You are alive. What is the problem?"

"I suffered horribly, that's the problem!"

He caught my hand before I could poke him again, turned it up, and grazed his lips across the underside of my wrist, then bit it, sharply. I snatched it away, skin stinging. "Such a naked, defenseless wrist," he said. "How many times have I offered you the Cuff of Cruce? Not only would it prevent lesser Unseelie from harming you, with it, you could have summoned me and I would have saved you. I told you this at our first encounter. I have offered you my protection repeatedly. You have refused me at every turn."

"A cuff can be removed." I sounded bitter because I was. I'd learned that lesson the hard way.

"Not this—" He closed his mouth but it was too late. He'd slipped. All-powerful Prince V'lane of the Supercilious Fae had slipped.

"Really?" I said dryly. "So once it's on me, I'm stuck with it forever. That's the tiny little inconvenient catch you've never happened to mention to me before?"

"It is for your own safety. As you said, a cuff could be removed. How would that serve you? Better that it cannot be taken off."

Barrons and V'lane had both been up to the same trick all along: trying to put their permanent mark on me. Barrons had succeeded. I'd be darned if V'lane would. Besides, I was pretty sure Mallucé would have cheerfully sawed off my arm to remove the cuff, which made me really glad I hadn't been wearing it. "You want me to trust you, V'lane? Give me another way to summon you. A way that costs me nothing."

He sneered. "And make a Fae prince answerable to a *sidhe*-seer?"

"Allow me to put it into perspective for you. I saw the Book again the other night, and had no way to contact you."

"You saw it? When? Where?"

"How do I summon you?"

"You dare much, *sidhe*-seer."

"You ask much, Fae."

"Not as much as I could."

Had I lost a few seconds there, or had he been leaning closer all the time? His mouth was inches from mine. I could feel his breath on my skin. He smelled of exotic, drugging spices.

"Back off, V'lane," I warned.

"I am preparing to give you the way to summon me, human. Stand still for it."

"A kiss? Oh, please! I'm not that—"

"My name on your tongue. I cannot teach you to say it. Humans do not possess the ability to form such sounds. But I can give it to you. With my mouth, I can place it on your tongue. Then you have but to release my name to the wind, and I will appear."

He was so close that the heat of his body was sunshine on my skin. Was nothing simple? I didn't want a cuff. I didn't want a kiss. I wanted nice normal methods of communication. "How about a cell phone?"

"No towers in Faery."

I narrowed my eyes. "Did you just make a joke?"

"You walk among the worst of my kind, yet tremble at the prospect of a simple kiss."

"I'm not trembling. See any trembling here?" I thrust my trembling hands in my coat pockets, and gave him a dead-level, cocky stare. I doubted anything from V'lane was simple. Especially not a kiss. "How about a mystical cell phone, that doesn't use towers?" I pressed. "Surely, with all that power you're so smug about, you can create—"

"Shut up, MacKayla." He grabbed a handful of curls at the back of my head and yanked me toward him. I couldn't get my hands out of my pockets fast enough, so I slammed into his chest. I considered Nulling him, but if he really was going to give me a way to contact him, I wanted it. It was part of my egg-diversifying plan. I wanted all the backup, potential weapons, and odds in my favor that I could get. If I got into a jam again, like I'd been in beneath the Burrens, V'lane could save me in a matter of seconds. It had taken Barrons hours to track me and get to me, following the beacon of my tattoo.

Speaking of which . . .

V'lane's knuckles grazed the base of my skull where Barrons had branded me; his eyes narrowed, and he inhaled sharply. For a moment, he seemed to shimmer, as if he was struggling to hold form and not revert to another. "You think to allow his mark upon your body but refuse mine?" he hissed. He closed his mouth over mine.

The Unseelie Hunters are especially terrifying to *sidhe*-seers because they know where we live inside our heads. They instinctively know exactly where to find the small, frightened child in us all.

The Seelie princes know where we live, too, but it's the grown woman they're after. They hunt us in our own bodies, tracking us without mercy into the darkest corners of our libido. They seduce the Madonna; they celebrate the whore. They serve our sexual needs tirelessly, gorging on our passion, amplifying it, and slamming it back at us a thousand-fold. They are masters of all our desires. They know the limits of our fantasies; they take us to the edge and leave us there, hanging by shredded fingernails above a bottomless gorge, begging for more.

His tongue touched mine. Something hot and electric jolted through my mouth, and pierced my tongue. It swelled inside me, filling my mouth. I choked on it, and orgasmed instantly, as hot and electrifying as whatever he'd just done to my tongue. Pleasure ripped through me with such exquisite precision that my bones steamed and turned to water. I would have collapsed, but he took my weight, and I was in a dreamy, surreal place for a few moments, where his laughter was black velvet and his need was as vast as the night, then I was clear and me again.

There was something potent and dangerous in my mouth, on my tongue. How was I supposed to talk around it?

He drew back. "Give it a moment. It will settle in."

It settled with all the subtlety of multiple orgasms on the cusp of a steel thorn; pleasure inseparable from pain. Aftershocks quaked through me. I glared at him, more shaken by his touch than I cared to acknowledge.

He shrugged. "I dampened myself greatly. It could have been much more...what is your word? Traumatic. Humans were not meant to carry a Fae's name on their tongue. How does it feel, MacKayla? You have a piece of me in your mouth. Would you like another?" He smiled, and I knew he didn't mean a word, or whatever it was that lay there coiled, slumbering but barely, in a porcelain cage.

When I was fourteen, I chipped a tooth in cheerleader practice. My dentist was on vacation, and it was nearly two weeks before I could get it fixed. During the interminable wait, my tongue incessantly worried the jagged edge of the enamel. That was how I felt now: I had an aberration in my mouth, and I wanted to scrape it out because it was wrong, it didn't belong there, and as long as it was on my tongue, I wouldn't be able to scrape the Fae prince from my mind.

"It makes me want to spit," I said coolly.

His face tightened, and the temperature plunged so sharply my breath frosted the night air. "I have honored you. I have never before given such a gift. Do not belittle it."

"How do I use it?"

"Need me, open your mouth, and I will be there." I didn't see him move but suddenly his lips were against my ear. "Tell no one I gave it to you. Mention it, and I will take it away." He vanished before he finished speaking. His words danced on the air like the Cheshire cat's smile.

"Hey, I thought you wanted to know about the *Sinsar Dubh*!" I was so startled by his abrupt departure that I spoke without thinking. I regretted it immediately. My words hung as heavy as Georgia humidity in the night. *"Sinsar Dubh"* seemed to echo sibilantly, soughing on the night wind, racing the darkness to darker ears, and I suddenly felt as if I'd stamped a red *X* on myself.

I had no idea where V'lane had gone, or why he'd disappeared so suddenly, but I decided I'd be wise to do the same myself.

Before I could move, a hand closed on my shoulder. "I do, Ms. Lane," Barrons said grimly. "But first I'd like to know what the fuck you were doing kissing him."

FOUR

I turned, scowling. Barrons has a habit of popping up, without warning, when I least expect it, at the most inconvenient times. I absorbed him in slow degrees, the only way to look at him. As a whole, he's jarringly present in the space he occupies, as if ten times the man occupies a normal man-sized space. I wonder why. Because there's an Unseelie stuffed inside him? I wonder how old he *really* is.

I should be afraid of him. And sometimes in the middle of the night when I'm alone and I think about him—especially when I picture him carrying the dead woman's body, and the look on his bloody face—I am.

But when he's standing in front of me, I'm not.

I wonder if it's possible for a person to do some kind of "numbing" spell, create a glamour so complete that it deceives all the senses, even *sidhe*-seer ones.

"There's something on your lapel." I dabbed at it.

He's also meticulous, never a man to sport lint or stains on his clothes, but tonight his dark suit had a shiny spot on the left side. I was dabbing at a... man, for lack of a better word...who'd had birthdays untold, and walked in Unseelie Hallows, carrying around corpses. It felt as absurd as brushing a wolf's teeth, or trying to mousse his fur. "And I wasn't kissing him."

And I'd like to know what the feck you were doing with that woman in that mirror, I thought. But I didn't say it. There's a legal term my dad likes to use: *res ipsa loquitur*—the thing speaks for itself. I knew what I knew, and now I was watching him. And my back. Very carefully.

He knocked my hand away. "Then why was his tongue in your mouth? Was he conducting a clinical test of your gag reflex?" He smiled, but not nicely. "How *is* your gag reflex, Ms. Lane? Are you a hair trigger?"

Barrons likes to use sexual innuendo to try to shut me up. I think he expects the well-raised southern belle in me will think *eew* and back off. Sometimes, I do think *eew,* but I don't back off. "I'm a spitter, if that's what you're asking." I flashed him a too-sweet smile.

"Didn't look that way to me. I think you're a swallower. His tongue was halfway to China and you were still taking it."

"Jealous?"

"Implies emotional investment. The only investment I have in you is my time, and I'm expecting a big payoff. Tell me about the *Sinsar Dubh.*"

I glanced at my hand. It had come away from his lapel wet. I angled it in the light. Red looks black at night. I sniffed it. It smelled like old pennies. Gee, blood. No surprise there. "Have you been in a fight? No, let me guess; you saved a wounded dog, again?" I said dryly. That was the excuse he'd used last time.

"I had a nosebleed."

"Nosebleed, my petunia."

"Petunia?"

"Ass, Barrons. As in you are one."

"The Book, Ms. Lane."

I looked into his eyes. Was there a Gripper in there? Something very old looked back. "There's nothing to tell."

"Why did you call after him?"

"I haven't seen him since the last time we saw the Book. I keep V'lane informed. You're not the only shark in the sea."

He raked me with a contemptuous glance. "It's a Fae prince's fundamental nature to enslave a woman with sex, Ms. Lane. It's a woman's fundamental nature to be enslaved. Try to rise above it."

"Oh, it is *not* a woman's fundamental nature to be enslaved!" Everywoman reared up in me, battle-ready.

He turned and walked away. "You wear my brand, Ms. Lane," floated over his shoulder, "and if I'm not mistaken, you now wear his. Who owns you? I don't think it's you."

"It is, *too*," I yelled at his retreating back, but he was already halfway down the street, vanishing into the darkness. "I *don't* wear his brand!" Did I? Exactly what had V'lane embedded in my tongue? I fisted my hands, staring after him.

Behind me, militant footfalls approached. I reached instinctively for my spear. It was back where it was supposed to be, holstered beneath my arm again. I needed to figure out how V'lane was taking it. Had he returned it when he'd kissed me? Wouldn't I have felt it? Could I persuade Barrons to ward, so it couldn't be taken from me? He seemed to have a vested interest in my having it.

A troop of ugly gray-skinned Rhino-boys marched by, and I busied myself digging in my purse, partly to keep from watching them, counting their numbers, and trying to decide if they were new in town or if I'd seen them before, and partly to keep my face concealed in shadow. I wouldn't be at all surprised if the Lord Master was circulating a **WANTED** poster of me, with a detailed sketch. It was probably time to change my hair again, start wearing ball caps or wigs.

I resumed my trek to the bookstore. It hadn't eluded my orgasm-drenched brain that V'lane had disappeared the moment Barrons had appeared. Maybe he wasn't a Gripper but an even *worse* Unseelie that I'd not yet encountered. In a world that kept growing darker every day, Barrons sure did seem to have a knack for keeping all the monsters at bay.

Because he was the biggest, baddest monster of all?

———

Monday morning I woke up slow and hard.

Most mornings, I spring out of bed. Despite the fact that my life hasn't turned out how I wanted it to, it's the only one I have, and I try to milk it for all it's worth. But some days, despite my best intentions to plunge into the day and grab what happiness I can—even if it's only a perfect latte topped with cinnamon-sprinkled foam, or twenty minutes dancing around the bookstore with my iPod jamming—I wake up feeling bruised, coated with bad dream residue that clings to me all day.

I was slick with it this morning.

I'd had the dream about the beautiful dying woman again.

And now that I'd had it, I couldn't believe I'd forgotten it for so long. For years, as a child, I'd dreamt it over and over, so often that I'd begun confusing the details with reality, and started expecting to see her somewhere when I was awake.

I had no idea what was wrong with the sad woman, just that it was something awful, and I would have given my right arm, my eyeteeth, maybe even twenty years off my life to save her. There wasn't a law I wouldn't have broken, a moral code I wouldn't have violated. Now that I knew Alina and I were adopted, I wondered if it wasn't a dream, but a memory, borne in my infancy and suppressed, creeping out at night when I couldn't control it.

Was this beautiful, sad woman our biological mother?

Had she given us up because she'd known she

was dying, and her sorrow was the pain she felt at being forced to give us to new parents?

But if she'd had to give us up because she was dying, why had she sent us so far away? If I was truly an O'Connor, as Rowena, Grand Mistress of the *sidhe*-seers claimed, it seemed likely Alina and I had been born in Ireland. Why would our mother have sent us out of the country? Why not let us be raised by people who could have taught us about our heritage, indoctrinated us like the other *sidhe*-seers? Why force our adoptive parents to swear to raise us in a small town, and never to let us go to Ireland? What had she been trying to keep us away from? Or what had she been trying to keep away from *us*?

Were there other memories my child's mind had blocked? If so, I needed to find them, knock them loose, and remember.

I went into the bathroom and turned on the shower. I spun the handle to full hot, and let the scalding spray steam the air. I was shivering, icy. Even as a child, the dream had always left me that way. It was bitterly cold wherever the dying woman was, and now I was cold, too.

Sometimes my dreams feel so real it's hard to believe they're just the subconscious's stroll across a whimsical map that has no true north. Sometimes it seems like Dreaming must be a land that really exists somewhere, at a concrete latitude and longitude, with its own rules and laws, treacherous terrains, and dangerous inhabitants.

They say if you die in a dream, your heart stops in real life. I don't know if that's true. I've never known anyone who died in a dream to ask. Maybe because they're all dead.

The hot spray cleansed my skin but left my psyche coated. I couldn't soap away the feeling that it was going to be a truly sucky day.

I had no idea just how sucky.

I learned in one of my college psych courses about comfort zones.

People like to find them and stay in them. A comfort zone can be a mental state: Belief in God is a lot of people's comfort zone. Don't get me wrong, I'm not knocking faith; I just don't think you should have it because it makes you feel safe. I think you should have it because you *do*. Because somewhere deep inside you, you know beyond equivocating that something greater, wiser, and infinitely more loving than we're capable of understanding has a vested interest in the Universe, in the way things turn out. Because you can feel that, as much as the forces of darkness might try to gain the upper hand, there *is* an Upper Hand.

That's my comfort zone.

But comfort zones can be physical places, too: like your dad's favorite recliner that your mom keeps threatening to send to Goodwill, with those sagging springs, the torn upholstery, and some kind of no-worry guarantee because the moment he settles into it every night, he relaxes; or your mom's breakfast nook, where the sun shines in at the perfect angle every morning as she sips her coffee, and she kind of glows sitting there; or the rose garden your elderly

neighbor prunes to perfection, despite the swelter-
ing summer heat, smiling the day away.

Mine is the bookstore.

I'm safe inside. As long as the lights are on, no
Shades can get in. Barrons warded the building
against my enemies: the Lord Master; Derek
O'Bannion, who wants me dead for stealing the
spear and killing his brother; the terrifyingly Satanic
Unseelie Hunters that track and kill *sidhe*-seers on
general principle; all of the Fae, even V'lane—and if
by some bizarre fluke something *did* get in, I've got
an arsenal plastered to my body and I've hidden
weapons, flashlights, even holy water and garlic in
strategic locations throughout the store.

Nothing can hurt me here. Well, there's the owner
himself, but if he's going to harm me, it won't be until he's done with me, and since I'm far from finding
the Book, he's far from done with me. There's a measure of comfort in that.

You want to know somebody? I mean, *really*
know somebody? Take away their comfort zone and
see what happens.

I knew I shouldn't have been up on the third
floor, cataloging books, with an untended cash register and an unlocked front door two floors below
me, but it had been a slow day and my guards were
down. It was daytime and I was in the bookstore.
Nothing could hurt me here.

When the bell over the front door tinkled, I called,
"Be right down," and inserted the book I'd been

about to catalog on its side on the shelf to mark my place. Then I turned and hurried for the stairs.

Something that felt like a baseball bat slammed me in the shins as I passed the last row of bookshelves.

I went flying, headfirst, across the hardwood floor. A banshee landed on my back, tried to grapple my wrists behind me.

"I've got her!" the banshee yelled.

My petunia, she did. I'm not as nice a person as I used to be. I twisted, grabbed a fistful of her hair, and yanked on it hard enough to give myself a sympathy headache.

"Ow!"

Women fight differently from men. You couldn't get me to hurt a woman's breasts for anything. I know how tender my own are when I'm PMSing. Besides, we feed babies with them. Using a handful of her hair as leverage, I wrenched her around, slammed her on her back on the floor, and grabbed her by the throat. I nearly choked her by default when a second banshee landed on my back, but this time, I sensed her approach and pistoned back my elbow, nailing her squarely in the abdomen. She doubled over and rolled away. A third one vaulted herself at me, and I punched her in the face. Her nose cracked beneath my fist and spurted blood.

Three more women appeared and the fight got really vicious, and I lost all my illusions about women fighting differently, or being the kinder, gentler sex. I didn't care where I hit, as long as my punches connected, and I was hearing thuds and grunts. The louder the better. Six against one wasn't playing fair.

I felt myself changing like I'd changed that day in the warehouse in the Dark Zone, when Barrons and I had first battled side by side, against the Lord Master's minions and Mallucé. I felt myself turning into a force to be reckoned with, a danger in her own right, even without the dark aid of Unseelie flesh. It still didn't stop me from wishing I had a bite of it handy.

I felt myself becoming *sidhe*-seer, growing stronger, tougher, moving faster than a human could, striking with the accuracy of a trained sharpshooter, the skill of a professional assassin.

Only problem was—their green Post Haste, Inc. uniforms were a dead giveaway—they were *sidhe*-seers, too.

Fight scenes bore me in movies and since I'm telling this story, I'm fast-forwarding through the details. I was outnumbered, but for some reason, they seemed a little afraid of me. I decided Rowena must have sent them, and perhaps she'd told them I was rogue, unpredictable.

Make no mistake, I took a beating. Six *sidhe*-seers is an army and they kicked my petunia six different ways to Sunday, but they couldn't keep me down.

How abruptly a situation can flip from bad to ir-revocable, leaving you standing there thinking, Wait a minute, who's got the remote? Where's my rewind? Can I just go back a lousy three seconds, and do things differently?

I didn't mean to kill her.

It was just that, once it penetrated that they were *sidhe*-seers, I kept trying to talk to them, but none of them would listen to me. They were determined to beat me unconscious, and I was equally determined *not* to be beaten unconscious. I wasn't about to let them drag me to the abbey against my will. I would go on my own terms, how and when I felt safe—and after this underhanded ambush of Rowena's, that might be never.

Then they started demanding my spear, poking and prodding me, trying to find out if I was wearing it, and something in me snapped as I realized that Rowena had sent my own people after me—not to bring me in, but to *take my weapon away from me,* as if she had the right! *I* was the one who stole it. *I* was the one who'd paid for it in blood. She thought to leave me defenseless? Over my dead body. No one was taking my hard-won power away from me.

I reached beneath my jacket to pull it out and wave it threateningly, to make them back off and listen to reason, and as I yanked it from my shoulder holster, the brunette in the ball cap lunged for me, and she and the spear . . . collided. Violently.

"Oh," she said, and her lips froze on the round shape of the word. She blinked, and coughed. Blood blossomed on her tongue, and stained her teeth.

We looked down at my hand, at the blood on her pinstriped blouse and the spear lodged in her chest. I don't know who was more mystified. I wanted to let go of it and back as far away as I could from the terrible thing it had done to her—those cold inches of killing steel—but not even under such circumstances could I force myself to let go of the spear. It was mine. My lifeline. My only defense in those dangerous, dark streets.

Her lids fluttered and she looked suddenly... sleepy, which I guess isn't so odd; death is the great sleep. She shuddered, and sort of wrenched herself backward, twisting. Blood gushed from the unplugged wound, and I stood there holding the stopper. Green goo from stabbing Unseelie was one thing. This was human blood, on her shirt, her pants, on *me*, everywhere. I felt hot and cold at the same time. Too many panicked thoughts collided in my mind, blanking it out. I reached for her but her eyes closed and she stumbled backward.

"I'll call an ambulance," I cried.

Two of the *sidhe*-seers caught her as she fell, and lowered her gently to the floor, snapping orders at each other.

I fished out my cell. "What's the emergency number here?" I should know it. I didn't know it. She was still, too still. Her face was white, her eyes closed.

"It's too late for that," one of them snarled up at me.

Screw medical help. "I can get something else to save her," I cried. I should have kept those stupid sandwiches! What had I been thinking? Fact was, I should probably start carrying live Unseelie chunks with me, everywhere. "Just keep her still." I would rush outside, grab the nearest dark Fae, drag it back here, and feed it to her. She would be fine. I would fix this. She wasn't dead. She couldn't be. Unseelie would heal her. As I lunged for the stairs, one of them grabbed me and jerked me back.

"She's dead, you fecking idiot," she hissed. "It's too late. You'll pay for this." She shoved me violently and I slammed into a bookcase.

I stared at the green-garbed women huddled around the body, and my future flashed before my eyes. They would call the police. I would be arrested. Jayne would lock me up and throw away the key. He'd never buy self-defense, especially not with a stolen, ancient spear. There would be a trial. My parents would have to fly over. This would destroy what was left of them: one daughter rotting in a grave, the other in a jail cell.

They gathered her up, and began carrying her toward the stairs, taking her down to the main floor.

They were disturbing the crime scene. If I were to have any hope at all of proving my innocence, I would need it intact. "I don't think you should do that. Aren't you going to call the police?" Maybe I could make it out of the country before they did. Maybe Barrons could fix this. Or V'lane. I had friends in high places. Friends who wanted me alive and free to do their bidding.

One of them shot me a murderous look over her shoulder. "Have you taken a good look at the Garda lately? Besides, humans don't police us," she sneered. "We police our own. Always have. Always will." There was an unmistakable threat in her words.

I poked my head over the balustrade and watched as they reappeared downstairs. One of them glanced up at me. "Don't try to leave; we'll just hunt you," she hissed.

"Oh, take a ticket and get in line," I muttered as they banged out the door.

"I need to borrow a car," I told Barrons when he walked in the front door that night, shortly after nine.

He was wearing an exquisitely tailored suit, an impeccable white shirt, and a blood-red tie. His dark hair was slicked back from his handsome face. Diamond cuff links glinted at his wrists. His body hummed with energy, saturating the air around him. His eyes were startlingly brilliant, restless, darting everywhere.

I've felt that body on top of mine, been the focus of that consuming gaze. I try not to think about it. I have a box inside me now that never used to exist. I never needed it before. It's down in my deepest, darkest corner, and it's airtight, soundproofed, and padlocked. It's where I keep thoughts I don't know what to do with, that could get me into trouble. Eating Unseelie hammers on the inside of that lid incessantly. I try to keep kissing Barrons in that box, too, but it gets out sometimes.

I would not put the death of the *sidhe*-seer in the box. It was something I had to deal with in order to move forward with my goals.

"Why don't you ask your fairy little boyfriend to take you wherever you want to go?"

That was a thought, but there were other thoughts attached to that thought that I hadn't thought through yet. Besides, back home whenever I got really upset about something, like breaking a nail the same day I'd spent good money on a manicure, or finding out that Betsy had gone to Atlanta with her mom and bought the same pink prom dress as me, totally ruining my senior experience, I used to get in my car, crank up the music really loud, and drive for hours until I'd calmed down.

I needed to drive now, to lose myself in the night, and I wanted to feel the thunder of hundreds of stampeding horses beneath me while I was doing it. My body was bruised in a dozen places; my emotions were black and blue all over. I'd killed a young woman today. Commission or omission, she was dead. I cursed the vagaries that had led me to choose that precise moment to unsheathe my weapon, and her, that exact moment to lunge. "I don't feel like asking my fairy little boyfriend."

Barrons' lips twitched. I'd almost made him smile. Barrons smiles about as often as the sun comes out in Dublin, and it has the same effect on me; makes me feel warm and stupid.

"I don't suppose you'd call him that the next time you see him, and let me watch his reaction?"

"Don't think that would work, Barrons," I said sweetly. "Nobody ever sticks around when you show up. Darndest thing. Almost as if everyone's afraid of you."

My saccharine humor exorcised the ghost of his smile. "Did you have a specific car in mind, Ms. Lane?"

I wanted blue-collar muscle tonight. "The Viper."

"Why should I let you take it?"

"Because you owe me."

"Why do I owe you?"

"Because I put up with you."

He smiled then, really smiled. I snorted and looked away. "The keys are in it, Ms. Lane. The keys to the garage are in the top drawer of my desk, right-hand side."

I glanced at him sharply. Was this a concession? Telling me where he kept his keys? The offer of a deeper, more trusting association?

"Of course you know that already," he continued dryly. "You saw them there the last time you snooped through my study. I was surprised you didn't try using them then, rather than breaking my window. You might have saved me some aggravation."

Barrons deserves to be aggravated. He's the most aggravating...whatever he is...I've ever met. The night I'd broken a window to get into his garage, it hadn't occurred to me to try those keys because I'd been so certain he was keeping some huge dark secret locked up in there, that he'd surely never let the keys just lie around. (He *is* keeping some huge dark secret in there, I just haven't figured out how to get to it yet.) He'd caught my nocturnal B&E on the video cameras hidden in the garage, and left the incriminating evidence outside my bedroom door. "Let me guess, you have video cameras hidden in the store, too?"

"No, Ms. Lane, but I can smell you. I know when you've been in one of my rooms, and I know your nature. You snoop."

I didn't try to deny it. Of course I snooped. How else was I supposed to find anything out? "You can't smell where I've been," I scoffed.

"I smell blood tonight, Ms. Lane, and it's not yours. Why is your face bruised? What happened today? Who bled in my bookstore?"

"Where's the abbey?" I countered, fingering the lump on my cheek. I'd iced it, but not soon enough. It was hard and painful to the touch. I'd taken most of the blows to my body. My ribs were a mess, it hurt to breathe deep, and my right thigh was one massive contusion. My shins had huge goose-eggs on them. I'd been afraid several of my fingers were broken, but aside from being a little swollen, they seemed okay now.

"Why? Is that where you plan to go tonight? Do you think that's wise? What if they attack you?"

"Been there, done that. How did you find me last night? Were you looking for me?" The question had been vexing me. Why had he shown up when I was with V'lane? It seemed too coincidental to have been coincidence.

"I was on my way to Chester's." He shrugged. "Coincidence. The bruise?"

Chester's. Where Inspector O'Duffy had spoken to a man named Ryodan who, according to Barrons, talked too much about things he shouldn't be talking about—Barrons himself. I made a mental note to find Chester's, track down the mysterious Ryodan, and see what I could learn. "I got in a fight with some other *sidhe*-seers. Evade if you want, Barrons, but don't treat me like an idiot."

"I knew you were nearby last night. I detoured to

make certain you were safe. How did the fight go? Are you... unharmed?"

"Mostly. Don't worry, I'm intact in all the ways you need me to be. Never fear, your OOP detector is here." My hand went to the base of my skull. "Is it the brand? Can you find me so easily by it?"

"I sense you when you're near."

"That sucks," I said bitterly.

"I can remove it if you wish," he said. "It would be... painful." His brilliant gaze met mine and we stared at each other a long moment. In those obsidian depths I saw the darkness of Mallucé's grotto, tasted my own death again.

Through the annals of history, women have paid a price for protection. One day, I won't have to. "I'll deal with it. Where's the abbey, Barrons?"

He wrote "Arlington Abbey" and an address on a scrap of paper for me, got me a map off the bookshelf, and marked it with an X. It was several hours from Dublin.

"Would you like me to accompany you?"

I shook my head.

He studied me a long moment. "Then good night, Ms. Lane."

"What about OOP detecting?" We hadn't done any in days.

"I'm busy with other things now. But soon."

"What are you busy with?" It was innocuous as questions go. Sometimes he answers those.

"Among other things, I'm tracking down the bidders on the spear," he said, reminding me that he'd gotten several names from Mallucé's laptop in the grotto; contenders in an auction for the immortal weapon. I imagined he was trying to find out what they had in their possession that we wanted, and we'd be robbing them as soon as he had the lay of the land, and a plan in place. OOP detecting loomed on the horizon. I was startled to realize I was rather looking forward to it.

Barrons inclined his dark head and left. I stared at the door after he'd gone. There were times that I wished I could go back to my earliest days with him, when I'd thought he was just an overbearing man, as in *hu*man. But he wasn't, and if there's one thing I've learned in the past few months, in some of the most painful ways, it's that there's no going back, ever. What's done is done, the dead stay dead (well, mostly; Mallucé had a few problems with that), and all the regrets in the world can't change a thing. If only they could, Alina would be alive and I wouldn't even be here.

I picked up the phone and dialed the number I'd looked up earlier. I wasn't at all surprised that someone answered at such a late hour, at Post Haste, Inc., the Dublin courier service that housed Rowena's bicycling *sidhe*-seers who kept tabs on what was happening in and around the city under guise of delivering letters and packages.

Their motherhouse, the abbey, was far from the city, and I was informed stiffly that the abbey was where Rowena was now.

"Fine. Tell the old woman I'll be there in two hours," I said, and hung up.

FIVE

The Viper isn't the most expensive or fastest car on the market, but it delivers on everything it promises. It's got great lines, a wicked attitude, and hits sixty in under four seconds. If I ever get home again, I won't know what to do with my Toyota. I'll need to pull a Fred Flintstone, and poke my feet through the bottom.

The last Viper that Barrons let me drive, and the one I thought I was getting this time, was gone. In its place was one of the new ones, hot off the assembly line, sleek, low, and muscley: the SRT-10 with 90 additional snorting horses for a total of 600 feisty stallions, and 560 ft-lb of torque.

It was black on black with heavily tinted windows, and looked like some kind of crouching metal beast, waiting—no, *begging*—to be taken and tested to its limits. I was momentarily awed to be holding its reins in my hands.

I stood for a moment, absorbing Barrons' incredible

car collection, listening hard, alert for any sounds or vibrations in the floor. There was nothing. Whatever creature dwelled beneath the garage either slumbered or lay sated. I envisioned a hulking darkness surrounded by a mound of cleanly picked bones, and shook my head to dispel the image.

I slid into the black leather interior of the two-seater, cranked it, listened to the engine, smiled, shifted into first, and pulled out of the garage. A complaint about the Viper (by people who would be better off sticking to 4-cylinder automatics and living vicariously through reality TV shows) is that the passenger compartment gets too hot because of the exhaust, and that it's excessively noisy when you open it up on the road.

I revved the engine. The throaty growl was magnified by the close quarters of the alley, and I laughed out loud. That's what the Viper's all about, muscle and machismo, and when you've got it in spades, you strut it.

Down to my right, the huge Shade puffed up, nearly eclipsing the building behind it. I muttered something that would make my mother cringe, but kept my hands on the steering wheel and gearshift. There would be no more flipping of the bird at monsters of unknown parameters. I'd heard of road rage cases resulting in murder over less, and I saw no point in antagonizing an already antagonistic Shade that was far more aware of me than I would have liked.

Driving a hot car is a lot like sex to me, or a lot like I keep thinking sex *should* be: a total body experience, overwhelming to all the senses, taking you places you've never been, packing a punch that leaves you breathless and touches your soul. The Viper was way more satisfying than my last boyfriend.

I cranked up the music and barreled into the night. I didn't think about what had happened today. I'd had all afternoon to think about it and had made my decisions. The time for thinking was over. It was time for action.

Twenty minutes from the abbey, in the middle of what we call B.F.E. back home, surrounded by too many sheep and too few fences for my comfort in such an expensive car, I pulled over to the side of the dark, narrow, two-lane road, looked around to make sure there was grass and foliage growing, reassuring myself it was a Shade-free zone, left the headlamps blazing anyway, and stepped out.

The thing on my tongue had been bothering me since V'lane had put it there. I didn't know how long I was going to be able to stand it. But at the moment, I was glad I had it.

Need me, open your mouth, and I will be there, he'd said. I'd never have believed I'd be using it less than twenty-four hours later, but there was something I had to do tonight, and I needed backup. Serious backup. I needed something that would rock Rowena's world, and Barrons just didn't fit the bill the way a Seelie prince did.

I tried to decide what might constitute needing him, in a way that would release whatever was piercing my tongue. Merely thinking about him? Couldn't be that. I'd been half thinking about him all day. He'd been simmering on the back burner of my mind's stove ever since he'd put his pot there, as he'd known he would. Maybe, in time, I'd grow inured to the intruder. I doubted it.

"V'lane, I need you," I told the night, and darned if the thing in my mouth didn't *move*.

I gagged. The thing uncoiled and slammed against the back of my teeth. I spit it out convulsively. Something soft and dark exploded from my mouth, hit the air, and was gone.

"*Sidhe*-seer."

I spun. V'lane was behind me. I opened my mouth and shut it again, pining for the good old days of cell phones. Perhaps, as experts warned, radiation really would fry my brain after decades of repeated use, but I was feeling fried already from using Fae methods of communication a single time.

I didn't bother reaching for my spear. Its cold weight in my shoulder holster was gone. He'd somehow lifted it from me the moment he'd appeared. If I'd known how quickly he would show up, I'd have held on to it, to see if that stopped him. I made a mental note to try it next time.

"Fae," I returned the salutation, if it could be called that, dryly. How had I ended up in a world with such strange methods of address? Of all the men I'd met in Dublin, only Christian called me Mac. "Give me my spear back." I knew he wouldn't but it didn't stop me from asking.

"I do not come to you armed with lethal human weapons." V'lane was in full Fae mode: glittering a dozen shades of alien, his iridescent eyes dispassionate with a thousand-yard stare, dripping heart-stoppingly incredible sex. Literally.

"You *are* a lethal human weapon."

His gaze said *There is that, and so it should be.* "Why have you called me?" He looked impatient, as if I'd interrupted him in the middle of something important.

"How badly do you want the Book for your queen?"

"If you have found it and think to hold out on me..."

I shook my head. "Not holding out. But everyone wants my help finding it, and I'm not sure who's the strongest, or who will help *me* the most. There are things I want, too."

"You question my power?" His eyes blazed the silver of sharp knives, and I had a sudden, strange vision—the tatters of a genetic memory?—of a Fae flaying a human's skin from his body with a glance. *If they catch you, bow your head before them,* we'd taught our children, *and never look into their eyes.* Not because we'd been afraid they might be mesmerized—a Fae didn't need to make eye contact to do that—but because if our children were going to die horribly, we didn't want them to see their fate glinting in those sharp, inhuman eyes.

"Why did you leave when Barrons showed up?" I asked.

"I despise him."

"Why?"

"It is not your concern. Are you such a fool that you think to summon me to interrogate me?"

I shivered in my light sweater and jacket. The temperature had just dropped sharply. Fae royalty are so powerful that their pleasure or displeasure affects the weather, if they allow it. I'd recently learned that the Unseelie Hunters, with their great leathery wings, forked tongues, and fiery eyes, command this power, too. "I called you because I need your help. I'm just wondering if you can do what I need you to do."

"I will keep you alive. And I will not let you... what is it you disliked so greatly when you couldn't summon me before? Ah, you said you suffered horribly. I will not permit that."

"That's not enough. I need you to keep everyone alive tonight, and not let anyone suffer horribly. And I need to know you won't return here one day and hurt them in the future." *Sidhe*-seers had been hiding from the Fae for thousands of years, and I was about to take one of the most powerful straight into their hidden lair. Would I be branded traitor? Cast out? Oh, duh, I already was. Those who should have been my allies in this battle were now gunning for me, thanks to Rowena. I wouldn't have to do this if she hadn't pushed me so far.

His alien eyes narrowed and he glanced around. Then he laughed.

I caught myself pulling my sweater up, smiling vapidly. My breasts ached and my nipples throbbed. "Turn it off," I growled. "We have a deal, remember? You said you would turn it off around me all the time."

He shimmered and was once again the man I'd seen the night before, in jeans, boots, and biker jacket. "I forgot." There was neither truth nor contrition in his words. "You are going to the abbey."

"Crimeny," I exploded, "does everyone know

everything but me?" I consoled myself with the thought that at least now I didn't have to feel bad about betraying their location to V'lane. He already knew it.

"It would seem so. You are young. Your minuscule time is a yawn in my life." He paused then added, "And Barrons'."

"What do you know about Barrons?" I demanded.

"That you would be far wiser to depend on me, MacKayla." He moved toward me and I stepped back. Even in his muted, humanlike form, he was pure sex. He glided past me, stopped at the Viper, and traced his hand over the sleek metallic curve of the hood. V'lane standing next to a black-on-black Viper was a thing to see.

"I want you to go to the abbey with me," I told him. "As backup. I want you to be my protection. You will not harm any of the *sidhe*-seers there."

"You think to give me orders?" The temperature plunged again, and snow dusted my shoulders.

I reconsidered. It wouldn't kill me to phrase it nicely. Mom always said you draw more flies with honey than vinegar. "Will you promise me that you won't hurt any of the *sidhe*-seers?" Grimacing mentally, I added, "Please?"

He smiled, and a nearby tree pushed out velvety-looking, fragrant white blossoms that drenched the night air with pungent spices. They overgrew rapidly, plummeted to the ground in a lush fall of alabaster petals, and swiftly decomposed. Life to death in a matter of seconds. Was that how he saw me? "I will grant you this. I like it when you say 'please.' You will say it again."

"No. Once was enough."

"What will you do for me in exchange?"

"I'm doing it. Helping you find the Book."

"Not enough. You wish to command a Fae Prince as a lapdog? It costs, MacKayla. You will let me fuck you."

I jerked, and for a moment I was so angry I couldn't speak. It didn't help that his words had caused a slick, erotic thrill to flutter in my belly. Had he amped himself up again? Shot some kind of Fae sex-dart at me when he'd said it? "No. Not even if Hell freezes over will I offer you sex with me in exchange for anything. Got it? Some things are non-negotiable and that's one of them."

"It is merely coitus, a physical act, the same as eating or voiding waste. Why attach such importance to it?"

"Maybe for a Fae it's merely a physical act, and maybe for some people, too, but not me."

"Because sex has been so stupendous in your brief life? Because you have had lovers that have made your body burn, and set your soul on fire?" he mocked.

I notched my chin higher. "Maybe I haven't felt that, exactly, yet, but I will one day."

"I will give it to you now. Ecstasy that you would die for, but I will not permit it. I will stop before that happens."

His words chilled me: He was just another vampire, promising to stop before he drained the last drops of blood that kept my heart beating. "Forget it, V'lane. I'm sorry I summoned you. I'll take care of things myself. I don't need you or anybody." I opened the car door.

He slammed it so quickly that I nearly lost a finger. I was startled by his sudden violence. He crushed me back against the Viper, and touched my face. His eyes were razor sharp, hostile; his fingers feather-light. "Who bruised you?"

"I had a fight with some *sidhe*-seers. Quit crowding me."

He traced a finger over my cheekbone, and the ache vanished. He dropped his hand to my rib cage and pain no longer spiked through me with each breath. When he slid his palm across my thigh, I felt the hemorrhaged blood drain from the contusion. He pressed his legs to mine and my shins were no longer bruised. My flesh burned in the wake of his touch.

He dropped his head forward, lips close to mine. "Offer me something in exchange for what you ask of me, MacKayla. I am a prince and we have our pride." Though his touch was soft, I felt the rigidity in his body, and knew I'd pushed him as far as he would go.

In the Deep South, we understand pride. We lost everything once, but by God, we held on to our pride. We heaped fuel onto the fire of it, stoked it as high as a crematorium. And we immolate ourselves on it sometimes. "I know how the Book is moving around. I haven't told anyone." The length of V'lane's body against mine was unhinging doors in my mind, showing me rooms I was better off not knowing existed.

His lips brushed my cheek and I shivered. "Barrons doesn't know?"

I shook my head, turned it away. His lips moved to my ear. "No. But I'll tell you."

"And you won't tell Barrons? It will be our secret?"

"No. I mean yes. In that order." I hate it when people pile questions on top of each other. His mouth was fire on my skin.

"Say it."

"I won't tell Barrons and it will be our secret." No loss there; I hadn't planned to tell him, anyway.

V'lane smiled. "We have a deal. Tell me."

"*After* you help me."

"Now, MacKayla, or you go in alone. If I am to accompany a Null inside *sidhe*-seer walls, I require payment in advance." There was no room for negotiation in his voice.

I hated parting with any of my aces in the hole, but if I had to give V'lane a piece of information that I'd rather not give him, in order to keep Rowena from going after my back every time it was turned, so be it. I couldn't guard against all the dangers in the city. The Fae were bad enough, but at least I could see them coming. Rowena's minions were perfectly normal-looking humans who could get too close before I even knew they were a danger. While my instincts to lash out at a Fae were strong, my instincts to strike at a human weren't, and I didn't want them to get better. Humans weren't my enemy. I needed to send Rowena and her *sidhe*-seers a great, big "Back Off" message, and V'lane was the perfect courier.

Still, I didn't have to tell him everything. I pushed him away and slid out from between him and the Viper. He watched my retreat with a mocking smile. I felt better with a dozen paces between us, and began to recount select portions of what I'd seen, lying in the sour-smelling puddle. I told him that it was moving from person to person, making them commit crimes.

But I didn't tell him the three faces the Book had presented, or the severity of the crimes, or that it was killing the carrier before it moved on. I let him believe it was passing itself off from one live human to the next. That way if he decided to try to track it, too, I'd have an edge. I needed all the edges I could get. I knew V'lane didn't really consider humans viable life forms, and I had no more reason to trust him than I did Barrons. V'lane might be Seelie, and Barrons might keep saving my life, but I had far too many unanswered questions about them both. My sister had trusted her boyfriend right up to the end. Had she made excuses for the Lord Master, the way I'd been making them for Barrons? *So what if he never answers any of my questions? He's told me more about what I am than anyone else. So what if he kills ruthlessly? He only does it to keep me safe*...I could string together half a dozen at a moment's notice. V'lane, too: *So he's a death-by-sex Fae; he's never really harmed me. So what if he gets off on making me strip in public places? He saved me from the Shades*...

I'm a bartender. I like recipes. They're concretes. Was the drink recipe for seduction one shot charm and two shots self-deception, shaken, not stirred?

"You remained conscious the entire time?"

I nodded.

"Still you cannot approach it?"

I shook my head.

"How do you plan to find it again?"

"I have no idea," I lied. "Dublin has over a million people in it, and the crime rate has been skyrocketing. Assuming it stays around the city, which I'm not even sure we can assume" (this was a lie; I don't know why I was so sure of it, but I believed the Book had no intention of leaving Dublin's chaotic streets at the moment, nor at any time in the near future) "we're looking for a needle in a haystack."

He studied me a moment, then said, "Very well. You have upheld your end of the bargain. I will keep mine."

We got in the car and headed for the abbey.

Arlington Abbey was constructed on consecrated ground in the seventh century, when a church originally built by Saint Patrick in A.D. 441 had burned down. The church, interestingly, had been built to replace a crumbling stone circle some claimed had, long ago, been sacred to an ancient pagan sisterhood. The stone circle had allegedly been predated by a *shian*, or fairy mound, that had concealed within it an entrance to the Otherworld.

The abbey was plundered in 913, rebuilt in 1022, burned in 1123, rebuilt in 1218, burned in 1393, and rebuilt in 1414. It was expanded and fortified each time.

It was added onto in the sixteenth century, and

again extensively in the seventeenth, sponsored by an anonymous, wealthy donor who completed the rectangle of stone buildings, enclosing the inner courtyard, and added housing—much to the astonishment of the locals—for up to a thousand residents.

This same unknown donor bought the land around the abbey, and turned the enclave into the self-sustaining operation it is today. The abbey boasts its own dairy, orchards, cattle, sheep, and extensive gardens, the highlight of which is an elaborate glass-domed hothouse rumored to house some of the world's rarest flowers and most unusual herbs.

And that was all I'd been able to find out about the place in the twenty minutes I had to surf the Internet before leaving for the destination Barrons had given me.

Today, Arlington Abbey was owned by a subcorporation of a much larger corporation that was part of the vast holdings of an even larger corporation. Nobody knew anything about its modern-day operations. Oddly, no one seemed to find that odd. I found it spectacularly odd that a country that took such loving care of its abbeys, castles, standing stones, and countless other monuments asked no questions about the most extraordinarily well preserved abbey within its boundaries. But they didn't, and there it sat, in the middle of nearly a thousand acres, silent and mysterious and private, and nobody bothered it.

I wondered what tremendous importance this site had for *sidhe*-seers that they'd doggedly protected it, even under guise of Christianity, and rebuilt it each time it had been destroyed, fortifying it ever stronger until now it loomed, a forbidding fortress over a still, dark lake.

In the passenger seat, V'lane flinched and seemed to flicker.

I glanced at him.

"We will leave the car here," he said.

"Why?"

"Those at the abbey are...bothersome...with their attempts to defy my race."

Translation: The abbey was warded. "Can you get past their wards?"

"They cannot prevent my entry. We sift place. They cannot ward against that."

Okay, that was disturbing, but I'd come back to it. First things first. "Barrons said you can sift time, too." Actually, he'd said the Fae *used* to be able to, but couldn't anymore. "That you can go back into the past." Where Alina was still alive. Where I could save my sister, and this terrible future could be prevented, and we could resume our blissfully ignorant lives, unaware of what we were, happy with our family back in Ashford, Georgia, and we'd never leave. We'd get married, have babies, and die in the Deep South at a ripe old age. "Is that true? Can you go back in time?"

"At one time certain ones among us could. Even then, we were limited, but for the queen. We no longer possess that ability. We are as trapped in the present as humans."

"Why? What happened?"

He flinched again. "Stop the car, MacKayla. I do not enjoy this. Their wards are many."

I pulled over, and killed the engine. When we got out, I looked at him across the roof of the car. "So, wards are uncomfortable to you, but that's all? They don't actually keep you out?" Could he enter the bookstore anytime he wanted? Were Barrons' wards keeping me safe from *any* of the Fae?

"That is correct."

"But I thought you couldn't get into the bookstore. Were you just pretending the night the Shades got in?"

"We have been discussing *sidhe*-seer wards. The magic your people know and the magic Barrons knows are not the same." His gaze glinted like sharp steel at the mention of my employer. "Come. Give me your hand so I may sift you in. And mind your intent. If you Null me inside those walls, you will regret it. Again, MacKayla, see the trust I grant you? I permit you to take me inside your *sidhe*-seer world, where I am feared and hated, and I go at your mercy. There is no other among my kind who would consider it."

"No Nulling. I promise." Barrons had yet another edge over the rest of us. Why didn't that surprise me? Was that how he'd managed to conceal the Unseelie mirror from me? With deeper, darker magic than *sidhe*-seers knew? I couldn't get too bent out of shape over it, however, because it meant I really *was* safe in the bookstore. How complex I was becoming: grateful for power wherever it could be found, provided it worked for me. "Are we clear on what I'm going to do, and what you're *not* going to do?"

"As clear as your transparent desires, *sidhe*-seer."

Rolling my eyes, I skirted the car and took his hand.

At home in Ashford, I have a great group of friends.

I don't have a single one in Dublin.

The one place I thought I might make friends was at the abbey, among my own kind. Now, thanks to Rowena, that opportunity was closed to me. She'd been messing up my life since the first night I'd arrived in Ireland, when I'd nearly betrayed myself in a pub to the first Fae I'd ever seen and, instead of taking me in and teaching me what I was, she'd told me to go die somewhere else.

Then she'd stood passively by while V'lane had nearly raped me in a museum.

Then she'd sent her *sidhe*-seers to spy on me (like I wasn't one, too!) and finally, she'd added insult to injury—sending them to attack me and take my weapon, forcing me to harm one of my own. Not once had Rowena welcomed me. Not once had she shown me anything but disdain and distrust—for no good reason!

These women were never going to forgive me for killing one of them. I knew that, and I wasn't here to ask them to. It's not the hand you're dealt that matters. It's how you play the cards.

I was here to set the record straight.

Rowena had made a statement this afternoon. By

sending her *sidhe*-seers after me in force, with orders to subdue me and steal my weapon, she'd said: *You are not one of us and the only way you can become one of us is complete subjugation to my will. Give me your weapon, obey me in all things, and I'll consider letting you into the fold.*

I was here to make my own statement back: *Screw you, old woman.* To drive my point home I'd brought as my protector a Fae Prince capable of destroying them all (not that I would ever let him). If she was a wise woman, she wouldn't mess with me again, and she'd call off her attack dogs. I already had enough people and monsters messing with me.

Darn it all, I'd wanted friends and I'd wanted them among my own kind!

I'd wanted girls like Dani, only older, to confide in, to talk to, to share secrets of our heritage with. I'd wanted to *belong* here. I'd wanted to learn about the O'Connors, the bloodline I was supposedly descended from, and the last living member of.

"Take me in," I told V'lane, bracing myself to be "sifted."

I asked V'lane why the Fae call it sifting, and he said it was the only human word that encapsulated the basics of what they do. The Fae sift the limitless dimensions, like grains of sand through their fingers, letting a little spill here, a little spill there, sorting them until they have hold of the ones they want. When they have chosen, things change.

I asked if that meant he chose the "grain" of place where he wanted to be, and moved there by the power of thought. He didn't get the idea of moving there. According to him, neither we, nor the dimensions moved. We simply...changed. And there it was again, the two prevalent Fae concepts: stasis or change.

Sifting felt like dying. I simply stopped existing completely, then was there again. It was painless, but deeply disturbing. One moment I was outside, standing next to the Viper, in near darkness; the next, my night-enlarged pupils gorged on a blaze of lights, momentarily blinding me, and when I could see again, I was inside the brilliantly lit walls of Arlington Abbey.

Women were screaming. Many and loudly. It was deafening.

For a moment, I was afraid they were under attack. Then I understood: *I* was the attack. I was hearing the sound of hundreds of *sidhe*-seers sensing an immensely powerful Fae inside their warded walls. I'd forgotten about that tiny detail; of course they would sense V'lane, and they'd raise the hue and cry.

"Shall I shut them up?" V'lane said.

"No. Leave them alone. They'll stop in a minute." I hoped.

They did.

At my direction, he'd sifted us into the rear of the abbey, where I'd hoped to find the dormitories. My guess, based on the sketches I'd seen online, had been accurate. One by one, doors opened, heads popped out, mouths closed, gaped, and closed again.

A familiar head of curly red hair emerged from a nearby room. "Oh, you are *so* fecking dead!" Dani exclaimed. "You were in serious trouble before, but now she's going to kill you."

"Watch your language, Dani," chastised the woman who appeared in the doorway behind her.

Dani rolled her eyes.

"I'd like to see her try," I said.

The outer corners of the gamine redhead's mouth twitched.

"How dare you come here? How dare you bring that *thing* in here?" demanded a pajama-clad *sidhe*-seer, stabbing a finger at V'lane. Another head popped into view behind her, nose heavily bandaged. I knew that woman. My fist had met her face earlier today. Her eyes were bloodshot from crying, and narrowed on me with hostility.

When he stiffened, I placed a hand on his arm, careful to harbor no Nulling intent, in a show of solidarity I hoped would defuse his aggression.

The corridor was now filled with *sidhe*-seers in various stages of undress. Not because of V'lane, but because it was after midnight and I'd woken them. Apparently, he was proving true to his word. Not a single *sidhe*-seer was undressing. I didn't feel the ghost of a sexual tingle. Nonetheless, they were all staring fixedly at him.

"I didn't dare come here without Prince V'lane." The use of his title pleased him; I felt muscle slide smoother beneath his skin. "Rowena sent six of you after me today."

"I saw the ones that returned," the pajama-clad woman snapped. She glanced over her shoulder at her bandaged roommate, then back at me, her gaze frigid. "Those that *lived* were badly beaten. There's not a scratch on you. Not a single bruise." She paused, then spat, "*Pri-ya.*"

"I am *not* Pri-ya!"

"You travel with a Fae Prince. You touch him freely, of your own accord. What else could you be?"

"Try a *sidhe*-seer who's working with a Fae Prince in order to help Queen Aoibheal find the *Sinsar Dubh* so she can fix the mess we're all in," I said coolly. "V'lane approached me on the Seelie queen's behalf, because I can sense the Book when it's near. I've been—"

She gasped. "You can sense the *Sinsar Dubh*? Is it near? Have you seen it?"

Sidhe-seers up and down the corridor turned to each other, exclaiming.

"Can't any of *you* sense it?" I glanced around. The faces turned toward me reflected astonishment. It mirrored my own. I'd thought surely there would be others like me. One or two, at least.

Dani shook her head. "The ability to sense Fae objects is extremely rare, Mac."

Her roommate said stiffly, "The last *sidhe*-seer with that ability died a long time ago. We've not been successful at breeding those bloodlines."

Breeding those bloodlines? The soft Irish lilt didn't soften the words a bit. They were cold. Made me think of white coats and labs and petri dishes. It was no wonder I was so highly sought after. No wonder Barrons was so determined to keep me alive, and I had a Fae prince playing lapdog, and the Lord Master hadn't yet launched a full-scale attack against me. They all *needed* me alive. I was Tigger. I was the only one.

"You killed Moira!" the woman in the door across the hall accused.

V'lane regarded me with acute interest. "You killed one of your own?"

"No, I didn't kill Moira." I addressed the *sidhe-seers*, who were all regarding me with open hostility, with the exception of Dani. "*Rowena* killed Moira when she sent her after me to beat me up and take my spear." The woman had a name: Moira. Did she have a sister, too, who was now mourning her like I grieved for Alina? "I'm just as horrified by what happened today as you are."

"Sure you are," someone scoffed.

"She doesn't even say she's sorry," another spat. "Just comes in here with her fancy Fae guard and blames our leader. I'm surprised she didn't bring a Hunter along, too."

I'd give them an apology if they wanted one. "I'm sorry I unsheathed my spear and was holding it. I'm even sorrier she decided to lunge for me right then. If she hadn't, she'd be alive."

"If you hadn't refused to give us the spear, she would, too," someone called.

"The spear isn't yours," another woman cried. "Why should *you* have it? There are only two weapons that kill Fae. More than seven hundred of us share the sword. You have the other. Do what's right. Give it to those who were born and bred to have it!"

Others concurred.

Born and bred, my petunia. As if I were something less! "*I'm* the only one who can sense the

Book, and I have to be out there every night, hunting for it. Do you have any idea what Dublin's like right now? I wouldn't survive a night without it. Besides, I'm the one who risked my life to steal it."

My accuser sniffed and turned away, folding her arms. "Stealing. Working with a Fae Prince. Killing one of our sisters. You are not one of us."

"I say she is, and she just got off to a bad start," Dani said. "She didn't have anyone to help her figure things out. How would you guys have done in the same situation? She's just trying to survive, like we all are."

I smiled. I'd once asked her the same thing and she'd acted all snotty and perfect, but apparently she'd gotten my point. I admired her courage, defending me like that. Barely thirteen or fourteen, and she had the balls of a bull. It was also the longest run of sentences I could recall hearing her string together, unplugged by a single cussword.

"Go back to bed, kid," someone called.

"I am *not* a fecking kid," Dani bristled. "I've killed more of them than any of you."

"What's your kill count now, Dani?" Last time we talked, she'd had forty-seven Unseelie kills to her credit. With her *sidhe*-gift of heightened speed, armed with the Seelie Hallow, the Sword of Light, she had to be a formidable fighter. I'd like the chance to find out one day, to battle at her side. The two of us could seriously watch each other's backs.

"Ninety-two," she said proudly. "And I just got this big, nasty fecker with dozens of mouths and a huge, disgusting dick—"

"All right, Dani, that's *it*," her roommate said

sharply, forcibly turning her from the door. "Back to bed."

"You got the Many-Mouthed Thing?" I exclaimed. "Way to go, Dani!"

"Thanks," she said proudly. "He was tough to kill. You wouldn't believe—"

"Bed. Now." Her roommate shoved Dani into the room and pulled the door shut behind her, remaining in the hall.

"You know she's just standing on the other side of the door, listening," I said. "What's the point?"

"Stay out of our business, and get that *thing* out of here."

"Well said," came the voice of steel I'd been waiting for.

Sidhe-seers fell back, allowing a silver-haired woman through. I'd wondered how long it would take her to get here. I'd wagered two or three minutes. It had taken her five. I'd wanted a few minutes alone with the *sidhe*-seers, unimpeded by Rowena, to clear my name. I'd said what I had to say to her followers. Now I had a few things to say to their leader.

I glanced up at V'lane. He returned the look, face impassive, but his eyes were blades, hundreds of sharp shiny edges that could spill blood in the blink of a lethal eye.

With a rustle of her long white robes, the old woman stopped in front of me. Her age was impossible to pinpoint; she might be sixty, she might be eighty. Her long silvery hair was intricately plaited in a crown above a finely wrinkled face. Glasses rested on a small pointed nose, magnifying the fierce intensity and intelligence in her piercing blue eyes.

"Rowena," I said. She was wearing what I guessed must be Grand Mistress garb: a white hooded robe, with emerald trim, and a misshapen shamrock—the symbol of our Order's pledge to See, Serve, and Protect—emblazoned on the breast.

"How dare you?" Her voice was low, controlled, and furious.

"Oh, you should talk," I said, in the same tight voice.

"I invited you to assume your place among us and waited for you to accept my offer. You didn't. I could only conclude you had turned your back on us."

"I told you I would come and I was planning to, but a few things came up." Things like being hunted down, abducted, locked up, and tortured to death. "It was only a few days."

"It was a week and a half! Days matter now, even hours."

Had it really been a week and a half? Time flew when you were dying. "Did you give them orders to kill me if it was the only way they could get my spear?"

"Och, it was not I who spilled *sidhe*-seer blood to-day!"

"Oh, yes, it was. You sent them after me. You sent six of your women to attack me. I would never have killed any of them, and they know it. They saw it happen. Moira collided with my spear. It was a terrible accident. But it was just that—an accident."

She slipped her glasses from her nose, and let

them rest on her chest, suspended by a chain of delicate seed pearls behind her neck. Without taking her gaze from my face, Rowena addressed her enclave. "She's calling murder an accident, she is. Betraying us to our enemies and guiding them past our wards. This woman is our enemy, too."

"I have known where your kind hide for millennia," V'lane purred. "Your wards are laughable. They could not prevent a nightmare of me from getting in. You stink of old age and death, human. Shall I weave you dreams of it, haunt you with them?"

Rowena stared past him. "I do not hear it speaking." To me, she said, "Give me the spear and I will permit the two of you to live. You will remain here with us. *It* will leave and never return."

Snow dusted my cheeks. Soft gasps filled the corridor. Some of the *sidhe*-seers held out their hands, palms upward, to catch the whirling, icy flakes. I guessed none of them had seen a Fae prince before.

V'lane's voice was even colder than the unnatural snow caused by his displeasure. "Do you think to kill me with the sword you have hidden in your robes, old woman?"

I groaned inwardly. Great. Now he had *both* weapons. Should I Null him and try to take them back?

Rowena reached for the blade. I could have told her not to bother. V'lane raised the sword she sought in a flash of silver, and rested the razor-sharp tip in the wrinkled hollow of her throat.

The Grand Mistress of the *sidhe*-seers went very, very still.

"I know your kind, old woman. And you know

mine. I could make you kneel before me. Would you like that? Would you like your lovely little *sidhe-*seers to watch you writhe naked in ecstasy before me? Shall I make them all writhe?"

"Stop it, V'lane," I said sharply.

"She did not save you from me," he said, reminding me of the time he'd nearly raped me in the museum. "She stood by and watched you suffer. I merely mean to—how do you say it?—return the favor. I will punish her for you. Perhaps then you will forgive me a little."

"I don't want her punished, and it wouldn't be a favor. Stop it."

"She interferes and offends you. I will eliminate her."

"You will not. We have a deal, remember?"

Sword poised at her throat, hilt balanced on his palm, he glanced at me. "Indeed, I remember. You are helping me aid your race. For the first time in seven thousand years, Fae and Man are working together for a common cause. It is a rare thing, and necessary if we both wish to survive with our worlds intact." He looked back at Rowena. "Our combined efforts will accomplish what all your *sidhe*-seers put together cannot. Do not make me angry, old woman, or I will abandon you to the Hell that is coming if MacKayla fails to find the *Sinsar Dubh.* Cease trying to steal her weapon from her, and start protecting her. She is the best hope for your race. Kneel."

I didn't care for that "best hope for your race" stuff. I test poorly. I've never functioned well under pressure.

He forced Rowena, white-lipped and shuddering, to her knees. I could see the battle raging within her small, sturdy frame. Her robe trembled, her lips peeled back from her teeth.

"Stop it," I said again.

"In a moment. You will never again come before me bearing weapons, old woman, or I will forgo the promises I have made, and destroy you. Help her in her quest to help me, and I will let you live."

I sighed. I didn't need to take a look around to realize that I had made no friends here tonight. In fact, I was pretty sure I'd made things worse. "Just give her back the sword, V'lane, and get us out of here."

"Your wish, my command." He took my hand and sifted us out.

The instant we rematerialized a few dozen yards from the Viper, I slammed him with the palms of both hands, willing him to freeze with every ounce of that foreign place inside my skull.

Unlike the first time I'd tried Nulling him the night we'd met, he stayed frozen longer than a few heartbeats. I was so surprised that I didn't move myself, until he began to move, and I hit him again, putting everything I had into my desire to neutralize Fae. If intention was what counted, I was strong in that department. I'd been intending to grow up one day, for years. I had intentions down pat.

I timed it. He stayed frozen for seven seconds. I searched him quickly for my spear, patting him down, sending little "Stay frozen, you bastard" messages with my palms along the way.

No spear.

I stepped back and allowed him to unfreeze.

We stared at each other across the ten feet I'd put between us and I saw many things in his eyes. I saw my death. I saw my reprieve. I saw a thousand punishments in between, and knew the moment he decided to take no action against me.

"It's really hard for you to view me as a valid life form, isn't it?" I said. "What would make you take me more seriously? How many years would I have to live to count as whatever it is you credit as being worthwhile?"

"Longevity is not the defining factor. I do not credit most of my own race as worthwhile; a view born not of arrogance but of eons spent among those who are the worst of fools. Why did you Null me, *sidhe*-seer?"

"Because you majorly screwed up my plan in there."

"Then perhaps the next time you should confide in me the subtler nuances of your plan. I believed you wanted to establish the upper hand, and I endeavored to aid you in achieving that end."

"You made them think I was allied with you. You made them fear me."

"You are allied with me. And they should fear you."

My eyes narrowed. "Why should they fear me?"

He smiled faintly. "You have barely begun to understand what you are." Abruptly, he vanished.

Then his hand was in the curls at the back of my head, and his tongue was pushing in my mouth, and that hot, dark, frightening thing was piercing my tongue and embedding itself there, and I exploded in a violent orgasm.

He was ten feet away again, and I was sucking air like a fish out of water and floundering as badly. Shock waves of such intense eroticism rocked me that I was momentarily immobilized. If I'd tried to move, I would have collapsed.

"It only works once, MacKayla. I must replace my name on your tongue each time you use it. I assumed you did want it back?"

Furious, I nodded. Figured he'd not told me about that little catch.

He disappeared. This time he did not reappear.

I felt for my spear. It was back.

I stood still, waiting for the last of the aftershocks to pass. I wondered if I'd actually succeeded in Nulling V'lane tonight, or if he'd been faking it. I was growing increasingly paranoid, wondering if everyone was playing games with me. Surely anything that could move that fast could evade my sophomoric efforts at *sidhe*-seer magic. Or had I genuinely taken him by surprise? What might he gain by pretending? An ace in the hole? That maybe someday I'd really *need* to Null him, and that would be the day I'd find out it didn't work, and never had?

I turned around and began walking toward the Viper. I hadn't glanced in its direction since we'd materialized. I did now, and gasped.

The Wolf Countach was parked on the far side of it, deep in the shadows, and Jericho Barrons was leaning back against it, arms crossed over his chest, dressed from head to toe in black, every bit as dark and still as the night.

I blinked. He was still there. Hard to peel apart from the darkness, but there.

"What in the...how...where did you come from?" I sputtered.

"The bookstore."

Duh. Sometimes his answers make me want to strangle him. "Did V'lane know you were standing there?"

"I think the two of you were a little too busy to see me."

"What are you doing here?"

"Making sure you didn't need backup. If you'd told me you were taking your fairy little boyfriend, I wouldn't have wasted my time. I resent it when you waste my time, Ms. Lane."

He got in his car and drove away.

I followed him most of the way back to Dublin. Near the outskirts, he kicked his horses into a gallop I couldn't match, and I lost him.

SIX

It was a quarter till four when I drove the Viper down the back alley behind the bookstore. The predawn hours between two and four are the hardest on me. For the past few weeks, I've been waking up every night at 2:17 A.M. on the dot, as if it's my official preprogrammed time slot to have an anxiety attack, and the world will fall apart, even worse than it already is, if I don't pace my bedroom and worry it safe.

The bookstore is unbearably quiet then, and it's not hard to imagine that I'm the only person alive in the world. Most of the time I can handle the mess I call my life, but in the butt-crack of the night even I get a little depressed. I usually end up sorting through my wardrobe, meager as it is, or paging through fashion magazines, trying not to think. Putting outfits together soothes me. Accessorizing is balm to my soul. If I can't save the world, I sure can make it pretty.

But last night, haute couture from four different countries couldn't distract me, and I'd ended up snuggled under a blanket on the window seat with a dry volume about the history of the Irish race, including several lengthy, pedantic essays about the five invasions and the mythic Tuatha Dé Danaan, cracked open on my lap, staring out the back window of my bedroom at the sea of rooftops, watching the Shades slink and slither out of the corner of my eye.

Then my vision had played a trick on me, and blacked out the horizon as far as I could see, extinguishing every light, blanketing Dublin in absolute darkness.

I'd blinked, trying to dispel the illusion, and finally was able to see lights again, but the illusory blackout had seemed so real that I was afraid it was a premonition of things to come.

I pulled the Viper into the garage and parked in its allotted space, too tired to even halfheartedly appreciate the GT parked next to it. When the floor trembled beneath my heel, I stomped my foot and told it to shut up.

I opened the door to step out into the alley, flinched, slammed the door shut again, and stood there on the cusp of hyperventilating.

The garage where Barrons houses his fabulous car collection is located directly behind the bookstore, across an alley approximately twenty-five feet wide. Multiple floodlights on the exteriors illuminate a path between the two, affording safe passage from the Shades on even the darkest night.

Unfortunately, we haven't yet devised a means of perpetual light. Bulbs burn out, batteries die.

Several of the lights on the façade of the garage had outlived their usefulness during the night: not enough that I'd noticed in the glare of the Viper's headlights and the soft spill coming from the bookstore's rear windows, but enough to have created a sliver of opportunity for a truly enterprising Shade, and unfortunately, I had one of those shadowing my doorstep.

I was tired, and I'd been sloppy. I should have looked up and checked the spotlights on the buildings the moment they'd come into view. Thanks to the burned-out bulbs, a thin line of darkness now ran down the center of the alley, where the light cast by the adjacent buildings failed to meet, and the massive Shade that was as obsessed with me as I was with it had managed to pour itself into the crack, creating an inky black wall that soared three stories high and extended the entire length of the bookstore, barring me from crossing the alley.

I'd opened the door to find it towering over me, a greedy, dark tsunami, waiting to come crashing down and drown me in its lethal embrace. Although I was 99.9% sure it couldn't do that—that it was trapped in its menacing wall-shape by the light on both sides of it—there was that petrifying .1% doubt in my mind. Each time I'd thought I'd known its limits, I'd been wrong. Most Shades recoiled from the mere *possibility* of the palest, most diffuse light. Just waving one of my flashlights in the direction of the Dark Zone usually caused them to scatter.

But not this one. If light was pain, this enormous,

aggressive Shade was getting tougher, its pain threshold increasing. Like me, it was evolving. I only wished I was as dangerous.

I reached inside my jacket, fisted a flashlight in each hand, and yanked the door open again.

One of my flashlights wouldn't turn on. Dead batteries. When it rains, it pours. I tossed it and grabbed a second from my waistband. Two more came out with it, crashed to the ground, clattered down the steps and spun out into the alley, unlit, wasted.

I had two left. This was ridiculous. I needed a better way to keep myself safe than toting unwieldy flashlights with me everywhere I went.

I turned on another, and ordered myself to step out onto the pavement.

My feet didn't obey.

I aimed one of my flashlights directly at it. The inky wall recoiled and a hole exploded in it the exact diameter of the beam. I could see it was barely an inch thick.

I heaved a sigh of relief. It still couldn't tolerate direct light.

I studied it. I wasn't completely barred from getting to the bookstore. I could walk down to the left, parallel to the towering, dark cloud until I reached the end of the building, where the lights of the greengrocer next door prevented it from spreading farther, then go around to the front door and let myself in.

Problem was I wasn't sure I had the nerve, and I wasn't entirely sure it would be smart. What if, when I was nearly to the end of the Shade-wall, the light on the grocer's building burned out? Normally, I'd relegate the odds of that happening to the realm of the absurd, but if there was one thing I'd learned over the past few months, it was that absurd really meant "more likely to happen to MacKayla Lane." I wasn't about to risk it. I had my flashlights, but I couldn't shine them on every part of my body at once, and I certainly couldn't shine them on all of *it*.

I could call V'lane. He'd helped me get rid of Shades once before. Of course with V'lane there was always a price, and I would have to let him embed his name in my tongue again.

I considered my cell phone. It had three numbers programmed in: Barrons, IYCGM, and IYD.

IYCGM, which was Barrons' not-so-subtle short-hand for If You Can't Get Me, would be answered by the mysterious Ryodan who—although Barrons contended he talked too much—hadn't confided anything useful to *me* in our recent, brief phone conversation. I had no desire to lure anyone else close to the overly aggressive Shade. I wanted a few days reprieve between deaths on my conscience.

IYD was If You're Dying, and I wasn't.

I was sick of depending on others to save me. I wanted to take care of myself. It was only a few hours until dawn. The Shade could stay out there all night for all I cared.

I stepped back into the garage, closed and locked the door, flipped on the brightest tier of interior lights, considered the collection a moment, then crawled into the Maybach to sleep.

It occurred to me, as I drifted off, that my feelings about the car had certainly changed. I no longer cared that it had formerly belonged to the Irish mobster Rocky O'Bannion, from whom I'd stolen my spear and whom I was indirectly responsible for killing, along with fifteen of his henchmen, in the very alley where the monster Shade now lurked. I was just grateful it was comfortable to sleep in.

We expect Evil to announce itself.

Evil is supposed to adhere to certain conventions. It's supposed to cause a chill of foreboding in the intended recipient of its visit; it should be instantly recognizable; and it's supposed to be hideous. Evil should glide out of the night in a black hearse, fog streaming from its dark flanks, or dismount from a skeletal Harley, leather-clad, wearing a necklace of freshly scalped skulls and crossbones.

"Barrons Books and Baubles," I answered the phone brightly. "You want it, we've got it, and if we don't, we'll find it." I take my job very seriously. After snatching six hours of sleep in the garage, I'd made my way across the alley to the bookstore, showered, and opened shop, business as usual.

"I'm certain of that. You finding it, that is, or I wouldn't have phoned."

I froze, hand on the receiver. Was this a joke? He was *phoning* me? Of all the possible confrontations with Evil I'd imagined, this was not one of them. "Who is this?" I demanded, unable to believe it.

"You know who I am. Say it."

Though I'd heard the voice only twice before—the afternoon in the Dark Zone when I'd almost died, and more recently in Mallucé's lair—I would never forget it. Contrary to what Evil was supposed to be, it was a seductive, beautiful voice, mirroring the physical beauty of its owner.

It was the voice of my sister's lover—and murderer.

I knew his name, and I'd die before I'd call him Lord Master. "You *bastard*."

I slammed down the phone with one hand and was already using my other to punch up Barrons on my cell. He answered instantly, sounding alarmed. I got right to the point. "Can the Druid spell of Voice be used over the telephone?"

"No. The spell's potency doesn't carry through—"

"Thanks, gotta go." As I'd expected, the store phone was already ringing again. I thumbed my cell off, and left Barrons sputtering. I was safe from being coerced over the phone lines, and that was what I'd needed to know, fast, before the Lord Master had been able to use it on me.

Just in case it was a paying customer, I said, "Barrons Books—"

"You should have asked me," came that seductive, rich voice. "I would have told you that Voice is diluted by technology. Both parties must be in physical proximity to each other. At the moment, I'm too far away."

I wasn't going to give him the satisfaction of knowing that was what I'd been afraid of. "I dropped the phone."

"Pretend what you will, MacKayla."

"Don't address me by name," I gritted.

"What should I call you?"

"Don't."

"You have no curiosity about me?"

My hand was shaking. I was talking to my sister's murderer, the monster that was bringing all the Unseelie through his mystic dolmens and turning our world into the nightmare it was. "Sure. What's the quickest, easiest way to kill you?"

He laughed. "You have more fire than Alina. But she was clever. I underestimated her. She concealed your existence from me. She never spoke of you. I had no idea there were two with talents like hers."

We'd been equals in our ignorance. She'd concealed his existence from me, too. "How did you find out about me?"

"I'd heard rumors of another *sidhe*-seer, new to the city, with unusual abilities. I would have tracked you eventually. But the day you came to the warehouse, I smelled you. There was no mistaking your bloodline. You can sense the *Sinsar Dubh*, the same way Alina could."

"No, I can't," I lied.

"It's calling you. You feel it out there, getting stronger. You, however, won't get stronger. You'll weaken, MacKayla. You can't handle the Book. Don't even think of trying. You can't begin to imagine what you'd be dealing with."

I had a pretty fair idea. "Is that why you called me? To warn me off? I'm quaking in my boots." This conversation was wigging me out. I was on the phone with the monster that had killed my sister— the infamous Lord Master—and he wasn't cackling maniacally or threatening villainously. He hadn't come after me with an army of dark Fae, backed by his black-and-crimson-clad personal guard. He'd phoned me and was speaking in beautiful, cultured tones, softly, and without hostility. Was this the true face of Evil? It didn't conquer, it seduced? *He lets me be the woman I always wanted to be,* Alina had written in her journal. Would he ask me out to dinner next? If he did, would I accept, to get a chance at killing him?

"What do you want most in the world, MacKayla?"

"You dead." My cell phone rang. It was Barrons. I thumbed IGNORE.

"That's not what you want most. You want that *because* of what you want most: your sister back."

I didn't like where this was going.

"I called to offer you a deal."

Deals with the devil, Barrons had recently reminded me, never went well. Still, I couldn't stop myself from asking, "What?"

"Get me the Book, and I'll get you your sister back."

My heart skipped a beat. I held the phone away from my ear and stared at the receiver, as if seeking some kind of inspiration, or answer, or maybe just the courage to hang up the phone.

Your sister back. The words hung in the air.

Whatever I was looking for, I didn't find it. I returned the phone to my ear. "The Book could bring Alina back from the dead?" I was chock-full of superstitions inspired by childhood fables; resurrecting the dead was always accompanied by gruesome caveats, and even more gruesome results. Surely something so evil couldn't restore something so good.

"Yes."

I wasn't going to ask. I *wasn't*. "Would she be the same as she was before? Not some scary zombie?" I asked.

"Yes."

"Why would you do that, when you're the one who killed her in the first place?"

"I didn't kill her."

"Maybe you didn't do it yourself, but *you* sent them after her!"

"I wasn't done with her." There was the barest hesitation. "And I had no plans to kill her when I was."

"Bull. She found you out. She followed you into the Dark Zone one day, didn't she? She refused to help you anymore. And you killed her for it." I was certain of it. I'd thought about it every night before I went to sleep, for months. It was the only conclusion that made sense of the voice mail message she'd left me, a few hours before she'd died. *He's coming,* she'd said. *I don't think he'll let me out of the country.*

"You've felt the power of my coercion. I might have lost her willing cooperation, but I never needed it to begin with." Imperious arrogance dripped from his voice, as he reminded me how easily he'd controlled me. No, he wouldn't have needed her cooperation. With that terrible, will-stealing Voice, he could have made her do anything he wanted, anything at all.

My cell phone rang again.

"Answer it. Barrons hates waiting. Think about my offer."

"How do you know Barrons?" I demanded.

The line was dead.

"Are you all right?" Barrons growled, when I answered my cell.

"Fine."

"Was it him?"

"The great LM?" I said dryly. "Yes."

"What did he offer you?"

"My sister back."

Barrons didn't say anything for a long moment. "And?"

I was quiet for an even longer moment. "I told him I'd think about it."

Silence fell between us and lengthened. Strangely, neither of us hung up. I wondered where he was, what he was doing. I strained my ears but couldn't hear any background noise. Either his cell phone had great noise reduction capabilities, or he was somewhere very quiet. An image flashed through my mind: Barrons, big and dark, naked against white silk sheets, arms folded behind his head, phone propped at his ear, crimson and black tattoos ranging across his chest, down his abs. Leg tangled with some woman's.

Nah. He'd never let a woman stay the night. No matter how good the sex was.

"Barrons," I said at last.

"Ms. Lane."

"I need you to teach me to resist Voice." I'd asked him this before, but he'd only given me one of his noncommittal replies.

There was another of those long silences, then, "In order to attempt that—and I assure you it will be no more than an attempt, one at which I highly doubt you'll succeed—I'll have to use it on you. Are you prepared for that?"

I shivered. "We'll lay some basic ground rules."

"You like those, don't you? Too bad. You're in my world now, and there are no basic ground rules. You learn how I teach you, or not at all."

"You're a jackass."

He laughed, and I shivered again.

"Can we start tonight?" I'd been safe today, with the Lord Master on the phone. But if, instead of calling, he'd strolled up behind me on the street and commanded me to be silent, I wouldn't have even been able to open my mouth long enough to release V'lane's name.

I frowned.

Why *hadn't* he walked up behind me? Why hadn't he sent his army after me? Now that I thought about it, the only two times he'd ever tried to capture me were when I'd practically delivered myself to him, and he'd believed I was alone, almost as if I'd been an opportunity too convenient to pass up. Was the Lord Master in no hurry to get close to me? Did he fear my spear after seeing what it had done to Mallucé? *I'd* feared it intensely when I'd eaten Unseelie. I hadn't wanted it anywhere near me. But with Voice he could easily strip it away. He'd wanted Alina's willing participation, and now he seemed to want mine. Why? Because it was easier if I was willing, or was it more complicated than that? Did Voice work only to a certain extent, and there was something he needed from me that he wouldn't be able to coerce? Or maybe—a chill of foreboding accompanied this thought—I was only a small part of his much larger plans, and he'd already made other arrangements for me, and it just wasn't the right time yet. Maybe he was even now constructing a cage around me that I couldn't see. Would I wake up one morning, and walk straight into it? I'd been duped by Mallucé. I'd believed him a figment of my imagination until the last.

I shoved my fearful thoughts away before they could multiply. I certainly wanted to get close to *him*. I was going to kill him. And his nasty trick of Voice was a barrier I was going to have to be able to get past.

"Well," I prompted, "when can we start?" I didn't trust Barrons, but he'd had plenty of opportunities to use Voice on me in the past, and hadn't. I didn't believe he'd use it to harm me now. At least not much. The potential gain was worth the risk.

"I'll be there at ten." He hung up.

It was nine-fifteen by the time I finished my invention, forty-five minutes before Barrons was due to arrive.

I turned it on, sat back, scrutinized it a few moments, then nodded.

It looked good.

Well, it didn't really. It looked...strange, like something out of a sci-fi movie. But it worked, and that was all that mattered to me. I was sick of not being safe in the dark. I was sick of watching my flashlights go spinning away from me. This *couldn't* spin away. And if I was right about its capabilities, I'd be able to walk straight through a Shade-wall with it on.

There was one final test I needed to perform.

It was a great invention and I was proud of it. The idea had come to me this afternoon, during a slow spell. I'd been stressing over the enormous Shade outside the bookstore, when suddenly a light had gone off in my head, or rather, several dozen.

I'd flipped the sign and locked up at seven on the dot, raced down the street to the sporting goods store on the corner, and bought everything I needed, from the biking helmet, to batteries, to brackets and caving lights, to tubes of superglue, to Velcro bands as an added precaution.

Then I'd come back to the bookstore, dialed my iPod to the latest playlist I was crazy about, cranked it up to a smidge below deafening, and gone to work.

I shook my invention. I dropped it. I kicked it, and still all parts remained intact. Superglue: after duct tape, a girl's best friend.

I was satisfied. With three quarters of an hour until my Voice lessons, I had time to test the device, and still make it upstairs to freshen up a bit, not that I cared how I looked around Barrons. It's just that in the Deep South, women learn at a young age that when the world is falling apart around you, it's time to take down the drapes and make a new dress.

Every truly inspired invention needed a catchy name, and I had just the right one for mine. Who needed the Cuff of Cruce to walk among the Shades?

I slipped the biking helmet on my head and

strapped it securely beneath my chin. It fit snugly so it couldn't fall off in the heat of battle. I could do a flip (if I *could* do a flip) and the thing would stay stuck to my head. I'd superglued dozens of Click-It lights all over the surface of the helmet. Brackets stuck out several inches from both sides and the rear, with spelunker lights attached, pointing downward.

I swept my arms out and took a deep bow: Presenting the *MacHalo*!

With all the lights turned on, the helmet created a perfect halo of light around my entire body, down to my feet. I loved it. If it hadn't been so bulky, I might have tried sleeping in it. As an added precaution, I strapped on the Velcro wrist and ankle bands I'd cut little pouches in, and sewn Click-It lights into. All I had to do was hit my wrists and ankles together and the lights clicked on.

I was ready.

But first, I wanted a test run inside the store before I went outside.

I clicked myself on from head to toe, hurried to the panel, and began flipping off the interior lights in the front part of the bookstore. Not the exterior ones, just the interior. Even though I knew the building was still surrounded in light outside, it was hard to make myself do it. My fear of the darkness had grown beyond a rational thing. That happens when you know a shadow can eat you alive if you touch it.

My hand hesitated over the last row of switches for a long, difficult moment.

But I had my MacHalo, and I knew it would work. If I gave fear a toehold, it would screw me. I'd learned that lesson from Barrons, and had it driven home by Mallucé: Hope strengthens. Fear kills.

I flipped off the last row, plunging the bookstore into complete darkness.

I blazed as bright as a small sun in the room!

I laughed. I should have thought of it before. There wasn't an inch of me, not a centimeter, that wasn't lit up. My halo radiated outward a good ten feet in all directions. And I was right; if I had the courage, I could walk right through a Shade-wall. None of the vampiric life-suckers could get close to me in this getup!

My iPod began playing "Bad Moon Rising" by Creedence Clearwater Revival, and I did a little dance, giddy with success. I had one more weapon in my arsenal to make me safer, and I'd thought of it myself.

I whirled around the bookstore, miming the epic fighter I was now going to be, armed with my clever MacHalo, no longer afraid of dark alleys in the night. I leapt chairs and darted around bookcases. I pounced sofas, I hurdled ottomans. I stabbed imaginary enemies, immune to Shade-danger by the brilliance of my own invention. There's not much room in my life for good, plain, stupid fun, and there hasn't been much to celebrate lately. I take advantage of both when I can.

" 'Hope you got your things together,' " I sang, stabbing a pillow with my spear. Feathers exploded into the air. " 'Hope you are quite prepared to die!' " I spun in a dazzling whirl of lights, landed a killer back-kick on a phantom Shade, and simultaneously punched the magazine rack. " 'Looks like we're in for nasty weather!' " I took a swan dive at a short, imaginary Shade, lunged up at a taller one—

—and froze.

Barrons stood inside the front door, dripping cool old-world elegance.

I hadn't heard him come in over the music. He was leaning, shoulder against the wall, arms folded, watching me.

" 'One eye is taken for an eye...' " I trailed off, deflating. I didn't need a mirror to know how stupid I looked. I regarded him sourly for a moment, then moved for the sound dock to turn it off. When I heard a choked sound behind me I spun, and shot him a hostile glare. He wore his usual expression of arrogance and boredom. I resumed my path for the sound dock, and heard it again. This time when I turned back, the corners of his mouth were twitching. I stared at him until they stopped.

I'd reached the sound dock, and just turned it off, when he exploded.

I whirled. "I didn't look *that* funny," I snapped.

His shoulders shook.

"Oh, come on! Stop it!"

He cleared his throat and stopped laughing. Then his gaze took a quick dart upward, fixed on my blazing MacHalo, and he lost it again. I don't know, maybe it was the brackets sticking out from the sides. Or maybe I should have gotten a black bike helmet, not a hot pink one.

I unfastened it and yanked it off my head. I stomped over to the door, flipped the interior lights back on, slammed him in the chest with my brilliant invention, and stomped upstairs.

"You'd better have stopped laughing by the time I come back down," I shouted over my shoulder.

I wasn't sure he even heard me, he was laughing so hard.

"Can Voice make you do something that you find deeply morally objectionable? Can it override everything you believe in?" I asked Barrons, fifteen minutes later when I came back down. I'd made him wait, partly because I was still stinging from his laughter, and partly because it pissed me off in general that he was early. I like it when a man's on time. Not early. Not late. Punctual. It's one of those lost dating courtesies, not that Barrons and I are dating, but I think dating courtesies are common courtesies that should be practiced in most all civilized encounters. I pine for the days of good, old-fashioned manners.

I made no mention of his laughter, the MacHalo, or my absurd dance. Barrons and I are pros at ignoring anything and everything that passes between us that might smack of emotion of any kind, even so simple a feeling as embarrassment. Sometimes I can't believe I was ever beneath that big, hard body, kissing him, getting glimpses into his life. The desert. The lonely boy. The lone man. Don't think it hadn't occurred to me that having sex with Barrons might just answer some of my questions about who and what he was. It had. And I'd promptly stuffed that idea into my padlocked box. For a gazillion reasons that need no explaining.

"It depends on the skill of the person employing Voice, and the strength of his victim's convictions."

Typical Barrons answer. "Elucidate," I said dryly. I've been learning new words. I've been reading a lot lately.

As I moved deeper into the room, his gaze dropped to my feet, and worked its way back to my face. I was wearing faded jeans, boots, and a snug pink Juicy T-shirt I got on sale at TJ Maxx last summer that said *I'm a Juicy girl.*

"I bet you are," he murmured. *"Take off your shirt,"* he said, but this time his voice resonated with a legion of voices. It rippled outward, past me, filling the room, stuffing every corner, cramming it full of voices that were all telling me to obey, pressuring every cell in my body to comply. I *wanted* my shirt off. Not the same way I wanted it off around V'lane, rooted in sexual compulsion, but merely because I... well, I didn't know why. But I wanted it off right now, this very instant.

I began to lift the hem of my tee, when I thought, Hang on a minute, I'm not going to show Barrons my bra, and pulled my shirt back down.

I smiled, faintly at first then bigger, pleased with myself. I stuffed my hands in the back pockets of my jeans and gave him a cocky stare. "I think I'm going to be pretty good at this."

"TAKE OFF YOUR SHIRT."

The command hit me like a brick wall and destroyed my mind. I sucked in a violent, screeching breath and ripped my shirt from neckline to hem.

"Stop, Ms. Lane."

Voice again, but not the brick wall: rather a command that lifted the brick wall from me, freeing me. I sank to the floor, clutching the halves of my torn T-shirt together, and dropped my head in my lap, resting my forehead against my knees. I breathed deeply for several seconds, then raised my head and looked at him. He could have coerced me like that anytime. Turned me into a mindless slave. Like the Lord Master, he could have forced me to do his bidding whenever he'd wanted. But he hadn't. The next time I discovered something horrifying about him, would I say, yeah, but he never coerced me with Voice? Would that be the excuse I made for him then?

"What are you?" It burst out before I could stop myself. I knew it was wasted breath. "Why don't you just tell me and get it over with?" I said irritably.

"One day you'll stop asking me. I think I'll like knowing you then."

"Can we leave my clothes out of the next lesson?" I groused. "I only packed for a few weeks."

"You wanted morally objectionable."

"Right." I wasn't sure his demonstration had served its purpose. I wasn't sure taking my shirt off in front of him was.

"I was illustrating degrees, Ms. Lane. I believe the Lord Master has achieved the latter level of proficiency."

"Great. Well, in the future spare my tees. I only have three. I've been washing them out by hand and the other two are dirty." BB&B didn't have a washer or dryer, and so far I'd been refusing to tote my stuff to the Laundromat a few blocks down, although soon I was going to have to, because jeans didn't wash well by hand.

"Order what you need, Ms. Lane. Charge it to the store account."

"Really? I can order a washer and dryer?"

"You may as well hold on to the keys to the Viper, too. I'm certain there are things you need a car for."

I eyed him suspiciously. Had I lost another few months in Faery, and this was Christmas?

He bared his teeth in one of those predatory smiles. "Don't think it's because I like you. A happy employee is a productive employee, and the less time you waste going out to the Laundromat or... doing whatever errands it is... someone like you does... is more time I can use you for my own purposes."

That made sense. Still, while it was Christmas, I had a few more items on my wish list. "I want a backup generator, and a security system. And I think I should have a gun, too."

"Stand up."

I had no will. My legs obeyed.

"Go change."

I returned wearing a peach tee with a coffee stain over the right breast.

"Stand on one leg and hop."

"You suck," I hissed, as I hopped.

"The key to resisting Voice," Barrons instructed, "is finding that place inside you no one else can touch."

"You mean the *sidhe*-seer place?" I said, hopping like a one-legged chicken.

"No, a different place. All people have it. Not just

sidhe-seers. We're born alone and we die alone. That place."

"I don't get it."

"I know. That's why you're hopping."

I hopped for hours. I wearied, but he didn't. I think Barrons could have used Voice all night, and never worn down.

He might have kept me hopping until dawn, but at quarter till one in the morning my cell phone rang. I thought instantly of my parents, and it must have shown on my face, because he released me from my thrall.

I'd been hopping for so long that I actually took two hops toward my purse where I'd left it on the counter near the cash register, before I caught myself.

It was about to roll into my voice mail—a thing I've hated ever since I missed Alina's call—so I thumbed it on inside my purse, tugged it out, and clamped it to my ear.

"Fourth and Langley," Inspector Jayne barked.

I stiffened. I'd been expecting Dad, figuring he'd just forgotten to factor in the time difference. We alternated calling each other every other day, even if only for a few minutes, and I'd forgotten last night.

"It's bad. Seven dead, and the shooter's holed up in a pub, threatening to kill more hostages, and himself. Sound like the kind of crime you wanted me to tell you about?"

"Yes." *Himself*, Jayne had said. The shooter was a man, which meant I'd missed whatever crime the woman who'd picked it up the night I'd been watching had committed, and the Book had already moved on. I wondered how many times it had changed hands since. I would search back issues of newspapers for clues. I needed all the information I could get, to try to understand the Dark Book, in hopes of anticipating its future moves.

The line went dead. He'd done what he'd promised and no more. I stared down at my cell phone, trying to figure out how to get rid of Barrons.

"Why was Jayne calling you at this hour?" he said softly. "Have you been inducted as an honorary member of the Garda since they last arrested you?"

I glanced over my shoulder with disbelief. He was standing at the opposite end of the room, and the volume on my phone was set to low. Maybe he'd picked up on the tones of the inspector's voice from that distance, but there was no way he'd heard any of the details. "Funny," I said.

"What aren't you telling me, Ms. Lane?"

"He said he thinks he might have a lead on my sister's case." It was a weak lie, but the first that came to mind. "I have to go." I reached behind the counter, grabbed my backpack, tossed in my MacHalo, strapped on my shoulder holster, transferred my spear from my boot to beneath my arm, then slid into a jacket and headed for the back door. I would get the Viper and drive to Fourth and Langley as fast as I could. If the shooter was still at the scene, the *Sinsar Dubh* would be, too. If the shooter was already dead by the time I got there, I'd drive up and down the streets and alleys in the immediate vicinity, ranging outward in a tight pattern, waiting for a tingle.

"The fuck he did. He said Fourth and Langley. Seven dead. Why do you care?"

What kind of monster had ears like that? Couldn't I have gotten a half-deaf one? Scowling, I continued toward the door.

"You will stop right there, and tell me where you're going."

My feet stopped, independent of my will. The bastard had used Voice. "Don't do this to me," I gritted, sweat breaking out on my forehead. I was fighting him with all I had, and weakening quickly. I wanted to tell him where I was going nearly as badly as I wanted to kill the Lord Master.

"Don't make me," he said in a normal voice. "I thought we were working together, Ms. Lane. I thought we were allied in a common cause. Did that phone call from the inspector have something to do with the *Sinsar Dubh*? You aren't keeping something from me, are you?"

"No."

"Final warning. If you don't answer me, I'll rip it from your throat. And while I'm at it, I'll ask anything else I feel like asking, too."

"That's not fair! I can't use Voice on you," I cried. "You're only teaching me to resist it."

"You'll never be able to use it on me. Not if I teach you. Teacher and student develop immunity to each other. There's quite an incentive for you, eh, Ms. Lane? Now talk. Or I'll take the information I want, and if you fight me, it'll hurt."

He was a shark who'd scented blood and he

wasn't going to stop circling until he'd devoured me. I had no doubt he would do as he was threatening, and if he got started forcing answers from me, I was afraid of what he might ask. He'd heard the address. With or without me, he was going there. It would be better if I went, too. I'd think of a plan along the way. "Get in the car. I'll tell you while we're driving."

"My bike's out front. If traffic's bad, it's faster. If you've been holding out on me, you're in deep trouble, Ms. Lane."

Of that, I had no doubt. But I wasn't sure who was going to be more pissed at me before the night was through: Barrons because I hadn't told him sooner, or V'lane because I'd broken my promise to him and told Barrons at all. The alien thing piercing my tongue felt intrusive and dangerous in my mouth.

Dublin was a dark, bizarre circus that I was walking through on a high wire, and if there was a safety net somewhere below me, I sure couldn't see it.

SEVEN

Like jacked-up pickup trucks in the Deep South, Harleys are an ode to testosterone: The bigger and louder the better. Down south, trucks and bikes roar, *Look at me! Hot damn, I'm big and noisy and wild and, yeehaw, wouldn't you like a piece of me?*

Barrons' Harley didn't roar. It didn't even purr. A chrome and ebony predator, it glided soundlessly into the night, whispering, *I'm big and silent and deadly, and you'd better hope I don't get a piece of you.*

I could feel fury in the set of his shoulders beneath my hands as we careened through narrow alleys, around corners, laying the bike so low I had to tuck up my feet and keep my legs crushed to the sides for fear of scraping off a few layers of skin, but as with everything else Barrons undertook, he was a master of precision. The bike did things for him I wasn't sure a bike could do. Several times I almost wrapped my arms and legs around him and clambered onto his back, for fear of falling off.

His body bristled with anger. The fact that I knew something about the Book that I hadn't told him was as deep a transgression as transgressions could go, as far as he was concerned. I'd learned the last time we'd had a brush with the *Sinsar Dubh* that it was his end-all/be-all, for whatever reason. Despite the unnerving dark energy rolling off him, eventually I hugged him with all my might just to stay on the bike. It was like embracing a low-level electrical current. Sometimes I wonder if Barrons has any real awareness of risk of injury. He doesn't live like he does.

"It's not like you don't keep secrets from me!" I finally shouted against his ear.

"I don't keep ones from you that involve the fucking Book," he snarled over his shoulder. "That's our deal, isn't it? If nothing else, we're honest with each other about the Book."

"I don't trust you!"

"And you think I trust *you*? You haven't been out of fucking diapers long enough to be trusted, Ms. Lane! I'm not even sure you should be allowed to handle sharp objects!"

I punched him in the side. "That's not true. Who ate Unseelie? Who survived no matter the cost? Who keeps getting out there facing all kinds of twisted monsters, and still manages to find something to smile about while she does it? *That* takes real strength. That's more than you can do. You're grumpy and broody and secretive all the time. You're no joy to live with, I can tell you that!"

"I smile sometimes. I even laughed about your … hat."

"MacHalo," I corrected tightly. "It's a brilliant invention, and it means I don't need you or V'lane to keep me safe from Shades, and that, Jericho Barrons, is worth its weight in gold: not needing either of you for something!"

"Who came to teach you Voice tonight? Do you think you could find another teacher? Those who can use that power don't share it. Whether you like it or not, you *do* need me, and you've needed me since the day you set foot in this country. Remember that, and *stop pissing me off.*"

"You need me too," I growled.

"That's why I'm teaching you. That's why I gave you a safe place to live. That's why I keep saving your life, and try to give you the things you want."

"Oh, the th-things I w-want," I stammered because I was so mad I tried to spit all the words out at once. "How about answers? Try giving me those!"

He laughed, and the sound bounced back off the brick walls of the narrow alley down which we sped, making it sound like men were laughing all around me, and it was creepy. "The day I give you answers will be the day you no longer need them."

"The day I no longer need them," I told him icily, "will be the day I'm dead."

By the time we arrived at the crime scene, the shooter had blown his head off, what hostages had survived were being treated, and the grim duty of counting and collecting bodies had begun.

The street was closed around the pub from one end of the block to the next, crammed with police cars and ambulances, and crawling with Garda. We parked and dismounted a block from the scene.

"I'm assuming the Book was here. Do you feel it?"

I shook my head. "It's already gone. That way," I pointed west. An icy channel sluiced east through the night. I would lead him in the opposite direction, and eventually claim that I'd lost its "signal." I felt sick to my stomach, and not because of all the bodies and blood. The *Sinsar Dubh* is the ultimate in nausea. I reached in my pocket and thumbed out a Tums. I had the beginnings of a brutal migraine, and hoped it wouldn't spike.

"Later you're going to tell me everything you know. Somehow you've figured out how it's moving around the city, and it's linked to the crimes, isn't it?"

He was good. When I nodded gingerly, trying not to split my skull, he said, "And somehow you managed to coerce Jayne into feeding you information. How you accomplished that, frankly, confounds me."

"Gee, maybe I'm not as inept as you think I am." I popped another Tums in my mouth and made a mental note to start carrying aspirin, too.

After a pause, he said tightly, "Maybe you're not," which was very nearly an apology from Barrons.

"I fed him Unseelie."

"Are you fucking nuts?" Barrons exploded.

"It worked."

His eyes narrowed. "One might think you're developing situational ethics."

"You think I don't know what those are. My father's an attorney. I know what those are."

A faint smile curved his lips. "Get back on the bike and tell me where to go."

"I'll tell you where to go," I muttered sourly, and he laughed. As we sped down the street, away from the Dark Book, my headache began to ease. I was abruptly so aroused that I caught myself on the dangerous verge of rubbing my aching nipples against Barrons' back. I jerked away instantly and glanced over my shoulder. My heart sank. I reached for my spear. It was gone.

Barrons must have felt the tension in my body, because he glanced over his shoulder at me, and saw what I'd seen: the Fae Prince, sifting down the street behind us, one moment there, then gone, the next, a few dozen feet closer.

"It's bad enough that you didn't tell me about the Book, Ms. Lane, but tell me you didn't tell *him*."

"I had to. I needed him to do something for me, and it was all I had to offer up that I was willing to part with. But I didn't tell him everything." In fact, I'd deliberately led him astray, so how had he found me tonight? Dumb luck? He couldn't *possibly* be checking out every crime in the city!

Anger reclaimed Barrons' body, worse than before. He stopped so abruptly that I slammed into his back, fell off the bike, and went sprawling. By the time I stood up and dusted myself off, Barrons was off the bike; V'lane, too, had stopped, and was standing in the street about twenty-five feet away.

"Come here, Ms. Lane. Now."

I didn't move. I was pissed that he'd dumped me like that. It had made my head hurt even worse. Besides, a furious Barrons isn't something you want to stand next to any more than you'd want to cozy up to a pissed-off cobra.

"Unless you want him to sift in and take you, get close to me. Now. Or do you want to go with him?"

I glanced at V'lane and moved to Barrons' side. V'lane was so glacial with displeasure that a small blizzard was icing his end of the street, and I wasn't dressed for the weather. Okay, so maybe V'lane scares me a little more than Barrons does. V'lane uses his sexuality against me and I'm susceptible to it. Barrons doesn't. Even now, my hand was slipping to my fly, grazing the zipper, and I nearly whimpered. I sought that cool alien place in my pounding head. I'm strong, I told myself, a *sidhe-seer*. I will not give in.

Barrons draped an arm over my shoulder and I moved into the shelter of it. The thing on my tongue burned. My brand itched. At that moment, I despised them both.

"Stay away from her," Barrons growled.

"She comes to me of her own will. She calls me, chooses me." V'lane was in high glamour, gold and bronze and iridescent ice. He raked me with an imperious gaze. "I will attend to you later. You broke our bargain. There is a price for that." He smiled, but Fae don't really smile. They paste a humanlike expression on and it chills to the bone because it looks so unnatural on their unnaturally perfect faces. "Do not fear, MacKayla, I will—how do you say?—kiss it and make it better when I am through."

I removed my hand from my fly. "I didn't break our bargain intentionally, V'lane. Barrons overheard something he shouldn't have overheard."

"Omission or commission, what difference?"

"There is one. Even the courts of law permit the distinction."

"Human law. Fae law acknowledges no such thing. There are outcomes. The means by which they are achieved have no bearing. You said you did not know how to track the Book."

"I don't. I just followed a hunch tonight. Got lucky. You?"

"Impudence and lies, MacKayla. I suffer neither."

"You won't harm a hair on her head, or I'll kill you," said Barrons.

Really? With what? I wanted to ask. V'lane was a Fae. My spear was gone and Rowena had the sword.

The Book's icy pull was diminishing rapidly. It was moving swiftly. Its next victim was in a car, and a fast one. I had a smug, utterly beside-the-point car-lover thought: not faster than mine. *I* had a *Viper*. Its keys were in my pocket.

The smug thought faded. It offended every ounce of my being to let the Book get away, to allow it to go cruising off to destroy more lives. But no matter how insistently my *sidhe*-seer senses were screaming at me to track it, I didn't dare. Not with Barrons and V'lane here. I needed to know more about the Book. I needed to know how to get my hands on it, and do the right thing with it. Who was I kidding? I needed to know *what* the right thing was. Assuming I eventually got it, who could I trust with it? V'lane? Barrons? God forbid, Rowena? Would the Seelie Queen herself shimmer in and save the day? Somehow, I doubted it. Nothing in my life is easy anymore.

"You have no right to it," V'lane was telling Barrons.

"Might makes right. Hasn't that always been your motto?" Barrons said.

"You could never understand my motto."

"Better than you think, fairy."

"There is nothing you could do with it even if you managed to get it. You do not speak the language in which it was scribed, and could never hope to de-code it."

"Maybe I have the stones."

"Not all of them," V'lane said coldly, and I knew from the disdain in his voice that he had at least one, if not both of the other translation stones we'd been hunting. All four of the mystical translucent blue-black stones were necessary to "reveal the true na-ture" of the *Sinsar Dubh*. Barrons had one already when I met him. I'd recently stolen the second one from Mallucé, the event that had precipitated the hostilities between us.

Barrons smiled. Clever man. Until that moment, he'd suspected but not been certain. "Maybe I learned enough from your *princess* that I don't need all four," Barrons sneered, and there was a world of insinuation in his words. Even I, who had no idea what he was insinuating, heard the insult in them, and knew it cut deep. There was history between V'lane and Barrons. They didn't despise each other just because of me. There was more than that going on here.

Ice dripped from V'lane's iridescent robes, flowed down the cobbled street and expanded, covering the pavement from gutter to gutter with a thin black sheet that cracked like gunshots as it encased the warmer stone.

Good, let them fight. Let the Book disappear and carry my problems with it. To add fuel to the fire, I said, "Why do you two hate each other so much?"

"Have you fucked her yet?" V'lane ignored me completely.

"I'm not trying to."

"Translation: Your efforts have failed."

"No, they haven't," I said. "He hasn't tried. FYI, boys, and I use that term loosely, there's more to me than sex."

"Which is why you're still alive, Ms. Lane. Keep cultivating those parts."

Since I had them both together, for a novel change, I had a hunch I wanted to test. "What *is* Barrons?" I asked V'lane. "Human, or something else?"

The Fae Prince looked at Barrons, and said nothing.

Barrons shot me a sharp look.

"So, Barrons," I said sweetly, "tell me about V'lane. Is he a good guy or a bad guy?"

Barrons looked away and said nothing.

I shook my head, disgusted. It was as I'd suspected. *Men.* Were they the same among all species, whether human or not? "Both of you have something on the other, and neither of you will rat it out, in order to keep your own secrets safe. Unbelievable. You hate each other, and still stick together. Well, guess what? Screw you. I'm done with you both."

"Big words from a little human," V'lane said. "You need us."

"He's right. Deal with it, Ms. Lane."

Great. Now they were uniting forces against me. I preferred V'lane disappearing when Barrons appeared. Did this mean V'lane wasn't afraid of Barrons, after all? I eyed the space between them. If Barrons were to step forward, would V'lane step back? I could hardly suggest it. After a moment's consideration, I moved out from beneath Barron's arm, and stepped behind him. I felt him relax a little. I think he thought I was seeking the shelter of his body, using the movement to show that I'd chosen a side. I imagined he looked pretty self-satisfied right now.

I shoved him forward as hard as I could. V'lane glided instantly back.

Barrons jerked a furious look over his shoulder at me.

I smiled. I don't think many women push Barrons around.

"What games are you playing, *sidhe*-seer?" V'lane hissed.

The Fae Prince feared Barrons. I tried to process that thought but I'm not sure I succeeded.

"Can you still feel the Book?" Barrons asked, a muscle jumping in his jaw.

"Yes, where has it gone?" demanded V'lane. "Which way?"

"You wasted too much time arguing," I lied. I still had a faint tingle. It had stopped somewhere. "It passed beyond my radar a few minutes ago." I wasn't sure either of them believed me, but what could they do?

Actually, it occurred to me, they both could do something really nasty to me if they felt like it: Barrons could use Voice, force me to tell him the truth, and make me hunt it, and if I understood a death-by-sex Fae's thrall, V'lane could amp up the sex thing and steer me around like a horny little divining rod.

So, why weren't they? Because they really *were* decent guys with decent motives, albeit very screwed-up personalities? Or because they didn't want each other around when they used me to track it, and neither could think of a way to get rid of the other at the moment?

Were we all letting it get away, to keep each other from getting it? Wow. I used to have a hard time with high school geometry. Life was way more complicated than math.

"Move," Barrons said. "Get on the bike."

I didn't like his tone.

"Where will you go, Ms. Lane, if not with me or him? Back home to Ashford? Will you strike out on your own? Get a flat? Will your father have to come pack up after you, like you cleaned up after your sister?"

I turned and began walking. He followed me, close enough that I could feel his breath on the back of my neck. "He'll sift you," he said in a low growl, "if you give him the chance."

"I don't think he'll risk getting within twenty feet of you," I said coolly. "And you didn't have to remind me that my sister's dead. That was a cheap shot."

I got on the Harley.

Go with V'lane and be punished for violating our bargain?

I'd take my chances with Barrons. For now.

EIGHT

"Some of your mail missed the slot," Dani said as she pushed open the front door of Barrons Books and Baubles, and wheeled her bike inside.

I glanced up from the book I was reading (Irish invasions again, some of the most boring research I'd ever done, except for some of the bits about the Fir Bolg and Fomorians) and, after looking behind her to make sure she was alone, smiled. Her curly auburn hair was windblown, her cheeks were flushed with cold, and she'd topped her green pin-striped Post Haste, Inc., courier uniform with a jauntily perched company cap, and her eternal I'm-bored-and-way-too-cool-for-words expression.

I like Dani. She's different from the other *sidhe*-seers. I've liked her since the day I met her. There's something kindred in us, besides the fact that we're both on vengeance quests: her for her mother, and me for my sister.

"Rowena would kill you for coming here, you

know." I frowned, as a suspicion occurred to me. "Or did she send you?"

"Nah. I snuck away. I don't think anyone followed me. You're top dog on her shit list, Mac. If she'd sent me, she'd've sent me with the sword."

I caught my breath. I never wanted to battle Dani. Not because I was afraid I might not win—although with her superhuman speed, I supposed it was possible—but because I never wanted to see that exuberant, flippant spark extinguished by my hand, or any other. "Really?"

She flashed a gamine grin. "Nah. I don't think she wants you dead. She just wants you to grow the feck up and obey her every word. She's waiting for the same thing from me. She doesn't get that we *are* grown the feck up. We're just not good little tin soldiers like the rest of her fluff-brained army. If you have a mind of your own, Rowena calls you a child. If you don't have a mind of your own, *I* call you a sheep. *Baaa*," she said, making a face. "The abbey's so full of 'em it stinks of sheep shit on a summer day."

I swallowed a laugh. It would only encourage her. "Stop cussing," I said. Before she could get pissy, I added, "Because pretty girls don't have ugly mouths, okay? I cuss sometimes, too. But I do it sparingly."

"Who cares if I'm pretty?" she sneered, but I saw right through her. The first time I'd seen her she'd had makeup on and been in street clothes and I'd thought she was older than she was. In her uniform and without all that black eyeliner, I could see she was thirteen, fourteen at the most, and frozen briefly at that awkward stage all of us suffer for a time. I'd had a gangly period, too, where I'd been convinced the Lane genes had betrayed me, and unlike Alina, I was going to grow up ugly and have to spend the rest of my life eclipsed by my older sister while people said sadly, and never quite quietly enough, "Poor MacKayla, Alina got the brains *and* the beauty."

Dani was trapped in adolescent limbo. Her torso hadn't yet caught up with her legs and arms, and although her hormones were wreaking havoc on her skin they had yet to shape her hips and bust. Caught between child and woman was a rough place to be, and she had to fight monsters on top of it. "You're going to be gorgeous one day, Dani," I told her, "so clean up your language, if you want to hang out with me."

She rolled her eyes, leaned her bike against the counter, tossed a rolled-up wad of mail on the counter, and sauntered cockily off toward the magazine rack, but not before I caught the startled, thoughtful look in her eyes. She would remember what I'd said. She would cling to it during her worst moments and it would get her through, the same way my Aunt Eileen's promise that I would one day be pretty had gotten me through.

"Found it on the sidewalk," she tossed over her shoulder. "Fecking postmen can't even hit the slot." She punctuated it with a glance that was a dare to correct her, and I might have, but she plucked a *Hot Rod* magazine from the stand.

Nice choice. I'd gone for the same thing at her age.

"Do you know you're sitting on the edge of a whole neighborhood of nasty Unseelie?"

"You mean the Shades?" I said, absently flipping through the mail. "Yeah. I call it a Dark Zone. I've found three of them in the city."

"You come up with the coolest names. Doesn't it creep you out that they're so close?"

"Creeps me out that they exist at all. Have you seen what they leave behind?"

She shuddered. "Yeah. Rowena sent me out with a team looking for some of us who didn't make it home one night."

I shook my head. She was too young to be seeing so much death. She should be reading magazines and thinking about cute guys. As I thumbed through the fliers and coupons, I spotted an envelope stuck in the middle. I'd seen that kind of envelope before: thick, plain, off-white vellum.

No return address.

It had a Dublin postmark, stamped two days ago. **MacKayla Lane c/o Barrons Books and Baubles,** it said.

I ripped it open with trembling hands.

I talked to Mac tonight.

I closed my eyes, mentally braced myself, then opened them again.

It was soooo good to hear her voice! I could picture her lying on her bed, sprawled across the rainbow quilt Mom made for her years ago that's frayed at the edges from a hundred washings, but she refuses to give it up. I could close my eyes and smell the caramel-apple pie with pecan crumb crust Mom was baking. I could hear Daddy in the background, watching baseball with old man Marley from next door, yelling at the Braves as if the batter's ability to hit the ball depended on how loud they could shout. Home feels like it's a million miles away, not four thousand—a mere plane ride, eight hours and I could see her.

Who am I kidding? Home's a million <u>lifetimes</u> away. I want to tell her so badly. I want to say, Mac, come over here. You're a <u>sidhe</u>-seer. We're adopted. There's a war coming and I'm trying to stop it, but if I can't I'm going to have to bring you over here anyway, to help us fight. I want to say, I miss you more than anything in the world, and I love you <u>so much</u>! But if I do, she'll know something's wrong. It's been so hard to hide it from her, because she knows me so well. I want to reach through the phone lines and hug my baby sister. Sometimes I'm afraid I'll never get to do it again. That I'll die here and there'll be a lifetime of things left unsaid and undone. But I can't let myself think that way because—

I fisted my hand, crushing the page into a wad. "Watch the counter, Dani," I barked, and raced for the bathroom.

I slammed the door, locked it, sat on the toilet, and hung my head between my knees. After a moment, I blew my nose and dried my eyes. Her handwriting, her words, her love for me, had slid an unexpected knife straight through my heart. Who was sending me these stupid, painful pages, and why?

I uncrumpled the page, smoothed it on my legs, and continued where I'd left off.

—if I do, I'll lose hope, and hope's all I've got. I learned something important tonight. I thought I was hunting the Book, and that would be the end of it. But now I know we've got to re-create what once was. We've got to find the five foretold by the Haven's prophecy. The <u>Sinsar Dubh</u> alone isn't enough. We need the stones <u>and</u> the book <u>and</u> the five.

That was the end of the page. There was nothing on the other side.

I stared at it until it blurred out of focus. When did grief end? Did it ever? Or did you just get numb from hurting yourself on it so many times?

Would I grow emotional scar tissue? I hoped so. At the same time I hoped not. How could I betray my love for my sister by not suffering every time I thought about her? If I stopped hurting, would that mean I'd stopped loving her a little?

How had Alina known about the Haven? I'd only recently learned of its existence and what it was: the High Council of *sidhe*-seers. Rowena claimed she'd never met my sister, yet Alina had written in her journal about the governing body of the very organization Rowena ran, and she'd somehow learned of a prophecy foretold by them.

What were the five? What was the Haven's prophecy?

I clutched my head and massaged my scalp. Evil books and mysterious players and plots within plots, and now prophecies, too? Before I'd needed five things: four stones and a Book. Now I needed ten? That wasn't merely absurd, it was unfair.

I stuffed the page in the front pocket of my jeans, stood up, freshened my face, took a deep breath, and went out to relieve Dani of her clerk duties. If my eyes were too bright when I stepped behind the counter, either she didn't notice, or she understood a thing or two about grief, and left me alone.

"Some of the girls want to meet with you, Mac. That's why I came today. They asked me to ask you because they figured you wouldn't even let them in the door, and they're freaked out that you know a prince." Her feline eyes narrowed. "What's he like?" Her young voice was hushed with a dangerous blend of fascination and awakening hormones.

V'lane was the *sidhe*-seer equivalent of Lucifer; and even if his motives in Mankind's current predicament mirrored ours, he was to be feared, shunned, and, a deep part of me insisted, destroyed. Seelie and Unseelie alike, the Fae were our enemies. They always had been, and always would be. Why, oh why, do we find the most dangerous, forbidden men the most irresistible?

"Fae princes kill *sidhe*-seers, Dani."

"He hasn't killed *you*." She shot me an admiring look. "It looked like you had him eating out of your hand."

"No woman could have that Fae eating out of her hand," I said sharply, "so don't be daydreaming about it."

She ducked her head guiltily, and I sighed, remembering what it was like to be thirteen. V'lane would have been the object of every one of my teenage fantasies. No rock star, no actor, could have competed with the golden, immortal, inhumanly erotic prince. In my daydreams, I would have wowed him with my cleverness, seduced him with my budding femininity, succeeded in winning his heart where no other woman could because, of course, in my fantasy, I would have endowed him with the heart he didn't have.

"He's so beautiful," she said wistfully. "He's like an angel."

"Yep," I agreed flatly. "The one that fell." My words did nothing to change the expression on her face. I could only hope she never saw him again. I could see no reason that she would. At some point, in the near future, she and I were going to have a long talk about life. She was overdue. I almost laughed. I'd been overdue too. Then I'd come to Dublin. "Tell me more about this meeting they want, Dani." What were they after?

"After you left that night, everybody got into a huge fight. Rowena sent everybody back to bed, but once she left, it started up again. Some of the girls wanted to hunt you down and get even. But Kat— she was with Moira that day—said that you didn't mean to do it, and it would be wrong, and a lot of girls listen to her. Some of 'em aren't happy with Rowena. They think she keeps too tight a rein on us.

They think we should be out in the streets, doing what we can to stop what's going on, instead of just biking past it every day, watching. She almost *never* lets us go out to kill."

"With only one weapon, I can see why." I hated agreeing with the old woman, but I concurred on that score.

"She keeps the sword herself. She doesn't like to be without it. I think she's afraid."

I could understand that, too. Last night, after I'd gotten on the bike and we'd sped off, I'd checked for my spear. Despite his obvious displeasure with me, V'lane had kept his word and returned it at parting.

I showered with it strapped to my thigh.

I slept with it in my hand.

"We could *fight*, Mac. Maybe we can't kill them without the sword, but we sure could kick some fecking ass, and maybe they'd think twice about settin' up shop in our city. I could save dozens of people every day, if she'd just let me. I see 'em walking down the street, holding hands with a human"—she shuddered—"and I know that person's gonna die. I could save them!"

"But the Unseelie you stopped would only move on to another victim, if you didn't kill it, Dani. You'd be saving one person to sentence another." I'd thought this through myself. I felt the same things. We were hopelessly outnumbered with only two weapons.

Her mouth twisted. "That's what Rowena says, too."

Ugh. I was *not* like Rowena. "In this case, she's right. Diverting them isn't enough. We need more weapons. More ways to kill them, and I can't give up my spear, so if they're using you to bait some kind of trap..." I warned. "I didn't kill Moira. It *was* an accident. But I won't let anyone take my spear away."

"They're not trying to trap you, Mac. I swear. They just want to talk to you. They think there's stuff happening that you don't know about, and they think you might know some stuff we don't. They want to trade info."

"What do they think I don't know?" I demanded. Was there some threat I was unaware of? A new, even worse enemy out there, gunning for me?

"If I tell you anything else, they'll get mad at me, and half the abbey's usually mad at me. I'm not pissing off the other half. They said they'd meet on neutral ground, and that you could choose where. Will you do it?"

I made a show of considering it but my mind was already made up. I wanted to know what they knew, and desperately wanted access to their archives. Rowena had given me a glimpse into one of their many books about the Fae the day Dani had taken me to meet her at PHI. She'd shown me the first few sentences of an entry about V'lane, and I'd been itching to get my hands on it ever since, and finish the rest of it. If information about the *Sinsar Dubh* existed, it was a good bet the *sidhe*-seers had it, somewhere. Not to mention my hope that somewhere in the abbey were answers to my questions about my mother, and heritage. "Yes. But I'll need a show of faith."

"What do you want?"

"Rowena has a book in her desk—"

Dani stiffened instantly. "No fecking way! She'd know! I'm not taking it!"

"Not asking you to. You have a digital camera?"

"Nope. Sorry. Can't do." She folded her arms.

"I'll loan you mine. Photograph the pages about V'lane and bring them to me." My plan would serve the dual purposes of getting me more information, and proving that she was willing to defy Rowena for me. It would also make her read about the object of her misguided fantasies, and hopefully cure her of them.

She stared at me. "If she catches me, I'm dead."

"Don't let her catch you, then," I said. Then I softened, "Do you think you can do it, Dani? If it's really too dangerous..." She *was* only thirteen, and I *was* pitting her against a woman with years of wisdom and experience, ruthless intentions, and a spine of steel.

Her lambent eyes gleamed. "I'm superfast, remember? You want it, I'll get it." She glanced around the bookstore. "But if things get really bad, I'm coming to live with you."

"Oh no, you're not," I said, trying not to smile. She was *such* a teenager.

"Why not? It looks cool to me. No rules, either."

"I'd drown you in rules. All kinds of rules. No TV, no loud music, no boys, no magazines, no snacks or soda, no sugar, no—"

"I get it, I get it," she said sourly. Then she brightened. "So, I can tell 'em you'll meet?"

I nodded.

Dani watched the counter for me, while I ran upstairs and got my Kodak. I changed the settings so it would take the highest resolution photos possible, and told her to make sure she got the entire pages, so I could download them onto my computer, zoom in on the images, and read. I told her to call me as soon as she had them; we'd set a place and time to meet.

"Be safe, Dani," I said, as she wheeled her bike out the door. There was a storm brewing in the streets of Dublin, and I didn't mean those dense black clouds currently crawling across the rooftops. I could feel it. Like a bad moon really *was* rising, and even worse trouble was on the way. Ever since I'd danced to that song the other night, I hadn't been able to shake it from my head. It was such boppy, happy-sounding music to be accompanied by such grim predictions.

She glanced back over her shoulder at me. "We're kinda like sisters, aren't we, Mac?"

A knife twisted in my gut. There was such a hopeful look on her face. "Yeah, I guess we are." I didn't want another sister. Ever. I didn't want to worry about anyone but me.

Still, I did the closest thing to praying I knew how to do, and whispered a silent invocation to the universe to watch over her, as I closed the door.

The dark clouds creeping over the city exploded, thunderheads crashing, raindrops biting with October's chill teeth, flash-flooding the pavement, gushing down the gutters, overflowing the grates, and sweeping all my customers away.

I cataloged books until my vision blurred. I made myself a cup of tea, turned on the gas logs, cozied up to the fire, and paged through a book on Irish fairy tales, hunting for truth in the myth, while picking at a lunch that was the UK equivalent of Ramen noodles. I haven't had much of an appetite since I ate Unseelie. Not for food, anyway.

Last night Barrons and I hadn't said a word to each other all the way back to the bookstore. He'd dropped me at the front and watched me walk in. Then, he'd given me a smile that was all teeth and nastiness, and driven straight into the Dark Zone, managing to say, "Fuck you, Ms. Lane," without even bothering to open his mouth. He knows how much his refusal to tell me why the Shades don't eat him irks me.

I want to be so fearless. *I* want to be so bad and tough that all the monsters leave me alone.

I tugged Alina's journal entry from my pocket and read it again, more slowly this time.

Her worst fear had come true, and here I was, left alone with a lifetime of things unsaid and undone. I'd never gotten that hug. I knew I needed to push past the emotional punch and focus on the Haven's prophecy, the five, and the new questions her journal entry raised, but I was detoured by memories. There'd been so many nights that I'd sprawled on my bed, talking to Alina on the phone. Mom was always making good stuff, filling the house with the mouth-watering aroma of yeast, caramel cream sauces, and spices. Dad was always yelling at the Braves with old man Marley during baseball season. I would have prattled aimlessly about boys and school and my idiotic complaints about whatever I used to complain about, believing the whole time she and I were immortal.

What a shock when life ends at twenty-four. Nobody's ready for it. I missed my rainbow quilt. I missed my mom. God, I missed—

I stood, crammed the page back in my pocket, and pruned my dark thoughts in the seedling stage before they could sprout. Depression gets you nowhere but tangled in an overgrown garden that can choke the life out of you.

I moved to the window and stared out at the rain. Gray street. Gray day. Gray rain, splashing grayly on gray pavement. What was that Jars of Clay song on my iPod? *"My world is a flood. Slowly I become one with the mud."*

As I stared, unblinking into the grayness, a brilliant shaft of sunlight splintered the rain, directly in front of me.

I looked up, seeking its source. The beam pierced the dark clouds, a radiant lance shot down from heaven, forming a perfect golden circle on the dreary, drenched sidewalk, inside which there was no rain, no storm, just sunshine and warmth. I thumbed a Tums from my pocket. My tea and noodles were abruptly an unpleasant stew in my stomach.

Speaking of the *sidhe*-seer's equivalent of Lucifer...

"Funny," I said. But I wasn't laughing. Fae-induced nausea coupled with an impossible illusion spelled one thing: V-l-a-n-e. The only thing missing was a frenzy of Fae lust, and I braced myself for it. His name piercing my tongue suddenly tasted sweet as honey, felt smooth and supple and sexy in my mouth. "Go away," I told the illusory shaft of sun, focusing my *sidhe*-seer center on it. It didn't evaporate.

Then V'lane was standing in it, but he wasn't Fae, and he wasn't the biker man. He was a version of himself I'd never seen before: He looked human, and he was definitely muted. Still, he was inhumanly beautiful. He was wearing white swim trunks that contrasted perfectly with his gold skin, and flaunted his flawless body. His hair slid like silk over his bare shoulders. His eyes were amber, warm with invitation.

He'd come to punish me. I knew that. And *still* I wanted to step outside, splash through the rain and join him in his sunny oasis. Hold his hand. Run away for a while, maybe to Faery, where I could play volleyball and drink beers with a perfectly convincing illusion of Alina. I stuffed that thought back in my padlocked box and checked the chains. They weren't holding so good today.

I will attend to you later, he'd said last night. *You broke our bargain. There is a price for that.*

"Leave me alone, V'lane," I called through the window. It echoed off the glass back at me, and I wasn't sure he heard. Maybe he could read lips. Suddenly the windowpane separating us was gone. Drops of wind-driven rain needled my face, my hands.

"You are forgiven, MacKayla. Upon reflection, I realized it was not your fault. You were not responsible for Barrons' interference. I do not expect you to be able to control him. To demonstrate my understanding, I have come, not to punish you, but to give you a gift."

His "gifts" all had strings attached, and I told him so, with a tongue that tasted of nectar.

"Not this one. This is for you and only for you. I will gain nothing from it."

"I don't believe you."

"I could have harmed you long before now if I wished."

"So? Maybe you're just putting it off. Sucking me in for the grand finale." I brushed rain from my face, and pushed my hair back. It was simultaneously curling and drooping, becoming an unmanageable mess. "You can put the window back anytime."

"I took your hand and accompanied you into the halls of my enemies, trusting you not to Null me. Return the honor, *sidhe*-seer." The temperature was dropping. "I gave you my name, the means to summon me at will." The rain turned to sleet.

"Not inspiring trust with your little display of temper." A strong gust of wind dumped a sudden bucket of rain on me. "Oh! You did that on purpose!" I dragged a sleeve across my face, mopping at it. It didn't help. My sweater was soaked.

He didn't deny it. Just cocked his head, studied me. "I will tell you about the one you call Lord Master."

"*I* don't call him Lord Master and never will," I

bristled. I battled the urge to leap out the window, grab him, and demand to know whatever he knew.

"Would you like to know who he is?"

"You said you'd never heard of him when I told you about him." I studied my nails, knowing if he knew how badly I wanted the information, he'd make it harder to get. Probably try to trade it for sex.

"I have learned much since then."

"So, who is he?" I said, in a bored voice.

"Accept my gift."

"Tell me what your 'gift' is first."

"You have no plans for the afternoon." He glanced at the flooded street beyond his warm, sunny oasis. "You will have no customers. Will you sit in your chair and pine for lost things?"

"You're pissing me off, V'lane."

"Have you ever seen the Caribbean Sea? There are hues in those waves that nearly vie with Faery."

I sighed. No. I'd dreamed of it, though. Sun slanting off water was one of my favorite things in the world, whether it was swimming-pool-blue or shades-of-tropic. During the winter in Ashford, I used to go to the local travel agent's office in town and thumb through the pamphlets, dreaming of all the exotic, sunny places the husband I hadn't met yet was going to take me. Part of the reason I was so depressed in Dublin was from simple lack of sun. My time in the subterranean caves beneath the Burren had sapped me. I not only love sun, I *need* it. I think if I'd grown up in the colder, drearier North, I'd have been a completely different person. Sure, the sun comes out here, but not nearly as often as it does in Georgia, and not the same way. Dublin doesn't get those months of long, blissfully blazingly hot summer days, crowned by a sky so blue it hurts to look at, and a sultry heat that warms you to the core. My bones are cold here. So is my heart.

A few hours in the tropics, plus information about the Lord Master?

The rain slanting in through the windowless hole pricked my skin with the icy spines of a dozen porcupines. Would he really forgo retaliation against me for breaking our bargain? I was in no position to shut the Seelie prince out of my life. Whether I trusted him or not, I needed to be on decent terms with him, and if he really was offering me a Get Out of Jail Free card, I'd be crazy not to take it. I couldn't cower in the bookstore from him every time he showed up. I was going to have to confront him on unwarded ground eventually.

"Put the window back." I wasn't going to be blamed by Barrons for another missing window, or risk that big nasty Shade out back getting in.

"Do you accept my gift?"

I nodded.

When the pane was back, I went to the counter, swapped my soaking cardigan for a dry jacket over my damp shirt, and bent to extract the spear from my boot and holster it beneath my arm. It was gone.

Apparently the bookstore being warded only kept him *out*. It didn't keep him from performing his tricks in or on the store itself. I made a mental note to discuss this problem with the intractable owner and keeper of the wards. Surely with all his secrets and inexplicable abilities Barrons could do better than that.

I flipped the sign to **CLOSED,** locked up, splashed through the puddles, stepped into the sun and, when V'lane offered his hand, nullified my intent to Null, and laced my fingers with his.

I was in Cancún, Mexico, sitting in a disappearing-edge swimming pool, on a bar stool that was actually *under* the water, watching palm trees sway in a sultry breeze against the unmistakable aqua splendor of the Caribbean Sea; drinking coconut, lime, and tequila from a scooped-out pineapple, with the salt spray of breaking surf and sun kissing my skin.

Translation: I'd died and gone to heaven.

Dublin, the rain, my problems, my depression: All of it had vanished in the blink of a Fae Prince's sift.

My bikini today, courtesy of V'lane, was leopard print, three embarrassingly tiny triangles. A gold belly chain, inset with amber, draped my hips. I didn't care how nearly naked I was. The day was blindingly bright and beautiful. The sun was warm and healing on my shoulders. The double shots of Cuervo Gold in my drink weren't hurting, either. I was glowing golden inside and out.

"So? Who is he? You said you'd tell me about the Lord Master," I prompted.

His hands were on me then, rubbing suntan oil into my skin that smelled of the coconut and almond, and for a short time I forgot that I even *had* a tongue that could ask questions.

Even when he's fully muted, there's magic in a death-by-sex Fae's hands. They make you feel like you're being touched by the only man who could ever know you, understand you, give you what you need. Illusion, deception, and lie, perhaps, but it still *feels* real. The mind may know the difference. But the body doesn't. The body is a traitor.

I leaned into V'lane's touch, moving under his strong, sure strokes, purring inwardly while he petted me. His iridescent eyes burned a shimmering shade of amber, like the gems on my belly chain, grew sleepy, heated, promising me sex that would blow my mind away.

"I have a suite, MacKayla," he said softly. "Come." He took my hand.

"I bet you say that to all the girls," I murmured, and pulled away. I shook my head, trying to clear it.

"I despise girls. I like women. They are infinitely more...interesting. Girls break. Women can surprise you."

Girls break. I had no doubt he'd broken more than a few in his time. I'd not forgotten the book in Rowena's study that credited this very Fae with being the founder of the Wild Hunt. The thought jarred me back to reality. "Who is he?" I asked again, scooting to the farthest edge of my bar stool. "Stop touching me. Honor your promise."

He sighed. "What is it you humans say? All work and no play—"

"—might just keep me alive," I finished dryly.

"*I* will keep you alive."

"Barrons says the same thing. I'd prefer to be able to do it myself."

"You are a mere human, a woman at that."

I felt my jaw jut. "Like you said. Women can surprise you. Answer my question. Who is he?" I motioned the bartender for a fresh pineapple—hold the tequila—and waited.

"One of us."

"Huh?" I blinked. "The Lord Master is *Fae*?"

V'lane nodded.

Although I'd gotten a Fae read off the Lord Master the two times we'd met, I'd also gotten a human read, similar to what I sensed in Mallucé and Derek O'Bannion. I'd thought the Fae part was because the Lord Master ate Fae, not because he *was* Fae. "But I don't sense full Fae from him. What's the deal?"

"He is no longer. He who calls himself the Lord Master was formerly a Seelie known as Darroc, a trusted member of the queen's High Council."

I blinked. He was *Seelie*? Then what was he doing leading the *Un*seelie? "What happened?"

"He betrayed our queen. She discovered he was working secretly with the Royal Hunters to overthrow her, and return to the old ways, and old days in which no Fae bowed to an insult of a Compact, or had any use for humans other than passing diversion." Alien, ancient eyes studied me a moment. "Darroc's special diversion was playing with human women for a long, cruel time, before destroying them."

An image of Alina's body as it had looked lying on the morgue table rose up in my mind. "Have I told you how much I hate him?" I hissed. For a moment I couldn't say any more, couldn't even think past him hurting my sister and leaving her to die. I breathed deep and slow, then said, "So, what, you threw him out of Faery and dumped him on us?"

"When the queen uncovered his treason, she stripped him of his power and immortality, and banished him to your realm, condemning him to suffer the brevity and humiliation of a mortal life, and die—the cruelest sentence for a Fae, crueler even than ceasing to exist by immortal weapon, or . . . simply vanishing the way some of us do. To die was insult to injury. Mortal indignity is the greatest indignity of all."

He was *so* arrogant. "Was he a prince?" A death-by-sex Fae like V'lane? Was that how he'd seduced my sister?

"No. But he was old among our kind. Powerful."

"How can you know that, if you've drunk from the cauldron?" I pointed out an obvious bit of illogic. A side effect of extreme longevity, V'lane had told me, was eventual madness. They dealt with it by drinking from the Seelie Hallow, the cauldron. The sacred drink wiped their memories clean, and let them start over with a brand-new Fae life, and no memory of who they'd once been.

"The cauldron is not without flaws, MacKayla. Memory is . . . how did one of your artists say it?— persistent. It was fashioned to ease the onus of eternity, not leave us blank. When we drink from it, we emerge speaking the first language we knew. Darroc's is mine: the ancient one, from the dawn of our race. In such a way, we know things about each other, despite the divestiture of memories. Some attempt to plant information about themselves for their next incarnation to find. The Fae Court is an unpleasant place to be, stripped of ability to discern friend from foe. We prolong drinking as long as possible. Tatters from earlier times sometimes remain. Some must drink twice, three times, to be cleansed."

"How can I find Darroc?" I asked. Now that I knew his name, I would never call him anything but that, or a mocking "LM" again.

"You cannot. He is hiding where even we have been unable to track him. He slips in and out of Unseelie through portals unknown to us. We are hunting him, the other Seelie princes and I."

"How can a mere human elude you and move in and out of Fae realms?" I goaded. I was angry. They'd made this mess. They'd dumped Darroc into our realm because they'd been having problems, and it was my world that was suffering, my sister who'd been killed because of it. The least they could do was clean up after themselves, and fast.

"My queen did not strip his knowledge from him, an oversight she now regrets. She believed he would die quickly. It is why we did not suspect him of being the one behind the trouble in your realm. Once human, Darroc had no immunity against the many illnesses that plague your kind, and those who live as gods tend to underestimate the brutality of the herd when they walk among it."

"He's not the only one who underestimated something," I said frostily. Herd, my petunia. With so much inhuman power at their fingertips, they certainly were humanly fallible, and we humans were the ones paying for it.

V'lane ignored the jibe. "We believed if he did not

contract a mortal illness, he would anger a human with his arrogance, and become one of your violent crime statistics. Contrary to our expectations, since Darroc has been mortal, he has acquired immense power. He knew where to look, and how to get it, and he has always had allies among the Royal Hunters. He promises them freedom from the Unseelie prison where they are stabled; a promise no other Fae would make. Hunters cannot be trusted."

"And other Fae can?" I said dryly.

"Hunters go beyond all bounds." Here V'lane momentarily flickered, as if struggling not to revert to another form. "They have taught Darroc to eat the flesh of Fae to steal Fae power!" He paused, and for a fleeting moment, the temperature plunged so sharply that I couldn't draw a breath and the ocean, as far as I could see it, iced. Abruptly, all was normal again. "He will die very slowly when we find him. The queen may make him suffer immortally for it. We do not savage our own."

I looked away hurriedly and stared out at the sea, owning the same sin, feeling it flashing in incriminating neon letters on my forehead: FAE EATER. Darroc had taught Mallucé, Mallucé had taught me, and I'd taught Jayne. I had no desire to suffer immortally, or otherwise. "What can I do to help?"

"Leave it to us to find Darroc," V'lane said. "You must do as the queen has charged you and find the Book. The walls between our realms are dangerously thin. If Darroc succeeds in bringing them down, the Unseelie will escape their prison. Without the *Sinsar Dubh*, we are as powerless to reimprison our dark brethren as you. Once loose, they will consume your world and destroy your race."

He paused before adding grimly, "And, quite possibly, mine."

NINE

At quarter to ten, I was waiting for Barrons to arrive, and my Voice lessons to begin. We'd set a standing engagement, and although I knew he was probably still angry with me, I expected him to show.

I didn't mind hopping. He could make me squawk like a chicken, for all I cared. If he made me feel stupid enough, I'd figure out how to resist him.

Christian had been right. If the walls came down, all the Unseelie would be freed. And I'd been right, too: The Seelie couldn't reimprison them without the *Sinsar Dubh*. Despite the grimness of our situation, I was once again focused, determined Mac. I'd stolen some sun—real human sun, not Faery stuff like last time with V'lane—and stashed it away, solar energy for my cells. A junkie, I'd gotten my fix.

Thumbing my nose at the chilly weather outside, which I had no intention of venturing into, I was wearing my favorite short white skirt, pretty sandals, and a lime-gold sleeveless top that tinted the green of my eyes a lighter, more intense shade. My skin was burnished gold from my hours in the sun. I looked and felt great. After showering, and doing my makeup and hair, I'd talked to Dad for a while. In Ashford, it was suppertime, and it had been 88 degrees today. In Dublin it was 38, but knowing Cancún was a mere "sift" away made it a lot easier to handle.

In my refreshed state of mind, I'd decided to divulge some information to Barrons. Try fishing with a baited hook instead of demanding answers, do things his way. I was going to show him the page from my sister's journal that I'd received today. V'lane had slipped. Surely every now and then Barrons did, too. Maybe his face would betray something. Maybe he knew what the five were. Maybe he'd have some idea who had Alina's journal. I didn't believe *he* did. I couldn't see any reason he would choose those specific entries to send to me. Then again, I couldn't see any reason *anyone* would choose them, but someone had.

If I shared something with him, maybe he'd return the favor. Perhaps he felt the answers were innocuous enough that they didn't matter. Sunny Mac felt it was worth a try.

The bell above the door tinkled.

Barrons stepped in. He swept a gaze from my head to my feet, slowly. His face tightened, then he worked his way back up, just as slowly. I guess he didn't like my clothes. He rarely does. Left to my own devices, I dress too happy to suit his tastes. Ms.

Rainbow and Mr. Night. That's what we look like walking around together.

To defuse any tension left over from last night, I offered him a smile, and a friendly, "Hey," letting him know I was willing to start this night off fresh, and hoped he was, too.

I sensed his violence a split second before he attacked me, and then it was too late. He slammed the door behind him. Dead bolts ratcheted into place.

"Tell me every detail of the last time you saw the Sinsar Dubh."

Voice compacted my body in a head-to-toe vise, and squeezed brutally. Shit, shit, shit.

I doubled over, the breath slammed out of me. A legion of voices rebounded in the room, careening off the walls, intensifying as they zoomed left and right, up and down, then through me, burrowing into my skin, rearranging things in my head, making my mind *his*. Dominating. Seducing. Selling me the lie that his will was mine, and I lived to obey it.

Sweat beaded on my brow and upper lip, and slicked my palms. The harder I tried to fight the compulsion, the less possible it was to inflate my lungs, to move any part of my body at all. A paper doll, I hung, folded, limp, spineless. And like a paper doll, he could tear me in half, if he wanted to.

"Stop fighting me, Ms. Lane, and it'll go easier. Unless you enjoy the pain."

In my mind I spewed a geyser of curses, but not a word came out. I had no breath to fuel it. He'd topped the level he'd used on me last night—the level of proficiency he'd said the Lord Master had achieved—and he'd done it with a voice of silk. Like the difference between other men's motorcycles and his, Barrons walks softly—but he carries the biggest stick I've ever seen.

"Nice tan, Ms. Lane. How's V'lane? Did you have a good time today? I take you to graveyards, but he takes you to the beach—is that what our problem is? Our little dates aren't good enough for you? Does he romance you? Feed you all those pretty lies you're so hungry for? I've been neglecting you lately. I'll be remedying that. *Sit. Over there.*" He pointed to a chair near the fire.

I jerked upright and tiptoed tightly toward the indicated seat, not because I felt dainty, but because that's what happens when you try to lock down your leg muscles to prevent your feet from rising and falling, but your body moves anyway. One resistant step after the next, I minced toward the chair. I reached it and collapsed into it like a rag doll. My throat muscles convulsed and I tried to force out words. "D-don't . . . d-do—"

"You will not speak unless it is in direct answer to one of my questions."

My lips sealed. I couldn't believe he was doing this to me. How ironic that V'lane had asked me to trust him today, I had, and he hadn't betrayed me. I'd been ready to open up a little to Barrons tonight, tell him a few things, and he'd betrayed me. V'lane had muted his sexuality to preserve my will. Barrons had just stripped it away with a single command, no different from the Lord Master.

"Tell me what you saw the night you encountered the Sinsar Dubh," he repeated.

Straining in my skin, nearly suffocating myself

with my attempts to resist, I spilled every detail, every last thought, every perception. From the humiliation of lying in that vile puddle in my pretty clothes, to the various forms the Book had taken, to the look it had given me, to my decision about how to track it. Then, to make things worse, I volunteered my entire "intervention" with Inspector Jayne.

"Don't move," he said, and I sat ramrod-straight in my chair, unable to even scratch my nose while he pondered his thoughts. There was violence in the room with us, a killing violence. I didn't get it. What had I done to piss him off so much? He hadn't been half this angry last night, and he'd had every opportunity to grill me forcibly then. He hadn't. He'd just driven off.

"Where did you go today?"

Sweat dripping down my face, I told him that, too. I wanted to speak of my own free will, to call him every name in the book, to tell him we were through, he and I, and that *I* was the one who deserved answers, not him. But he'd sealed my lips with a command, and I could only answer what he asked.

"Did V'lane tell you anything?"

"Yes," I said flatly, biting it off there. I'd obeyed the compulsion to the letter. I didn't have to offer more.

"What did he tell you?"

"That the Lord Master was once a Fae, named Darroc."

He snorted. "Old news. *Did he tell you anything about me?"*

Old news? He'd been sitting on information about the Lord Master that he hadn't shared with me? And he got pissed at *me* for not telling him everything I knew? If he didn't kill me when he was done with me, he was dead. He was a walking encyclopedia with a cover I couldn't crack. Useless. Dangerous. "No."

"Did you fuck him?"

"No," I gritted.

"Have you ever fucked him?"

"No," I ground out. I'd never had two men more obsessed with what was happening in my sex life, or rather, *not* happening.

Some of the violence in the air abated.

My eyes narrowed. Was this it? The source of his rage? Was Barrons jealous? Not because he cared, but because he thought of me as a possession, his personal and private *sidhe*-seer, and there would be no other men's erections interfering with her OOP detections?

He gave me a cold look. "I needed to know if you were Pri-ya. That's why I asked."

"Do I look Pri-ya?" I snapped. I had no idea what a Fae addict looked like, but I somehow doubted I was the Poster Girl for it. I figured them for something more like the Goth girls I'd seen hanging out at Mallucé's vampire lair: pierced, tattooed, and heavily made-up, dressed in vintage clothing, mostly black.

He started, measured me a moment, then laughed. "Good for you, Ms. Lane! You're learning."

I started, myself, realized what I'd just done. I'd said something that hadn't been an answer to a

direct question! I tried to do it again, mentally forming the words, but I couldn't force them out. I didn't
know how I'd done it in the first place.

"Who were you going to see the night you saw the
Sinsar Dubh?*"*

Oh, no. This wasn't fair. He didn't get to know
everything. "A guy that knew Alina," I said between
clenched teeth.

"Tell me his name."

No, no, no. "Christian MacKeltar."

"Are you fucking kidding me?" He exploded from
his chair and glared down at me.

Since he'd used Voice, I was obligated to say,
"No," although I knew the question had been
rhetorical. The killing violence was back, over a simple name. Why? What significance did Christian's
name have to him? Did he know him? Closing my
eyes, I sought the *sidhe*-seer place in my head. It was
no help. I still couldn't speak. How could I feel so
much power in that hot, alien part of my mind, yet
find nothing there of use to me in this situation?

"How did you meet Christian MacKeltar?"

"He works at the ALD at Trinity. I met him when
you sent me to pick up the invitation to the auction
from his boss, but she wasn't there."

His nostrils flared. "He must be a recent hire.
They've been spying on me."

He hadn't used Voice, nor had he asked a question, so I said nothing.

"Have the MacKeltars been spying on me?"

Squeezing my eyes shut, I said, "Yes."

"Have you been spying on me, Ms. Lane?"

"As much as I can."

"What have you learned about me?"

I went poking around in my head again but whatever place I was supposed to discover remained a mystery to me. Aware that I was digging my own grave, one spadeful of information at a time, I told him. That I knew he wasn't human. That I knew he was impossibly old. That I'd watched him step out of the Unseelie Sifting Silver he kept in his study, carrying the savagely brutalized corpse of a woman. That, like the Shades, the demons in there had fled his path.

He laughed. As if it was some kind of *joke* that I knew all his dark secrets. He didn't try to explain or justify one bit of it. "And I didn't think you could keep your own counsel. You knew these things and never said a word. You're becoming interesting. *Are you working with the MacKeltars against me?*"

"No."

"Are you working with V'lane against me?"

"No."

"Are you working with the sidhe-*seers against me?"*

"No."

"Are you working with anyone against me?"

"No."

"Where do your loyalties lie, Ms. Lane?"

"With myself," I shouted. "With my sister! With my family, and screw all of you!"

The violence in the room abated.

After a moment, Barrons resumed his seat in the chair across from me, absorbed my painfully stiff posture, and smiled without humor. "Very well, Mac. *Relax.*"

Mac? He'd called me Mac? I fought for breath.

"Am I about to die?" I wheezed. "Are you going to kill me?"

He looked startled. I'd done it again. Spoken of my own will. He'd released my body, but not his hold on my mind and mouth. I could still feel it, compelling me, hurting me.

Then he snorted. "I tell you to relax and you think I'm going to kill you? You're crippled by a woman's illogic." He added as a seeming afterthought, *"You may speak freely now."*

The stranglehold on my throat was gone, and for a few moments I simply enjoyed the sensation of breath moving in and out of my lungs, of knowing my tongue was once again my own. I could feel V'lane's name, piercing the meat of it, and realized that from the moment Barrons had used Voice to bind my will, it had somehow faded, receded beyond my reach. "I am not. The only two times you ever called me Mac is when I was near death. Since there's no other threat around right now, you must be about to kill me. It's perfectly logical."

"I didn't call you Mac."

"Yes, you did."

"I called you Ms. Lane."

"No, you didn't."

"Yes, I did."

I clenched my jaw. Sometimes, despite Barrons' eternal old-world sophistication, and my glamour-girl cool, he and I very nearly devolve into childish fights. Frankly, I didn't give a rat's petunia what he'd called me, and wasn't about to sit here and argue about it. I was free, and furious. I exploded from my chair, launched myself at him, and slammed both palms against his chest. I put every ounce of determination to Null into my hands that I could summon. My *sidhe*-seer core blazed like a small fiery sun in my head. Was he or wasn't he Unseelie?

I hit him so hard that his chair toppled backward and we went skidding across the floor toward the fireplace, stopping inches from the grate. If he froze at all, it was for so brief a moment that I couldn't decide if I'd nulled him, or merely startled him into a brief second of immobility.

Figured. More non-answers where Barrons was concerned.

I reared back, straddling him, and punched him in the jaw as hard as I could. He started to speak and I punched him again. I wished I'd eaten Unseelie. I was going to go eat ten of them tonight then come back here and finish him off, the hell with answers.

"How *dare* you saunter in here and force me to give you answers when you've never given me a single one?" I hissed. I punched him in the stomach, hard. He didn't even wince. I punched him again. Nothing.

"You stand there all tan and glowing and wonder why I use Voice on you?" he bellowed. "Where the hell do *you* get off? You've been with V'lane again. How many slaps in the face do you think I'm going to take, Ms. Lane?" He grabbed my fist and held it when I tried to punch him again. I swung at him with the other. He caught that, too. "I warned you not to play us against each other."

"I'm not playing you! I'm trying to survive. And I don't slap you when I go off with V'lane!" I tried to yank my fists from his hands. "It doesn't have anything to do with you. I'm trying to get answers, and since you won't give me any, you can't blame me for going somewhere else."

"So, the man who doesn't get laid at home has the right to go off and cheat?"

"Huh?"

"Which word didn't you understand?" he sneered.

"You're the one who's crippled by illogic. This isn't home, it never will be, and nobody's getting laid!" I practically shouted.

"You think I don't know that?" He shifted his body beneath me, making me painfully aware of something. Two somethings, in fact, one of which was how far up my short skirt was. The other wasn't my problem. I wriggled, to shimmy my hem down, but his expression perished the thought. When Barrons looks at me like that, it rattles me. Lust, in those ancient, obsidian eyes, offers no trace of humanity. Doesn't even bother trying.

Savage Mac wants to invite it to come out and play. I think she's nuts. *Nuts*, I tell you.

"Let go of my hands."

"Make me," he taunted. "Voice me, Ms. Lane. Come on, little girl, show me some power."

Little girl, my ass. "You *know* I can't. And that makes what you did to me tonight even more unforgivable. You might as well have raped me. In fact, that's exactly what you did!"

He rolled hard and fast, and I was on my back beneath him, with my hands pinned above my head, the weight of his body crushing me to the floor, his face inches from mine. He was breathing harder than the exertion merited.

"Make no mistake, Ms. Lane, I didn't rape you. You can lie there on your pretty little P.C. ass and claim with your idealistic little P.C. arguments that any violation of your will is rape and that I'm a big, bad bastard, and I'll tell you that you're full of shit, and you've obviously never been raped. Rape is much, much worse. Rape isn't something you walk away from. You crawl."

He was off me and on his feet, stalking out the door before I'd even managed to catch enough breath to reply.

PART TWO

The Darkest Hour

"Nightfall.

What a strange word.

'Night' I get.

But 'fall' is a gentle word.

Autumn leaves fall, swirling with languid grace

To carpet the earth with their dying blaze.

Tears fall, like liquid diamonds

Shimmering softly, before they melt away.

Night doesn't fall here.

It comes slamming down."

—*Mac's journal*

TEN

I slept fitfully and dreamed of the sad woman again.

She was trying to tell me something but an icy wind kept stealing her words each time she opened her mouth. Laughter rippled on the chilling breeze, and I thought I recognized it, but I couldn't lift the name from my mind. The harder I tried, the more frightened and confused I became. Then V'lane was there, and Barrons too, with men I'd never seen before, and suddenly Christian appeared, and Barrons moved toward him, with murder in his eyes.

I woke up, iced to the bone, and in a state of alarm.

My subconscious had put something together that hadn't penetrated my conscious mind: Today was Thursday, Christian was returning from Scotland, and Barrons was onto him, because of me.

I had no idea what Barrons might do to him, and didn't want to find out. The lie-detecting Keltar was no match for...whatever my employer was. Teeth chattering, I grabbed my cell off the night table, and called the ALD. The dreamy-eyed boy answered, and told me Christian wasn't due in until afternoon. I asked for an apartment, home, or cell number, and he said the personnel files were locked up in the department head's office. She was gone for a long holiday weekend, and wouldn't be back until Monday.

I left an urgent message for Christian to call me the instant he walked in.

I was about to tug the covers up, snuggle down, and try to shiver myself warm, when my phone rang.

It was Dani.

"She almost caught me, Mac!" she said breathlessly. "She didn't leave PHI at all yesterday. She slept in her office, and I was up all fecking night, waiting for a chance to get in. Then a few minutes ago she finally went downstairs, for breakfast, I thought, and I slipped in but I couldn't find the book you wanted. There was another one in her desk, so I took pictures of it, but I didn't get many because she came right back, and I had to go out the fecking window and I tore my uniform and banged myself up something wicked. I couldn't get what you asked for but I tried, and I got something else. That counts, doesn't it? Will you still meet up with us?"

"Are you okay?"

She snorted. "I kill monsters, Mac. I fell out of a stupid window."

I smiled. "Where are you?" I could hear horns

honking in the background, the sounds of the city waking up.

"Not far from you." She told me. I knew the intersection.

I glanced at the window. It was still dark out. I hated her being out there in the dark, regardless of her superspeed, and I doubted she had the sword. "There's a church across the street." It was brilliantly lit. "I'll meet you in front of it in ten minutes."

"But the rest of 'em aren't here!"

"I'm just coming for my camera. Can you get the girls together this afternoon?"

"I can try. Kat says you have to pick a place where the other . . . couriers . . . won't see us."

I named several cafés, all of which she nixed as too risky. We finally settled on a below-street pub, aptly named The Underground, that offered darts and pool tables, but no windows.

I hung up, brushed my teeth, splashed water on my face, tugged on jeans, and zipped a fleece-lined jacket over my PJ top, then jammed a ball cap on my head. My blond roots were showing. I made a mental note to stop in a drugstore on the way back and grab a couple boxes of color. It was depressing enough that I had to have dark hair. I wasn't going to cheese it up with a sloppy dye job.

It was 7:20 when I hit the pavement. The sun wouldn't rise until 7:52 A.M. It would set at 6:26; I've become a bit obsessed with the precise timing of natural light, and keep a chart of it on my wall, next to the map where I track Unseelie hot spots and Book activity. I stayed to the lights as much as I could, moving from the pool cast by one streetlamp to the next, a flashlight in each hand, my spear heavy and comforting in my shoulder harness. My MacHalo was for deep night work only. If the people passing by thought it was bizarre that I was carrying lit flashlights, I didn't care. I was staying alive. They could smirk all they wanted. A few of them did.

As I hurried down the street, I pictured myself three months ago, compared it to what I looked like now, and laughed. The businessman hurrying along next to me glanced over. He met my eyes, jerked a little, and stepped up his pace, leaving me behind.

It had rained during the night, and the cobbled streets were shiny in the predawn light. The city perched on the expectant edge of day about to explode: buses honking, taxis vying for space with commuters, people checking their watches and rushing to their jobs, other people ... or things ... already doing theirs, like those Rhino-boys sweeping the streets, and picking up trash.

I watched them surreptitiously, struck by the oddity of it. The non-*sidhe*-seer passerby would see only the human glamour they projected, of the still half-asleep city employee, but I saw their stumpy gray limbs, beady eyes, and jutting jaws as plain as the skin on the back of my hand. I knew they were watchdogs for higher-ranking Fae. I didn't get why they were doing human dirty work. I couldn't see a Fae stooping to it, Light or Dark Court. The many low-level Unseelie were chafing my *sidhe*-seer senses. Usually Rhino-boys don't bother me too much, but in mass numbers they make me feel like I have an ulcer. I poked around inside my head, wondering if I could mute it somehow.

That was better! I could turn the volume down. Very cool.

Dani was leaning jauntily against a streetlamp in front of the church, bike propped against her hip. She had a painful-looking knot on her forehead; the undersides of her forearms were scraped raw, and dirty; and she'd torn holes in the knees of her pinstriped pants as if she'd gone sliding on all fours down an asphalt roof, which, she told me breezily, she had. I wanted to take her back to the bookstore, clean and bandage her up. I told my bleeding heart to get over it. If we ever ended up fighting back to back, I'd need to trust her to deal with all but critical wounds.

Dani slapped the camera into my hand with a cocky grin, and said, "Go ahead, tell me what a great job I did."

I suspected she didn't hear praise often. Rowena didn't seem the type to waste breath on a job well done, when she could save it for a job badly done. I also doubted Dani got much nurturing from the other *sidhe*-seers. Her mouthy defensiveness made her hard to cuddle, and her sisters-in-arms had their own worries on their minds. I thumbed on the camera, glanced at the measly seven pages she'd photographed, of the wrong stuff, and said, "Great job, Dani!"

She preened a moment, then hopped on her bike and pedaled off, skinny legs pumping. I wondered if she ever used her superspeed while biking and, if she did, would you see only a flash of green whizzing by? Kermit the Frog on steroids. "Later, Mac," she said over her shoulder. "I'll call you soon."

I headed back to the bookstore by way of the drugstore. It was light enough to put away my flashlights. I did, then stared down at my camera, zooming in on the photos, trying to figure out what she'd gotten.

I knew better than to walk with my head down. I didn't even dare carry an umbrella in the rain for fear of what I might bump into.

When I careened off the shoulder of a man standing near a dark, expensive car parked at the curb, I exclaimed, "Oh, sorry!" and kept right on going, blessing my luck that it had been a human I'd bumped into, not a Fae—when I realized I had my "volume" way down—and it *hadn't* been a human.

I whirled, whipping my spear from my jacket, willing the people passing by—most with their noses buried in a newspaper, or on their cell phones—not to see me, as if maybe I could throw a little glamour of my own. Melt into the shadows with the other monsters.

"Bitch," spat Derek O'Bannion, his swarthy features contorted with hatred. But his cold, reptilian gaze acknowledged my weapon and he made no move toward me.

Ironically, that weapon is the spear I stole from his brother, Rocky, shortly before Barrons and I led him and his henchmen to their death-by-Shade behind the bookstore. Capitalizing on Derek's hunger for revenge, the LM recruited him as a replacement for Mallucé, taught him to eat Unseelie, and sent him after me to get the spear. I'd convinced the younger O'Bannion brother that I would kill him if he so much as blinked at me wrong, and I'd let him know just how terrible that death would be. The spear killed anything Fae. When a person ate Unseelie, it turned *parts* of the person Fae. When those parts died, they rotted from the inside out, poisoning the human parts of the person, and ultimately killing them. The one time I'd eaten Fae, I'd been terrified of the spear. I'd seen Mallucé up close and personal. He'd been marbled with decay. Half his mouth had rotted, parts of his hands, legs, and stomach had been a decomposing stew, and his genitals . . . ugh. It was a horrific way to die.

O'Bannion yanked open the car door, muttered something to the driver, then slammed it again. The engine turned over and twelve cylinders purred to the quiet life of understated wealth.

I smiled at him. I love my spear. I understand why boys at war name their guns. He fears it. The Royal Hunters fear it. With the exception of the Shades, who have no substance to stab, it will kill anything Fae, allegedly even the king and queen themselves.

Someone I couldn't see pushed the rear car door open from the inside. O'Bannion rested his hand on the top of the window. He was far more riddled with Fae than he had been a week and a half ago. I could feel it.

"Little addictive, huh?" I said sweetly. I dropped my spear, pressed it to my thigh, to dissuade potential busybodies from calling the Garda. I wasn't willing to sheathe it. I knew how fast and strong he was. I'd been there myself, and it had been *incredible*.

"You should know."

"I only ate it once." Probably wasn't so wise to admit that just then, but I was proud of the battle I'd been winning.

"Bullshit! Nobody who's tasted the power would give it up."

"We're not the same, you and I." He wanted dark power. I didn't. Deep down, I just wanted to go back to being the girl I used to be. I would trespass into darker territories only if my survival depended on it. O'Bannion considered embracing the darkness a step up.

I feinted a jab at him with my spear. He flinched, and his mouth compressed to a thin white line.

I wondered, if he stopped eating it now, would he revert to fully human, or, after a certain point, was it too late, and the transformation couldn't be undone?

How I wished I'd let him walk into the Dark Zone that day! I couldn't fight him here and now, in the middle of rush hour. "Get out of here," I stabbed air again, "and if you see me on the street, run as fast and as far as you can."

He laughed. "You stupid little cunt, you have no idea what's coming. Wait till you see what the Lord Master has in store for you." He ducked into the car, and glanced back at me, with a smile of malevolence and . . . sick anticipation. "Trick or treat, bitch," he said, then laughed again. I could hear him laughing, even after he'd closed the door.

I tucked the spear in my harness then stood on the sidewalk, gaping, as he drove away.

Not because of anything he'd said, but because of what I'd seen as he'd settled back into the supple, camel-colored leather seats.

Or, rather, *who* I'd seen.

A woman, beautiful and voluptuous, in the way of aging movie stars from a time long gone by, when actresses had been worthy of the title Diva.

My "volume" was on high. She was eating Fae, too.

Well, now I knew: While Barrons might have killed the woman he'd been carrying out of the mirror, he hadn't killed Fiona.

I opened Barrons Books and Baubles at eleven on the dot, with a new 'do. I'd colored it two shades lighter than Arabian Nights this time and looked closer to my age again (black hair makes me look older, especially with red lipstick), then run down the street for a quick cut, and now a few longish wedges of bang framed my face. The result was feminine and soft, completely at odds with how I felt inside. The rest of it I'd twisted up and stabbed with a hair pick. The result was flirty, casual elegance.

My nails were cut to the quick, but I'd brushed on a quick coat of Perfectly Pink, and glossed on matching lipstick. Despite these concessions to my passion for fashion, I felt drab in my standard uniform of jeans, boots, a black tee under a light jacket, with spear holstered, and flashlights tucked. I missed dressing up.

I sat back on the stool behind the cashier counter, and eyed the tiny jars of wriggling Unseelie flesh lined up there.

I'd managed to cram a lot into my morning. After the drugstore, I'd hit a corner convenience, bought baby food, dyed my hair, showered, emptied the contents, and washed the jars. Then I'd gone out again, attacked a Rhino-boy, cut off part of his arm and stabbed him, putting him out of both our miseries, and making sure he didn't live to tell any tales of a human girl stealing Fae power. Then I'd sliced and diced the stump of arm into bite-size pieces.

If only I'd kept some handy, as I'd wanted to after feeding Jayne, Moira might not have died. If something unexpected and awful happened while I was in the bookstore, I wasn't going to be caught unprepared this time; I wanted a dose of superpower close at hand. It wasn't as if it would ever expire. It was the only snack I knew of with an immortal shelf life.

My hunting and gathering expedition had nothing to do with Derek O'Bannion or Fiona, or the reminder of how weak I was compared to them. It was proactive. It was smart. It was just plain, good common sense. I slid the small fridge out from beneath the rear counter and tucked several jars behind it, before sliding it back in. The others I would stash away upstairs later.

After catching myself staring at them for several minutes without blinking, I stuffed the jars in my purse. Out of sight, out of mind.

I opened my laptop, hooked up my camera, and began uploading the pages. While I waited, I called the ALD again, to make sure the dreamy-eyed boy really understood the urgency of the message I'd asked him to relay. He assured me he did.

I tended to customers for the next several hours. It was a busy morning and sales were brisk. It wasn't until early afternoon that I got to sit down, and take a look at the pages Dani had photographed.

I was disappointed by how small they were, barely the size of recipe cards. The scribbled lines were cramped tightly together, and when I finally managed to begin deciphering the small, slanted script, I realized what I had was a pocket notebook of observations and thoughts penned in a badly butchered version of the English language. The spelling made me suspect the author had had little in the way of formal education, and had lived many centuries ago.

After studying it for some time, I opened my own journal, and began to write down what I believed was a fair translation.

The first page picked up in the middle of a lengthy diatribe about *The Lyte* and *The Darke*—which I swiftly realized meant the Seelie and Unseelie—and how dastardly and "Evyle" they both were. I already knew that.

However, halfway through the page, I found this:

Sae I ken The Lyte maye nae tych The Darke nae maye The Darke tych The Lyte. Whyrfar The Darke

*maye nae bare sych tych, so doth the sworde felle et low.
Whyrfar the Lyte may nae bare sych Evyle, sae The
Beest revyles et.*

Okay, so that sounded like the Seelie hated the Unseelie and vice versa. But not quite. There was something more here. I puzzled over it several moments. Did it mean the Seelie couldn't actually touch the Unseelie, and vice versa? I read on.

*Tho sworde doth felle thym bothe, yea een Mastr and
Myst! Ay t'hae the blade n ende m'suffrin!*

The sword killed both Unseelie and Seelie, up to the highest royalty. I knew that, too. So did the spear.

*Sae maye ye trye an ken thym! That The Lyte maye
nae tych The Beest, nr The Darke the sworde, nr
The Lyte the amlyt, nr the Darke the spyr . . .*

So may you try and know them, I scribbled my translation. *The Light (Seelie) may not touch the Beast (Book?) and the Dark (Unseelie) may not touch the sword.* "I get it!" I exclaimed. This was important stuff! *The Seelie can't touch the amulet,* I wrote, *and the Unseelie can't touch the spear.*

What it was saying was that the Seelie couldn't touch the Unseelie Hallows and Unseelie couldn't touch the Seelie Hallows—and *that* was how you could tell them apart!

I'd just found the perfect way to lay my questions to rest about whether or not Barrons might be a Gripper! If he was, he couldn't touch the spear.

I lay my pen aside, thinking back. Had I ever seen him touch it? Yes! The night he'd stabbed the Gray Man, while I'd hung, suspended by my hair.

I narrowed my eyes. Actually, I hadn't seen him touch it that night. When he'd returned it to me, the hilt was still stuck in my purse, with the spear protruding from it. He'd handled it through the fabric. And although he'd said he was going to wear it to the auction, strapped to his leg, I'd never pulled up his pants leg and gone looking for it. For all I knew, he might have left it laying on the desk, right where I'd placed it for him, and where I'd later reclaimed it.

Okay, but the night we'd stolen the spear, surely he'd touched it at some point, hadn't he? I closed my eyes, replaying the memory. We'd gone underground and broken into the Irish mobster Rocky O'Bannion's treasure chamber. Barrons had made *me* pluck it from the wall, and carry it to the car. He'd instructed me to break the rotting shaft from the spearhead. I'd been carrying it ever since.

I opened my eyes. Clever, clever man.

I had to put him in a position where he had no choice but to hold the spear. To take it. Touch it. I would settle for no less than skin on steel. If he were a Gripper—or an Unseelie of any kind—he wouldn't be able to do it. It was that simple.

So how was I going to trick him into taking it?

These pages had been worth Dani's efforts for this tidbit alone. I was glad the book on V'lane had been gone, and this had been there in its place.

I resumed reading. It was slow going but fascinating.

The author of the pocket notebook was no *sidhe-seer*. Its scribe was a man, or rather a young boy, who'd been so beautiful he was mocked by the warriors of his time, though loved by the lasses who'd taught him his letters.

At ten and three, he'd had the misfortune of capturing the eye of a Faery princess, while taking a shortcut through a dark and tangled wood.

She'd charmed and seduced him off to Faery, where she'd swiftly transformed into something cold and frightening. She'd kept him locked in a golden cage at court, where he'd been forced to watch the Fae play with their human "pets." Among their games, their favorite was turning mortals Pri-ya: into creatures who begged for the touch of a Fae, any Fae—in fact, for the touch of anything at all, for the "vilest of things to be done to them, and to do foul things to each other," according to the young scribe. These creatures had no will, no mind, no awareness of anything but sexual need. They knew neither morality nor mercy, and were as likely to turn on one another as rabid animals. The boy had found them terrifying and feared being given to what had become of his human companions. He had no way of tracking time but he watched hundreds come and go, and began a growth of manly hair, which was when the princess began once more to look his way.

When the Fae were no longer amused with their pets they cast them from Faery to die. In this manner, the letter of the Compact wasn't violated. They didn't actually *kill* the humans they captured. They just didn't save them. I wondered how many had died in madhouses, or been used for exactly what they wanted, and killed by their own kind.

The boy listened to all that was said, recorded all he heard, because when the dying were discarded, their possessions went with them, and, although he'd lost hope for himself, he hoped to warn his people. (The child hadn't known that hundreds of years would have passed by the time he was released from Faery.) He hoped something he recorded might save one of them, perhaps hold the key to one day destroying his terrifying, merciless abductors.

A chill kissed my nape. That his plan had worked meant the boy was long dead. And as he'd hoped, his notebook had found its way back to the world of Man, and eventually into the hands of a *sidhe*-seer, to be passed down through the centuries, and end up in Rowena's desk. Why was it in her desk? Just some light reading at lunchtime, or was she looking for something?

I glanced at the clock. It was two-thirty, well into afternoon. I snatched up my cell phone and dialed the ALD again. There was no answer. Where had the dreamy-eyed boy gone? Where was Christian? I snapped my laptop closed, and was thinking of heading over there when my cell rang. It was Dani, and the girls were already at the pub waiting for me, so could I hurry?

When I descended the stairs into the shadowy, substreet-level pub, I found seven women in their mid- to late twenties waiting for me, not including

Dani. Two had been present the day Moira had died: the tall, gray-eyed brunette with the unwavering gaze that kept sweeping the pub—and I doubted she missed much—and the skinny, dark-eyed girl with platinum hair, heavy black eyeliner, and matching nail polish, who was rocking slightly in her chair to a rhythmic beat, although her iPod and earbuds lay on the table. The only exit was the entrance I'd come in and, with no windows, the place felt dark and claustrophobic to me. As I took my seat, I could see they were as uncomfortable as I was with our close, dimly lit surroundings. Five cell phones lay on the table, emitting wan glows. There were two Notebooks open, running on battery power, displaying bright white screens. It was all I could do not to pull out my flashlights, turn them on, and slap them down on the table, adding my share to the lot.

We nodded stiffly to each other. I got straight to the point. "Do you have unrestricted access to the library Rowena told me about?" I asked the group of women. I wanted to know just how useful an alliance between us might be.

The brunette answered, "It depends on your place in the organization. There are seven circles of ascension. We're in the third, so we can enter four of the twenty-one libraries."

Twenty-one? "Who could possibly use that many books?" I said irritably. I'd bet there was no handy card catalog around, either.

She shrugged. "We've been collecting them for millennia."

"Who's in the seventh circle? Rowena?"

"The seventh is the Haven itself, the High Council of...you know..." That level gray gaze swept the pub uneasily.

I glanced around, too. There were five customers in the place. Two were shooting pool, the other three were brooding into their beers. None of them were paying any attention to us, and there wasn't a Fae in sight. "If you don't feel comfortable talking in a public place, why did you ask me to pick one?"

"We didn't think you'd meet in private after what happened. I'm Kat, by the way," the brunette said. "This is Sorcha, Clare, Mary, and Mo." She pointed to each in turn. The skinny Goth was Josie. The petite brunette was Shauna. "That's the lot of us," Kat said, "though if you prove useful, and your loyalties are true, more will join us."

"Oh, I'm useful," I said coolly. "The question is, are you? And as for loyalties, if yours are with the old woman, I suggest you rethink them."

Her gaze cooled to match mine. "Moira was my friend. But I saw what I saw, and you didn't mean to kill her. Doesn't mean I have to like it, and doesn't mean I have to like *you*. It does mean I'm after doing everything I can to stop the walls from coming down, and if that means I have to join forces with the only person I know can sense the *Sin*—er, Book—here I am. But back to loyalties; where are yours?"

"Where any *sidhe*-seers should be. With the humans we're supposed to protect." I didn't say what else I was thinking—in exactly this order: my family, my vengeance, the rest of the world.

She nodded. "Very good. The leader of a cause is

never the cause itself. But make no mistake, we listen to Rowena. She's been training most of since we were born. Those she didn't teach from birth, she's spent years gathering and educating."

"Then why are you going behind her back, and meeting with me?"

All eight, including Dani, shifted uncomfortably and either glanced away or fiddled with something; a coffee mug, a napkin, a cell phone.

It was Dani who finally broke the silence. "We used to guard the Book, Mac. It was ours to protect. We lost it."

"What?" I exclaimed. "You *lost* it?" I'd been blaming the Fae for the mess we were in, for making Darroc human, but the *sidhe*-seers were complicit, too? "How did you lose it?" Then again, knowing what I knew of it, how had they contained it to begin with? How had any *sidhe*-seer gotten close to it? Weren't they all repelled by it, like me?

"We don't know," Kat said. "It happened twenty-some years ago, before any of us came to the abbey. Those who lived through those dark days share little detail about them. One day it was there, hidden beneath the abbey, then it was gone."

So that was why Arlington Abbey had been continuously rebuilt and fortified ever stronger—because beneath it they'd been protecting the greatest menace known to Man! How long had it been there, hidden in ground, guarded by whatever was held sacred by each age? Since it had been a *shian*? Before even that?

"Or so we've heard," she continued. "Only the Haven knew it was there to begin with. The night it vanished, they say terrible things happened. *Sidhe*-seers died, others disappeared, and rumors flew, until the entire abbey knew what had once been hidden beneath their very feet. That was when Rowena formed PHI, and opened branches all over the world, with couriers out in the streets, listening for even a vague rumor of it. She's been trying to track it since. For many years, there was no account of it, but recently it surfaced, right here, in Dublin. There are many of us who fear it was our predecessors' failure to contain it that has caused the problems we're having now, and only by getting it back do we have any chance to fix them. If you can sense the Book, Mac, then you really *are* our best hope, like..." She trailed off, as if reluctant to say the word aloud. She stared into her coffee but I saw what she struggled to hide: pure, raw fascination. Like Dani, she was smitten. She cleared her throat. "Like the Fae you brought that night said." She wet her lips. "V'lane."

"Rowena says you're dangerous," Josie said hotly, raking a black-nailed hand through a fringe of pale bangs. "We told her you could sense it but she doesn't want you to go after it. She says if you find it, you won't do what's right, that you want revenge. She says you told her that your sister was killed in Dublin, so she did some checking, and your sister was a traitor. She was working with *him,* the one who's been bringing all the Unseelie through."

"Alina wasn't a traitor!" I cried. Every occupant in the place turned to look at me. Even the bartender dragged his attention from the small TV behind the bar. I closed my eyes and took a deep breath. "Alina

didn't know who he was," I said, carefully modulating my voice. "He tricked her. He's very powerful."
How had Rowena found out about Alina's involvement with the LM?

"So you say," Kat said softly.

Those were fighting words. I rose from my seat, hands splayed on the table.

She rose, too. "Easy, Mac. Hear me out. I'm not accusing you, or your sister. If I truly believed you traitors to our cause, I wouldn't be here. I saw the look on your face when Moira—" She broke off, and I saw deep, unspoken grief in her eyes. They'd been close. Still, she was here, trying to connect with me, because she believed it was best for our cause. "We're not here to speak of the dead but to plan for the living," she continued after a moment. "I know that things are not always what they seem. We learn that from birth. But you can see the bind we're in. We need you, but we don't know you. Rowena is against you and, while we normally support her in all things, her attempts to recover the Book have failed. She has tried many times. We need results, and time is of the essence. You asked Dani for a show of faith, and she gave you it. Now we're asking you to return the favor."

I bit back an instinctive refusal. "What do you want?" I'd vowed never to prove myself to the old woman, but these women were not Rowena. I badly wanted to be invited to the abbey again. They were the only people I knew who were like me. I'd been banned from the only club I'd ever wanted to join. With V'lane's name on my tongue, I wouldn't be at their mercy at the isolated fortress. If things took a threatening turn, he'd be there to rescue me the moment I opened my mouth.

"Can you sense *all* Fae objects?"

I shrugged. "I think so."

"Have you heard of the D'Jai Orb?"

When I nodded, she leaned forward and said urgently, "Do you know where it is?"

I shrugged. I'd been holding it in my hands a little over two weeks ago, but I had no idea where it was right now, only that it was in Barrons' possession. "Why?"

"It's important, Mac. We need it."

"Why? What is it?"

"A relic from one of the Seelie Royal Houses that contains some kind of Fae energy that Rowena believes can be used to reinforce the walls. We need it fast, before Samhain."

"Sowen. What's sowen?"

"If you can get the Orb and bring it to us, we'll tell you everything we know, Mac. Even Rowena will have to believe in you then."

ELEVEN

I hurried back to the bookstore, deep in thought.
Not, however, with my head down. I wasn't making that mistake again today. I won the struggle not
to frown at two Rhino-boys that were repairing a
streetlamp. What was their deal? Shouldn't they be
supporting their dark brethren, the Shades, and
busting out the lights, instead of fixing them?

I couldn't believe the *sidhe*-seers had been
guardians of the Book and lost it. How had it been
lost? What had happened that night twenty-some
years ago?

My meeting with the *sidhe*-seers had answered
few questions, and raised more.

What was sowen? How did the D'Jai Orb fit in?
How had Barrons gotten it? What did he plan to do
with it? Sell it to the highest bidder? Could I steal it
from him? Did I want to burn that bridge? Were
there any bridges *left* between us?

If the Orb was my passport to *Sidhe*-seer Central, I

was determined to get it, by fair means or foul. Was Rowena manipulating their efforts to befriend me? Had she allowed Dani to photograph those pages and give them to me, seemingly on the sly?

My short time in Dublin had me looking for games within games everywhere I turned. I'd sure like to get Christian into the same room with a few people and employ his lie-detecting abilities while I asked questions.

Speaking of the Scot, I tried calling him again. There was no answer, again. Grrr. Wondering what exactly constituted "afternoon" in the dreamy-eyed boy's world, I let myself into the store, opened my laptop, and logged onto the Net.

My search for "sowen" yielded no results. I tried half a dozen different spellings, and was about to give up when a Google search result caught my eye. It was about trick-or-treating, which brought to mind O'Bannion's earlier crack.

I looked up Halloween and bingo, there it was: sowen—gee, why didn't *I* think of spelling it S-a-m-h-a-i-n?

Samhain had its origins, like many modern holidays or celebrations, in pagan times. As the *sidhe*-seers had been inclined to erect churches and abbeys on their sacred sites, the Vatican had been wont to "Christianize" ancient, pagan celebrations in an if-you-can't-beat-them-and-don't-want-to-join-them-rename-it-and-pretend-it-was-yours-all-along campaign.

Scrolling past the various names, etymology, and pictures of jack-o'-lanterns and witches, I read.

Samhain: the word for November in the Gaelic language marks the beginning of the dark half of the Gaulish year, with Beltane adventing the light half.

Great. So, these past few months *hadn't* been the dark ones?

Technically, Samhain refers to November 1, christened All Saints' Day by the Vatican, but it's Samhain night—Oiche Shamhna, October 31st, that has long been the focus of ritual and superstition.

Celts believed All Hallows' Eve was one of the liminal (Latin, meaning threshold) times of the year, when spirits from the Otherworld could slip through, and when magic was most potent. Since the Celts held that both their dead and the terrifying, immortal Sidhe resided in mounds beneath the earth, on this night both could rise and walk freely. Festivals were held and large communal bonfires were lit to ward off these evil spirits.

I read entry after article, astonished by how many countries and cultures held similar beliefs. I'd never given any thought to the origins of Halloween, just happily collected the candy, and in later years had a blast with the costumes and parties, and enjoyed the great tips if I was working.

Bottom line was the walls between our world and the "Otherworld" were dangerously thin on the last day of October, at their most vulnerable at precisely midnight, the crack between one half of the year and the next, the threshold between light and dark, and if anything was going to try to get through, or if any-one—say an evil ex-Fae with vengeance issues—wanted to bring them crashing down around our ears, that was the time to try it.

Certain nights of the year, lass, Christian had told me, *my uncles perform rituals to reinforce our pledge and keep the walls between our realms solid. The last few times, some other dark magic rose up, and prevented the tithe from being fully paid. My uncles believe the walls won't last through another incomplete ritual.*

Certain nights. Wouldn't last through another in-complete ritual.

Was Samhain the night the MacKeltars' next rit-ual was to be performed? Were we *that* close to dis-aster—two short weeks away? Was this the meaning of O'Bannion's snide threat?

I thumbed redial and called the ALD again. Again, there was no answer. The waiting had been making me crazy all day, and now I didn't just need to warn him, I needed answers. Where *was* he?

Powering down my laptop, I locked up and headed for Trinity.

Surprisingly, I dozed off, slumped sideways against the wall outside the locked offices of the ALD. I think it was because I felt like Mac 1.0 there, in the brightly lit hallway, on a college campus, sur-rounded by the happy sounds of youth that didn't have a clue what was waiting for them out in the real world.

I woke to someone touching my face and my in-ner *sidhe*-seer exploded.

The next thing I knew, Christian was on the floor beneath me, and my spear was at his throat. My muscles were rigid. I was ready for a fight; my adrenaline had no outlet. Dreams had shattered the moment I'd felt myself touched. My brain was cold, clear, and hard.

I took a deep breath, and ordered myself to relax.

Christian nudged the spear from his throat. "Easy, Mac. I was just trying to wake you. You looked so sweet and pretty asleep." His smile was fleeting. "I'll not be making that mistake again."

We separated awkwardly. As I've said before, Christian is a man, and there's no mistaking it. I'd been straddling him much the way I'd straddled Barrons recently. Either my spear hadn't intimidated him or he'd managed to . . . well, rise above it.

Speaking of my weapon, his gaze was fixed on it with fascination. It was emitting a soft, luminous glow. "It's the Spear of Destiny, isn't it?" He looked awed.

I slid it back in my shoulder harness and said nothing.

"Why didn't you tell me you had it, Mac? We'd been bidding on it, trying to buy it. We thought it was out there on the black market. We need it now more than ever. It's one of only two weapons that can kill—"

"I know. It kills Fae. That's why I have it. And I didn't tell you because it's mine and I'm not giving it up."

"I didn't ask you to. There's nothing I could do with it, anyway. I can't see them."

"Right. And that's why you shouldn't have it."

"A little touchy, are we?"

I flushed. I was. "Someone tried to steal it from me recently, and it went badly," I explained. "Where have you been, anyway? I've been calling you all day. I was getting worried."

"My plane was delayed." He unlocked the door, and pushed it open. "I'm glad you're here. I was going to call you as soon as I got in. My uncles have an idea they want me to talk to you about. I think it's a terrible idea, but they insist."

"Samhain is the night your uncles have to perform the next ritual, isn't it?" I said, as we stepped inside. "And if they don't get it right, the walls between our worlds are going to come down and we're all screwed." I shivered. It had sounded weirdly like I'd just made a proclamation: *The walls between our worlds are going to come down and we're all screwed.*

Christian closed the door behind me. "Smart girl. How'd you figure it out?" He gestured to a chair opposite his but I was too wound up to take it. I paced instead.

"The *sidhe*-seers mentioned Samhain. They want…" I trailed off and looked at him hard, searching his gaze for … I don't know … maybe a big, block-lettered message that said YOU CAN TRUST ME, I'M NOT EVIL. I sighed. Sometimes you just have to take a leap of faith. "They want the D'Jai Orb to try to reinforce the walls. Would it work?"

He rubbed his jaw and it made a rasping sound. He hadn't shaved in several days and the shadow beard looked good on him. "I don't know. It's possible. I've heard of it, but I don't know what it does. Who are these *sidhe*-seers? You've found more of your own, then?"

"You're kidding, right?" He knew so much about Barrons, and the Book, that I'd assumed he also knew about Rowena and her couriers, and probably V'lane, too.

He shook his head.

"You said you followed Alina. Didn't you see other women out there, watching things that weren't there?"

"I had reasons to watch your sister. She had a photocopy of a page of the *Sinsar Dubh*. I've had no cause to watch others."

"I got the impression your uncles knew everything."

Christian smiled. "They'd like that. They think quite highly of themselves, too. But no, for a long time we believed all the *sidhe*-seers had died out. A few years ago, we discovered we'd been wrong. How many have you come across?"

"A few," I hedged. He didn't need to know. V'lane and Barrons knowing about the abbey was bad enough.

"Not the truth, but it'll do. You can keep the numbers to yourself. Just tell me this: Are there enough to put up a fight if we need them to?"

I didn't sugarcoat the sour fact. "Not with only two weapons. So, what's this terrible idea of your uncles'?"

"A while back, they had a run-in with Barrons,

and they've been toying with the idea since. They're no longer toying. Uncle Cian says power is power, and we need all of it we can get."

I narrowed my eyes. "What kind of run-in? Where?"

"At a castle in Wales, a month and a half ago. They'd been chasing the same relics for some time, but never actually tried to rob the same place, on the same night."

"*Those* were your uncles? The other thieves that were after the amulet, the night Mallucé took it?" The night V'lane had snatched me out, sifted me off to a beach in Faery!

"You know where the amulet is? Who is Mallucé? And they aren't thieves. Some things shouldn't be loose in the world."

"Mallucé is dead and no longer matters. The Lord Master has it now."

"Who's the Lord Master?"

I was astonished. What *did* he know? Anything of use? "He's the one who's been bringing the Unseelie through, the one who's been trying to tear the walls down!"

He looked blank. "*He's* the one who's been doing the magic against us?"

"Duh," I said.

"Doona be 'duh'ing me, lass," he growled, his burr thickening.

"How can you know so many things, but none of the important ones? *You're* the ones who are supposed to be protecting the walls!"

"Right, the walls," he said. "And we've been

doing it. To the best of our ability. With our own blood. Can't try much harder than that, lass, unless you want us to revert to the archaic ways and sacrifice one of our own, an idea I just went home to explore, but was forced to conclude wouldn't work. What about the *sidhe*-seers? Aren't they supposed to be doing something, too?" He cast my accusation of slacking off on the job right back at me.

"Yes. As a matter of fact they were. *They* were supposed to be protecting the Book." I distanced and acquitted myself.

He opened his mouth, closed it again, then exploded, "*You're* the ones who had the *Sinsar Dubh* to begin with? We knew somebody was guarding it; we just didn't know who. Och, for the love of Christ, lass, what did you do with it? *Lose* the bloody thing?"

I clarified my pronouns again. "*They* lost it. I'm not part of them."

"You certainly look like a *sidhe*-seer to me."

"Don't be trying to blame me, Scotty," I snapped. "Your uncles were supposed to be keeping the walls up. The *sidhe*-seers were supposed to be guarding the Book. The Fae were supposed to strip the LM's memory before they dumped him on us, and *I* was supposed to be home with my sister playing volleyball on a beach somewhere. It's not my fault. *None* of this is my fault. But for some idiotic reason, I seem to be able to do something about it. And I'm trying, so get off my back!"

We faced off, breathing fast and shallow, glaring at each other, two young people living in a world that was coming apart at the seams, doing their best to stop it, but realizing rapidly just how long the odds were. Tough times make for tough words, I guess.

"What's your terrible idea?" I said finally, in an effort to get things back on track.

He inhaled and released it slowly. "My uncles want Barrons to help them hold the walls on Samhain. They say he's Druid trained, and not afraid of the dark side."

I laughed. No, he certainly wasn't afraid of the dark side. Some days I was pretty sure he *was* the dark side. "You're right. It's a terrible idea. Not only does he know you guys have been spying on him, Barrons is mercenary to the core. He doesn't give a rat's petunia about anyone but himself. Why would *he* care if the walls come down? Everybody's afraid of him. He has nothing to lose."

"What did you just say?"

"In a nutshell, he doesn't care."

"You said he knows we've been spying on him? How?"

I gave myself a mental smack in the forehead. I'd completely forgotten the reason I'd come here in the first place. I hastily recounted how Barrons had used Voice to interrogate me about my recent activities, and that visiting Christian had been one of them. I told him I'd been trying to reach him all day, to warn him, and when I hadn't managed to get in touch with him by four, I'd come by to wait for him. When I finished, Christian was regarding me warily.

"You let him do that to you? Push you around

like that? Force answers from you?" The tiger-gold gaze swept me up and down, the handsome face tightened. "I thought you were...a different kind of girl."

"I *am* a different kind of girl!" Or at least I had been when I first came to Dublin. I wasn't sure what kind of girl I was now. But I hated the look in his eyes: aloofness, censure, disappointment. "He's never done it before. We have a complicated...association."

"Doesn't sound like an association to me. Sounds like a tyranny."

I wasn't about to discuss the complexities of life with Barrons, with anyone, especially not a living, breathing polygraph test. "He's trying to teach me to resist Voice."

"Guess you aren't very good at it. And good luck. Voice is a skill that can take a lifetime to learn."

"Look, you guys were planning to talk to him anyway. I'm sorry, okay?"

He measured me. "Make up for it, then. Talk to him for us. Tell him what we want."

"I don't think you can trust him."

"I don't, either. I told my uncles that. They overruled me. The problem is we aren't sure we can keep the walls up, even with Barrons' help." He paused, then said grimly, "But we *know* we can't without him." He opened a notepad, tore off a scrap of paper, wrote on it, and handed it to me. "Here's where you can reach me."

"Where are you going?"

"You think Barrons won't be coming after me? I just wonder what's taken him this long. My uncles told me if he ever got wise to me, I should get out, fast. Besides, I told you what I came back to say, and they can use me at home." He moved toward the door, opened it, then paused and looked back at me, golden eyes troubled. "Are you having sex with him, Mac?"

I gaped. "Barrons?"

He nodded.

"No!"

Christian sighed and folded his arms over his chest.

"What?" I snapped. "I've never slept with Barrons. Subject that to your little lie detector test. Not that I see how it's any of your concern."

"My uncles want to know exactly where you stand, Mac. A woman who's having sex with a man is a compromised source of information, at best. At worst, she's a traitor. That's how it's my concern."

I thought of Alina, and wanted to protest that it wasn't true, but what had she betrayed to her lover, believing them to be on the same side? "I've never had sex with Barrons," I told him again. "Satisfied?"

His gaze was remote, a tiger assessing its prey. "Answer one more question, and I might be: Do you *want* to have sex with Barrons?"

I gave him a hard look and stormed from the room. It was such a stupid question, and so far out of line, that I refused to dignify it with a response.

Halfway down the hall, I drew up short.

Dad's told me all kinds of wise-sounding things over the years. I haven't understood a lot, but I filed it all away because Jack Lane doesn't waste breath, and I figured one day some of it might make sense.

You can't change an unpleasant reality if you won't ac-knowledge it, Mac. You can only control what you're willing to face. Truth hurts. But lies can kill. We'd been having a talk about my grades again. I'd told him I didn't care if I ever graduated. It wasn't the truth. The truth was I didn't think I was very smart, and I had to work twice as hard as everyone else to get passing grades, so I'd spent most of high school pre-tending not to care.

I turned slowly.

He was leaning in the doorway, arms folded, looking young and hot and everything a girl could want. He arched a dark brow. What a gorgeous guy. *He* was the one I should be thinking about having sex with.

"No," I said clearly. "I don't want to have sex with Jericho Barrons."

"Lie," Christian said.

I headed back to the bookstore, flashlights on, watching everyone and everything. My brain was too stuffed with thoughts to be able to sort them out. I walked, and watched, hoping my gut would piece things together into a plan of action, and notify me when it was done.

I was passing the Stag's Head pub when two things occurred: the black ice of a Hunter dusted me, and Inspector Jayne squealed to a stop in a blue Renault, flung open the passenger door, and barked, "Get in!"

I glanced up. The Hunter hovered, great black

wings churning ice in the night air. It terrified me in my special *sidhe*-seer place. But I'd seen and done a lot since my last encounter with one of them, and I wasn't the same anymore. Before it could speak in my mind, I sent it a message of my own: *You'll choke on my spear if you make one move toward me.*

It laughed. With a *whuf-whuf* of leathery, midnight sails, it rose into the twilight and vanished.

I got in the car.

"Slump," Jayne fired at me.

Raising both eyebrows, I slumped.

He drove to a brightly lit back parking lot of a church—I could see the steeple from where I crouched—pulled in between cars, and turned off the lights and engine. I sat up. The parking lot sure was packed for a Thursday night. "Is it some kind of religious day?"

"Stay down," he barked. "I won't be seen with you."

I withdrew to the floorboards again.

He stared straight ahead. "The churches've been packed for weeks. The crime hike is scaring people." He was silent a moment. "So, how bad is it? Should I get my family out?"

"I would, if it were my family," I said frankly.

"Where should I take them?"

I didn't know what the rest of the world out there was like in terms of Unseelie, but the *Sinsar Dubh* was *here,* an evil centrifuge, distilling people to their darkest essences. "As far from Dublin as you can."

He continued staring straight ahead in silence, until I began to fidget impatiently. I was getting a cramp in my leg. There was something else he wanted. I wished he'd hurry up and get to it before my foot went to sleep.

Finally, he said, "That night, that you...you know...I went back to the station and...saw the people that I work with."

"You saw that some of the Garda are Unseelie, " I said.

He nodded. "Now I can't see them anymore but I know who they are. And I tell myself you did something to me, somehow, and it was all a hallucination." He rubbed his face. "Then I see the reports coming in, and I watch what they do, or rather *don't* do, like investigate a bloody damn thing, and I..."

When he trailed off, I waited.

"I think they killed O'Duffy to shut him up, and tried to make it look like a human did it. Two more Garda have been killed. They'd begun asking a lot of questions, and..." He trailed off again.

The silence lengthened. Abruptly, he looked straight at me. His face was red, his eyes bright and hard. "I'd like to have tea with you again, Ms. Lane."

I stared. That was the last thing I'd expected. Had I created an addict? "Why?" I said warily. Was he craving it like I was? Could he sense the tiny jars of wriggling flesh in my purse, yet to be deposited on the upper floors of the store? I could. I'd been feeling the dark pull of it beneath my arm all afternoon.

"I swore to uphold the peace in this city. And I will. But I can't this way. I'm a sitting duck," he said bitterly. "You were right, I didn't know what was out there, but now I do. And I don't sleep at night anymore, and I'm angry all the time, and I'm useless, and it's more than my job to fight it, it's who I am. It's who Patty was, too, and that's why he died. His death should mean something."

"It could end up meaning *your* death," I said softly.

"I'll take that chance."

He didn't even know my "tea" would give him superpowers. He just wanted to be able to see them again. I could hardly blame him. I'd created this problem by feeding it to him in the first place. How would I feel in his shoes? I knew the answer to that: after an initial period of denial, exactly the same. Jayne wasn't the ostrich I'd pegged him as, after all.

"If you betray yourself, they'll kill you," I warned.

"They might kill me anyway, and I won't even see them coming."

"Some of them are pretty horrific. They can startle you into betraying yourself."

He gave me a tight smile. "Lady, you should see the crime scenes I've been on lately."

"I need to think about it." Eating Unseelie had many repercussions. I didn't want to be responsible for what the good inspector might become.

"You're the one who opened my eyes, Ms. Lane. You owe me. You get one more heads-up on the house, but after the next crime, it's no tea, no tips."

He dropped me a few blocks from the bookstore.

The interior lights of Barrons Books and Baubles were at the closed-for-business level when I let myself in, which was enough to keep Shades away but little more.

I moved to the counter, dropped my flashlights, and stripped off my jacket. There were some papers on it that hadn't been there earlier. I riffled through them. They were receipts for a backup generator, a state-of-the-art security system, and a proposal for installation. The bill was astronomical. An appointment was noted for the work to begin the first week of November.

I didn't hear him behind me. I felt him. Electric. Wild. One foot in the swamp. Never going to crawl all the way out. And I wanted to have sex with whatever he was. Where was I supposed to put *that* in my head? I wadded the thought up, stuffed it in my padlocked box, and tested the chains. I was going to need a few more.

I turned and we had one of those wordless conversations that were our specialty.

Nice apology, I said, *but not enough.*

It's not an apology. I don't owe you one.

Our wordless conversation ended there. We're getting worse at them. Distrust clouds my eyes, and I can't see past it.

"Do you have news for me, today, Ms. Lane?" said Barrons.

I thrust my hands in my pockets. "No run-ins with the Book."

"No calls from Jayne?"

I shook my head. He could Voice me on that one,

and I'd still be able to say no. He'd asked the wrong question. I took perverse pleasure in that.

"Any contact with V'lane?"

"Aren't you Question Boy tonight? Why don't you try judging my actions?" I said. "Speaking of which, I've decided I see the wisdom of your advice."

"Has Hell frozen over?" he said dryly.

"Funny. I'm not going to ask you questions tonight, Barrons. I'm going to ask you for three actions." It seemed my gut had come up with a plan. I hoped my instincts were sound.

Interest uncoiled like a dark snake in his eyes. "Go on."

I reached beneath my jacket, removed my spear from the shoulder harness, and held it out to him. "Here. Take this."

Here it was, the moment of truth. So simple. So telling.

Dark eyes narrowed; the snake in them moved. "Who have you been talking to, Ms. Lane?" he said softly.

"No one."

"Tell me what you're after or I won't play your little game."

There was no room for negotiation in his voice. I shrugged. It was past time to force this confrontation. "I've heard that an Unseelie can't touch a Seelie Hallow."

"So, now I'm not eating them," he said, reminding me of a prior accusation I'd made against him, "I *am* them? You've quite the imagination, Ms. Lane."

"Just take it," I said irritably. The suspense was

killing me. I knew he wouldn't. *Couldn't.* Barrons was a Gripper. That was all there was to it.

Long, strong, elegant fingers closed around steel. He took the spear.

Astonished, certain his features would be contorted in pain, my gaze flew to his face.

There wasn't a flicker of a lash, not the smallest shift of a muscle. Nothing. If anything, he looked bored.

He offered it back. "Satisfied?"

I refused to take it. Maybe if he kept holding it, something would happen.

He waited.

I waited.

Eventually I started to feel stupid and took the spear back. He thrust his hands in his pockets and regarded me coolly. I was deflated. Barrons wasn't Unseelie. Until that moment, I hadn't realized how completely I'd made my case against him, and convicted him. It explained everything: his longevity, his strength, his knowledge of the Fae, why the Shades left him alone, why V'lane feared him, why the Lord Master had walked away—all of it made sense, if Barrons was an Unseelie. But he wasn't. I'd just proved it. And now I had to go back to square one and start trying to figure out what he was all over again.

"Try not to look so disappointed. One might almost think you wanted me to be Unseelie, Ms. Lane. What's your second request?"

I wanted him to be *something*. I wanted to be able to peg him and put him *somewhere* and quit being

torn in half, one moment believing him my aveng-
ing angel, the next, certain he was the devil himself.
I couldn't live like this, not knowing who to trust.
Off-kilter, I blurted, "I want you to give me the D'Jai
Orb."

"Why?"

"So I can give it to the *sidhe*-seers."

"You trust them?"

"In this," I qualified. "I believe they'll use it for
the greater good."

"I despise that phrase, Ms. Lane. Atrocities have
been committed in its name. What is the greater
good but tyranny's chameleon? For eons it has
changed skins to sate the current ruler's hunger for
political and spiritual dominion."

He had a point there. But in this case, the greater
good was my whole world, as I knew it, and I
wanted to keep knowing it. I clarified. "They think
they can use it to reinforce the walls on Halloween."

"Very well. I will bring it to you tomorrow night."

I almost fell over. "Really?" Two surprises:
Barrons wasn't Unseelie, and he'd just agreed to
hand over a priceless relic, asking nothing in return.
Why was he being so nice? Was *this* his apology for
last night?

"What's the third thing you want, Ms. Lane?"

This one was going to be a little trickier. "What do
you know about the walls between realms?"

"I know they're paper-thin at the moment. I
know some of the smaller, less powerful Fae have
been slipping through the cracks, without the Lord
Master's help. The prison continues to contain the
most powerful."

His comment sidetracked me. "You know, that just doesn't make sense. Why are the *less* powerful ones able to escape? I'd think it would be the other way around."

"The walls were created from a formidable magic," he said, "which no Fae has been able to match since. At great cost to herself, the queen wove living strands of the Song of Making into the walls of the prison, which slams the magic of the Unseelie back at them. The stronger the Unseelie, the stronger the wall; by attempting to break free, they actually join forces with their gaoler."

Cool trick. "So, do you know why the walls are so thin?"

"Aren't you Question Girl tonight?"

I gave him a look.

He smiled faintly. "Why are the walls so thin?"

"Because when the Compact was struck, humans were appointed to help maintain them. But those responsible for keeping them up with their rituals—the most important of which take place every Halloween—have been attacked by dark magic each time they've performed it over the past few years. They've exhausted the limits of their knowledge and power. If it happens again this · year—and there's every reason to expect it will—the walls will come down completely. Even the prison walls."

"What does this have to do with me, Ms. Lane?"

"If the walls come down completely, all the Unseelie will get out, Barrons."

"So?"

"You told me once you didn't want that to happen."

"Doesn't mean it's my problem." He was looking bored again.

"This is the third action I want. I want you to *make* it your problem."

"In what manner?"

"They think you can help them. Can you?"

He considered it. "Possibly."

I wanted to strangle him. "*Will* you?"

"Motivate me."

"If nothing else, it'll keep me safer. A safer OOP detector is a happier one. Happier is more productive."

"You haven't detected anything of use to me for several weeks."

"You haven't asked me to," I said defensively.

"There's an OOP you know I want, yet you withheld information from me about it."

"You have that information now. What's the problem?" Had I just sounded like V'lane?

"The problem is I still don't have the OOP, Ms. Lane."

"I'm working on it. I'll be able to work faster, the safer I am. If the walls come down, every Unseelie out there will be hunting it, getting in my way. You told me once that you didn't want more of them in your city. Was that a lie?"

"Point made. What do you want from me?"

"I want you to join them on Halloween and help them perform the ritual. And I want you to promise not to harm them." Because of the delicate way I'd shaped our conversation, it sounded as if I was asking him to help the *sidhe*-seers.

He measured me a long moment, then said, "I'll

swap you an action for an action. Get me within sight distance of the *Sinsar Dubh,* and I'll help your little friends."

"Help my little friends," I countered, "and I'll get you within sight distance of the *Sinsar Dubh.*"

"I have your word?"

"You trust my word?"

"You're an idealistic fool. Of course."

"You have my word." I'd deal with the problem of the promise I'd just made in the future. Right now, I needed to keep the walls up, and make sure the human race *had* a future.

"Then we have a deal. But your action doesn't hinge on the outcome of mine. I will do my best to help them with their ritual, but I can't assure you success. I know nothing of their abilities, and it's magic I've not done before."

I nodded. "I accept your condition. You'll help them, and not harm them?"

"You trust my word?" he mocked.

"Of course not. You're a cynical bastard. But they seem willing to."

The faint smile was back. "I'll help them and not harm them. Take a note, Ms. Lane: You undermine yourself as a negotiator when you permit your opponent to see emotion. Never betray emotion to an enemy."

"Is that what you are?"

"It's how you treat me. Be consistent and follow through on the finer nuances." He turned away and moved toward the fire. "Who am I to assist and protect? The old witch herself?"

"It's not the *sidhe*-seers."

He stopped and went very still. "Who is it?"

"The MacKeltars."

He was silent a long moment. Then he began to laugh, softly. "Well played, Ms. Lane."

"I had a good teacher."

"The best. *Hop on one foot, Ms. Lane.*"

Voice lessons had begun.

I had a feeling they might be brutal tonight.

TWELVE

'E ven Rowena will have to believe in you, then.'
Isn't that what you said, Kat? I did what you
asked. I got the Orb. And now you're telling me the
old woman *still* won't let me into her libraries?" I
was so furious I nearly slammed down the phone.

"She said you'll be welcome once the Orb has
served its purpose, and the walls are standing
strong." Kat had been apologizing for several minutes, but it had done nothing to defuse my temper.

"That's bogus and you know it! What if the walls
come down anyway? I can't help it if whatever she
plans to do doesn't work! I kept my part of the bargain."

On the other end of the phone line, Kat sighed.
"She said I had no right to speak for her in the first
place. And I'm sorry I did, Mac. I didn't intend to
mislead you, please believe that."

"What else did she say?" I asked tightly.

She hesitated. "That we were to cease all contact

with you until after Samhain, and if we didn't, then we no longer had a home at the abbey. That we could live in Dublin with you. She means it, too."

I had a momentary flash of Barrons Books and Baubles overrun by young *sidhe*-seers, and the look on the intensely private owner's face. A fleeting smile touched my lips before anger erased it. "And what did you say?"

"I said I didn't think we should have to choose, or shut out a sister *sidhe*-seer when times were as dangerous as these, and I didn't understand why she despised you so much. And she said she can see moral decay as clearly as she can see the Fae, and you're..."

"I'm what?"

Kat cleared her throat. "Rotten to the core."

Unbelievable! My rate of moral decay was about as high as my tooth decay—I didn't have a single cavity. The woman hated me. She'd disliked me since the first, and my visit with V'lane had only made things worse.

I eyed the Orb, resting on the counter in a box padded with bubble-wrap. I was glad I'd refused to turn it over until I'd secured an invitation to return to the abbey from the Grand Mistress herself. "Then she can't have the Orb," I said flatly.

"She said that was what you'd say, and that it proved her point. She said you'd choose your pride over saving our world from the Fae," said Kat.

What a clever, manipulative old bat! She'd had decades to perfect her politics. Until a few months ago the only politics I'd ever worried about were the two waitresses who always pretended they'd had terrible nights so they wouldn't have to tip me out, as if my flair for swift, exceptional drink-making had played no part in their financial success.

"I told her she was wrong. That you care about us, and about the world. She's being unfair, Mac. We know that. But we...well, we still need the Orb. We may not be able to get you inside the abbey, but we'll...uh..." her voice dropped to a near-whisper, "we'll help you as much as we can. Dani said she thinks she can get more pages from the book. And we might be able to slip a few others out, if you tell us what you're looking for."

My hand curled and uncurled. The spear felt heavy in my harness. "I need to know everything there is to know about the *Sinsar Dubh*. How you guys got it in the first place, how you were keeping it contained and where. I want to know every rumor, legend, and myth that has ever been told about it."

"Those books are in the forbidden libraries. Only the Haven has access!"

"Then you'll have to figure out how to break in."

"Why don't you ask, er...you know...*him*...to sift you in?" Kat said.

"I don't want to involve V'lane in this." I'd considered that already, and the mere thought of him in the same room with all those books about his race made me cringe. Arrogance alone might make him destroy them. *Humans have no right to know our ways*, he would sneer.

"You don't trust him?"

His name was bittersweet, invasive on my tongue. "He's Fae, Kat! He's the ultimate in self-serving. We may be after the same goal of keeping the walls up, but to him humans are just a means to an end. Besides, the entire abbey would know we were there, and I'd be looking for a needle in a haystack, without enough time and seven hundred *sidhe*-seers closing in." It was a bad idea, all the way around. "Do you know who the members of the Haven are, and if any of them might be persuaded to help?"

"I doubt it. Rowena selects them, for their loyalty to her. It didn't used to be that way. I heard we used to vote on the council members back in the day, but after we lost the Book, things changed."

Talk about tyranny. I *really* wanted to know what had happened twenty years ago, how the Book had been lost, who was to blame. "I also need to know about the Haven's prophecy, and the five."

"I've never heard of either," Kat said.

"See if you can dig up something. And anything about the four translation stones, too." I had a lot of questions I needed answered. Not to mention all the ones about where I'd come from. But for now, those were going to have to wait.

"Will do. What about the Orb, Mac?"

I stared broodingly at it. If I toughed it out until Halloween, and refused to let Rowena have it, might she relent and share information with me? I doubted it, but even if she did, what would that accomplish? What good would information serve at such a late hour? As the old woman had said, time was of the essence. I needed information *now*.

If the walls crashed, would the LM send every Unseelie in existence out hunting for the Book? Would the streets of Dublin run so thick with dark

Fae that no *sidhe*-seer would dare enter them, not even me?

We couldn't let things get that far. The walls *had* to stay up.

Maybe having the Orb in advance would help Rowena perfect the ritual she planned to perform. Between the *sidhe*-seers, Barrons, and the MacKeltars, surely they could get the ritual right one more time, and buy me until next Halloween—an entire *year*—to figure things out. I swallowed my pride. *Again.* I was really beginning to resent the greater good.

Besides, there was an abbey full of *sidhe*-seers as worried as I was. I wanted them to know I was firmly on their side. Just not their leader's. "I'll drop it by PHI sometime tomorrow, Kat," I said finally. "But you guys owe me. A big one. *Several* big ones. And tell Rowena it's a darn good thing one of us is grown-up enough to do the right thing."

At seven o'clock Saturday evening, I was sitting in the front conversation area of the bookstore, legs crossed, foot kicking air impatiently, waiting for Barrons.

Your problem, Ms. Lane, he'd said last night, after he'd handed me the Orb, *is you're still being passive. Sitting around, waiting for phone calls. Although Jayne wasn't an entirely bad idea—*

Jayne was a brilliant idea and you know it.

—time is not on our side. You must be aggressive. You promised me a sighting. I want it.

What do you suggest?

Tomorrow we hunt. Sleep late. I'll be keeping you up all night.

I'd shrugged off a thrill of unwanted sexual awareness at his words. No doubt Barrons could keep a woman up all night. *Why night? Why not hunt the Book during the day?* Where did he go? What did he do?

I've been tracking crimes in the dailies. Night is its time. Has Jayne ever called you during the day?

There was that. He hadn't.

Seven o'clock, Ms. Lane. You'll have an hour of Voice first.

I stood up, stretched, caught sight of my reflection in the window, and admired the picture. My new jeans were French and fit like a dream, my sweater was pink and soft, my boots were Dolce & Gabbana, my jacket was Andrew Marc, made of the supplest black leather I'd ever seen, and I'd woven a brilliant pink, yellow, and purple silk scarf through my hair and taken my time with my makeup. I looked and felt great.

Barrons was still apologizing, or maybe just trying to get on my good side. This morning when I'd awakened there'd been four shopping totes and two hanging garment bags outside my bedroom door, full of new clothes. It wigged me out that Barrons had shopped for me. Especially considering what was in some of those bags. The man had exceptional taste and an eye for detail. Everything fit. That wigged me out, too.

The bell over the door tinkled and Barrons stepped in. He was night in an Armani suit, silver-toed boots, black shirt, and dark eyes.

"Not bothering with the mirror tonight?" I said breezily. "Or have you forgotten I know you walk around in it?"

"Kneel before me, Ms. Lane."

His words surrounded me, infiltrated me, drove me to my knees, like a human before a Fae.

"Doesn't that just burn?" He gave me one of his scarier smiles. "Kneeling to me must offend every ounce of your perky little being."

I'd show him perky. Jaw clenched, I tried to rise. I tried to scratch my nose. I couldn't even do that. I was as locked in place as a person in a body-encompassing straitjacket. "Why does your command lock down my whole body?" At least my vocal cords were working.

"It doesn't. My order only holds you on your knees. The rest of you is free to move. You're over-muscling yourself, struggling so hard you're locking up. When someone uses Voice on you, they've got you only to the letter of their command. Remember that. Close your eyes, Ms. Lane."

It wasn't an order, but I did it anyway. I managed to wiggle my fingers then my entire hands. I poked around inside my head. The *sidhe*-seer place burned hot but everything else was dark. The *sidhe*-seer place didn't have a thing to do with resisting Voice.

"Who are you?" he demanded.

What an odd question. Didn't he know everything about me? I'd like to be able to Voice *him* on that one. "I'm Mac. MacKayla Lane." Perhaps O'Connor in my blood, but Lane in my heart.

"Strip away the name. Who are you?"

I shrugged. Ha—now only my knees were rooted.

The rest of me was moving freely. I swung my arms, to make sure he knew it. "A girl. Twenty-two. A *sidhe*-seer. A daught—"

"Labels," he said impatiently. "Who the fuck are you, Ms. Lane?"

I opened my eyes. "I don't get it."

"*Close your eyes.*" Voice ricocheted from wall to wall. My eyes closed as if they were his. "You exist only inside yourself," he said. "No one sees you. You see no one. You are without censure, beyond judgment. There is no law. No right or wrong. How did you feel when you saw your sister's body?"

Rage filled me. Rage at what had been done to her. Rage at him for bringing it up. The thought that no one could see or judge me was liberating. I swelled with grief and anger.

"Now tell me who you are."

"Vengeance," I said in a cold voice.

"Better, Ms. Lane. But try again. *And when you speak to me, bow your head.*"

I was bleeding by the time the night's lesson was over. In several places. They were self-inflicted wounds.

I understood why he'd done it. This was tough, well, not love, but tough life lessons. I *had* to learn this. And I would do whatever it took.

When he'd made me pick up the knife and cut myself, I'd seen a glimmer of light in the darkness inside my skull. I'd still cut myself, but something deep inside me had stirred. It was there, somewhere, if I could just dig deep enough to get to it. I wondered who I'd be by the time I got there. Was this why Barrons was the way he was? Who had put Jericho Barrons on his knees? I could hardly even picture it.

"Did you hurt yourself when you learned?" I asked.

"Many times."

"How long did it take you?"

He smiled faintly. "Years."

"That's unacceptable. I need this now. At least to be able to resist, or I'll never be able to get near the LM."

I thought he was going to argue with me about getting near the LM but he said only, "That's why I'm skipping years of training, taking you far ahead into difficult territory. Tonight was only the beginning of . . . pain. If you're not okay with where it's going, tell me here, and now. I won't ask again. I'll push you as far as I think you can go."

I took a deep breath and exhaled slowly. "I'm okay with it."

"Go bandage yourself, Ms. Lane. Use this." He withdrew a small bottle of ointment from his pocket.

"What is it?"

"It will speed the healing."

When I returned, he held open the door, and ushered me into the night.

I glanced instinctively to the right. My gargantuan Shade was a dark cloud on top of the building next door. It loomed menacingly, and began to slither down the brick façade.

Barrons stepped out behind me.

The Shade retreated. "What *are* you?" I said irritably.

"In the Serengeti, Ms. Lane, I would be the cheetah. I'm stronger, smarter, faster, and hungrier than everything else out there. And I don't apologize to the gazelle when I take it down."

Sighing, I moved for the bike but he turned left. "We're walking?" I was surprised.

"For a few hours. I want a look at the city, then we'll come back for a car."

Unseelie were everywhere in the damp, cobbled streets. The ever-increasing crime rate didn't seem to be keeping anyone at home. The juxtaposition of the two worlds—carefree humans, some half drunk, others only beginning their night on the town, laughing and talking, mingling with the predatory, grimly focused Unseelie draped loosely in glamour that I now had to work to see, as opposed to having to work to see *past*—painted the night with the slick menace of a traveling carnival.

There were Rhino-boys, and those creepy-looking street vendors with the huge eyes and no mouths; there were winged things, and things that scampered. Some were in high glamour, walking down the sidewalk with human companions. Others perched on buildings, birds of prey, selecting a kill. I half-expected one of them to recognize us, sound the alarm, and descend in force.

"They're self-serving," Barrons said, when I mentioned it. "They obey a master as long as he's in their face. But an Unseelie's true master is its hunger, and this city is a banquet. They've been trapped for hundreds of thousands of years. There is little left of them but hunger at this point. It's consuming to feel so empty, so . . . hollow. It blinds them to all else."

I looked at him sharply. He'd sounded strange there at the end, almost as if he felt . . . sorry for them.

"When did you last kill one of them, Ms. Lane?" he said suddenly.

"Yesterday."

"Was there trouble you didn't tell me about?"

"No. I just cut him up for parts."

"*What?*" Barrons stopped and looked down at me.

I shrugged. "A woman died the other day. She wouldn't have, if I'd had it handy. I won't make that mistake again." I was secure in my conviction that I was doing the right thing.

"The woman in my store?" When I nodded, he said, "And just where are you keeping these . . . parts, Ms. Lane?"

"In my purse."

"Do you think that's wise?"

"I think I just said I did," I said coolly.

"You do realize if you eat it again, you won't be able to sense the one thing we need?"

"I've got it under control, Barrons." I hadn't even looked at the jars since lunch.

"One never has an addiction under control. If you eat it again, I will personally kick your ass. Got it?"

"If I eat it again, you can *try* to personally kick my ass." Being able to hold my own with Barrons had been one of the many upsides to eating Unseelie. I often craved it for that reason alone.

"I'll wait till it wears off," he growled.

"What fun would that be?" I would never forget the night we'd fought, the unexpected lust.

We looked at each other and for a moment those clouds of distrust lifted and I saw his thoughts in his eyes.

You were something to see, he didn't say.

You were something to feel, I didn't reply.

His gaze shuttered.

I looked away.

We walked briskly down the sidewalk. Abruptly, he grabbed my arm and detoured me down a side alley. Two dark Fae were doing something near a trash can. I really didn't want to know what.

"Let's see how good your fighting skills are, Ms. Lane, when you're not pumped up on Unseelie steroids."

But before I could lose myself in the bliss of killing a few of the bastards, my cell phone rang.

It was Inspector Jayne.

THIRTEEN

The next few days settled into a strange routine, and sped by with me mostly in a daze.

Barrons came each night and taught me Voice. And each night, unable to find my backbone, I came away with fresh wounds.

Then we hunted the *Sinsar Dubh.*

Or rather *he* hunted the *Sinsar Dubh,* and I continued taking great pains to avoid it, as I had the other night when Jayne had called to tip me off, steering Barrons in the opposite direction, keeping us far enough away that I wouldn't betray subtle signs of its proximity, like flailing in a puddle, clutching my head, or foaming at the mouth.

At some point, each day, V'lane appeared to question me about the fruits of my labors. I made sure I had no fruits. He began bringing me gifts. One day he brought me chocolate that wouldn't make me gain weight, no matter how much I ate. Another day he brought me dusky, spicy-smelling flowers from Faery that would bloom immortally. After he left, I threw them both out. Chocolate *should* make you fat and flowers *should* die. Those were things you could count on. I needed things to count on.

When I wasn't busy being yo-yoed back and forth between the two of them, I tended the bookstore, badgered Kat and Dani for information, and continued pushing my way through stacks of books about the Fae, having exhausted my Internet search for anything of use. There was so much role-playing and fanfic online that it was impossible to distinguish fact from fiction.

I was getting nowhere, a car spinning its tires in the mud, all too aware that, even if I got out of the mud, I didn't know where to go.

The tension and indecision in my life became unbearable. I was edgy, and snapped at everyone, including my dad when he called to tell me Mom finally seemed to be getting better. They were decreasing her Valium, and increasing her antidepressants. She'd cooked breakfast Sunday: cheese grits (how I missed those!), pork chops, and eggs. She'd even made fresh yeast bread. I pondered that breakfast after I hung up. Tried to place it somewhere in my life, while I munched a power bar.

Home was a gazillion miles away.

Halloween was ten days away.

Soon, the *sidhe*-seers would be doing their thing at the abbey. Barrons and the MacKeltars would be doing theirs, in Scotland. I hadn't yet decided where I would be. Barrons had asked me to accompany him, no doubt to OOP-detect the MacKeltar

estate while we were there. I was considering crashing the abbey. I wanted to be somewhere, doing
my part, whatever that might be, even if my part
was only keeping Barrons and the MacKeltars
from killing each other. Christian had phoned yesterday to tell me things were moving ahead, but if
they survived the ritual, they might not survive
each other.

Come All Hallows' Eve, the walls would stand or
fall.

Weirdly, I'd begun looking forward to Halloween,
because at least my waiting would be over. Limbo
would end. I'd know what I had to deal with. I'd
know exactly how good or bad things were going to
be. I'd know if I could be relieved—a year would
buy me plenty of time to figure out what to do—or if
I should be terrified. Either way, I'd have concretes.

I had no concretes where the Book (beast!) was
concerned. I didn't know how to get it or what to do
with it.

I had no concretes where Barrons or V'lane were
concerned. I didn't trust either of them.

Making matters worse, each time I glanced out
the window, or stepped outside, I had to battle the
intense biological imperative to slay monsters. Or
eat them.

Rhino-boys were everywhere, looking absurd in
city employee uniforms, stumpy arms and legs popping buttons and straining seams. I felt a constant
mild nausea from their presence. Reluctant to turn
my "volume" down again, I'd begun taking Pepcid
with my morning coffee. I'd even tried switching to

decaf to calm my nerves. That had been a monumental mistake. I needed my caffeine. I made it one day.

Something had to give. I was a jumpy, broody, temperamental mess.

I can't tell you how many times over those endless, angsty days, I decided to trust Barrons.

Then tossed him out in favor of V'lane.

I made my cases painstakingly, with lengthy lists of pros and cons neatly tabulated in my journal in three columns, tallying their "good" actions, "bad" actions, and those of "indeterminate nature." The latter was by far the longest column for them both.

One day I even persuaded myself to throw in the towel, give Rowena my spear, and join up with the *sidhe*-seers. There was not only safety in numbers; I could pass off the crushing responsibility of decision-making, and hand it over to the Grand Mistress. If the world subsequently went to hell in a handbasket, at least *I* was off the hook. That was the Mac I knew. I never wanted to be in charge. I wanted to be taken care of. How had I gotten myself stuck in this mess where I was supposed to take care of everyone else?

Fortunately by the time Rowena returned my call, I was even grumpier, she was her usual pissy self, we'd swiftly gotten into one of our standoffs, and I'd come to my senses, pretending I'd only called to make sure she'd gotten the Orb, since she hadn't been there when I'd dropped it by. *If you called expecting thanks, you'll be getting none from me,* she'd snapped and hung up, reminding me of all the many reasons I couldn't stand her.

Each day, I made one more slash mark on my calendar, and October 31 marched closer.

I remembered past Halloweens, the friends, the
parties, the fun, and wondered what it would bring
this year.

Tricks? Or treats?

Oh, yeah, something had to give.

At noon on Wednesday, I was at a spa in St.
Maarten, getting a massage—V'lane's latest gift
from whatever Human Dating Manual he was reading. Was it any wonder I was rapidly losing any
sense of reality? Monsters and mayhem and mas-
sages, oh my.

When it was over, I dressed and was escorted to a
private dining room in the hotel where V'lane met
me on a terrace overlooking the ocean. He pulled
back a chair and seated me before a table drenched
with linen, fine crystal, and finer food. Mac 1.0
would have felt many things: flattered, flirtatious, in
her element. I felt hungry. I picked up a knife,
stabbed a strawberry, and ate it off the blade. I might
have used my spear but, as usual, it vanished the
moment he appeared. I felt more naked without it
fully clothed than I did nude, and if given the
choice, I would have walked through the resort bare
as I'd been born, if it had meant keeping the spear.

For the past few days, V'lane had been in his most
humanlike form when we'd met, heavily muted. He,
too, was trying to get on my good side. Ironically, the
more he and Barrons tried, the less I trusted them

both. Heads turned when the Fae Prince moved through the public places he took me. Even turned off, women stared after him with voracious eyes.

I dug into the spread with gusto, piling a plate with strawberries, pineapple, lobster, crab cakes, crackers, and caviar. I'd been living on popcorn and ramen noodles too long. "What exactly is the *Sinsar Dubh*, V'lane, and why does everyone want it?"

V'lane's eyelids lowered halfway and he looked to the side. It was a human look, secretive, contemplative, as if he were sorting through a wealth of information, trying to decide how much, if anything, to share. "What do you know of it, MacKayla?"

"Virtually nothing," I said. "What's . . . in it . . . that everyone wants so badly?" It was hard to think of it as a book, with an "it" for information to be "in" when scored into my mind was the dark shape of the Beast, not pages at all.

"What did it look like when you saw it? A book? Ancient and heavy, bound by bands and locks?"

I nodded.

"Have you seen the creature it becomes?" He absorbed my face. "I see you have. You neglected to tell me that."

"I didn't think it was important."

"Everything that concerns the *Sinsar Dubh* is important. What legends do humans tell of our origins, *sidhe*-seer?"

It was a sure sign he was displeased when he called me by title, not name. I told him what little I'd learned from the Irish Book of Invasions.

He shook his head. "Recent history, grossly

inaccurate. We have been here far longer than that. Do you know the history of the Unseelie King?"

"No."

"Then you do not know who he is."

I shook my head. "Should I?"

"The Unseelie King was once the King of the Light, the Queen's consort, and Seelie. In the beginning, there was *only* Seelie."

He had me. I was riveted. This was true Fae lore straight from a Fae. Stuff I doubted I'd ever find in the *sidhe*-seer archives. "What happened?"

"What happened in your Eden?" he mocked. "What always happens? Someone wanted more."

"The king?" I guessed.

"Ours is a matriarchal line. The king held vestigial power. Only the queen knew the Song of Making."

"What's the Song of Making?" I'd heard of it from Barrons and seen references in the books I'd been reading but still didn't know what it was.

"Impossible to explain to your stunted consciousness."

"Try," I said dryly.

He gave me one of his affected shrugs. "It is life. It is that from which we come. It is the ultimate power to create, to destroy, depending on how it is used. It sings into existence...change."

"As opposed to stasis."

"Exactly," he said. Then his eyes narrowed, "You mock me."

"Only a little. Do Fae really only understand those two things?"

A sudden, icy breeze buffeted the terrace and tiny

crystals of frost settled over my plate. "Our perception is not limited, *sidhe*-seer. It is so vast it defies
your paltry language, as does my name. It is because we comprehend so much that we must distill
things to their essential natures. Do not presume to
think you understand our nature. Though we have
long consorted with your race, we have never
shown our true face. It is impossible for you to truly
behold us. If I showed you—" He stopped abruptly.

"Showed me what, V'lane?" I said softly. I
popped a bite of cracker spread with lightly frosted
caviar in my mouth. I'd never had it before. I
wouldn't be having it again. Rhino-boy was more
palatable. I hastily downed a strawberry chased by
a gulp of champagne.

He offered me a smile. He'd been practicing. It
was smoother, less alien. The day heated up again;
the frost melted. "Irrelevant. You wanted to know of
our origins."

I wanted to know about the Book. But I was eager
to hear anything else he was willing to share. "How
do you know the history of your race, if you've
drunk from the cauldron?"

"We have stores of knowledge. After drinking,
most seek immediately to become reacquainted
with who and what we are."

"You forget to remember." How strange. And
how awful, I thought, to be so paranoid, to have
lived so long madness settled in. To be reborn but
never truly wiped clean. To come back fearful, in a
place of such strange and treacherous politics. "The
Seelie King wanted more," I prompted.

"Yes. He envied the queen the Song of Making, and petitioned her to teach it to him. He had become enamored of a mortal of whom he did not wish to be deprived until he had sated his desire for her. It did not appear to be waning. She was...different to him. I would merely have substituted another. He asked the queen to make her Fae."

"Can the queen do that? Make someone Fae?"

"I do not know. The king believed she could. The queen refused, and the king tried to steal from her that which he sought. When she caught him, she punished him. Then she waited for his obsession to pale. It did not. He began...experimenting on lesser Fae, in hopes of teaching himself the Song."

"What kind of experiments?"

"A human might grasp it as an advanced form of genetic mutation or cloning, without DNA or physical matter to mutate. He tried to create life, MacKayla. And he succeeded. But without the Song of Making."

"But I thought the Song *is* life. How could he create life without the Song?"

"Precisely. It was imperfect. Flawed." He paused. "Yet it lived, and was immortal."

I got it, and gasped. "He made the Unseelie!"

"Yes. The dark ones are the Seelie King's children. For thousands of years he experimented, concealing his work from the queen. Their numbers grew, as did their hungers."

"But his mortal woman must have been long dead by then. What was the point?"

"She was alive, kept so in a cage of his making.

But trapped, she withered, so for her, he created the Sifting Silvers and gave her worlds to explore. Although time passes outside them, within them it does not. One might spend a thousand centuries in there, and walk out not one hour older."

"I thought the mirrors were used for travel between realms."

"They are used for that, too. The Silvers are... complicated things, doubly so, since they were cursed. When the queen felt the power of the Silvers spring into existence, she called the king to court and demanded he destroy them. Creation was her right, not his. In truth, she was disturbed to discover he had grown so powerful. He claimed to have made them as a gift for her, which pleased her, as he had paid her no tribute in eons.

"But the king gave her only a portion of the Silvers. The other he kept hidden from her, for his concubine, where he planted lush gardens and built a great, shining white house upon a hill with hundreds of windows, and thousands of rooms. When his mortal grew restless, he made her the amulet, so she could shape reality with her will. When she complained of loneliness he made her the box."

"What does it do?"

"I do not know. It has not been seen since."

"Are you saying he also made her the Book? But why?"

"Patience, human. I tell this tale. The king's experiments continued. Eons passed. He created more... aberrations. Over time, of which we have a fortunate abundance, they began to improve until some of them were as beautiful as any Seelie. The Unseelie royalty were born, the princes and princesses. Dark counterparts to the Light. And like their counterparts, they wanted what was rightfully theirs: power, freedom to come and go, dominion over lesser beings. The king refused. Secrecy was a necessary part of his plan."

"But someone went to the queen," I guessed. "One of the Unseelie."

"Yes. When she learned of his treachery, she tried to strip him of his power but he had grown too strong, and learned too much. Not the Song, but another melody. A darker one. They battled fiercely, sending their armies against each other. Thousands of Fae died. In that age, we still had many weapons, not merely the few that remain. Faery withered and blackened; the skies ran with the lifeblood of our kind; the planet itself upon which we lived wept to see our shame, and cracked from end to end. And still they fought until he took up the sword and she took up the spear and the king killed the Faery Queen."

I inhaled sharply. "The queen is dead?"

"And the Song died with her. She was slain before she was able to name her successor and pass on her essence. When she died, the king and all the Unseelie vanished. Before dying, she had managed to complete the walls of the prison, and with her last breath uttered the spell to contain them. Those Unseelie that eluded the spell's radius were hunted by the Seelie, and killed."

"So, where does the Book come into all this?"

"The Book was never meant to be what it was. It was created in an act of atonement."

"Atonement?" I echoed. "You mean for killing the queen?"

"No. The king's atonement was to his concubine. She slipped from the Silvers and took her own life. She hated what the king had become so much that she left him the only way she could."

I shivered, chilled by the dark tale.

"They say the king went mad and when his madness finally abated, he beheld the dark kingdom he had created with horror. In her name, he vowed to change, to become the leader of his race. But he knew too much. Knowledge is power. Immense knowledge is immense power. So long as he had it, his race would never trust him. Aware they would not let him near the Cauldron of Forgetting, and even if they did, they would destroy him the second he drank from it, he created a mystical book into which to pour all his dark knowledge. Freed of it, he would banish it to another realm where it could never be found and used for harm. He would return to his people, their Seelie King, beg their forgiveness, and lead them into a new age. The Fae would become patriarchal. The Unseelie, of course, would be left to rot in their prison."

"So that's what the Book is," I exclaimed, "part of the dark king himself! The worst part."

"Over the eons it changed, as Fae things do, and became a living thing, far different from what it was when the king created it."

"Why didn't the king destroy it?"

"He had made...how do you say it?...his doppelgänger. It was his equal and he could not defeat it. He feared one day it might defeat him. He cast it out, and for much time it was lost."

I wondered how it had come to be in the *sidhe*-seers' care. I didn't ask, because if V'lane didn't know it had been there, I didn't want to be the one to tell him. He despised Rowena, and might decide to punish her, and other *sidhe*-seers could suffer in the process. "Why does the queen want it? Wait a minute, if the queen is dead, who is Aoibheal?"

"One of many who came after, and tried to lead our race. She wants it because it is believed that, somewhere in all its darkness, the Book contains the key to the true Song of Making that has been lost to my race for seven hundred thousand years. The king was close, very close. And only with living strands of that Song can the Unseelie be reimprisoned."

"And Darroc? Why does he want it?"

"He thinks foolishly to possess its power."

"Barrons?"

"The same."

"Am I supposed to believe you're different? That you would blithely hand all that power to the queen, with no thought for yourself?" Sarcasm laced my words. V'lane and self-serving were synonyms.

"You forget something, MacKayla. I am Seelie. I cannot touch the Book. But she can. The queen and king are the only two of our race that can touch all the Hallows, Seelie and Unseelie. You must obtain it; summon me, and I will escort you to her. We alone have any hope of rebuilding the walls should they come down. Not the old woman, nor Darroc, nor Barrons. You must place your trust, as I have, in the queen."

It was dark when I returned, massaged, manicured, pedicured, and waxed. There were a dozen long-stemmed red roses wrapped in tissue paper waiting for me, propped in the alcoved entrance to the bookstore. I bent to pick them up, then stood in the lighted cubby, fumbling with the card.

Help me find it, and I will give you your sister back.
Refuse and I will take what you prize most.

Well, well, all my suitors were calling. There was a disposable cell phone tucked into the leaves with a text message waiting: **Yes or no?** The reply number was zeroed out; I could text him back, but I couldn't call him.

"V'lane?" came Barrons' voice from behind me.

I shook my head, wondering what "I prized most" was, afraid to contemplate it.

I felt the electricity of his body behind me as he reached around me and took the card from my hand. He didn't move away, and I battled the urge to lean back into him, seeking the comfort of his strength. Would he wrap his arms around me? Make me feel safe, if only for a moment, and if only a delusion?

"Ah, the old 'what you prize most' threat," he murmured.

I turned around slowly, and looked up at him. He

stiffened and sucked in a shallow breath. After a moment, he touched my cheek.

"Such naked pain," he whispered.

I turned my face into his palm and closed my eyes. His fingers threaded into my hair, cupped my head, and brushed the brand. It heated at his touch. His hand tightened at the base of my skull and squeezed, and he raised me slowly to my tiptoes. I opened my eyes and it was my turn to inhale sharply. Not human. Oh, no, not this man.

"Never show it to me again." His face was cold, hard, his voice colder.

"Why? What will you do?"

"What it is my nature to do. Get inside. It's time for your lesson."

After I'd received yet another failing grade, Barrons and I cruised the streets.

I'd gotten no tips from Jayne since his last call, four nights ago. I read the paper each morning. If I recognized the *Sinsar Dubh*'s calling card, and I was pretty sure I did, it was jumping to a new victim every night. I knew what the good inspector was doing: He was waiting for his "tea."

I was waiting for divine inspiration to strike at any moment, and show me the way, who to trust, what to do. I had no doubt Jayne would get what he wanted before I did.

I was wrong.

We'd been at it for almost six hours, driving up and down, muscling through the city in the Viper. After so many nights, I knew every street, every alley, every parking lot. I knew the location of every convenience store and petrol station that was open between dusk and dawn. There weren't many. Crime might not be keeping the partyers at home—the drunk and lonely are hard to corral; I know that from bartending—but it was certainly sending the small-business owners and their employees packing well before nightfall.

It made me sad to see Dublin battening her hatches. Just last night, we'd discovered a two-block Dark Zone that wasn't on my map, by driving through it. I mourned each newly darkened block as a personal loss, a few inches off my hair, a drabber outfit. We were both changing, this boisterous, *craic*-filled city and I.

Normally, when we went hunting, Barrons drove in case I lost control of my primary motor functions, but it had been getting more difficult to turn him away from near brushes with the Book, so I'd insisted on driving tonight.

He made a lousy passenger, barking directions I ignored, but it was better than the alternative. Last night when we'd had a near brush with the Book, I'd pretended to have an abrupt desperate need to use the bathroom—the only petrol station open was one we'd fueled at, in the opposite direction—and he'd given me an unnervingly searching look. I suspected he was getting suspicious. After all, he could read the paper, too. This morning's crime had been less than a mile from where I'd had him turn around last night. Although he didn't know my radar had been getting stronger, I had no doubt he was going to put two and two together eventually.

And so I was driving, my *sidhe*-seer senses on high alert, waiting for the faintest tingle, so I could subtly turn us away, when something totally unexpected happened.

The *Sinsar Dubh* popped up on my radar, and it was moving straight toward us.

At an *extremely* high rate of speed.

I whipped the Viper around, tires smoking on the pavement. There was nothing else I could do.

Barrons looked at me sharply. "What? Do you sense it?"

Oh, how ironic, he thought I'd turned us *toward* it. "No," I lied, "I just realized I forgot my spear tonight. I left it back at the bookstore. Can you believe it? I *never* forget my spear. I can't imagine what I was thinking. I guess I wasn't. I was talking to my dad while I was getting dressed and I totally spaced it." I worked the pedals, ripping through the gears.

He didn't even try to pat me down. He just said, "Liar."

I sped up, pasting a blushing, uncomfortable look on my face. "All right, Barrons. You got me. But I *do* need to go back to the bookstore. It's ... well ... it's personal." The bloody, stupid *Sinsar Dubh* was gaining on me. I was being chased by the thing I was supposed to be chasing. There was something very wrong with that. "It's ... a woman thing ... you know."

"No, I don't know, Ms. Lane. Why don't you enlighten me?"

A stream of pubs whizzed by. I was grateful it was too cold for much pedestrian traffic. If I had to slow down, the Book would gain on me, and I already

had a headache the size of Texas that was threatening to absorb New Mexico and Oklahoma. "It's that
time. You know. Of the month." I swallowed a moan
of pain.

"*That* time?" he echoed softly. "You mean time to
stop at one of the multiple convenience stores we
just whizzed past so you can buy tampons? Is that
what you're telling me?"

I was going to throw up. It was too close. Saliva
was pooling in my mouth. How far behind me was
it? Two blocks? Less? "Yes," I cried. "That's it! But I
use a special kind and they don't carry it."

"I can smell you, Ms. Lane," he said, even more
softly. "The only blood on you is from your veins,
not your womb."

My head whipped to the left and I stared at him.
Okay, that was one of the more disturbing things
he'd ever said to me. "Ahhh!" I cried, letting go of
both the wheel and the gearshift to clutch my head.
The Viper ran up on the sidewalk and took out two
newspaper stands and a streetlamp before crashing
to a stop against a fire hydrant.

And the blasted, idiotic Book was *still* coming. I
began foaming at the mouth, wondering what
would happen if it passed within a few feet of me.
Would I die? Would my head *really* explode?

It stopped.

I collapsed against the steering wheel, gasping,
grateful for the reprieve. My pain wasn't decreasing
but at least it was no longer increasing. I hoped the
Book's next victim would hurry along and tote it off
in the other direction, fast. Hardly *sidhe*-seerlike, but
I had problems.

Barrons kicked open the door, stalked to my side, and yanked me out. "Which way?" he snarled.

I would have fallen to my knees but he held me up. "I can't," I managed to say. "Please."

"Which way?" he repeated.

I pointed.

"Which way?"

He'd Voiced me. I pointed the other way.

Grabbing a fistful of my hair, he took off, dragging me behind him. Closer, closer still. "You're going...to....kill...me," I cried.

"You have no idea," he growled.

"Please...stop!" I was stumbling, blind to everything but the pain.

He released me abruptly and I fell to my knees, gasping, crying. It hurt so bad. Shrieking in my head. Ice in my veins. Fire under my skin. Why? Why did the Book hurt me? Surely I was no longer *that* pure and good! I'd been lying to everyone. I'd killed a *sidhe*-seer—granted, it had been by accident, but it was still innocent blood on my hands, along with all of O'Bannion's men. I'd been thinking lustful thoughts about men no sane woman would think lustful thoughts about. I'd been carving up other living creatures to eat to steal their...

Strength. That was what I needed. Unseelie strength and power; the darkness that was kith and kin to the Book, living inside me.

Where was my purse?

I fumbled for it through the pain. It was in the car. I'd never make it there. I couldn't even stand up. I whimpered with the agony of simply trying to raise my head. Where was Barrons? What was he doing?

The air was ice. The pavement beneath me frosted, and I felt it move up my knees, and creep over my thighs. An arctic wind whipped at my hair, tore at my clothes. Debris battered me.

What was Barrons doing? I had to see!

I sought the *sidhe*-seer place in my head. The mere existence of the Book inflamed it. It was everything we feared in the Fae. Everything we existed to defend against.

I inhaled fast and deep, sucking down breaths so icy they burned my lungs. I tried to embrace the pain, and convince myself I was one with it. What had Barrons said? I overmuscled things. I had to relax, quit fighting it. Let it crash over me and ride it like a wave. It was easier said than done, but I managed to push back on my knees, and raise my head.

In the middle of the cobbled street, thirty-five feet away, was the Beast.

It looked at me. *Hello, Mac,* it said.

It knew my name. How did it know my name? Fuck. Fuck. Fuck.

The shrieking in my head stopped. The pain vanished. The night stilled. I was in the eye of its storm.

Barrons was five feet from it.

I wish I could describe it to you. I'm glad I can't. Because if I could find the words for it, they would be stuck in my head forever, and I don't want anything about it stuck in my head. Its visage is terrible enough, but once it's no longer in front of you, your brain can't quite hold on to it. The way it moves, the way it looks at you. The way it mocks. The way it knows. We see ourselves in other people's eyes. It's the nature of the human race; we are a species of reflection, hungry for it in every facet of our existence. Maybe that's why vampires seem so monstrous to us—they cast no reflection. Parents, if they're good ones, reflect the wonder of our existence and the success we can become. Friends, well chosen, show us pretty pictures of ourselves, and encourage us to grow into them.

The Beast shows us the very worst in ourselves and *makes us know it's true*.

Barrons was leaning.

The Beast became the innocent hardcover.

Barrons bent to one knee.

The hardcover became the *Sinsar Dubh*, with bands and padlocks. It waited. I could feel it waiting.

Barrons reached.

For the first time in my life, I prayed. *God, no, please, God, no. Don't let Barrons pick it up and turn evil because if he does, we're all lost. I'm dead, the walls are down, and the world is a bust.*

I realized, then, that the reason I'd been so conflicted since the night I'd watched Barrons step out of the Unseelie mirror was because, in my heart, I didn't really believe he was evil. Don't get me wrong, I didn't think he was good, either, but bad is potential evil. Evil is a lost cause. I hadn't been willing to trust my heart because I'd been afraid I'd make Alina's mistakes, and as I was dying, the bodiless narrator of my life would remark, Gee, there goes the second Lane girl, dumber than the first. The most confused we ever get is when we're trying to convince our heads of something our heart knows is a lie.

His fingers were inches from the *Sinsar Dubh*.

"Barrons!" I shouted.

He flinched and looked back at me. His eyes were black on black.

"Jericho," I cried.

Barrons shook his head, once, a violent jerk from side to side. Moving like a man with bones fractured in every limb, he pushed himself slowly to his feet, and began backing away.

Suddenly the Book morphed into the Beast and rose, and rose, and rose until it towered over us, eclipsing the sky.

Barrons turned then, and ran.

The pain was back, crushing, crucifying. The night turned cold and life-sucking, and the wind returned, screaming with the voices of the unavenged dead.

I felt myself scooped up.

I flung my arms around Barrons' neck and held on as he ran.

At four o'clock in the morning, we were sitting in front of a fire in the bookstore, in the rear conversation area, behind bookcases where no passersby might see us, not that any were expected at four o'clock in the morning on the edge of a Dark Zone.

I was snuggled in a nest of blankets, staring into the flames. Barrons brought me a cup of hot cocoa he'd microwaved, using two packets of instant from Fiona's old stash behind the cash register. I accepted it gratefully. Every few minutes, I jerked with a convulsive chill. I doubted I would ever get warm again.

"She's with O'Bannion, you know," I told him through lips that burned with cold. Even Barrons looked chilled, pale.

"I know," he said.

"She's eating Unseelie."

"Yes."

"Do you care?"

"Fio is her own woman, Ms. Lane."

"What if I have to kill her?" If she came after me now, I'd have no choice but to stab her.

"She tried to kill you. If her plan had worked, you would have been dead. I underestimated her. I didn't think her capable of murder. I was wrong. She wanted you out of the way and was willing to sacrifice anything I might want, or need, to accomplish it."

"Were you her lover?"

He looked at me. "Yes."

"Oh." I swirled the cocoa with my spoon. "She was a little old, don't you think?" I rolled my eyes at myself as soon as I said it. I was going by appearances, not reality. Reality was Barrons was at least twice her age; who knew how much more?

His lips curved faintly.

I began to cry.

Barrons looked horrified. "Stop that immediately, Ms. Lane."

"I can't." I sniffled into my cup of cocoa so he couldn't see my face.

"Try harder!"

I gave a great sniff and shudder, and turned it off.

"I have not been her lover for...some time," he offered, watching me carefully.

"Oh, get over yourself! That's not why I cried."

"Why, then?"

"I can't do it, Barrons," I said hollowly. "You saw it. I can't get...that...that... *thing*. Who are we kidding?"

We stared into the flames for a time, until long after my cocoa was gone.

"What did it feel like to you?" I said, finally.

His mouth shaped a bitter smile. "All this time I've been hunting it, I've been telling myself *I* would be the exception. I would be the one who could touch it. Use it. I would be unaffected. I was so certain of myself. 'Just get me within sight distance of it, Ms. Lane,' I said, convinced I'd all but have it in the bag then. Well, I was wrong." He laughed, a sharp bark of a sound. "I can't touch it, either."

"Can't? Or won't?"

"A fine distinction. Irony, perfect definition: That for which I want to possess it, I would no longer want, once I possessed it. I would lose everything to gain nothing. I am not one for exercises in futility."

Well, at least I no longer had to worry about Barrons or V'lane getting the Book before I did. V'lane couldn't touch it because he was Seelie, and Barrons *wouldn't* touch it because he was smart enough to realize that whatever purpose he wanted it for would be instantly forfeit to the Beast's all-consuming nature. "Was it coming after us?" I asked.

"I don't know," he said. "It certainly looked like it, though, didn't it?"

I nestled deeper into my blankets. "What are we going to do, Barrons?"

He gave me a dark look. "The only thing we can do, Ms. Lane. We're going to keep those fucking walls up."

FOURTEEN

When I unlocked the front door Thursday morning to open for business—a measure of how desperately I wanted to be a normal girl in a normal world—Inspector Jayne was waiting for me.

I stepped back to let him in, closed the door, then, with a gusty sigh, ceded the absurdity of my actions, and flipped the sign back to **CLOSED**. I wasn't normal and it wasn't a normal world, and pretending wasn't going to accomplish a thing. It was time to call yet another of my own bluffs. The bookstore lulled me with temporary comfort that I had no right to. I should be anxious, I should be afraid. Fear is a powerful motivator.

I took the inspector's damp coat and motioned him to a seat near the fire. "Tea? Er, I mean, normal tea?"

He nodded and sat.

I brought him a cup of Earl Grey, took a seat across from him, and sipped at my own.

"Aren't we the pair?" he said, blowing his cup to cool.

I smiled. We certainly were. It seemed a year ago that he'd dragged me down to the station. Months since he'd accosted me in the alcove with his maps. "It has downsides," I told him, meaning eating Unseelie. He knew what I meant. It was what he'd come here for.

"Doesn't everything?"

"It makes you superstrong, but the Fae can't be killed, Jayne. You can't engage them. You must be satisfied merely seeing them. If you start trying to kill them, they'll know you know, and they'll kill you."

"How strong does eating it make you? As strong as one of them?"

I considered it. I didn't know, and told him that.

"So, it might?"

I shrugged. "Regardless, you still can't kill them. They don't die. They're immortal."

"Why do you think we have prisons, Ms. Lane? We're not allowed to kill the serial murderers, either."

"Oh." I blinked. "I never thought of imprisoning them. I'm not certain anything would hold them." Except an Unseelie prison woven from the fabric of the Song of Making. "They sift, remember?"

"All of them?"

He'd made another good point. I'd never seen a Rhino-boy sift. I supposed it was possible only the more powerful Fae could do it; the princes and the one-of-a-kinds like the Gray Man.

"Isn't it worth a try? Maybe we lowly humans

can come up with a few surprises. While you do your thing, others can be doing theirs. The word in the street is that something bad is coming, soon. What's going on?"

I told him about Halloween, and the walls, and what would happen if they came down.

He placed his cup and saucer on the table. "And you would have me go out there defenseless?"

"It has other downsides, too. I'm not sure what they all are, but one of them is that if you get wounded by one of the immortal weapons, you'll..." I described Mallucé's death for him. The decomposing flesh, the dying body parts.

"How many of these immortal weapons are there, Ms. Lane?"

"Two." How far he'd come from denying missing parts of the maps to so casually speaking of dining on monsters and immortal weapons!

"Who has them?"

"Uh, me and someone else."

He smiled faintly. "I'll take my chances."

"It's addictive."

"I used to smoke. If I can quit that, I can quit anything."

"I think it changes you somehow." I was pretty sure eating Unseelie was why I'd been able to get closer to the *Sinsar Dubh*. There was a lot about eating Dark Fae I wasn't clear on, but *something* had made the Book perceive me as ... tarnished, diluted.

"Lady, you've changed me more than an early heart attack. Quit stalling. No more tips, remember?"

For the time being, I didn't want tips. I had no desire to know where the Book was, other than as a means of avoiding it.

"You didn't give me a choice when you opened my eyes," the inspector said roughly. "You owe me for that."

I studied his face, the set of his shoulders, his hands. How far I'd come, too. Far from seeing an enemy, an impediment to my progress, I saw a good man sitting in my store, having tea with me. "I'm sorry I made you eat it," I said.

"I'm not," he said flatly. "I'd rather die seeing the face of my enemy than die blind."

I sighed. "You'll have to come back every few days. I don't know how long it lasts."

I went to the counter, rummaged in my purse. He accepted the jars a bit eagerly for my taste, revulsion married to anticipation on his face. I felt like a supplier to a junkie. I felt like a mom, sending her child off to face the perils of first grade. I had to do more than pack his lunch and put him on the bus; I had to give him advice.

"The ones that look like Rhinos are watchdogs for the Fae. They spy, and lately, for some bizarre reason, they've been doing utility work. I think the ones that fly prey on children, but I'm not sure. They follow them, behind their shoulders. There are dainty, pretty ones that can get inside you. I call them Grippers. If you see one coming toward you, run like hell. The shadowy dark ones will devour you in an instant if you stumble into a Dark Zone. At night, you've *got* to stay to the lights..." I was half hanging out the door, calling after him. "Start carrying flashlights at all times. If they catch you in the dark, you're dead."

"I'll figure it out, Ms. Lane." He got in his car and drove away.

At eleven o'clock, I was in Punta Cana, walking on the beach with V'lane, wearing a gold lamé bikini (me, not V'lane; tacky, I know; *he* chose it) with a hot pink sarong.

I'd released his name to the wind and summoned him shortly after Jayne had left, desperate for answers, and not at all averse to a little sunshine. I'd been thinking about the walls all night and most of the morning. The more we knew about them, the better our odds were of fortifying them. The surest bet for information was a Fae Prince, one of the queen's most trusted, and one who'd not drunk from the cauldron for a long, long time.

First, he demanded to know the latest about the *Sinsar Dubh* and I told him, withholding the fact that Barrons had been with me to avoid a potential pissing contest. I told him there was no point in my continuing to pursue it right now, because I had no clue how to get close to it, and since he couldn't, either, there was no way to get it to the queen. As I said that, a question occurred to me that was so obvious I couldn't believe I hadn't thought of it before.

"You said the queen can touch it, so why doesn't she come after it herself?"

"She dares not leave Faery. She was attacked recently, and it left her severely weakened. Her enemies in the mortal world are too numerous. She has fled court and sought an ancient place of refuge and protection within our realm. It is also a place of high magic. There, she believes she can re-create the Song. None but those few she trusts can enter. She must be kept safe, MacKayla. There is no other to lead in her place. All the princesses are gone."

"What happened to them?" In a matriarchal line, that was a disaster.

"She sent them searching for the Book, along with others. They have not been seen or heard from since."

And they thought *I* could do this? If Fae Princesses couldn't hold their own against the many dangers out there, what chance did I have?

"There's something I don't understand, V'lane. The walls of the Unseelie prison were put up hundreds of thousands of years ago, weren't they?"

"Yes."

"Wasn't that a long time before Queen Aoibheal erected the ones between our realms?"

He nodded.

"Well, if they existed independently once before, why can't they now? Why will the prison walls go down, too, if the LM succeeds in bringing those between our worlds down? Why will *all* the walls fall?"

"The walls have never existed independently. The walls between our worlds are an extension of those prison walls. Without the Song, the queen was unable to fabricate barriers on her own. Separating worlds requires immense power. She had to tap into the magic of the prison walls, and entrust a portion of the new walls' fortification to humans. A pact of magic inevitably yields stronger results than a solo undertaking. It was risky, but over the protests of her council, she deemed it necessary."

"Why did the council protest?"

"When first we came here, you were like the rest of life on this world: savages, animals. But one day you developed language. One day the dog did not wag its tail and bark. It spoke. She felt that made you higher beings. She granted you rights and ordered us to coexist. It did not work but, rather than exterminating you—which two thirds of her council was in favor of—she separated us, as part of your new rights."

It was obvious V'lane didn't think we'd deserved any rights at all. "Sorry we wrecked your racial supremacy," I said coolly. "It was our world first, remember?"

Snow dusted my shoulders. "You say that often. Tell me, human, precisely what do you think that establishes? That by dint of fate you happened to begin life on this planet entitles you to it? Under our care your world flourished. We made it verdant; for us Gaea bloomed. Your race has smogged it up, carved it up, concreted it up, and now you overpopulate it. The planet weeps. Your kind knows no restraint. We do. Your kind knows no patience. We are the most patient race you will ever encounter."

His words chilled me. The Fae could take thousands of years getting around to reimprisoning their dark brethren but the human race would never survive that long. More reason why we had to keep the prison break from occurring. "What's the LM doing that's weakening the walls?"

"I do not know."

"What can we do to fortify them?"

"I do not know. There were agreements reached between the queen and the humans she hid and protected. They must honor those agreements."

"They have been, and it's not working."

He shrugged a golden shoulder. "Why do you fear? If the walls come down, I will keep you safe."

"I'm not the only one I'm worried about."

"I will protect those you care for in . . . Ashford, is it not? Your mother and father. Who else matters to you?"

I felt the tip of a blade caress my spine at his words. He knew of my parents. He knew where I was from. I despised any Fae, good or bad, knowing anything about the people I love. I understood how Alina must have felt, trying so hard to keep us hidden from the dark new world she'd stumbled into in Dublin, including the boyfriend she'd trusted. Had her heart battled her head over him? Had she sensed somewhere deep down that he was evil, but been seduced by his words and charmed by his actions?

Nah, he'd duped her. Despite his assertions otherwise, he'd certainly used Voice on her. There was no other explanation for the way things had turned out.

"I want more than that, V'lane," I said. "I want the whole human race to be safe."

"Do you not believe your people would benefit from a reduction in numbers? Do you not read your own newspapers? You accuse the Fae of barbarism, yet humans are unparalleled in their viciousness."

"I'm not here to argue for the world. That's not in my job description. I'm just trying to save it."

He was angry. So was I. We didn't understand each other at all. His touch was gentle but his eyes were not when he pulled me into his embrace. He took his time with my tongue. I'm ashamed to say I leaned into it, lost myself in a Fae Prince's kiss, and came four times when he gave me back his name.

"One for each of the princely houses." With a mocking smile, he vanished.

The aftershocks were so intense it took me several moments to realize something was wrong. "Uh, V'lane," I called to the air. "I think you forgot something." Me. "Hello? I'm still in Punta Cana."

I wondered if this was his way of forcing me to use his name again, so he could replace it again. *My apologies,* sidhe-*seer,* he'd say. *I have many other concerns on my mind.* My ass. If his mind was as vast as he constantly claimed it was, he wasn't entitled to memory lapses.

My spear was back. People were staring at me. I guess it wasn't every day they got to watch a bikini-clad, spear-toting woman talking to the sky. I took a good look around and stared myself, realizing it was probably my suit, not my spear, that was most out of place. I'd been so engrossed in my conversation with V'lane that I hadn't noticed we were on a nude beach.

Two men walked by and I blushed. I couldn't help it. They were my father's age. They had penises. "Come on, V'lane," I hissed. "Get me out of here!"

He let me stew for a few more minutes before returning me to the bookstore. In a gold lamé bikini, of course.

My life changed then, took on yet another routine.

I no longer had any desire to run the bookstore, or sit in front of a computer, or bury myself in stacks of research books. I felt like a terminal patient. My bid to gain the *Sinsar Dubh* had not only failed, it had forced me to admit that it was hopelessly beyond my reach at the present time.

There was nothing I could do but wait, and hope that others could do their part, and buy me more time to figure out how to do mine—*if* it was even possible. What had Alina known that I didn't know? Where was her journal? How had she planned to get her hands on the Dark Book?

Seven days left. Six. Five. Four.

I couldn't shake the feeling that there was something going on out there, staring me straight in the face, that I was missing. I might have gotten pretty good at thinking outside my tiny little provincial box, but I suspected there was a much larger box that I needed to think outside of now, and to do that, I had to *see* the box.

Toward that end, I spent my days, armed to the hilt, collar turned up against the cold, walking the streets of Dublin, elbowing my way past tourists who continued to visit the city despite the gloom and the cold and the high crime rate.

Slipping between Unseelie horrors, I popped into

a pub for a hot toddy, where I eavesdropped shamelessly on conversations, human and Fae alike. I stopped in a corner dive for fish and chips and chatted up the grill cook. I stood on the sidewalk and made small talk with one of the few remaining human newsstand vendors—coincidentally the same elderly gentleman who had given me directions to the Garda when I'd first arrived here—and who now confided in his lovely lilt that the headlines of the scandal rags were right; the Old Ones *were* returning. I toured the museums. I visited Trinity's astounding library. I sampled beers at the Guinness brewery and stood up on the platform, staring out at the sea of roofs.

And I had a startling realization: I loved this city.

Even swimming as she was with monsters, deluged by crime, tainted by the violence of the *Sinsar Dubh*, I loved Dublin. Had Alina felt this way? Terrified of what might come, but more alive than she'd ever been?

And more alone.

The *sidhe*-seers weren't returning my calls. Not even Dani. They'd chosen. Rowena had won. I knew they were afraid. I knew she and the abbey were all most of them had ever known, and that she would skillfully manipulate their fears. I wanted to storm over to PHI and fight. Call the old woman out; argue my case with the *sidhe*-seers. But I didn't. There are some things you shouldn't have to ask for. I'd given them their show of faith. I expected some in return.

I walked the streets. I watched. I made notes in my journal about the various things I saw.

Even Barrons had abandoned me, off looking into

some ancient ritual he believed might help on Samhain.

Christian called and invited me out to MacKeltar-land, somewhere in the hills of Scotland, but I couldn't bring myself to leave the city. I felt like her vanguard, or maybe just the captain going down with her ship. His uncles, Christian told me grimly, were tolerating Barrons, but barely. Nonetheless, they'd agreed to work together for the duration. His tone made it clear that once the ritual was over, there might be an all-out Druid war. I didn't care. They could fight all they wanted once the walls were fortified.

Three days before Halloween, I found a plane ticket to Ashford outside my bedroom door. It was one-way. The flight was that afternoon. I stood holding it for a long time, eyes closed, leaning back against the wall, picturing my mom and dad, and my room at home.

October in south Georgia is fall at its finest: trees dressed in ruby, amber, and pumpkin; the air redolent with the scent of leaves and earth, and down-home southern cooking; the nights as clear as you can find only in rural America, far from the sky-dimming lights of city life.

Halloween night, the Brooks would host their annual Ghosts and Ghouls Treasure Hunt. The Brickyard would hold a costume contest, inviting the town to come as they *wished* they were. It was always a blast. People chose the strangest things. If I wasn't working and it was warm enough, Alina and I would throw a pool party. Mom and Dad were always cool about it, checking into a local bed-and-breakfast for the night. They'd made no secret of the fact that they rather looked forward to getting away from us all for a romantic night alone.

I lived my trip home while holding that ticket.

Then I called and tried to get Barrons' money refunded. The best they could do was reassign the funds, for a fee, to a future fare in my name.

"Did you think I'd run?" I asked later that night. Barrons was still wherever he was. I'd rung him up on my cell phone.

"I wouldn't blame you if you did. Would you have gone, if I'd made it round-trip?"

"No. I'm afraid something might follow me. I gave up the idea of going home a long time ago, Barrons. One day I will. When it's safe."

"What if it never is again?"

"I have to believe it will be."

There was a long silence. The bookstore was so quiet you could hear a pin drop. I was lonely. "When are you coming home?" I asked.

"Home, Ms. Lane?"

"I have to call it something." We'd had this exchange once before, standing in a cemetery. I'd told him if home was where the heart was, mine was six feet under. That was no longer true. My heart was inside me now, with all its hopes and fears and pains.

"I'm nearly done. I'll be there tomorrow." The line went dead.

Three o'clock in the morning.
I shot straight up in bed.

Heart hammering. Nerves screaming.

My cell phone was ringing.

"What the feck?" Dani snapped when I answered. "You sleep like the fecking dead up there! I been calling you for five fecking minutes!"

"Are you okay?" I demanded, shivering. I'd been in that cold place again. Shadowy dream remnants slipped away but the chill remained.

"Look out your window, Mac."

I pushed out of bed, grabbed my spear, and hurried to the window.

My bedroom, like the last one that Barrons trashed, is at the rear of the building, so I can watch the back alley out my window, and keep tabs on the Shades.

Dani was standing down there, in the narrow path of light between the bookstore and Barrons' garage, cell phone propped between her skinny shoulder and ear, grinning up at me. Shades watched her hungrily from their roost in the shadows.

She was wearing a long black leather coat that was straight out of a vampire movie, and much too big through the shoulders. As I watched, she slid something long and alabaster and shiningly beautiful out from under it.

I gasped. It could only be the Sword of Light.

"Let's go kick some fairy ass." Dani laughed, and the look in her eyes was anything but thirteen years old.

"Where's Rowena?" I dropped my PJ bottoms and thrust a leg into jeans, teeth chattering. I hate my Cold Place dreams.

"Ro's away. She left on a plane this afternoon. Couldn't take the sword with her. I snuck out. You wanna talk or you wanna come slay some Unseelie, Mac?"

Was she kidding? This was a *sidhe*-seer wet dream. Instead of sitting around, thinking, talking, researching—I could get out there and *do* something! I thumbed off my phone, layered two T-shirts beneath a sweater and a jacket, tugged on boots, grabbed my MacHalo on the way out and strapped it on, wishing I had one for her, too. No matter; if we ended up in the dark somewhere, I'd stick to her like *sidhe*-seer glue.

We took down eighty-seven Unseelie that night. Then we lost count.

FIFTEEN

I spent most of the day before Halloween cleaning up after the prior night's festivities. Unlike the aftermath of fun back home in Georgia, the remnants of a rollicking good time in Dublin weren't sticky plastic cups, crusts of half-eaten pizza, and cigarette butts dropped in beer bottles, but dead monsters and body parts.

Problem: When you kill a Fae, they cease projecting glamour, and contrary to pop culture's inane belief, the corpses do not disintegrate. They remain here, in our world, perfectly visible to all. In the pleasure of the kill, I forgot the corpses. So did Dani. It's not like they suddenly become visible to *me* when they die. They're always visible to me.

I learned from the morning news about the discovery of "movie props displayed in gruesome fashion around Dublin," rubbery monsters from the set of some "in-production horror movie, arranged as a prank, and people mustn't be alarmed, but call the

Garda; they've designated manpower to clean...er, pick them up."

My phone was ringing before the spot was over. It was Rowena. "Clean them up, you bloody imbecile!"

I was eating breakfast. "They just said the Garda are taking care of it," I muttered around a mouthful, mostly to irritate her. I'd been thinking the same thing. I needed to tidy up, and quickly. I was ashamed of myself for not realizing what I was doing.

"Did you leave a trail of bodies that can be traced to you?"

I winced. Probably. "I didn't know you cared, Ro," I said coolly.

"Was Dani with you last night?" she demanded.

"No."

"You did all that by yourself?"

"Uh-huh."

"How many?"

"I lost count. Over a hundred."

"Why?"

"I'm sick of doing nothing."

She was quiet for several moments, then, "I want you at the abbey for the ritual tomorrow."

I almost choked on a bite of crusty muffin top. *That* was the last thing I'd expected her to say. I'd been bracing for a lengthy accounting of my many failings, and had been contemplating hanging up before she had the chance to begin. Now I was glad I hadn't. "Why?"

There was another long silence. "There is strength in numbers," she said finally. "You are a powerful *sidhe*-seer." *Whether I like it or not* remained unsaid, but floated in the air.

Like the MacKeltars, she wanted all the power that she could get at her disposal.

I'd been thinking of crashing it anyway. I felt drawn to fight with them. If they were making a stand, I wanted to be there. I didn't feel drawn to join the MacKeltars the same way. I guess blood tells. Now I had an invitation. "What time?"

"The ceremony begins precisely one hour after sunset."

I didn't need to consult the calendar hanging in my bedroom upstairs to know the sun would rise tomorrow at 7:23 A.M. and set at 4:54 P.M. Nature rules me in ways she never used to. I can't wait for the long, bright days of summer again, and not just because of my love of the sun. These short, dreary days of fall and winter frighten me. December 22, the Winter Solstice, will be the shortest day of the year, at seven hours, twenty-eight minutes, and forty-nine seconds of daylight. The sun will rise at 8:39 and set at 4:08. That gives the Shades sixteen hours, thirty-one minutes, and eleven seconds to come out and play. More than *twice* as much as humans get. "When will we know for sure it worked?"

"Shortly after we open the orb," she said, but she didn't sound certain of that. It was unsettling to hear doubt in Rowena's voice.

"I'll think about it." That was a lie. I'd most definitely be there. "What's in it for me?"

"That you ask such a thing only reinforces my opinion of you." She hung up.

I finished my muffin and coffee, then headed out

to sweep up breadcrumbs, and keep the monsters from my door.

I stuffed Unseelie corpses in trash Dumpsters, hid them in abandoned buildings, and even managed to shove two into a concrete pour on a construction site when the workers took a coffee break.

I dragged the ones closest to the bookstore into the nearby Dark Zone. Even in broad daylight, it was hard for me to make myself go in there. I could feel Shades in all directions, the pulsating darkness of their voracious, terrible hunger. Where did they go? Were they wedged in tiny dark crannies of the bricks, watching me? Did they slither off underground? Were they piled up in dark corners inside the decrepit buildings? How small could they get? Might one be hiding in that empty soda can, at just the right angle to avoid the light? I'd never been a kick-the-can girl, and wasn't about to start now.

The streets were oddly empty. I would find out later that record numbers of people called in sick the last two days before Halloween. Fathers took long overdue personal days. Mothers kept their children home from school, for no good reason. I think you didn't need to be a *sidhe*-seer to feel the taut, expectant hush in the air, to hear the distant drumming of dark hooves on a troubled wind, moving closer, closer.

Closer.

I sliced, diced, and bottled a new stash of Unseelie while I was out. I'd expected Jayne days ago, but decided maybe the effects lasted longer in ordinary humans.

On my way back to the bookstore, I stopped at

the grocery to grab a few items, then popped into a bakery and picked up the order I'd placed yesterday.

Then I stood under the spray of a steaming hot shower, naked but for the thigh sheath I'd taken to wearing so I could give myself better than a one-handed hair washing, and scrubbed away the taint of dead Unseelie.

By midnight, Barrons hadn't shown up and I was feeling pissy. He'd said he'd be here. I'd planned for it.

By one, I was worried. By two, I was certain he wasn't going to show. At three-fifteen, I called him. He answered on the first ring.

"Where the hell are you?" I snapped, at the same time he snapped, "Are you all right?"

"I've been waiting for hours," I said.

"For what?"

"You said you'd be here."

"I was delayed."

"Maybe you could have called?" I said sarcastically. "You know, picked up the phone and said 'Hey, Mac, I'm running late.' "

There was a moment of silence on the other end of the line. Then Barrons said softly, "You've mistaken me for someone else. Do not wait on me, Ms. Lane. Do not construct your world around mine. I'm not that man."

His words stung. Probably because I'd done exactly that: structured my night around him, even played out in my head how it was going to go. "Screw you, Barrons."

"I'm not that man, either."

"Oh! In your *dreams*! Allow me to put this into words you taught me yourself: I resent it when you waste my time. Keys, Barrons. That's what I've been waiting for. The Viper's in the shop." And I missed it like I missed my long blond hair. We'd bonded, the Viper and I. I doubted I'd ever get it back. It had been heavily damaged from its high-speed trip down the sidewalk and, if I knew Barrons as well as I thought I did, he'd sell it before he'd drive it again, no matter how flawlessly it was repaired. I kind of felt the same way. When you spend that much money, you want perfection. "I need a car to drive."

"Why?"

"I've decided to go to the abbey for the ritual," I said.

"I'm not certain that's wise."

"It's not your decision."

"Maybe it should be," he said.

"I can't do anything to help the MacKeltars, Barrons."

"I didn't say you should. Perhaps you should remain in the store tomorrow night. It's the safest place for you."

"You want me to *hide*?" My voice rose with disbelief on the last word. Months ago, I might have happily hid. Watched late night TV while painting my fingernails and toenails to match, a divine shade of pink. Now? Not a chance.

"Sometimes caution is the wisest course," he said.

"Tell you what, Barrons: You come be cautious

with me, I'll stay in, too. Not because I want your company," I said before he could make a pithy comment, "but because of that whole good-for-the-goose-and-gander thing. I'm not going to gander helplessly."

"You're the goose, Ms. Lane. I'm the gander."

As if I could mistake his gender. "That was a double entendre," I informed him stiffly. "I was being clever. Gander has multiple meanings. What good is being clever when the person you're being clever to is too dense to get it?"

"I'm not dense," he said just as stiffly, and I sensed one of our childish fights looming on the horizon. "As a double entendre it didn't work. Look up double entendre."

"I *know* what double entendre means. And you can just shove your stupid birthday cake. I don't even know why I bothered!"

The silence was so protracted that I decided he'd hung up.

I hung up, too, wishing I'd done it first.

Twenty minutes later, Barrons stepped through the door from the back of the bookstore. Ice was crystallized in his hair, and he was pale from extreme cold.

I was sitting on the sofa in the rear conversation area, too aggravated to sleep. "Good. You've finally stopped pretending you don't use the mirror. It's about time."

"I only use the mirror when I must, Ms. Lane. Even for me, it is ... unpleasant."

Curiosity overrode irritation. "What constitutes 'must'? Where do you go?"

He glanced around. "Where is the cake?"

"I threw it away."

He gave me a look.

I sighed, got up, and got it out of the fridge. It was a seven-layer chocolate cake, with alternating raspberry and chocolate cream fillings, frosted pink, with a *Happy Birthday JZB* in the center, delicately scripted and adorned with flowers. It was beautiful. It was the only thing that had made my mouth water in weeks, besides Unseelie. I set it on the coffee table, then got plates and forks from the cabinet behind the counter.

"I'm confused, Ms. Lane. Is this cake for me, or for you?"

Yeah, well, there was that. I'd been planning on eating a lot of it myself. I'd spared no expense. I could have downloaded forty-seven songs from iTunes instead. "They were out of black icing," I said dryly. He wasn't reacting the way I'd planned. He didn't look the least bit touched or amused. In fact, he was regarding the cake with a mixture of horror and . . . grim fascination; the same way I regard monsters I'm about to kill.

I fidgeted. At the time I'd ordered it, it'd seemed like a good idea. I'd thought it was a humorous way of poking fun at our . . . relationship, while also saying, I know you're really old and probably not human at all, but whatever you are, you still have a birthday, just like the rest of the world.

"I believe candles are customary," he said finally.

I reached in my pocket, pulled out candles in the shape of numbers, and one I'd whittled to a stub of a period, and stuck them on top of the cake. He looked at me as if I'd sprouted a second head.

"*Pi*, Ms. Lane? I'd pegged you for failing high school math."

"I got a *D*. The little stuff always trips me up. But the big stuff stuck with me."

"Why pi?"

"It's irrational and uncountable." Funny girl, wasn't I?

"It's also a constant," he said dryly.

"They were out of sixes. Seems this time of year six-six-six is big," I said, lighting the candles. "Obviously, they haven't seen the real Beast, or they wouldn't be playing at worshipping it."

"Have there been more sightings?" He was still frowning at the cake, looking at it as if he expected it to sprout dozens of legs and begin scuttling toward him, thin-lipped, teeth bared.

"It's been transferring hands every day." There was a stack of papers by the couch. The crimes the newspapers were reporting made eating breakfast while reading it risky.

He lifted his gaze from the cake to my face.

"It's just a cake. I promise. No surprises. No chopped-up Unseelie in there," I joked. "I'll even eat the first slice."

"It's far from 'just' a cake, Ms. Lane. That you procured it implies—"

"—that I was having a sweet craving and used you for an excuse to indulge. Blow out the candles, will you? And lighten up, Barrons." How had I not realized the delicacy of the ice I was on? What in the world had made me think I could give him a birth-day cake and he'd be anything but weird about it?

"I'm doing this for you," he said tightly.

"I get that," I said. I was really glad I'd vetoed getting balloons. "I just thought it would be fun." I stood, holding the cake out to him in both hands, so he could blow out candles before they dripped wax on the pretty confection. "I could use a little fun."

I sensed violence in the room a split second before it erupted. In retrospect, I think he thought he had it caged, and was nearly as surprised as I.

Cake and candles exploded from my hands, shot straight up in the air, hit the ceiling, and stuck there, dripping gobs of icing. I stared up at it. My lovely cake.

Then I was trapped between the wall and his body, with no awareness of having gotten there. He's frighteningly quick when he wants to be. I think he could give Dani a run for the money. He had my hands pinned above my head, braceleted at the wrists by one of his. The other was around my throat. His head was down and he was breathing hard. For a moment, he rested his face in my neck.

Then he pulled back and stared at me and when he spoke his voice was low with fury. "*Never* do that again, Ms. Lane. Do not insult me with your silly rit-uals, and idiotic platitudes. *Never* try to humanize me. Don't think we're the same, you and I. We're not."

"Did you have to *ruin* it?" I cried. "I'd been look-ing forward to it all day."

He shook me, hard. "You have no business look-ing forward to pink cakes. That's not your world anymore. Your world is hunting the Book and staying alive. They're mutually exclusive, you bloody fool."

"No, they're not! It's only if I eat pink cakes that I *can* hunt the Book! You're right—we're *not* the same. I can't walk through the Dark Zone at night. I don't scare all the other monsters away. I need rainbows. You don't. I get that now. No birthdays for Barrons. I'll pen that in right next to *Don't wait on him* and *Don't expect him to save you unless there's something in it for him*. You're a jackass. There's a *constant* for you. I won't forget it."

His grip on my throat relaxed. "Good."

"Fine," I said, though I don't really know why. I think I just wanted the last word.

We stared at each other.

He was so close, his body electric, his expression savage.

I moistened my lips. His gaze fixed on them. I think I stopped breathing.

He jerked so sharply away that his long dark coat sliced air, and turned his back to me. "Was that an invitation, Ms. Lane?"

"If it was?" I asked, astonishing myself. What did I think I was doing?

"I don't do hypotheticals. Little girl."

I looked at his back. He didn't move. I thought of things to say. I said none of them.

He vanished through the connecting door.

"Hey," I shouted after him, "I need a car to drive!" There was no answer.

A large chunk of cake dropped from the ceiling and *splatted* on the floor.

It was mostly intact, just a little goopy.
Sighing, I got a fork and scraped it onto a plate.

It was noon the next day when I got out of bed,
cleared my monster alarm from in front of my door,
and opened it.

Waiting outside for me was a thermos of coffee, a
bag of doughnuts, a set of car keys, and a note. I un-
screwed the thermos top, sipped the coffee, and
unfolded the note.

> *Ms. Lane,*
> *I would prefer you join me in Scotland this
> evening, but if you insist on helping the old witch,
> here are keys, as you requested. I moved it for you.
> It's the red one, parked in front of the door. Call if
> you change your mind. I can send a plane as late as
> 4:00.*
> *CJ*

It took me a moment to figure out the initials. *Constant Jackass.* I smiled. "Apology accepted, Barrons,
if it's the Ferrari."

It was.

SIXTEEN

"Liminal" is a fascinating word. Times can be liminal: Twilight is the transition from day to night; midnight is the crack between one day and the next; equinoxes and solstices and New Year's Day are all thresholds.

Liminal can also be a state of consciousness: for example, those moments between waking and sleeping, also known as threshold consciousness, or hypnagogia, a state during which a person might think herself fully alert, but is actually actively engaged in dreaming. This is the time that a lot of people report a convulsive jerk, or a feeling of physically falling.

Places can be liminal: airports with people constantly coming and going, but never staying. People, too, can be liminal: Teens, like Dani, are temporarily stuck between child and adult. Fictional characters are often Liminal Beings, archetypes that straddle two worlds, marking or guarding thresholds, or are physically divided by two states of existence.

Between-ness is a defining characteristic of liminal. Limbo is another. Liminal is neither here nor there but exists between one moment and the next, poised in that pause where what's passing hasn't yet become what's becoming. Liminal is a magical time, a dangerous time, fraught with possibility... and peril.

Halloween seemed to drag on forever. Ironic, considering I had slept until noon. I had four measly hours to kill until four o'clock, when I would leave the city to head for the abbey, yet it stretched interminably.

I called Dani as soon as I got up. She was excited that I was coming, and told me the ritual was scheduled to begin at six-fifteen.

"So, what is it? A lot of chanting and weirdness?" I asked.

She laughed and said, pretty much so. Invocations had to be recited and tithes paid before the Orb could be opened and its Fae essence released to fortify the walls. I asked what kind of tithes, and she got a little cagey. I wondered if Rowena planned to use my blood or something. I wouldn't put it past her.

I called Christian and he said all was a go. His uncles had begun the Druid rites at dawn, although Barrons wouldn't be joining them until later in the day.

I called Dad, and we talked for a long time about cars and my job and the usual light stuff that makes up our conversations lately. I hate that Barrons Voiced him into a worry-free stupor, and I'm grateful for it. If Dad had said one halfway deep or insightful thing to me today, I might have burst into tears and told him all my problems. This is the man who kissed every bump or bruise I ever had, even the imaginary ones when I was little, and just wanted a Princess Jasmine Band-Aid and to be cuddled and cooed at, sitting on his lap.

After a while, I asked for Mom. There was a long pause, and I was afraid she wouldn't come to the phone—then she did, and I can't describe the joy I felt at hearing her voice for the first time in months!

Though she chose her words with uncharacteristic tentativeness, she was coherent, clearheaded, and obviously not drugged. Dad said she still tired very easily so I kept the conversation short and sweet, telling her nothing but happy news: My job was fabulous, I had a great employer, I'd gotten a raise, I was hoping to start my own bookstore when I came home, I was making concrete plans to finish college and get a degree in business, and no, I couldn't make Thanksgiving but yes, I would try as hard as I could to get home for Christmas.

Necessary lies. I understand them now. I could almost feel Alina, standing behind me, nodding her head, as I boosted our mother's spirits. Every time the phone had rung for me in Ashford, Georgia, and my sister had made me laugh and feel loved and safe, she'd been standing in Dublin, wondering if she'd be alive tomorrow.

After I hung up, I dug into the doughnuts and punched up a random playlist on my iPod. "Knocking on Heaven's Door" came up first, followed by "Don't Fear the Reaper." I turned it off.

I don't know what I did until three. I think I

passed a great deal of time sitting and staring into
the fire. Liminal sucks. You can't grasp it with your
hands and shape it. You can't make midnight come
faster, or grow up sooner, or avoid the in-betweens.
You can only hang in there, and get through them.

I showered, put on makeup, and sleeked my hair
back into a short ponytail. I tugged on black jeans, a
T-shirt, a sweater, boots, and a jacket. I grabbed my
backpack and stuffed my MacHalo in. I was going to
be out late. I holstered my spear in my shoulder harness, tucked in two of Barrons' short, sheathed
knives I'd pilfered from an upstairs display case into
my waistband, and loaded myself with diced
Rhino-boy, jars in my jacket pockets, plastic Baggies
in my boots. I strapped my Velcro bands with the
Click-It lights around my ankles and wrists. I even
slipped a vial of holy water into the front pocket of
my jeans. In this town, you never know what's coming. As they say back home, I was loaded for bear.
All kinds.

I went downstairs, glanced out the window, and
did a double take, wondering if I'd lost track of time.
It had been clear and light in the cold wintry way of
early November, when I'd gone upstairs. Now, at
three forty-five, it was nearly dark outside. A storm
had blown in while I'd been blow-drying my hair. It
wasn't raining yet, but the wind was kicking up,
and it looked like we might get a real ripper any
time.

I picked up the car keys and glanced around the
bookstore to make sure I wasn't forgetting anything.
As my gaze swept the four-story room, I shrugged
off a sudden, broody fear that I might never see

Barrons Books and Baubles again. Like I loved the city, I'd grown to love my store. The hardwood floors gleamed beneath the sconces and cut-amber lamps. The books were all shelved in their proper places. The magazine rack was freshly stocked. The fires were off. The sofas and chairs were invitingly positioned in cozy arrangements. The mural above me was lost in shadows. One day I was going to climb up there and see what it was. The store was tidy and quiet, stuffed with fictional worlds to be explored, business-ready and waiting for the next customer.

I headed for the back door.

It would be waiting for me when I got back tomorrow, when the walls were strong, and I had a whole year to figure things out. I would start keeping regular hours again, and get to work on my plans to set up a Web site and catalog the rare editions upstairs. No more slacking.

But right now, an Italian stallion was waiting for me, stomping and snorting. Out back, a Ferrari was calling my name. There were two hours of road between me and where I was going, and that was *one* liminal I was going to love every minute of.

SEVENTEEN

I made it twelve blocks.

My end of town, next to the Dark Zone, had been deserted as a war zone. Now, I knew why.

The streets an eighth of a mile east of BB&B were so packed with people and Unseelie that motor traffic didn't have a hope of getting through. Most of the Fae were in full human glamour, trying to incite riot, and succeeding.

Garda pushed among them, demanding order with raised batons. There're enough troubled youth in Dublin—in any city, for that matter—that even a small angry mob can combust and spread like wildfire. Especially on Halloween when all the freaks come out, hiding behind better masks.

While I watched, a few of the Garda—who were actually Unseelie in glamour—began viciously beating a group of youths with their batons, incensing the crowd. Other Unseelie began smashing out store windows, looting and encouraging others to take what they wanted. I called out to a few kids hurrying by to join the fracas. No one seemed to know what the rioting was about, nor did they care. I was afraid to get closer, for fear of damaging the car. Or me.

Bile boiled in my stomach from the compressed multitude of Fae. At least the *Sinsar Dubh* wasn't around to incapacitate me. The mob was expanding, pushing outward, and it occurred to me that getting stuck in the middle of it, sitting in a Ferrari, was a really bad idea. I backed up, hastily turned around, and drove away, glad I'd left a few minutes early.

I dug out a map of the city from my backpack and flipped on the interior light. Although the storm still only threatened, the cloud cover had turned day to night a full hour earlier than I'd expected.

Ten blocks north of the bookstore, I encountered another mob. I backed up, swung the car around, and headed west. It was no go. That way out of town was just as bad.

I pulled over in a parking lot to study the map, then headed southwest, intending to skirt the edge of the Dark Zone on my way out and, if I had to, put on my MacHalo and drive through part of it to get out of town. But as I approached the perimeter of the abandoned neighborhood, I slammed the brakes and stared.

The entire edge of the zone was a dense black wall of Shades, pressing at the pools of the light cast by the streetlamps on Dorsey Street. It stretched left and right as far as I could see, a massive barricade of death.

I put the car in reverse and backed away. I would

go through it only if I had to. I wasn't yet ready to admit defeat.

I spent the next fifteen minutes driving the ever-decreasing circumference of my world, hemmed in by danger on all sides. The edges of the Dark Zones had met and merged with the mobs, and I watched in horror as Unseelie in human glamour drove people into those waiting, killing shadows.

It finally occurred to me to get out of the flashy red car that was beginning to attract a dangerous amount of attention, so I sped back to BB&B where I planned to swap it for something nondescript, and figure how to escape the city.

As I turned down the side street leading to the store, I slammed the brakes so hard I nearly gave myself whiplash.

Barrons Books and Baubles was dark!

Completely. It was surrounded by night on all sides.

Every exterior light on the bookstore was out.

I stared blankly. I'd left them all on. I eased off the brake and inched closer. In the gleam of headlights, glass glittered on the cobbled street. The lights weren't off. Someone had broken them all out, or—considering how high they were mounted—shot them out. Or...someone had sent those flying Fae, maybe even Hunters, to do the job. Were they perched up there right now, on the cornices, looming over me? There were so many Fae in the city that my *sidhe*-sensor felt bombarded, overwhelmed by presences too numerous to count or differentiate. I peered up, but the roof of the store was lost in darkness.

Although the interior lights were on, they were set at the subdued, after-hours level, and what spilled onto the pavement through the beveled glass door and windows was not enough to deter my enemy. One more city block had fallen to the Shades: mine.

Barrons Books and Baubles was part of the Dark Zone.

Would the Shades' more substantial brethren enter BB&B tonight, smash it up, break out the interior lights, and render it unsalvageable? Could they? I knew Barrons hadn't warded it against everything, just the bigger risks.

My eyes narrowed. This was unacceptable. The Fae would not take my sanctuary! I would *not* be turned out into the streets. They would get their nasty, shady petunias out of my territory and they would do it now. I spun in a screech of tires, and drove in the other direction. Four blocks from the Dark Zone's new perimeter, the mob pushed me back. I floored it in reverse, narrowly missing parked cars, stopping beneath a pool of bright streetlamps. I could hear angry shouts, breaking glass, and the thunder of the approaching mob. I would not be swallowed up by it. But I had to act fast.

I stepped out of the car, plunged my hand beneath my jacket, and fisted it around my spear. I wasn't losing it this time.

A cold, windborne mist pricked my face and hands. The storm had begun. But it wasn't just storm I sensed in the air. Something was wrong, terribly wrong, besides angry mobs and hordes of

Unseelie, and Shades overtaking my home. The wind was strange, blowing from multiple directions, reeking of sulfur. The fringes of the chaotic, destructive crowd surged around the corner, two blocks from where I stood.

"V'lane, I need you!" I cried, releasing his name.

It uncoiled from my tongue and swelled, choking me, then slammed into the back of my teeth, forcing my mouth wide.

But instead of soaring into the night sky, it crashed into an invisible wall and plummeted to the pavement, where it lay fluttering weakly, a fallen dark bird.

I nudged it with the toe of my boot.

It disintegrated.

I turned my face to the wind, east and west, north and south. It eddied around me, buffeting me from all sides, slapping me with hundreds of tiny hands, and I suddenly could *feel* the LM out there, working his dark magic to bring the walls down. It was changing things.

I flexed the *sidhe*-seer place in my mind, focused, turned inward, seeking, hunting, and for an instant I actually got a flash of him, standing at the edge of a stark, sheer black cliff, in an icy place, red-robed, hands raised—and was that a heart held high, dripping blood?—chanting, summoning arts powerful enough to crash a prison wrought from living strands of the Song of Making, and it was doing something to all magic, even Fae, making it go terribly wrong.

I squeezed my inner eye shut before it got me

killed. I was standing in the middle of a street in a rioting Dublin, trapped in the city, alone.

V'lane would not be sifting in to save the day.

The mob was less than a block away. The marauding front-liners had just noticed my car and were roaring like maddened beasts. Some toted baseball bats, others swung batons taken from fallen Garda.

They were going to beat my Ferrari to smithereens.

There wasn't time to dig out my cell phone and try to call Barrons. They would be on me in seconds. I knew what happened to rich people during riots. I also knew they wouldn't believe I wasn't rich. I wasn't about to get beheaded with the aristocracy just because every now and then I got to drive a nice car that didn't even belong to me.

I grabbed my backpack from the car, and ran.

A block away another mob approached.

I plunged into it, and lost myself inside it. It was a horrible, smelly, hot, surging mass of humanity. It was rage unstoppered, frustration unleashed, envy unsuppressed. It howled with victory as it looted, smashed, and destroyed.

I couldn't breathe. I was going to throw up. There were too many people, too many Fae, too much hostility and violence. I swam in a sea of faces, some feral, some excited, others as frightened as I imagined I must look. Fae are monsters. But we humans hold our own. Fae might have incited this riot, but we were the ones keeping it alive.

The cobbled stones were slippery from the misting rain. I watched in horror as a young girl fell, crying out. She was trampled in seconds as the crowd swept on. An elderly man—why on earth was he out here?—went down next. A teenage boy was jostled into a streetlamp, rebounded, lost his balance, and vanished from view.

For time uncounted then, I was driven by a single imperative: Stay on your feet. Stay alive.

I rode the crowd, an unwilling mount, feet trapped in the stirrups, from one block to the next. Twice I managed to break free, fight my way to the outer fringes, only to be drowned in the herd again, propelled forward by its relentless stampede.

I feared two things: that they would gallop me straight into a Dark Zone, or that the *Sinsar Dubh* would make a sudden appearance, and I'd fall to my knees, clutching my head. I couldn't decide which death would be worse.

My cell phone was in my backpack, but there wasn't enough room to maneuver in the crowd and get to it. I worried that if I slipped my pack from my shoulders, it would be jerked from my hands and carried off. My spear was cold and heavy under my arm, but I was afraid if I whipped it out, I might be speared by it in the crush.

Unseelie.

I had baby food jars of it in my pockets.

With its dark life in my veins I would be able to break free of the mob.

We were nearing the edge of the Temple Bar District. The Dark Zone wasn't far. Were we being deliberately driven? If I were able to float above this riot, would I see Unseelie herding us from behind, cattle to the slaughter?

"Sorry," I muttered. "Oops, didn't mean to hit you." Without pissing off anyone badly enough to get myself punched, I managed to extract a jar from my pocket. I'd twisted the lids too tight to open them one-handed. I jostled for space, and popped the lid. Someone shoved into me and I lost my hold on it. I felt it hit my boot and then it was gone.

Gritting my teeth, I dug for another one. I had three in my pockets. The rest were sealed in plastic bags tucked inside my boots. I'd never be able to get to them in the crush. I was more careful with this jar, easing it out, clutching it for dear life—which I hoped it was. I had to get out of the crowd. I knew my landmarks. I was two blocks from the Dark Zone. I managed to pop the lid but was unwilling to duck my head to eat it, for fear of taking an elbow in the eye, freezing or stumbling in pain, and going down.

I raised the bottle close to my body, tossed my head back, gulped and chewed. I gagged the entire time I chewed. No matter that I'd been craving it; it was work to get it down, crunchy with gristle and cystlike sacs that popped when I chewed. It wriggled in my mouth, and crawled like spiders in my stomach. When I lowered the jar, I was looking straight into the eyes of a Rhino-boy, around the heads of two humans and, from the expression on his beady-eyed, bumpy gray face, he knew what I'd just done. He must have seen the pink-gray flesh moving in the jar as I'd tossed it back.

I guessed word was getting around, between

Mallucé, and the LM, and O'Bannion and now Jayne eating them. He bellowed, ducked his head, and charged. I spun, and began violently pushing my way through the crowd. I managed to get the third bottle out, and gulped that, too, as I fought toward freedom.

The only other time I'd eaten Unseelie, I'd been mortally wounded, and close to death, so I didn't know what to expect. Last time, it had taken several large mouthfuls just to begin the healing, and nearly ten minutes to complete the journey from dying to more alive than I'd ever been. Tonight I was whole and uninjured. Strength and power slammed into me like I'd taken a needle of adrenaline straight to my heart. A chilly heat suffused me as the potency of Fae spiked my blood.

Savage Mac raised her head, and looked out through my eyes, thought with my brain, and re-arranged my limbs into a sleeker composition: powerful, predatory, padding on certain paws.

Within moments, I was free of the crowd, but in the distance, I could hear another approaching. The city had gone crazy tonight. I would learn later that Fae in human glamour had broken into houses and businesses all over town, attacked owners and residents, and driven them out into the streets, forcing the riots to begin.

I glanced back. It appeared I'd lost the Rhino-boy in the crush. Or maybe he'd decided he was more interested in the destruction of an entire mob, than measly me. Behind me was the Dark Zone. Ahead was another mob, its front wave led by Rhino-boys smashing out streetlamps with baseball bats. To my left were sounds of violence. To my right was a pitch-black alley. I slipped off my backpack, dug out my MacHalo, strapped and buckled it beneath my chin, then hit the Click-It lights, one after another, until I blazed like a small beacon. I smacked my wrists and ankles together, lighting up my hands and feet.

The mob rushed me in a great wave.

I took off down the dark alley.

I lost track of time for a while then, racing down streets and alleys, drawing up short, doubling back, trying to avoid the mobs, and evade the troops of Rhino-boys, with whom I had repeated close calls, since I could no longer sense them, now that my *sidhe*-seer senses were deadened by my gruesome meal.

They marched militantly, rounding up the stragglers to herd into the mobs. I crisscrossed the same blocks dozens of times, hiding in doorways and Dumpsters. I had a terrible moment where I got hemmed in between two groups of them, and was forced to sidle behind cardboard boxes in the shadows of a trash bin, and turn off all my lights to let the horde of Unseelie crash by.

I tasted death sitting there in the darkness, wondering if there were Dark "Spots"—really tiny areas where only one or two Shades lived—and any moment it might slither from a crack and get me, and the thought was almost worse than flinging myself into the middle of the passing Unseelie, which, by the way, I unzipped my Baggies and ate some of, sitting there with my knees tucked up in the darkness behind the steel bin. Maybe, as I'd once joked to Barrons, Shades really didn't like dark meat, and they'd leave me alone.

After the troops passed, I crawled out and clicked myself back on.

Yes, people were being driven. Gathered and herded. Lambs to the slaughter. *My* people.

And there wasn't a thing I could do about it. Eating Unseelie might have transformed me from a pocketknife into an Uzi, and turned me into a walking weapon, but I was still only *one* weapon, and acutely aware of it. I was defense, not offense. There was no offense to be made in this city tonight. Not even Savage Mac, the cockiest of cocky, felt punchy. She felt threatened, feral. She wanted to find a cave to hide in until the odds were more in her favor. I was inclined to agree. Survival was our prime directive.

The first time I'd eaten Unseelie, nothing had fazed me. But that night I'd only had to worry about a single rotting vampire, plus I'd had Barrons by my side. Tonight, I was trapped in a rioting city of hundreds of thousands of people, it was Halloween, the Unseelie were numerous and horribly *organized*, V'lane was unreachable, and Barrons was a country away.

I finally found myself in a semilit deserted alley, with no militant footfalls or sounds of rioting nearby. I ducked into a doorway lit by a single, naked overhead bulb, to take care of something that badly needed taking care of. I removed my pack carefully, dropped it, ripped off my jacket, and gingerly, delicately removed my spear harness, which I placed on the ground.

The entire time I'd been running and hiding, its heavy weight had been a burning terror against my body. What if I fell? What if I got caught in a crowd again and someone jostled me? What if the tip pierced my skin? Hello, Mallucé. Good-bye, sanity. I might be tougher than I used to be, but I had no doubts about my ability to cope with rotting to death.

I stripped off my sweater and T-shirt, then put my sweater, jacket, and MacHalo back on and belted the spear harness on the outside of my coat, without touching anything but the leather straps.

I tied the T-shirt I'd removed around the bottom part of the harness, forming an additional layer of protection between the tip and me.

Ironic, the thing I love most, that makes me feel so powerful under normal circumstances, becomes my greatest liability, and the thing I fear most when I pilfer dark power. I can have one, or the other—but never both.

Carrying the dichotomy one step further, I could no longer sense the spear, which meant I could inadvertently hurt myself on it. However, I could also no longer sense the *Sinsar Dubh*, which meant it could no longer hurt me, and send me crashing to my knees, helpless, in a dangerous situation.

Duh. I stood in the doorway marveling, and not in a good way, at my own stupidity. If eating Unseelie made me unable to sense the *Sinsar Dubh*, then all I needed to do next time it popped up on my radar was get as close to it as I could, eat Unseelie, and get closer. Close enough to pick it up.

An image of the Beast as I'd last seen it materialized in my mind.

Yeah, right. Pick it up. Sure. What then? Put it in my pocket? I didn't have one large enough.

So, I knew how to get close to it without being incapacitated by pain. I still had no idea what to do then. If I touched it would I, too, turn psycho? Or was I a *sidhe*-seer/Null/OOP-detector mutant that was somehow exempt? A moot point right now, with my odds of surviving the night looking so grim.

I dug out my cell phone to call Dani and tell her what was happening in Dublin. There was no way I could make it to the abbey. I glanced at my watch and was stunned to find it was nearly seven o'clock. I'd been running and hiding for hours! The ritual might already be completed and if it was, *sidhe*-seers could come to the city and help me save some of the people being driven to death-by-Shade. *I* might not be able to make a difference, but seven hundred of us could. If they couldn't—or wouldn't—come because Rowena vetoed it for some idiotic reason, I would call Barrons and if he didn't answer, I'd call Ryodan, and if neither of them answered, it was probably time for IYD: if you're dying. A pall of death hung over Dublin like grief over a funeral. I could smell it, taste it on the air. If no *sidhe*-seers were coming in to join me, I wanted out, any way I could get there.

Dani answered on the second ring. She sounded

hysterical. "Feck, Mac!" she cried. "What did you *do* to us?"

I'd been adjusting the straps on my pack to accommodate my bulky external harness, and alarm made me drop it. "What's wrong?" I demanded.

"Shades, Mac! Fecking Shades came out of the fecking Orb when we opened it! The abbey's full of 'em!"

I was so stunned that I nearly dropped the phone. When I got it back to my ear, Dani was saying:

"Rowena says you betrayed us! She says you set us up!"

My heart constricted. "No, Dani, I didn't, I swear! Somebody must have set *me* up!" The thought iced my blood. There was only one person who could have, one person that walked among those dark vampires without fear. How easily he'd relinquished the relic. How quickly he'd agreed to give it to me. Yet he'd not given it to me that night. Thirty hours had passed between my request, and his delivery. What had he been doing during those hours? Spiking a *sidhe*-seer's drink with Shades? "How bad is it?" I cried.

"We've lost dozens! When we opened the Orb, they splintered, and we thought the light from the ritual killed them, but they fecking grew back together in the shadows. They're everywhere! In closets, in shoes, anywhere there's dark!"

"Dani, I didn't do this! I swear to you. I swear on my sister. You know what she means to me. You have to believe me. I would never do this. Never!"

"You said you'd come," she hissed. "You didn't. Where are you?"

"I'm stuck in the city, holed up between York and Mercer. Dublin's a nightmare, and I couldn't get out. People have been rioting for hours, and the Unseelie are driving them into the Dark Zones!"

She sucked in a breath. "How bad is it?" she echoed my question.

"*Thousands,* Dani! Beyond counting. If it keeps up like this—" I broke off, unable to make myself complete the thought. "If you guys come in, we can save some of them, but I can't do it by myself. There's too many Unseelie." But if the abbey was full of Shades, they couldn't leave. We couldn't afford to lose the abbey. The libraries were there, and God only knew what else. The lightbulb above me flickered and made a sizzling noise as if it had taken a power surge.

It's hard to say what makes the brain suddenly piece things together, but I had one of those moments where a series of images flashed through my mind and I was stupefied by the simplicity and obviousness of what I'd been missing: Rhino-boys collecting trash, repairing streetlamps, driving city trucks, replacing broken bricks in the pavement. "Oh, no, Dani," I breathed, horrified, "forget what I just said. Don't come into the city, and don't let anyone else. Not now. Not for any reason. Not until after dawn."

"Why?"

"Because they've been planning this. I've been seeing Unseelie in city jobs, and I didn't get it until now. It's not just the street sweepers, or the trash collectors." Where better to learn about one's enemy than from the leavings of their life, their refuse? The

FBI always infiltrated their suspects' daily lives, bugged their houses, and staked out their trash. "It's the utility workers, too." How long had the LM been orchestrating his macabre symphony? Long enough to have thought through every bit of it, and his time as a human had taught him well what our weaknesses were. "They've got control of the grid, Dani. They're going to turn the entire—" I held my phone away from my ear and looked at it.

Full battery.

No service. The cell phone towers had just gone down. I had no idea how much Dani had heard.

"—city into a Dark Zone," I whispered.

The lightbulb above me flickered again. I looked up at it. It sizzled, popped, and went dark.

EIGHTEEN

My world was falling apart around me.

I was cut off from V'lane, Barrons was looking like the ultimate traitor, the abbey was full of Shades, BB&B was a Dark Zone, the city had fallen to rioters and Unseelie, and it was about to descend into total darkness.

Once it did, nothing alive out in the streets would be safe. Nothing. Not even grass and trees. Well, I might be, illuminated by my MacHalo, armed with my spear (that could kill me horribly at this point), but what if a group of rioters or Unseelie attacked me en masse and rendered me defenseless? What could I hope to accomplish by wandering the city? Could I save lives? What would I do with them if I did? How would I keep them safe when the lights went out? Would they, like drowning people, claw and fight me to death to steal my lights? If I died, who would track the Book? I'm no coward. But I'm no fool, either. I know when to fight, and I know when to survive to fight another day.

Every cell in my body wanted to go up, get off the ground, far from the streets and alleys and lanes that would soon run dark with a flood of Shades, closer to the dawn that loomed on what seemed an impossibly far horizon.

Twelve hours. Plus some. I scoured the streets for my Alamo, refusing to ponder the outcome of *that* battle. I would do better.

I finally settled on an old church with a high steeple, an open belfry, and stone archways where I could perch, and watch my flanks. The tall, double front doors were locked. I liked them that way. There were no windows facing the street. I liked that, too. Here was my fortress, the best I could do, for now anyway.

I circled around the back, kicked in the door of the refectory, and slipped inside. After barricading the door with a heavy china cabinet, I swiped an apple and two oranges from a fruit basket on the dining table, and hurried through the dimly lit communal areas of the church.

It took me a while to find the entrance to the belfry, at the rear of the large chapel, beneath the choir balcony, in the thick of the massive organ pipes. The narrow door was almost completely concealed behind a bookcase that had been shoved in front of it, I suspected to prevent curious kids from making the climb. I pushed the bookcase aside—an easy nudge as pumped up on Unseelie as I was—and opened the door. It was pitch black beyond. Bracing myself, I stepped inside, lighting up the tower. No shadows recoiled, no inky darknesses slithered. I exhaled with relief.

A narrow, rickety wooden stair, more ladder than step, circled a hundred and fifty feet of stone wall to the belfry. It was actually *nailed* to the mortar in places; there were neither braces nor suspension for it, and it looked about as safe as a house of cards. I wondered when the last time was that anyone had actually ascended it. Did bells need to be serviced? Or was it more likely the last time anyone had climbed those stairs was fifty years ago?

No matter. I wasn't staying on the ground.

The rungs gave out in two places. Both times my heightened strength and reflexes saved me. Without Unseelie hammering through my veins, I would have slipped through the treads, plunged fifty feet, and broken something serious in the fall. Both times I was excruciatingly aware of the cold weight of the spear against my body. I hated having to carry it while I was like this. I was a water balloon with a pin taped to my side, rolling across the floor, tempting fate.

Perching precariously on the last rung, I strained to reach the trapdoor, pushed it up, hoisted myself through, and glanced around. I was in a room directly beneath the spire. Overhead was a second platform similar to the one I was on, above which hung two great brass bells. The room I was in appeared to be a utility room of sorts, with boxes of tools, and a broom closet that was partially open. I moved to it, made sure it was Shade-free, and closed it. Slightly cracked closet doors give me the creeps.

I climbed the final ladder, ascending to the bells.

I was surprised to find the storm was far north of the city now; the clouds had broken and moonlight, though wan, illuminated the belfry. I clicked myself off so I wouldn't be a blazing X-marks-the-spot-of-nubile-young-*sidhe*-seer. Four tall stone archways, twice as high as my head, framed the spire east, west, north, and south. I stepped into the one facing east, and shivered in the cold breeze, staring down at Dublin.

Fires burned in many places, and cars lay on their sides in the streets, and thousands upon thousands of rioters raged and looted, and destroyed. I watched them ebb and flow up and down city blocks. I watched a group of several thousand driven straight into a Dark Zone, forced into the waiting wall of pitch, where they were sucked dry of life down to a rind of human remains. I heard their cries of horror. I'll hear them till I die.

I stood looking out over Dublin as darkness took the city, grid by grid, district by district as if, somewhere in Dublin's basement, circuit breakers were being systematically thrown.

I remembered the night I'd curled in my window seat at BB&B, and my eyes had played a trick on me.

It was no trick now. Or rather, it was the greatest Halloween trick of all. There would be no treats handed out in Dublin tonight. *This* was what Derek O'Bannion had been talking about.

At 8:29 P.M., darkness reigned absolute.

Even the fires had been extinguished.

The sounds floating up were different now, the voices fewer, and frightened, not angry. Militant footfalls passed beneath me regularly. The Unseelie were still at it, collecting us, killing us. It took every ounce of self-control I possessed to *not* go down there to hunt in the darkness and try to save those humans that remained.

Out there, past a certain bookstore, a Dark Zone was spreading unchecked, taking over the city.

Dublin was without hope until 7:25 A.M.: Dawn.

I wondered what was happening with the MacKeltars. Was Barrons sabotaging that ritual, too? It made no sense to me. Why would Barrons want the walls down? *Did* Barrons want the walls down? Might the Orb have come to him already sabotaged, a prepackaged grenade, just waiting for the pin to be pulled? Where had he gotten it? Was I a hopeless fool, still trying to make excuses for him?

Were the walls already down? Was *this* the flood of Unseelie that had been freed from their prison, the ones wrecking the city? Or were they merely harbingers, and the worst was yet to come?

I dropped to the cold stone floor of the aperture, drew up my knees, folded my arms, and rested my chin on them, looking out at the city. My body bristled with the dark energy of Unseelie flesh, with the protective urges of a *sidhe*-seer, magnified by Fae steroids, demanding that I do something, *anything*.

I shuddered in the grip of my internal battle. I felt like I was crying, although no tears fell. I didn't know yet that tears are not possible for a Fae, or for anyone under the influence of it.

Seeing BB&B surrounded by Shades, swallowed up by a Dark Zone, had been bad enough. Seeing all of Dublin dark was overload. How many people would be left by dawn to try to reclaim it? Any? Did

Unseelie now guard wherever it was the utilities were controlled? Would we have to form armies to fight our way in and seize control from them? My world had changed tonight. I had no idea in how many ways, but I knew it was bad.

I sat in the cold stone opening, watching, waiting.

Three and a half hours later, the first of my questions was answered.

At eleven fifty-nine, the skin all over my body began to crawl. Literally. I scratched myself feverishly. Even deadened as my *sidhe*-seer senses were from my dark meal, I *still* felt it coming. No, the walls had not yet fallen. They were falling now.

The world was changing, becoming.

I felt a crushing sense of spatial distortion, stretching me, twisting, compressing. I was gigantic and paper-thin. I was small and round as a berry. I was inside out, my bones exposed. I was a bag of skin again.

Then the world felt suddenly much too large and horrifically skewed. The buildings below soared up at jagged, impossible angles, vanished down to pinpoints then erupted again. I watched as laws of physics were rewritten, as dimensions that were not meant to coexist crashed into each other and vied for dominance, contested for space to fill. I watched as the fabric of existence was ripped apart, and sewn back together again, aligned on diametrically opposing principles.

The universe screeched in protest as barriers collapsed, and realms collided; then the night was filled with another kind of screeching and I scrambled back, melting into the shadows, afraid of the shadows, but more afraid to turn my lights on, because the second of my questions was being answered: No, the Unseelie had not yet been freed from their prison. They were coming *now*, galloping down on a dark wind blowing from the horizon that had substance, the stuff of nightmares. Led by Death, Pestilence, Famine, and War?

They came.

I watched them come.

The ones who have no names, the abominations, those who are flawed yet live, those who hunger yet can never be sated, those who hate eternally, who need beyond bearing with their twisted limbs and psychopathic dreams, those who know but one joy: the hunt, the kill, the nectar of dust and ashes.

They soared over my head, high above the city, a vast, dark wave that stretched from one end of the horizon to the other, obliterating the sky, shrieking, howling, trumpeting their victory, free, free, *free* for the first time in nearly a million years! Free in a world warmed by sun, populated by billions of strong hearts beating, exploding with life, bursting with sex and drugs and music and glories untold that had been forbidden to them forever.

They came, the Wild Hunt, the winged ones, carrying their brethren in beaks and claws and other things that defied description, streaming from their icy hell, icing the world a slippery shining silvery frost in their wake.

I retreated into the belfry, my breath crystallizing on the bitterly cold air.

Then I retreated even farther, slinking to the lower platform, where I crept to the broom closet, pushed my way in between mops and pails, and shut the door.

Fingers numbed by cold, I shredded my T-shirt in the wan glow of one Click-It, stuffed pieces of it into every potentially telltale nook and cranny, then clicked myself on from head to toe until I filled the tiny room with light.

Heart pounding, eyes wide with terror, I backed into a corner, drew my knees to my chin, laid my spear harness on the floor beside me, and began the long vigil to Dawn.

PART THREE

Dawn

"Turned out I was wrong.

It wasn't the dark I should have been afraid of, at all."

—*Mac's journal*

NINETEEN

It was the second longest night of my life. The longest is yet to come.

I passed the time culling my memory for good ones, reliving them in vivid detail: those two years when Alina and I were in high school together; the trip we'd made as a family to Tybee Island, the guy I'd met there, who gave me my first real kiss, out in the waves where my parents couldn't see us; my graduation party; Alina's farewell bash before she'd left for Ireland.

Silence came long before dawn.

It was absolute; the hours from five to seven were so unearthly quiet I was afraid some cosmic calamity had befallen my closet; that a Fae realm had been victorious in the battle for the right to exist at my precise latitude and longitude, and me and the mops had been relegated Elsewhere. Precisely where Elsewhere might be I had no idea, but at 7:25 A.M., the moment of sunrise, it was still so utterly silent that when I placed my hand on the doorknob, it occurred to me to wonder if I might open it onto the vacuum of Space.

It would certainly simplify things.

I would be dead, and no longer have to worry about what the day might bring.

If I opened the door, I had to go *out there*. I didn't want to. My closet was cozy, safe, perhaps forgotten. What would I find out there? How would I get out of the city? What existed beyond Dublin's boundaries? Had we lost parts of the world last night, in a metaphysical battle between realms? Was Ashford, Georgia, still where it was supposed to be? Was I? Where would I go? Who would I trust? In the grand scheme of things, finding the *Sinsar Dubh* suddenly seemed a minor issue.

I cracked open the door, glimpsed the lower platform beyond, and exhaled with relief. Distastefully, with meticulous care, I strapped my spear harness back on. Unseelie marched through my blood, posturing aggressively. It would continue to do so for days, and I would fear my spear the entire time. I eased from the closet. After a thorough look around to make sure no Shades had assumed squatting rights during the night, I clicked myself off and ascended to the belfry.

When I stepped into the stone archway, I exhaled another sigh of relief.

The city looked mostly the same. The buildings stood. They hadn't been burned or demolished, and they hadn't vanished. Dublin might be worse for the wear, her party dress torn, hose run, stiletto heels broken, but she was in dishabille, not dead, and could one day be *craic*-filled and vibrant again.

There was no foot or motor traffic. The city looked abandoned. Though signs of rioting littered the streets, from cars to debris to bodies, there were neither people nor Fae moving around down there. I felt like the last person left alive.

There were no lights on, either. I checked my cell phone. No service. By nightfall, I was going to have to be holed up safely again.

I watched the city until day had fully dawned, and sunlight splintered off streets cobbled with broken glass. In the past forty-five minutes, no one and nothing had moved. It seemed the Unseelie foot soldiers had scrubbed Dublin clean of human life, and moved on. I doubted the Shades had gone. I could see greenery on the outskirts of the city. They'd probably gorged until the first rays of morning had forced them to retreat to their hidden cracks and crevices.

I blessed whatever fates had inspired me to make my MacHalo. It looked like it was going to be an integral part of keeping myself alive for a while. Impossible to stay to the lights when there were no lights to stay to.

First on my agenda was to find batteries, and cram my backpack full of them. Second was food. Third was wondering if Barrons could still track me by the tattoo at the base of my skull in a world that had merged with Faery realms, and if that was a good thing or a bad thing? Would V'lane come searching for me? Had the *sidhe*-seers survived? How was Dani? I didn't dare let my thoughts turn toward home. Until I found a phone that worked and could call, I couldn't handicap myself with those fears.

At the top of the rickety ladder, I slipped off my spear harness and dropped it the hundred-plus feet to the floor below, tossing it into the corner near the door. If the rungs gave way again, I would not fall on my own spear.

I descended slowly, carefully, and didn't breathe normally again until I'd reached the bottom. I'd eaten all the Unseelie I'd diced and jarred. I felt safer with a stash on me. I wanted more. Needed more. Who knew what battles I might encounter today?

I grabbed a loop of the spear harness, slid it over my shoulder, and stepped through the door, head cocked, listening for voices, movement, any sign of danger. The church was eerily quiet, flatly so. I inhaled, taking full advantage of my Unseelie-enhanced senses. There was a peculiar odor in the air, one I couldn't place. It appealed yet... disturbed me. It smelled kindred... but not quite. I hated not having my *sidhe*-seer senses. I hated not knowing if there might be Fae right around the corner, waiting to ambush me.

I moved furtively forward and added a fourth note to my mental agenda: new footwear. Tennis shoes. Rare are the boots crafted for stealth, and mine weren't.

Midway across the anteroom, I stopped. To my left was a wide flight of marble stairs, swathed by a carpeted runner that descended to tall double doors exiting the church.

To my right was the entrance to the chapel. Even beyond its closed doors, I could smell the inner sanctum, the faint, cloying scent of incense and that other, elusive, spicy scent that disturbed and intrigued me. In the dim light of the hushed morning, the white doors of the oratory seemed to glow with a soft, unspoken invitation.

I could turn left, and head out into Dublin's streets, or go right, and take a few moments to confer with a God I'd not spoken to much in my life. Was he listening today? Or had he shaken his head, packed up his Creation Kit, and headed off for a less screwed-up world late last night? What would I talk about? How cheated I felt by Alina's death? How angry I was at being alone?

I turned left. There were easier monsters to deal with in the streets.

At the top of the stair, lust blasted me, incinerated my will, awakening exotic, excruciating sexual need. For a change, I welcomed it.

"V'lane!" I exclaimed, yanking my hand from the top button of my jeans. I could feel him outside the church. He was moving toward me, down the sidewalk, up the outer stairs, about to enter. He'd found me! I caught myself thanking the God I'd just refused to talk to.

The doors opened and I was blinded by sunlight. My pupils constricted to pinpoints. Framed in the entrance, V'lane's hair shimmered a dozen shades of gold, bronze, and copper. He looked every inch the avenging angel in a way Barrons never could. *There* was that unusual scent; the one that beckoned and bedeviled me. Rolling off his skin. Did he always smell this way, and I could only pick it up now because I had Unseelie-heightened senses?

Spiked by his dark brethren, I wasn't sensing V'lane as a Fae. I felt no nausea. His appearance had been preceded only by his lethal sexuality. He was impacting me as he would any woman. It was no wonder heads turned when we went places. His allure was even stronger with my *sidhe*-seer senses dead, as if some special quality in my blood normally shielded me from his full effect, but couldn't when my veins ran with Fae.

Whatever the reason, his impact was formidable today. It was even more intense than the first time I'd encountered him, when I'd had no idea what he was. My legs felt weak. My breasts were heavy, aching, and my nipples burned. I wanted sex, *needed* sex. Violently. Had to have it. Didn't care about repercussions. I wanted to fuck and fuck until I couldn't move. Hadn't he said he could give it to me without hurting me? Mute himself, protect me from being harmed or changed?

"Turn it off," I forced myself to say, but I was smiling when I said it, and my command lacked heat.

I was so relieved to see him!

My sweater was on the floor. I bent to pick it up.

He moved from the shaft of brilliant sunlight and glided up the stairs. "*Sidhe*-seer," he said.

As the door closed behind him, and the anteroom returned to its dimly lit state, my pupils dilated, adjusted, and I realized my error. Gasping, I took a step back. "You're not V'lane!"

The exotic prince's gaze fixed on my breasts, sculpted by a lacy bra. I pressed my sweater to my chest. He made a sound deep in his throat and my knees buckled with sexual anticipation. Only with immense effort did I remain standing. I wanted to be on my knees. I *should* be on my knees. He wanted me on my knees. And hands. My head was vacuumed of thought. My lips and legs moved apart.

He stepped closer.

I fought a frantic battle with myself, managed to step back.

"No," he said. "I am not." Lids lowered over alien, ancient eyes, lifted. "Whatever that is."

"Wh-who are you?" I stammered.

He took another step forward.

I took another step back. There went my sweater again. Shit.

"The end," he said simply.

The doors leading to the inner sanctum opened behind me. I felt the draft of passage, and more of the strange, disturbing scent filled my nostrils.

Lust sledgehammered me, front and rear.

"We are all the end," a cold voice floated over my shoulder. "And beginning. Soon. Later. After."

"Time. Irrelevant," the other replied. "Round is round."

"We are always. You are not."

They might as well have been speaking a foreign language. I turned, hardly able to breathe. There was a lacy bra lying on the floor at my feet. It was mine. Shit again. The air was cool on my flushed skin. I would not ask "after what?" There were two of them. Two death-by-sex Fae. Two princes. Could I outrun them? Could I survive them? They could sift. I was between them. Could I Null them? Oh, God, not with my *sidhe*-seer abilities dead! "Do you know V'lane? He's a Seelie Prince," I managed to get out through lips that ached for touch, for fullness that had only been hinted at by the sensation of V'lane's name piercing my tongue. I wanted to drown in men. I wanted to be stuffed plumper than a sausage. Lips would do. So would other things. I looked from one of their crotches to the next. I shook my head, violently. My mouth was parched, my head spinning. "He protects me." Maybe they were friends of his. Maybe they could summon him. Maybe they feared him and would back off.

I wouldn't have been surprised by villainous laughs, sneers, ribald comments—after all, I was standing there naked from the waist up. I expected some comment, some expression, *any* expression, but they merely rotated their heads on their necks with eerie smoothness, and examined me in a manner so far from human that my blood ran cold and I stopped breathing.

I knew who they were. They were no friends of V'lane's. That alien gesture had given them away.

When I breathed again it was a great, sucking inhalation.

These were the Unseelie Princes. Fae that had never had the opportunity to study us, learn our habits, perfect glamour through mimicry; Fae that could employ our language but only void of reference or metaphor; that had learned about our world from a great distance, by proxy; that probably didn't even grasp the basic Fae concepts of stasis and change. Fae that had never been free, never drunk from the cauldron, never had sex with a human woman.

But they planned to have sex with me. It was pouring off them in immense, hungry, dark waves. Lust laced the room, explosive as dynamite, its fuse dangerously short. The air reeked of it. I was drawing it in with every breath, feeding an unquenchable, exquisite Fae fever.

A third one glided into the church.

What had Christian said? *Myth equates the heads of those four houses, the dark princes, with the Four Horsemen of the Apocalypse.*

Pestilence joined Death and Famine in God's house. Now only War remained unaccounted for. I hoped he would stay that way.

They closed in on me, a circle of three, morphing from one shape to the next as they came. Shifting shapes, colors, and...something else that might have been a dimensional nature. I see 3-D, not 4 or 5. My eyes couldn't explain to my brain what they were seeing so they just settled for pretending they weren't seeing it. V'lane said the Fae have never revealed their true face to us. That may have been what I glimpsed.

Swallowing my fear of the only weapon I had to use against them, I jerked out the spear, dropped the harness, and pivoted in a threatening circle.

"Stay back!" I commanded. "This is a Seelie Hallow. It can kill even princes! Just try me!" I stabbed at the nearest one. He paused, regarded the spear, then raised incandescent eyes to mine. He swiveled his head upon his neck, and glanced at the others, then back at the spear in a way that made me look, too.

I discovered with horror that my hand was turning it toward me, slowly, slowly, until the tip, the deadly, flesh-rotting tip was pointing straight at me. I tried to turn it away, to point it at him, but I couldn't move. My brain was issuing orders my body refused to obey.

Rape was horrific enough. There was no way I was going to die like Mallucé afterward.

When the tip was a mere quarter inch from my skin, I tried to fling the spear away, hoping I could, and they'd just forget about it. My release mechanism worked as my override had not—a thing that would make sense to me one day—and the spear clattered across the floor, through the door into the chapel. It crashed into the base of the pedestal of holy water with such impact that water sloshed over the side, and hissed and steamed when it hit the spear.

The princes adopted static form, became males so unutterably beautiful that looking at them was a moment of such exquisite perfection that it hurt my soul, and I gibbered wordlessly. They were naked except for glistening black torques that writhed like liquid darkness around their necks. Their supple, golden-skinned bodies were tattooed in brilliant, complicated patterns that rushed over their skin, kaleidoscopic storm clouds across a gilded sky. Lightning flashed in their glittering eyes.

Deep within me, I felt answering thunder.

I couldn't look at them. They were too much. I turned away but they were there again, forcing me to gaze upon their frightening, fantastic faces. My eyes widened, widened still.

I wept tears of blood that scaled my cheeks. I scrubbed at them with my fingers, and they came away seared, crimson.

Then the princes' mouths were on my fingertips, with tongues of soothing coolness and fangs of licking ice, and a beast far more primitive than Savage Mac, and far beyond my control, yawned and stretched her arms above her head, and awakened with a delicious sense of anticipation.

This was what she'd been born for. What she'd been waiting for all this time. Here. Now. Them.

Sex that was worth dying for.

I kicked off my boots. They peeled away my jeans and underwear, and turned me between them, kissing, tasting, licking, taking, feeding from the passion they fed in me, slamming it back at me, taking it, returning it again, and with each transfer between us it grew into something bigger than me, bigger than them, into a beast of its own.

With some distant part of my mind I recognized the horror of what was happening to me. I tasted on their perfect lips the emptiness within them, and understood that beneath the flawless, velvety, golden skin, far beneath the waves of Eros I was drowning in ... there was nothing but ... an ocean of ... me.

I glimpsed, even as I surrendered to it, the true nature of the Unseelie princes. They are voids of what they are not, and crave most: passion, desire, the fire of life, the capacity to feel.

Some essential component in them had been lost long ago, or perhaps frozen out of them by seven hundred thousand years of icy incarceration, or perhaps they'd come into being via the king's imperfect Song, equally imperfect and empty. Whatever the cause, the most intensely they could feel was through sex. They were maestros of lust, eternally denied music in their realm, surrounded by others also void, without a human's body to play the melody upon.

But with a human, so long as *she* felt, so did they, and they would gorge on her song, until the concert hall fell silent, the passion turned to ash, and she died, her body gone as cold as that place inside them where life could never be fully realized.

Empty, they would find another woman to play, and gorge again, giving her sex at its most elemental, at its purest, and most potent, channeling all that it was to be alive out of her, back into her, and out again. My orgasms were not petit mal but repeated births, a re-creation of myself every time I came. It was sex that was life that was blood that was God that filled every empty orifice I had, inside and out.

And it was killing me.

And I knew it.

And I had to have more.

We rolled and slid across the cool marble floor of the anteroom, my three dark princes and I, seeking purchase on the carpeted stairs, one beneath me, one behind, one inside my mouth.

They moved deep in me, filling me with sensations as kaleidoscopic as their tattooed bodies. I narrowed to a tiny blossom, exploded outward, and fragmented again and again into bits of shattered woman. They tasted of nectar, smelled of dark, drugging spices; their bodies were hard and sculpted and perfect, and if every now and then the ice of their black torques and pink tongues and white teeth were sharp nips of frostbite at my skin, it was a small price to pay for what they did inside me.

I felt my mind slipping; moments of my life flashed before my eyes, before dropping away to some forsaken place. I cried out, begging to be freed, but my mouth shaped only words of instruction, and demand: more, harder, faster, *there*.

My last month in Dublin, with all its hopes and worries and fears, flashed through my mind—and was forgotten. There went the day I'd spent in Faery with Alina, followed by all memory of Mallucé and Christian and the O'Bannions and Fiona and Barrons, and meeting Rowena in the bar, that first night in Ireland. My summer was flying backward past my eyes, falling away. Was there a fourth male kissing me now? Tasting me? Why couldn't I see him? Who was he?

I pricked myself on the day of Alina's death, then it was gone, too, and that day hadn't happened, and my life continued to unfurl backward.

I lost my college years to Pestilence's kisses. I bade farewell to high school with Famine spurting sweetly in my mouth. I lost my childhood in three Fae Princes' arms. If there was a fourth, I never saw his face. Only felt the strangeness of another, who wasn't quite the same.

And then I'd never been born.

I was only now.

This moment. This orgasm. This hunger. This endless emptiness. This mindless need.

I was aware that others had entered the anteroom but I could not see beyond my dark princes. Didn't care. More was good.

When my princes drew away from me, my body grew so cold I thought I would die. I writhed on the floor, begging for more.

Someone reached for me.

I grasped with both hands for the succor of touch, tossed a tangle of hair from my eyes, and looked up, straight into the face of the Lord Master.

"I think she'll obey me now," he murmured.

Obey him?

I'd die for him.

A Note to
the Reader

I foreshadowed this moment. And I've foreshadowed what's yet to come, but for those of you with flashlights running low on batteries, who feel the Shades closing in, and fear there's no hope in sight, consider this:

In *Bloodfever* Mac says, "Although it may not seem like it, this isn't a story about darkness. It's about light. Khalil Gibran says, *Your joy can fill you only as deeply as your sorrow has carved you.* If you've never tasted bitterness, sweet is just another pleasant flavor on your tongue. One day I'm going to hold a lot of joy."

And she will. That was my promise in her words.

For the latest news on Mac, future release dates, and the like, drop by www.karenmoning.com or www.sidhe-seersinc.com.

The latter is an interactive Web site, with hidden links, so you might have to do a little searching but it's well worth it. My Web designers are wonderfully talented, with a great sense of fun. You'll find a game to play, *Mac vs. the Shades*, Fever-world music downloads, Mac's complete (until the next *Fever* installment) glossary, the Wall, the Map Room, and much, much more.

At www.karenmoning.com you'll find a fantastic message board community where I sometimes drop in.

Stay to the lights,

Karen

Glossary from Mac's Journal

*AMULET, THE: Unseelie or Dark Hallow created by the Unseelie King for his concubine. Fashioned of gold, silver, sapphires, and onyx, the gilt "cage" of the amulet houses an enormous clear stone of unknown composition. A person of epic will can use it to impact and reshape reality. The list of past owners is legendary, including Merlin, Boudica, Joan of Arc, Charlemagne, Napoleon. Last purchased by a Welshman for eight figures at an illegal auction, it was all too briefly in my hands and is currently in the possession of the Lord Master. It requires some kind of tithe or binding to use it. I had the will; I couldn't figure out the way.

BARRONS, JERICHO: I haven't the faintest fecking clue. He keeps saving my life. I suppose that's something.

Addendum to original entry: He keeps a Sifting Silver in his study at the bookstore and when he walks through it, the monsters retreat from him just like the Shades. I saw him carry the body of a woman out of it. She'd been killed, brutally. By him? Or by the things in the mirror? He is at least several hundred years old, and possibly, *probably*, way older than that. I made him hold the spear to see if he was Unseelie, and he did, but I found out later from V'lane that the Unseelie King can touch *all* the Hallows (as can the Seelie Queen) and, although I can't fathom why the Unseelie King wouldn't be able to touch his own Book, maybe that's exactly why Barrons thought he *would* be able to touch it. Maybe it evolved into something more powerful than it began as. Also, I can't rule out that he might be some kind of Seelie/Unseelie hybrid. Do the Fae have sex and reproduce? Sometimes... I think he's human... gone *very* wrong. Other times I think he's nothing this world has ever seen. He's definitely not a *sidhe*-seer but he sees the Fae as plain as day, just like me. He knows Druidry, sorcery, black arts, is superstrong and fast, and has heightened senses. What did Ryodan mean by his comment about the Alpha & Omega? I've *got* to track that man down!

*CAULDRON, THE: Seelie or Light Hallow from which all Seelie eventually drink, to divest memory that has become burdensome. According to Barrons, immortality has a price: eventual madness. When the Fae feel it approaching, they drink from the cauldron and are "reborn" with no memory of a prior existence. The Fae have a record-keeper that documents each Fae's many incarnations, but the exact location of this scribe is known to a select few and the whereabouts of the records to none but him. Is that what's wrong with the Unseelie—they don't have a cauldron to drink from?

CRUCE: A Fae. Unknown if Seelie or Unseelie. Many of his relics are floating around out there. He cursed the Sifting Silvers. Before they were cursed, the Fae used them freely to travel through dimensions. The curse somehow corrupted the interdimensional channels and now not even the Fae will enter them. Unknown what the curse was. Unknown what damage it caused or what the risk in the Silvers is. Whatever it is, Barrons apparently doesn't fear it. I tried to get into the Silver in his study. I can't figure out how to open it.

CUFF OF CRUCE: A gold and silver arm cuff set with blood-red stones; an ancient Fae relic that supposedly permits the human wearing it "a shield of sorts against many Unseelie and other . . . unsavory things" (this according to a death-by-sex Fae—like you can actually trust one).

DANI: A young *sidhe*-seer in her early teens whose talent is superhuman speed. She has to her credit—as she will proudly crow from the rooftops given the slightest opportunity—forty-seven Fae kills at the time of this writing. I'm sure she'll have more by tomorrow. Her mother was killed by a Fae. We are sisters in vengeance. She works for Rowena and is employed at Post Haste, Inc.

Addendum to original entry: Her kills now number nearly two hundred! The kid has no fear.

DARK ZONE: An area that has been taken over by the Shades. During the day it looks like your everyday abandoned, run-down neighborhood. Once night falls, it's a death trap.

DEATH-BY-SEX FAE: (e.g., V'lane) A Fae that is so sexually "potent" a human dies from intercourse with it unless the Fae protects the human from the full impact of its deadly eroticism.

Addendum to original entry: V'lane made himself feel like nothing more than an incredibly sexy man when he touched me. They *can* mute their lethality if they so choose.

Addendum to original entry: This caste of Fae springs only from royal lines. They can do three things: protect the human completely and give them the most incredible sex of their life, protect them from dying and turn them *Pri-ya*, or kill them with sex.

They can sift space.

DOLMEN: A single-chamber megalithic tomb constructed of three or more upright stones supporting a large, flat horizontal capstone. Dolmens are common in Ireland, especially around the Burren and Connemara. The Lord Master used a dolmen in a ritual of dark magic to open a doorway between realms and bring Unseelie through.

DRUID: In pre-Christian Celtic society, a Druid presided over divine worship, legislative and judicial matters, philosophy, and education of elite youth to their order. Druids were believed to be privy to the secrets of the gods, including issues pertaining to the manipulation of physical matter, space, and even time. The old Irish "Drui" means magician, wizard, diviner. *(Irish Myths and Legends)*

Addendum to original entry: I saw both Jericho Barrons and the Lord Master use the Druid power of Voice, a way of speaking with many voices that cannot be disobeyed. Significance?

Addendum: Christian MacKeltar descends from a long, ancient bloodline of Druids.

FAE: (fay) See also Tuatha Dé Danaan. Divided into two courts, the Seelie or Light Court, and the Unseelie or Dark Court. Both courts have different castes of Fae, with the four Royal Houses occupying the highest caste of each. The Seelie Queen and her chosen consort rule the Light Court. The Unseelie King and his current concubine govern the Dark.

FIONA: The woman who ran Barrons Books and Baubles before I took over. She was wildly in love with Barrons and tried to kill me by turning out all the lights one night and propping a window open to let the Shades in. Barrons fired her for it—gee, now that I think about it, getting fired for trying to kill me sure feels like underkill. She's hooked up with Derek O'Bannion, and he's got her eating Unseelie. I have a bad feeling that she and I aren't done with each other.

FOUR STONES, THE: Translucent blue-black stones covered with raised runelike lettering. The key to deciphering the ancient language and breaking the code of the *Sinsar Dubh* is hidden in these four mystical stones. An individual stone can be used to shed light on a small portion of the text, but only if the four are reassembled into one will the true text in its entirety be revealed. *(Irish Myths and Legends)*

Addendum: Other texts say it is the "true nature" of the *Sinsar Dubh* that will be revealed.

GLAMOUR: Illusion cast by the Fae to camouflage their true appearance. The more powerful the Fae, the more difficult it is to penetrate its disguise. Average humans see only what the Fae want them to see, and are subtly repelled from bumping into or brushing against it by a small perimeter of spatial distortion that is part of the Fae glamour.

GRAY MAN, THE: Monstrously ugly, leprous Unseelie that feeds by stealing beauty from human women. Threat assessment: can kill, but prefers to leave its victim hideously disfigured, and alive to suffer.

Addendum to original entry: Allegedly the only one of its kind, Barrons and I killed it.

Addendum to original entry: It could sift space.

GRIPPER: Dainty, diaphanous Unseelie that is surprisingly beautiful. Grippers look like the modern media's representation of fairies—delicate, shimmering, nude beauties, with a cloud of gossamer hair, and lovely features, only they're nearly the size of a human. I named them Grippers because they "grip" us. They can step inside a human's skin and take them over. Once they've slipped inside a person, I can no longer sense them. I could be standing right next to a Gripper inside a person, and not even know it. For a while, I was afraid Barrons might be one. But I made him hold the spear.

HALLOWS, THE: Eight ancient relics of immense power fashioned by the Fae: four light and four dark.

The Light or Seelie Hallows are the stone, the spear, the sword, and the cauldron. The Dark or Unseelie Hallows are the amulet, the box, the mirror, and the book (*Sinsar Dubh,* or Dark Book). *(A Definitive Guide to Artifacts, Authentic and Legendary)*

Addendum to original entry: I still don't know anything about the stone or the box. Do they confer powers that could help me? Where are they? Correction to above definition, the mirror is actually the Silvers. *See* Sifting Silvers or Silvers. The Unseelie King made all the Dark Hallows. Who made the Light ones?

Addendum to original entry: See the story of the Unseelie King and his mortal concubine, as V'lane told it to me. (p. 77 this journal.) The king created the Silvers for her to keep her ageless and give her realms to explore. He created the amulet so she could reshape reality. He gave her the box for her loneliness. What does it do? The *Sinsar Dubh* was an accident.

HAVEN, THE: High council of *sidhe*-seers.

Addendum to original entry: Once selected by popular vote, now chosen by the Grand Mistress for their loyalty to her and the cause. They were the only ones besides Rowena who knew what was being kept beneath the abbey. Some of them died and/or disappeared when the Book escaped twenty-some years ago. How did it happen? I'm twenty-two. *Is it possible my mother was one of them?!!!*

IYCGM: Barrons gave me a cell phone with this number programmed in. It stands for If You Can't Get Me. The mysterious Ryodan answers when I call.

IYD: Another of Barrons' preprogrammed numbers; stands for If You're Dying.

LORD MASTER: My sister's betrayer and murderer! Fae but not Fae, leader of the Unseelie army, after the *Sinsar Dubh*. He was using Alina to hunt it like Barrons is using me to hunt OOPs.

Addendum to original entry: He offered me a trade: Alina back for the Book. I think he really could do it.

MACKELTAR, CHRISTIAN: Employed in the ancient languages department of Trinity. He knows what I am and knew my sister! Have no idea what his place in all this is, nor do I know his motives. Will find out more soon.

Addendum to original entry: Christian comes from a clan that once served as high Druids to the Fae and have been upholding the human part of the Fae/Man Compact for thousands of years, performing rituals and paying tithes. He knew Alina only in passing. She'd come to ask him to translate a piece of text from the *Sinsar Dubh*.

MALLUCÉ: Born John Johnstone, Jr. On the heels of his parents' mysterious death, he inherited hundreds of millions of dollars, disappeared for a time, and resurfaced as the newly undead vampire Mallucé. Over the next decade, he amassed a worldwide cult following, and was recruited by the Lord Master for his money and connections. Pale, blond, citron-eyed, the vampire favors steampunk and Victorian Goth.

MANY-MOUTHED THING, THE: Repulsive Unseelie with myriad leechlike mouths, dozens of eyes, and overdeveloped sex organs. Caste of Unseelie: unknown at this time. Threat assessment: unknown at this time but suspect kills in a manner I'd rather not think about.

Addendum to original entry: Is still out there. I want this one dead.

Addendum to original entry: Dani bagged the bastard!

Could he sift space? Which ones can and can't?

NULL: A *sidhe*-seer with the power to freeze a Fae with the touch of his or her hands (e.g., me). While frozen, it is completely powerless. The higher and more powerful the caste of Fae, the shorter the length of time it stays frozen.

O'BANNION, DEREK: Rocky's brother and the Lord Master's new recruit. He wants his brother's spear back and he wants to kill me for killing his brother. I should have let him walk into the Dark Zone that day.

Addendum to original entry: He's eating Unseelie and has hooked up with Fiona, who's also eating it!

O'BANNION, ROCKY: Ex-boxer turned Irish mobster, and religious fanatic. He had the Spear of Destiny* in a collection hidden deep underground. Barrons and I broke in one night and stole it. His death was the first human blood on my hands. The night we robbed him, Barrons turned out all the exterior lights around the bookstore. When O'Bannion came after me with fifteen of his henchmen, the Shades devoured them right outside my bedroom window. I knew Barrons was going to do something. And if he'd asked me to choose between them or me, I'd have *helped* him turn the lights out. You never know what you'll be willing to do to survive until you get backed into a corner and see what explodes out of you.

OOP: Acronym for Object of Power, a Fae relic imbued with mystical properties. Some are Hallows, some aren't.

OOP Detector: Me. A *sidhe*-seer with the special ability to sense OOPs. Alina was one, too, which is why the Lord Master used her.

Addendum to original entry: Very rare. Certain bloodlines were bred for this trait. Rowena's *sidhe*-seers say they've all died out.

Orb of D'Jai: No clue, but Barrons has it. He says it's an OOP. I couldn't sense it when I held it, but I couldn't sense anything at that particular moment. Where did he get it and where did he put it? Is it in his mysterious vault? What does it do? How does he get into his vault, anyway? Where is the access to the three floors beneath his garage? Is there a tunnel that connects buildings? Must search.

Addendum to original entry: Barrons gave it to me so I could give it to the *sidhe*-seers, to use in a ritual to reinforce the walls on Samhain.

Patrona: Mentioned by Rowena, I supposedly have "the look" of her. Was she an O'Connor? She was at one time the leader of the *sidhe*-seer Haven.

PHI: *Post Haste, Inc.,* a Dublin courier service that serves as a cover for the *sidhe*-seer coalition. ~~It appears~~ Rowena is in charge.

Addendum: After the Book was lost, Rowena opened branches of this courier service all over the world, in an effort to track and reclaim it. It was very clever, really. She has bicycling couriers serving as her eyes and ears in hundreds of major cities. The abbey/*sidhe*-seers have a very wealthy benefactor who funnels funds through multiple corporations. I wonder who it is.

PRI-YA: A human addicted to Fae sex.

Addendum: God help me, I *know*.

RHINO-BOYS: Ugly, gray-skinned Fae who resemble rhinoceroses with bumpy, protruding foreheads, barrel-like bodies, stumpy arms and legs, lipless gashes of mouths, and jutting underbites. They are lower mid-level caste Unseelie thugs dispatched primarily as watchdogs for high-ranking Fae.

Addendum to original entry: They taste horrible.

Addendum to original entry: I don't believe they can sift space. I saw them locked in cells in Mallucé's grotto and chained up. It didn't occur to me at the time how odd that was, then later I thought maybe Mallucé was somehow containing them with spells. But after Jayne made his comment about imprisoning Fae, I realized that not all Fae can sift and I'm starting to wonder if only the very powerful ones can. This could be an important tactical edge. Must explore.

ROWENA: In charge ~~to some degree~~ of a coalition of *sidhe*-seers organized as couriers at Post Haste, Inc. ~~Is she the~~ Grand Mistress? They have a chapter house or retreat in an old abbey a few hours from Dublin, with a library I *must* get into.

Addendum to original entry: She has never liked me. She's playing judge, jury, and executioner where I'm concerned. She sent her girls after me to take my spear away! I will *never* let her have it. I've been to the abbey but only briefly. I suspect many of the answers I want can be found there, either in the forbidden libraries that only the Haven is permitted to enter, or in their memories. I need to figure out who the Haven members are, and get one of them to talk.

ROYAL HUNTERS: A mid-level caste of Unseelie. Militantly sentient, they resemble the classic depiction of the devil, with cloven hooves, horns, long satyrlike faces, leathery wings, fiery orange eyes, and tails. Seven to ten feet tall, they are capable of extraordinary speed on both hoof and wing. Primary function: *sidhe*-seer exterminators. Threat assessment: kills.

Addendum to original entry: Encountered one. Barrons doesn't know everything. It was considerably larger than he'd led me to expect, with a thirty- to forty-foot wingspan and a degree of telepathic abilities. They are mercenary to the core and serve a master only so long as it benefits them. I'm not sure I believe they're mid-level, and in fact, I'm not sure they're entirely Fae. They fear my spear and I suspect are unwilling to die for any cause, which gives me a tactical edge.

RYODAN: Associate of Barrons and IYCGM on my cell.

Addendum: Top on my list of people to track down.

SEELIE: The "light" or "fairer" court of the Tuatha Dé Danaan governed by the Seelie Queen, Aoibheal.

Addendum: The Seelie cannot touch the Unseelie Hallows. The Unseelie cannot touch Seelie Hallows.

Addendum: According to V'lane the true queen of the Fae is long dead, killed by the Unseelie King, and with her died the Song of Making. Aoibheal is a lesser royal who is one of many that has tried to lead The People since.

SHADES: One of the lowest castes of Unseelie. Sentient but barely. They hunger—they feed. They cannot bear direct light and hunt only at night. They steal life in the manner the Gray Man steals beauty, draining their victims with vampiric swiftness, leaving behind a pile of clothing and a husk of dehydrated human matter. Threat assessment: kills.

Addendum to original entry: I think they're changing, evolving, learning.

Addendum: I know it is! I swear it's stalking me!

Addendum: They've learned to work together and shape themselves into barriers.

SHAMROCK: This slightly misshapen three-leaf clover is the ancient symbol of the *sidhe*-seers, who are charged with the mission to See, Serve, and Protect Mankind from the Fae.

SIDHE-SEER: (SHE-seer) A person Fae magic doesn't work on, capable of seeing past the illusions or "glamour" cast by the Fae to the true nature that lies beneath. Some can also see *Tabh'rs*, hidden portals between realms. Others can sense Seelie and Unseelie objects of power. Each *sidhe*-seer is different, with varying degrees of resistance to the Fae. Some are limited, some are advanced with multiple "special powers."

Addendum to original entry: Some, like Dani, are superfast. There's a place inside my head that isn't . . . like the rest of me. Do we all have it? What is it? How did we get this way? Where do the bits of inexplicable knowledge that feel like memories come from? Is there such a thing as a genetic collective unconsciousness?

SIFTING: Fae method of locomotion, occurs at speed of thought. (Seen this!)

Addendum to original entry: Somehow V'lane sifted me without my awareness that he was even there. I don't know if he was able to approach me "cloaked" somehow, then touched me at the last minute and I just didn't realize it because it happened so fast, or if perhaps instead of moving me, he moved the realms around me. Can he do that? How powerful is V'lane? Could another Fae sift me without me having any advance warning? Unacceptably dangerous! Require more information.

*SIFTING SILVERS OR SILVERS, THE: Unseelie or Dark Hallow, an elaborate maze of mirrors created by the Unseelie King once used as the primary method of Fae travel between realms, until Cruce cast the forbidden curse into the silvered corridors. Now no Fae dares enter the Silvers.

Addendum to original entry: The Lord Master had many of these in his house in the Dark Zone and was using them to move in and out of Faery. If you destroy a Silver does it destroy what was in it? Does it leave an open entry/exit into a Fae realm like a wound in the fabric of our world? What exactly was the curse and who was Cruce?

Addendum to original entry: Barrons has one and walks around in it!

*SINSAR DUBH, THE: (she-suh-DOO) Unseelie or Dark Hallow belonging to the Tuatha Dé Danaan. Written in a language known only to the most ancient of their kind, it is said to hold the deadliest of all magic within its encrypted pages. Brought to Ireland by the Tuatha Dé during the invasions written of in the pseudo-history *Leabhar Gabhåla,* it was stolen along with the other Dark Hallows, and rumored to have found its way into the world of Man. Allegedly authored over a million years ago by the Dark King of the Unseelie. (*A Definitive Guide to Artifacts, Authentic and Legendary*)

Addendum to original entry: I've seen it now. Words cannot contain a description of it. It is a book but it lives. It is aware.

Addendum: The Beast. Enough said.

*SPEAR OF LUISNE, THE: Seelie or Light Hallow (a.k.a. Spear of Luin, Spear of Longinus, Spear of Destiny, the Flaming Spear) The spear used to pierce Jesus Christ's side at his crucifixion. Not of human origin, it is a Tuatha Dé Danaan Light Hallow, and one of few items capable of killing a Fae—regardless of rank or power.

Addendum to original note: It kills *anything* Fae and if something is only part Fae, it kills part of it, horribly.

*SWORD OF LUGH, THE: Seelie or Light Hallow, also known as the Sword of Light, a Seelie Hallow capable of killing Fae, both Seelie and Unseelie. Currently, Rowena has it, and dispatches it to her *sidhe*-seers at PHI as she deems fit. Dani usually gets it.

Addendum: Saw it. It's beautiful!

TABH'RS: (TAH-vr) Fae doorways or portals between realms, often hidden in everyday human objects.

TUATHA DÉ DANAAN OR TUATHA DÉ: (TUA day dhanna or Tua DAY) (*See* Fae above) A highly advanced race that came to Earth from another world, comprising the Seelie and Unseelie.

UNSEELIE: The "dark" or "fouler" court of the Tuatha Dé Danaan. According to Tuatha Dé Danaan legend, the Unseelie have been confined for hundreds of thousands of years in an inescapable prison. Inescapable, my ass.

V'LANE: According to Rowena's books, V'lane is a Seelie Prince, Court of the Light, member of the Queen's High Council, and sometimes Consort. He is a death-by-sex Fae and has been trying to get me to work for him on behalf of Queen Aoibheal to locate the *Sinsar Dubh*.

VOICE: A Druid art or skill that compels the person it's being used on to precisely obey the letter of whatever command is issued. Both the Lord Master and Barrons have used this on me. It's terrifying. It shuts down your will, and makes you a slave. You stare helplessly out from your own eyes and watch your body doing things your mind is screaming at you *not* to do. I'm trying to learn it. At least to be able to resist it, because otherwise I'll never be able to get close enough to the Lord Master to kill him, and get vengeance for Alina.

*Denotes a Light or Dark Hallow

Pronunciation Guide

AN GARDA SIOCH'NA: In Dublin, garda, or on garda shee-a-conna. Outside Dublin, gardee.

AOIBHEAL: Ah-veel. (Not Irish Gaelic but an older language unique to the Fae.)

CRAIC: Crack.

CUFF OF CRUCE: Like the cruc in crucify.

DRUI: Dree.

FIR BOLG: Fair *bol* ugh.

LEABHAR GABHÅLA: Lour *Gow* ola (lour like flower, Gow like cow).

MALLUCÉ: Mal-*loosh*.

Irish pronunciations obtained from sources in Dublin at the Garda and Trinity. Any errors in pronunciation are mine.

Turn the page for a sneak peek at the next novel
in the Fever series, *Dreamfever*

Prologue

Mac: 11:18 a.m., November 1

Death. *Pestilence. Famine.*
They surround me, my lovers, the terrifying Unseelie Princes.

Who'd've thought destruction could be so beautiful? Seductive. Consuming.

My fourth lover—War? He ministers to me tenderly. Ironic for the bringer of Chaos, creator of Calamity, maker of Madness—if that is who he is. I cannot see his face, no matter how I try. Why does he hide?

He caresses my skin with hands of fire. I char, my skin blisters, bones fuse from sexual heat no human can endure. Lust consumes me. I arch my back and beg for more with parched tongue, cracked lips. As he fills my body, he quenches my thirst with drink. Liquid spills over my tongue, drips down my throat. I convulse. He moves inside me. I catch a glimpse of skin, muscle, a flash of tattoo. Still no face. He terrifies me, this one who keeps himself concealed.

In the distance, someone barks commands. I hear

many things, understand none. I know that I have fallen into enemy hands. I know also, soon, I will no longer know even that. *Pri-ya,* a Fae sex addict, I will believe there is no place, nothing else I would rather be.

If my thoughts were coherent enough to form sentences, I would tell you that I used to think life unfolded in a linear fashion. That people were born and went to . . . what's that human word? I dressed up for it every day. There were boys. Lots of cute boys. I thought the world revolved around them.

His tongue is in my mouth, and it's tearing apart my soul. Helpmesomeonepleasehelpmemakehimstopmakethemgoaway.

School. That's the word I'm looking for. After that, you get a job. Marry. Have . . . what are they? Fae can't have them. Don't understand them. Precious little lives. Babies! If you're lucky, you live a good, full life and grow old with someone you love. Caskets then. Wood gleams. I weep. A sister? Bad! Memory hurts! Let it go!

They're in my womb. They want my heart. Tear it open. Gorge on passion they can't feel. Cold. How can fire be so cold?

Focus, Mac. Important. Find the words. Deep breath. Don't think about what's happening to you. See. Serve. Protect. Others at risk. So many died. Can't be for nothing. Think of Dani. She's you inside, beneath that adolescent thumbs-in-the-pockets, one hip cocked, thousand-yard stare.

I orgasm without ceasing. I become the orgasm. Pleasure-pain! Exquisite! Mind-melting, soul-shredding, the more they fill me the emptier I am. It's slipping, all slipping, but before it goes, before it's gone completely, I get a hateful moment of clarity and see that

Most of what I believed about myself, and life, I derived from modern media, without questioning any of it. If I wasn't sure how to behave in a certain situation, I'd search my mind for a movie or TV show I'd seen, with a similar setup, and do whatever the actors had done. A sponge, I absorbed my environment, became a by-product of it.

I don't think I ever once looked up at the sky and wondered if there was sentient life in the universe besides the human race. I *know* I never looked down at the earth beneath my feet and contemplated my own mortality. I tunneled blithely through magnolia-drenched days, blind as a mole to everything but guys, fashion, power, sex, whatever would make me feel good right then.

But these are confessions I would make if I could speak, and I can't. I'm ashamed. I'm so ashamed.

Who the fuck are you? Someone shouted that question at me recently—his name eludes me. Someone who frightens me. Excites me.

Life's not linear at all.

It happens in lightning flashes. So fast you don't see those lay-you-out-cold moments coming at you until you're Wile E. Coyote, steamrolled flat as a pancake by the Road Runner, victim of your own elaborate schemes. A sister dead. A legacy of lies. An unwanted inheritance of ancient blood. An impossible mission. A book that is a beast that is ultimate power, and whoever gets their hands on it first decides the fate of the world. Maybe *all* the worlds.

Stupid *sidhe*-seer. So sure you had things headed in the right direction.

Here and now—not on some cartoon highway from which I can peel myself, stand up, and magically reinflate, but on the cold stone floor of a church, naked, lost, surrounded by death-by-sex Fae—I feel my most powerful weapon, the one I swore never to give up again—hope—slipping away. My spear is long gone. My will is . . .

Will? What's will? Do I know the word? Did I ever?

Him. He's here. The one who killed Alina. Please, please, please don't let him touch me.

Is he touching me? Is he the fourth? Why conceal himself?

When the walls come tumbling, tumbling down, that's the question that matters. *Who are you?*

I reek of sex and the scent of them—dark, drugging spices. I have no sense of time or place. They're inside me and I can't get them out, and how could I have been such a fool to believe that at the critical moment, when my world fell apart, some knight in shining armor was going to come thundering in on a white stallion, or arrive sleek and dark on an eerily silent Harley, or appear in a flash of golden salvation, summoned by a name embedded in my tongue, and rescue me? What was I raised on—fairy tales?

Not this kind. These are the fairy tales we were *supposed* to be teaching our daughters. A few thousand years ago, we did. But we got sloppy and complacent, and when the Old Ones seemed to go quietly, we allowed ourselves to forget the Old

Ways. Enjoyed the distractions of modern technology and forgot the most important question of all.

Who the fuck are you?

Here on the floor, in my final moments—MacKayla Lane's last grand hurrah—I see that the answer is all I've ever been.

I'm nobody.

Karen Marie Moning is the *New York Times* bestselling author of the Fever series, featuring MacKayla Lane. She has a bachelor's degree in society and law from Purdue University and is currently working on a new series set in the Fever world.

www.karenmoning.com